About the Author

Steve Monaghan was born in Bootle, Merseyside in 1958. He is a retired information security specialist, with experience in the private and government sectors in the UK and overseas which have given him a significant insight into the inner working of government, media and management.

Steve completed two periods of study with the UK's Open University, in 1999 obtaining a degree including Systems Analysis, Technology and Design and, in 2009, obtaining an MA in the Social Sciences, focussing on social policy, criminology, governance and the use of ideologies and their associated narratives.

Steve's first novel, *Samson's Syndrome* (2017), was the culmination of a period of research into current affairs prompted by the Western so-called 'humanitarian interventions' in various parts of the world. The main trigger point for *Samson's Syndrome* was the Ukraine crisis which began in February 2014 and continues unresolved as Steve's second novel, *A Phoney War*, goes into publication.

Information concerning the novels and future publications can be obtained from the Troubador – Matador website, Amazon websites, and also from the following social media pages:

Twitter: @StephenMonagha2
Facebook: fb.me/SJMauthor

A Phoney War

Steve Monaghan

Copyright © 2019 Steve Monaghan

The moral right of the author has been asserted.

Apart from any fair dealing for the purposes of research or private study, or criticism or review, as permitted under the Copyright, Designs and Patents Act 1988, this publication may only be reproduced, stored or transmitted, in any form or by any means, with the prior permission in writing of the publishers, or in the case of reprographic reproduction in accordance with the terms of licences issued by the Copyright Licensing Agency. Enquiries concerning reproduction outside those terms should be sent to the publishers.

This is a work of fiction. Names, characters, businesses, places, events and incidents are either the products of the author's imagination or used in a fictitious manner. Any resemblance to actual persons, living or dead, or actual events is purely coincidental.

Matador
9 Priory Business Park,
Wistow Road, Kibworth Beauchamp,
Leicestershire. LE8 0RX
Tel: 0116 279 2299
Email: books@troubador.co.uk
Web: www.troubador.co.uk/matador
Twitter: @matadorbooks

ISBN 978 1838591 267

British Library Cataloguing in Publication Data.
A catalogue record for this book is available from the British Library.

Printed and bound in the UK by 4edge limited
Typeset in 11pt Minion Pro by Troubador Publishing Ltd, Leicester, UK

Matador is an imprint of Troubador Publishing Ltd

CONTENTS

IN LIEU OF A PROLOGUE		**VII**
PART ONE	**MEDIA WARS (INVESTMENTS)**	**1**
1	LOVELY TO SEE YOU	3
2	THE UNTOUCHABLES	13
3	SUITED AND BOOTED	29
4	TWILIGHT OF THE CHRONICLE?	37
5	A RARE TALENT INDEED	51
PART TWO	**THE ASSASSINS**	**65**
6	OLD HABITS DIE HARD	67
7	COUNTER ESPIONAGE	76
8	CASING THE JOINT	86
9	MALICIOUS FABRICATION	95
10	MOTIVE, MEANS AND OPPORTUNITY	105
11	A HELPING HAND	116
PART THREE	**REBOOT TO FACTORY SETTINGS**	**129**
12	TAYLOR, FROM PANAMA	131
13	THE COLOUR OF FUNNY MONEY	144
14	SO LONG, FAREWELL	151
15	WHAT WE DID ON OUR HOLIDAYS	162

PART FOUR	THE BEST THINGS IN LIFE ARE FREE	175
16	ENEMIES OR OPPONENTS?	177
17	DECONSTRUCTING DMITRY	188
18	A SOLDIER'S TALE	211
19	A HEART OF DARKNESS	229
20	DEMOCRACY'S DIRTY LITTLE SECRETS	247
PART FIVE	GLAD HANDS AND NEW DISCOVERIES	259
21	FOR THE WANT OF A NAIL	261
22	THE HORROR, THE HORROR	270
23	DUTY OF CARE	281
24	SMOKE AND MIRRORS	298
PART SIX	MEDIA WARS (THE DIVIDENDS)	323
25	INFALLIBLE AND INEVITABLY INVINCIBLE	325
26	TOO MUCH INFORMATION	336
27	QUEEN BITCH	356
IN LIEU OF AN EPILOGUE		**371**

IN LIEU OF A PROLOGUE

Hands up who remembers 3 September 1939? It was a truly historical date.

This 3 September 1939 was the day when the United Kingdom's then prime minister, the Right Honourable Neville Chamberlain, announced on radio that "having received no such undertaking" from the Führer concerning the requisite removal of his armed forces from the conquered territories in Poland, "this country is now at war with Germany". The French government followed suit and declared war the next day.

War. Another bloody European war, barely twenty years after the Great War: 'the war to end all wars'.

Except that, for some countries, war seemed – how can one put it – somewhat 'distant'.

Even in the heartland of the European continent, between the main combatants (the UK, France and Germany), hardly a shot was fired. Instead, the main combatants took immediate measures to secure their own national interests and colonised territories.

A certain amount of manoeuvring for position took place. For instance, in the Middle East and North Africa, and in Norway, where the UK and France attempted (unsuccessfully) to prevent Germany from acquiring territory to safeguard the supply of raw materials from remote parts of Sweden to the Third Reich, and to prepare its U-boat war.

A war was also fought on the high seas, a war which was sometimes framed in the early days as a 'gentlemen's war' of sorts. During which Captain Hans Langsdorff behaved 'with honour', followed his orders from Berlin, scuttled his ship the *Admiral Graf Spee,* and shot himself.

The surprise conclusion to the Battle of the River Plate gave the impression that it might already be 'game over'; thereby feeding into a reassuring narrative that the war would probably not last very long, 'fortress UK' would probably escape relatively unscathed, Britannia would continue to rule the waves, and it was probably a good thing that it should end this way.

The sinking – in spectacular fashion – of *HMS Hood* and the dispatching to the bottom of the Atlantic Ocean of hundreds of thousands of tonnes of merchant shipping (courtesy of the German 'surface raiders' and the U-boats) likewise dispatched such optimism to the depths, in short order.

So, too, ended any residual optimism that the war would resemble anything like a 'gentlemen's war'.

The early months of the war in Europe were dubbed, in Germany, '*sitzkreig*': a form of slow-moving, probing warfare marked by repeated stalemates.

In the UK, the same period became known as 'The Phoney War', during which the British people were allowed and encouraged to indulge and overindulge themselves, as though not much had changed and nothing bad was really going to happen anyway.

Read *The Camomile Lawn* (1984) by Mary Wesley and watch the 1992 BBC TV adaptation of the novel to get a flavour of this aspect of The Phoney War and how it lingered even after the slaughter on the battlefield resumed in earnest. Or watch many of the black-and-white documentaries shown on TV decades later, or the nostalgic reveries of past glories in black-and-white movies such as *Dunkirk* (1958), *Green For Danger* (1946), *The Cruel Sea* (1953), et al.

A sudden blitzkrieg attack on Holland, Belgium and Luxembourg by the Wehrmacht, pinning the Allies down in June 1940, was swiftly followed up with an adroit manoeuvre as the panzers swept through the Ardennes, bypassing the great hope of France – the Maginot Line – and cornering the cream of the French Army and virtually the entire British Expeditionary Force near the French seaside town of Dunkerque.

Dunkerque became the scene of one of the greatest ever defeats for the British Army, but has since been commemorated for posterity as symbolic of the redoubtable British fighting 'Dunkirk' spirit.

When France fell, the scene was set (at least from the British perspective) for the main event – the Battle of Britain.

If the wartime German newsreels were anything to go by, the Battle of Britain should have comprised the utter destruction of the Royal Air Force as a prelude to the invasion of Britain by a fleet of clapped-out canal barges and modified nautical vessels requisitioned from their owners by the Wehrmacht and the Kriegsmarine; and protected from the might of the Royal Navy in the English Channel by half a dozen pocket battleships and motor torpedo boats, a fleet of submarines, and the much-vaunted air superiority expected from Goering's Luftwaffe.

When the Battle of Britain was called off by a defeated Führer, who had no doubt been taught a lesson from his English schoolmasters that he would never forget, ace Luftwaffe pilots were as surprised as anyone to receive notification that the invasion and subsequent conquest of France had been undertaken merely to cover Germany's back door, the Battle of Britain was merely a cleverly concealed feint, and the nightmarish main event would take place not on the Western Front but in the East.

Operation Barbarossa was scheduled for the summer of 1941, and its success in the East would ensure that, in the West, the British would be isolated – truly, as their politicians repeated at every opportunity, 'all alone' – and would have no choice but to sue for peace and an armistice on terms dictated by a victorious Germany. For Germany, the Battle of Britain might have been lost, but the war would have been won.

Okay, folks, don't panic. It never happened this way. Just saying.

However, there really was a period between September 1939 and June 1940 that is remembered as The Phoney War, and this phoney war was but the prelude to a half decade of mass slaughter.

✽

Cut to late September 2017.

A famous and highly regarded Hollywood actor faces the camera, paints a picture of the president of Russia as a former Soviet 'spy' who has become the leader of a nation of people who look a lot like many of us in the West, but whose culture is different from ours, whose history is separate from ours but which, from time to time, overlaps with ours.

A people who do not necessarily want to be like us or to behave exactly like us.

A people who were, in times past, designated in Adolf Hitler's *Mein Kampf* the role of *untermenschen*: namely, a people of a lower order entirely, who were worthy only to be enslaved, 'disposed of' or, to use the parlance of the day, 'resettled'.

A people who could never in a million years be expected to reach the great heights that we in the West had attained.

A people who, as far as we are encouraged to believe now in the twenty-first century, has no meaningful history; no culture; and nothing good to say about them, except that they and their leaders cause us so much grief.

What to do with these creatures? Is ethnic cleansing too good for them? Imagine the controversy! But we can't just leave it as it is. *They* are making a hell of a noise.

They won't let us 'democratise' Ukraine, and bring it into NATO (the North Atlantic Treaty Organisation) and into the European Union (EU), and thus bring it under *our* 'protection'. Even now, horror of horrors, *they* are in Syria. *They* tell us that *they* are in Syria legally and with the consent of the Syrian government, but that *we* are there illegally, neither with the consent of the Syrian government nor with a pertinent United Nations mandate.

And *they* tell us that *our* governments and *our* allies actually support the jihadist groups (including Al Qaeda and Islamic State of Iraq and Syria [ISIS]) in order to create chaos in the region, thereby providing a pretext for Western 'humanitarian intervention', and enabling the 'liberal' and 'democratic' Western elites to carve up the Middle East for their own benefit.

Worse still, Russian corporate media such as RT and Sputnik have outlets in the West, where they can counter the narrative of our corporate media with a narrative of their own. Furthermore, it is not as if our own corporate media – portrayed in the selfsame corporate media as victims of the evil Russians – are mere innocent babes in arms.

Now, instead of our own prime minister or the president of the United States (POTUS) telling us that we are at war with another great power, we have a Hollywood actor wrapping up his two-minute homily with a declaration that, "We are at war with Russia."

We have the POTUS announcing from the podium at the UN and in front of the entire world that the United States would be prepared to annihilate countries that do not do what the US tells them to do, and sends American carrier fleets scampering hither and thither to make the point.

Then, there is nothing. Silence. Absolute silence. A stunned world endeavours to recover from the news that a Hollywood actor has announced that, "We are at war with Russia," and that the US government is prepared to trash the planet in order to 'fix' it.

But, not for the first time this year, we have silence. Inaction. World War III has already begun. Our lords and masters have told us so. Their talking head from Hollywood made the unwelcome and pessimistic announcement that we are already at war with Russia. And, because our lords and masters themselves said it, it *must* be true and *cannot* be regarded as *fake news*. Right?

For some undisclosed reason, someone somewhere high up seems to be under the impression that this kind of talk is precisely what the world wants to hear.

Be afraid. Be very afraid.

"Pish and tosh," the more alert among us sing out in rejoinder, "surely not in this day and age."

"But everything has been decided," we are told. "It is the end of history; Mr Fukuyama told us so. Now we have reached the end of the line and full maturity. Believe it, masses; believe it, you swine; you miserable wretches. Enjoy your democracy now and don't complain. Rustics you are and rustics you will remain, and with times being a bit hard and everyone having to tighten their belts, we all have our part to play."

"But remember," the chronicler whispered, continuing his paraphrasing of the speech allegedly made by King Richard II to the survivors of the defeated peasant uprising of 1381, "if you do not play ball with us, you will remain in bondage, not as before but incomparably harsher. For as long as we live, we will strive with propaganda, financial inducements and, if push comes to shove, force of arms to suppress you so that the rigour of your servitude will be an example to posterity."

Well.

That's the thanks we get for trying to do the right thing, and now we have the trifling matter of World War III to contend with. What are we to do?

The final chapter of my first novel, *Samson's Syndrome* (2017), was entitled 'Breathing Space' – time to take stock, and rethink 'how the world works' and the modest role played in it by each and every one of us.

Samson's Syndrome was a fictional account of how easy it would be to inadvertently slip into a major war, but also how World War III might be averted.

It's sequel, *A Phoney War*, is a fictional account of what might happen while the world recovers from the shock of a close call, as the nuclear threat continues to dangle its blade over the heads of humankind.

A Phoney War takes place in the year 2016. This was the year of the surprise result of the June 'Brexit', the September Russian general election (remember that?) and the November US presidential election. These events act as necessary stepping stones within this tale of a modern-day phoney war; they are distinct events, yet is there a discernible thread which links them together? Fukuyama's 'end of history' – or, perhaps, *not* the 'end of history' – which is a break with a world order that was supposed to last forever, except that it is not. Well, to paraphrase the 1960s American rock band Love, 'forever' changes.

Samson's Syndrome revolved largely around a close, little world of men. Nonetheless, the women in the book can hardly be dismissed as shrinking violets. In *A Phoney War*, the roles are, at times, somewhat reversed, with the men playing a less prominent role as female characters seize the opportunity to take centre stage.

During a period of phoney war, people end up having to find non-lethal ways of waging the war, of forming their opinions and getting their points across, or of merely passing the time.

The latest in the *Fifty Shades* book series has been published in paperback and made into a movie. The former is selling like hot cakes and the latter is taking the box office by storm, proving that some are already well into the swing of the new age. Perhaps people have already started to get 'in the mood' to party in the spirit of a phoney war, *a la The Camomile Lawn*, while they still have time.

In *A Phoney War*, being indebted to the 'history of manners' outlined by the German sociologist Norbert Elias, the author is obliged to tone down the coverage of – how shall we label them – *explicit* behaviours that echo those referred to in the *Fifty Shades* book series.

But reader beware; the author cannot cater to all tastes and all expectations, so – for the sensitive reader in particular – prepare to be shocked occasionally.

But, please, no long faces. Having lived through it, we know that the year 2016 did not end with a nuclear Armageddon, so perhaps, for a while longer, we can relax and get out the port and stilton, the claret and cheddar, and the beer and savouries.

It is a time to relax but, as the scouts and guides forewarn, always *be prepared*.

So, in anticipation of an enjoyable and productive read, I welcome you to *your very own* phoney war.

Steve Monaghan
July 2019

PART ONE
MEDIA WARS (INVESTMENTS)

1
LOVELY TO SEE YOU

Flushed with success – having prevented, or at least delayed, the outbreak of World War III – the owners and the management of *The New Times* decided to invest in the future.

Starting with an upgrade of the troublesome and unreliable website.

An upgrade of the website implied a change of service provider and higher operating costs. Sir Harold Nevin had promised to arrange funding for the whole project, and, to get the ball rolling, John Morton MBE and Dmitry Krejevsky had agreed a bridging loan with the bank manager.

A wonderful package had been bundled together by the new service provider, including huge amounts of storage and a fast-retrieval facility for recovering archived material. Storage would be duplicated across more than one site to reduce the risk of data loss to virtually zero. An email server and a messenger chat facility dedicated to *The New Times* were included in the package. The whole website was protected with the most up-to-date encryption, vulnerability scanning and intrusion-detection services.

Going forward, the website of *The New Times* would be based upon a robust infrastructure. It would no longer share any computerised hardware, software and services with *The Chronicle* newspaper.

And that was not all. The new website could handle advanced application software. This included high-resolution video conferencing and – in line with an idea that had been brewing in the fertile mind of Dmitry Krejevsky for some time – the capability for live streaming.

Prior to going live, they had encountered a few glitches in some of the functionality, so the service provider sent round a technician to ensure that everything was working properly. The technician nursed the thing into place carefully. The whole installation process for the website – the migration of data from the old website to the new, the preliminary testing and the launch of the new website – was completed within two weeks. Dmitry Krejevsky and John Morton were impressed with the end product, and looked forward to the year 2016 with confidence.

Changes in personnel were also afoot. Dmitry Krejevsky would relinquish his role as editor-in-chief and become the chairman of The New Times Group. This new role placed him in the powerful position of keeping the direction of *The New Times* on the straight and narrow as it expanded its range of services.

The role of editor-in-chief could now be delegated to a trustworthy reporter, who was accountable directly to the chairman. Dmitry Krejevsky retained his role as principal expert on Russia, and, in addition to the new role of chairman, he assigned to himself formally the new role and title of human resources manager, in order to keep a tight rein on the vetting and recruitment of new staff. John Morton retained his positions of finance manager and Middle East expert. Zoe Neubauer's role within Europe (particularly Germany) remained unchanged.

Sir Tom Hamble – retired and reinvigorated by his knighthood, but, having failed to find a new 'adopted son' following the untimely death of Carl Waggoner almost two years earlier – had been offered the post of honorary president of The New Times Group. The idea crossed John Morton's mind during a cosy tête-à-tête with Hamble in the bar of a restaurant where they and their wives celebrated their New Year's Honours awards. Morton thought the appointment would provide *The New Times* with some cover, because he feared that many inside and outside the Establishment regarded *The New Times* as a threat to their very existence, and might at any time try to hamper its activity.

Morton's ploy was straight out of Sir Harold Nevin's playbook, and, after Morton raised the subject, Nevin immediately grasped the nettle and made the proposal to Hamble. Hamble's wife, Lady Joy, felt greatly reassured by this news because she had been worrying herself sick about what role in life her husband would assign to himself during his rather laid-back retirement.

Morton had learned a thing or two from Nevin; should Hamble decide to roam too far from the accepted norms of *The New Times*, then he could be easily persuaded to rein in his excesses (Shirley would merely have a word with Joy – and Tom Hamble would veer seamlessly back into line).

Hugh Lombard was promoted to editor-in-chief, with Shirley Bould as his personal assistant (PA). Lombard's promotion was agreed at a meeting between Krejevsky, Morton and Nevin, partly to leverage his previous experience as an associate editor but also in response to an attempt by Edward Ollerson – the editor-in-chief of *The Chronicle* newspaper – to poach Lombard with an offer of employment including a significant raise in his salary.

Edward Ollerson had 'accidentally on purpose' bumped into Lombard inside the latter's favourite haunt of a coffee bar and had suggested to Lombard that his sexual orientation was at odds with the editorial line of a news outlet that was well-disposed to the "present Russian government with its attendant homophobia". How, Ollerson had asked, could Lombard be a party to the repression of a minority of which he himself was a member?

Hugh Lombard fretted over the offer for more than a week, before pouring out his heart to Shirley Bould, over a cuppa.

"Ooh, you don't want to be going back there, dear," she warned. "I shudder to think what horrors that Edward Ollerson is cooking up. He has some dodgy people on his staff – as we all know." (Shirley was referring indirectly to the infamous Josh, among others.)

Shirley suggested that Hugh should, "talk with Mr Krejevsky to see what he can come up with."

Lombard did not want to do that. He would feel ungrateful after being offered a meaningful job at *The New Times* in December 2014, during a time of personal crisis, only to come across now as a cheap taker rather than a selfless giver. Furthermore, Hugh Lombard felt a bit unnerved by the 'legal expert' side of Dmitry

Krejevsky, particularly when the latter assumed an intimidating poker face below his furrowed brow, as though preparing to launch an exacting cross-examination – behaviour that made Hugh Lombard feel ill at ease.

So, instead, Lombard confided in John Morton, with whom he had been on cordial terms since they were both cub reporters and whom he trusted implicitly. It was a wise move because Morton listened sympathetically and was able to guide Lombard toward the correct decision.

"I agree with Shirley," Morton said. "Don't go back there. Whatever Edward Ollerson is up to will not become apparent until much later – at which point you will find yourself cornered and at your wit's end, and you would have burned your boats with Dmitry.

"In any case, we will be undergoing some changes in personnel over the next few months. One of my sons wants to become a journalist and will have a degree in modern history under his belt in August. We will probably take him on. Sir Harold Nevin has given us some names to expand the numbers of staff, who we might either employ directly or hire as freelancers. I can't tell you too much just yet, Hugh, but a high-profile vacancy at the top of the organisation is a virtual certainty. The salary will be higher than your current rate of remuneration, although we cannot compete with *The Chronicle*. I could put forward your name to Dmitry and Sir Harold, if you like."

When John Morton recounted Hugh Lombard's tale of woe to Dmitry Krejevsky and Sir Harold Nevin, Nevin immediately put his foot down. He was not in the mood to allow his pet project to be sabotaged by the likes of Edward Ollerson. *The Chronicle* would have to find someone else, instead of poaching Hugh Lombard, and every effort should be made to keep Lombard on board with *The New Times*.

Nevin announced a rise in income from sponsorships; the enlarged fund would enable Krejevsky to offer his old post to Lombard on a trial basis, with an immediate 10% pay rise and the prospect of an end-of-year bonus.

Lombard would have his own office, and greater scope for interaction with key personalities in the worlds of politics, business and the media. John Morton's son, Anthony, would return home from Sheffield University and join *The New Times* in the summer as a cub reporter. Lombard would be able to train Anthony in the dark arts of filching information from the array of contacts in his 'café of ill repute' and the doling out of disbursements in the appropriate manner.

In addition to Anthony Morton, another full-time newcomer was signed up. This was Vivienne Eissinger, the grandchild of one of the upper-class sponsors who had been persuaded by Sir Harold Nevin to increase his donation in return for a favour. As it turned out, the addition of Vivienne Eissinger to the staff was to play a key role in persuading Hugh Lombard to accept his promotion and enhanced package, and to remain with *The New Times*.

Friday, 1 April 2016. London.
At four o'clock in the morning, Hugh Lombard was hunched over his laptop on the table in his kitchen diner. The laptop's webcam was switched on, and the telecommunications channels were open.

The New Times was about to broadcast a live intercontinental debate spanning the continents of North and South America, Asia, and Oceania. The debate covered economic and political perspectives relating to a 'multipolar world order'.

It was Lombard's job to coordinate the teleconference from his home in London at this unearthly hour.

Behind Lombard – hiding from view the sink, the cooker and the fridge-freezer (the latter covered in fridge magnets and post-it notes) – a stylish six-leaf folding screen set the mood; each leaf was lacquered a glossy black around the edges, with the centre of each leaf outlining ancient scenes from an Asian adventure told in shadow play.

An ultra-high-resolution video camera was stationed on a shelf at one end of the kitchen diner in Lombard's apartment. This camera pivoted on a small tripod and could be controlled remotely by an operator who was in a different location. The high resolution proved to be impressive, but, to save time, Dmitry Krejevsky wanted to test the remote operation of the camera while the live intercontinental broadcast was in progress to evaluate the camera's potential for future use.

The broadcast was watched by over 20,000 people, who were logged into their computers across the globe. A technician was on hand at the premises of the website's service provider to ensure the process ran smoothly. The technician reported that the website was up and running – and showing no sign of strain.

Slick.

Thirty minutes into the broadcast, Dmitry Krejevsky noticed some noise: banging and loud voices. He was in constant contact with John Morton and Hugh Lombard via the website's online chat facility.

Lombard reported that the noise seemed to be coming from the lifts and staircase outside his front door. Then he reported that the noise was coming from inside his loft apartment. Suddenly, Lombard's kitchen diner was swarming with armed police officers wearing peaked caps with chequered bands above the rim and around the crown. A couple of helmeted riot police appeared momentarily before moving to secure the rear exit via the fire escape.

Lombard stood up with his mouth agape in astonishment. Plainclothes officers appeared on the scene, flashing their identity cards and asking if they were speaking to Mr Hugh Lombard.

"What the...!" Dmitry Krejevsky exclaimed. "We're being raided!"

Krejevsky's fingers hammered out an exchange of words on the keyboard, linking up with Morton via the website's online chat facility.

Meanwhile, around the world, 20,000 watchers were joined by thousands more as news of the raid spread and the live coverage of the event unfolded.

Stuck in his windowless operations room miles away from the action and oblivious to what was happening, the website's technician reported to Krejevsky an upsurge in hits to 25,000, then

30,000 and still climbing. The website was taking it all in its stride. It could handle it.

Lombard was lying face down on the floor of his kitchen diner. Then his hands were placed behind his back. Soon the handcuffs were applied. Finally, he was stood upright, as the police prepared to take him away.

Unknown to the police, the chaotic scenes were being captured live and in high resolution by the remotely controlled camera that was operated by Dmitry Krejevsky. The website had not crashed, and the camera worked; at least that was something positive. But what about Hugh Lombard's predicament?

Lombard's new cat, adopted recently from an animal rescue centre, sprang from its hiding place and fled terrified up the winding wooden staircase of Hugh Lombard's fashionable loft apartment. Then, everyone downstairs froze as the sound of slow, angry footsteps descended the staircase and reverberated around the loft apartment, as though the cat had transformed itself into some powerhouse superhero.

All eyes turned to the winding, wooden staircase, gazing in awe at the sight of a very tall, very elegant and very snooty-looking lady wearing an overnight face pack, who glared at the assembled throng with the most appalled and toffee-nosed expression. She wore a long, dark-blue dressing gown with dark-red trim and a high collar, which – together with her black hair that was swept back and secured with a large hair clip – projected an apparition of gothic, vampiric enticement.

"And precisely what is the meaning of this?" the lady demanded to know.

"Kenneth Yardley, Special Branch," volunteered one of the men, showing his credentials. "And who might you be, ma'am?"

"My name is Vivienne Eissinger. I must say, I am extremely distressed about the way I have been woken from my slumber, officer. Extremely distressed, I tell you."

Kenneth Yardley asked if there was anyone else in the apartment and explained to Vivienne Eissinger that she would have to accompany him to the police station.

The lady glared once more at the Special Branch officer, prior to succumbing to a resigned inevitability. "Very well, officer. However, first, I would like to pay a visit to the lavatory and to put on some fresh clothes."

A police sergeant instructed one of his young constables to escort the lady upstairs and to, "be a bit discreet if you don't mind, lad?"

Vivienne Eissinger led the way upstairs and entered the bathroom. "Oh, don't worry, officer. There's no need to close the door. I'll be with you in a trice," she stated. The lady bequeathed her instructions with a delicate touch of a fingertip onto the constable's young shoulder, before walking toward the toilet bowl, loosening her dressing gown and hoisting up her night dress to pee while standing up.

"What is it, Bates?" the sergeant said as he was confronted by his trembling young constable, who had staggered down the spiral staircase and into the kitchen diner in stunned silence.

"The lady is a fella," Bates stammered.

"What do you mean, Bates... a man?" the sergeant asked.

The constable nodded. Then the sergeant heard a click and turned to his right. The constable turned to his left. Together, they found themselves staring at, and being stared at by, the remotely controlled, high-resolution camera with its telephoto lens in the process of zooming in.

Lovely to see you!

Click!

Dmitry Krejevsky had caught the whole episode live on camera. It went viral by means of *The New Times* website. Globally. Immediately.

✽

It is seldom that The Great British Public wakes so early in the morning, even on a Friday, which is regarded commonly as the beginning of the weekend. Teenagers who would normally drag out to the last second the pulling aside of bedclothes and the act of reluctantly getting up for school were stirred into action by their older and more alert siblings.

Within two hours of the police raid, viewers discovered that the website of *The New Times* was no longer available. Dmitry Krejevsky had asked the technician to block access to prevent any mischief, such as a cyberattack. He also thought it prudent to take the website offline temporarily, to allow time for Sir Harold Nevin to pull strings behind the scenes. Dmitry Krejevsky did not want to be accused of acting recklessly by deliberately trying to embarrass the police or to be obstructing the police in what they would regard as the routine performance of their everyday duties.

Throughout the day, the internet buzzed with activity. Screenshots of the juiciest fragments of the affair were posted all over social media, and a lively debate thrived throughout the internet blogosphere. The breaking news was too early for the first editions of the daily newspapers, but that did not make a difference to how the incident would be reported in the Western corporate media. In short, it was not reported at all in the Western corporate media, because the UK's home secretary had intervened, slapped a ban on coverage of the incident and remained in touch with the press barons throughout the crisis.

The police and Special Branch officers who had taken part in the raid feared that they would be made scapegoats for what would be portrayed as a bungled operation. That would be more than a trifle disingenuous because, after all, the operation had been intelligence-led, and based upon data that had been gathered, analysed and interpreted by anonymous, faceless *secret police* officers based elsewhere, secluded in ivory towers far away from the action.

Furthermore, the police and Special Branch officers were only carrying out their instructions to the letter and according to the standard procedures that they had used on hundreds of previous occasions: smash open the front door, secure all exits, make arrests, gather evidence and execute closure. They were not aware of the camera recording the whole episode for the amusement of anyone who happened to be online at the time. Nor were they aware that Count Roland von Eissinger the Third, also known as Vivienne Eissinger (a darling of the British and German upper crusts), would intrude on the proceedings with such aplomb.

* * *

At the police station, Vivienne Eissinger made what is commonly termed 'such a stink' by insisting that she be fingerprinted *only* by a female police officer, and *only* in such a way that would cause the least damage to the nails and cuticles of her delicately manicured fingers.

The soap that was provided to wash off the ink was declared to be "simply atrocious", and, when the female police officer used the soap in a coarse manner in conjunction with a nail brush, that was absolutely the last straw.

Vivienne eventually settled herself down next to the female police officer in the interview room, and the latter managed to clean most of the ink off Vivienne's left hand with an emery board and some nail varnish remover, prior to exchanging seats with Vivienne to attend to her right hand.

The interview was trundling along at a snail's pace when the door opened gradually, and a crooked forefinger beckoned the interviewer.

* * *

At two o'clock in the afternoon, both Vivienne Eissinger and Hugh Lombard were released from police custody and ushered discreetly out of the back door into unmarked cars, which were driven at speed to the home of Sir Harold Nevin in the Buckinghamshire countryside.

After greeting them on arrival, Nevin told them, "Dmitry and John are flying back straight away. It is best that you remain here until they arrive. That will be tomorrow because they need to arrange flights from New York and Hong Kong, respectively."

2

THE UNTOUCHABLES

A silently fuming Vivienne Eissinger and a noticeably traumatised Hugh Lombard were instructed by Sir Harold Nevin to remain overnight in his stately home in the Buckinghamshire countryside.

"In fact," Nevin instructed, "I think you should stay for a few nights until this business has been cleared up. My chauffeur and one of my security officers will arrange for some of your belongings to be brought here."

This plan was executed quickly, for neither of Nevin's guests had showered, and they desperately wanted to freshen up and to put on some clean clothes.

Being on cordial terms with his peers in the Metropolitan Police and the security services, Nevin's private security officer had no trouble gaining access to Lombard's loft apartment when he arrived after driving there. However, the chauffeur was obliged to ring Nevin to check on some of the details of the required attire and wanted to know, "is the lady a star of stage and screen, or some other kind of luvvie?"

Nevin handed the phone to Vivienne Eissinger, who – wearing a scowl that would shatter solid granite – demanded that her entire wardrobe be requisitioned and packed carefully into suitcases, "by a lady officer, if you don't mind," but stipulated, "don't you *dare* let anyone near my laundry basket".

Nevin's security officer had to ring up the local police station to summon the services of a female officer, who duly arrived and packed the expensive paraphernalia as though she was doing it for her mother or an elderly relative.

The chauffeur and security officer returned to Nevin's abode subsequently, with the requested belongings.

Eventually – showered, shaved and wearing fresh clothes – the two former detainees sat down to dinner with Sir Harold Nevin and his wife, Lady Miranda.

✳

Dmitry Krejevsky was the first to arrive the next day. His rescheduled flight from New York had landed early, and he had managed to get some sleep on the extendable, lie-flat seat in business class. He was collected by Nevin's chauffeur and driven from Heathrow Airport straight to Nevin's house. The same procedure was applied to collect John Morton around midday, soon after his rescheduled flight from Hong Kong touched down.

At two o'clock in the afternoon, Nevin chaired a debriefing in his living room.

With a tremulous lump in his throat, Hugh Lombard described how he had been interrogated for three hours in the police station by Kenneth Yardley of Special Branch, "One or two other shady characters entered and left the room from time to time, and seated themselves next to the man from Special Branch; or, sometimes, came round to my side of the table and whispered suggestive allegations directly into my ear.

"They wanted to know the names of my contacts in the FSB [Federalnaya Sluzhba Bezopasnosti] – the Russian secret service. I told them I didn't know what they were talking about, but that didn't stop them. They went on and on. 'You are the editor-in-chief of *The New Times*,' they said. 'You and your friends must have good sources to provide you with the information you publish.'

"I didn't know what to say. It wasn't easy, I can tell you."

"All right, Hugh," Morton said. "No need to worry. It is over now. Just tell us what they said, in your own words and with as much detail as you can, so that we can build up a picture of what has happened. And, Hugh… try to relax."

Lombard recalled everything he could remember. His throat was dry. He sipped water frequently from a glass tumbler. For over thirty minutes, he described his experiences in the police interrogation room. Krejevsky and Morton made copious notes and compared their transcripts to ensure they tallied.

When Lombard wound up his tale of woe, Sir Harold Nevin was the first to speak.

"Unfortunately, this is the mentality of the people we are dealing with," declared Nevin. "None of us are supposed to have a brain between us. Everything we do is supposed to be dictated to us from Moscow and we just follow orders. There is no conception that, although a whole range of British interests are by their nature different from those of Russia, just for a moment and in certain cases our interests and those of Moscow might happen to coincide. Our adversaries simply have no idea that this is possible. They are even prepared to embroil our intelligence services and our police force in politically motivated actions that only serve to compromise the perceived impartiality of the police… and waste their time."

"But our adversaries do not apply the same rules to themselves," Morton put in. "If *they* have differences of opinion with the White House or with Downing Street, for example, *they* feel perfectly within their rights to express that criticism without beating their breasts with guilt over doing the bidding of the Russians."

"Quite." Nevin agreed.

The long hours of travel were beginning to catch up with Morton, and he allowed himself to take a back seat while the others discussed the police raid and its significance. Lombard was visibly shaken, but, in contrast to the support that Morton had received from his wife Alison during difficult times past, nothing remotely resembling any backing or encouragement was forthcoming from the new love interest in Lombard's life – Vivienne Eissinger – who sat erect and motionless in a high-backed chair that emphasised her aristocratic credentials. Vivienne Eissinger contributed nothing to the discussion, and Morton wondered whether she was having second thoughts about her appointment to the staff of *The New Times*.

Of even greater concern was the reaction of Dmitry Krejevsky while Lombard poured out his sorry tale with lips a-tremble and eyes almost welling up. Morton knew Krejevsky well enough by now to realise that the police raid was of lesser concern to him than whether Lombard would be able to handle the job, particularly if a similar incident took place further on down the line.

Krejevsky's line of enquiry was reasonable enough, and he was friendly and courteous in his manner of interviewing. However, to Morton, this interview resembled yet another interrogation; one more subtle and potentially more deadly for Lombard's future career than the interview in the police station, especially if Krejevsky smelled weakness in a key position for what had become for him a mission that must be accomplished at any cost.

※

At four o'clock in the afternoon, Nevin checked the pocket watch that he kept in a small compartment inside his cardigan. It was time to wrap things up. He asked Vivienne Eissinger to look after Hugh Lombard.

"If Hugh needs the brandy bottle, just give it to him," Nevin instructed.

Vivienne Eissinger assured Nevin that Hugh Lombard would be looked after, "as though he were my little brother".

After adjourning to the garden, Nevin, Krejevsky and Morton strolled around the paths separating the lawns from the flower beds. The daffodils had lost their flower heads, and their stalks had been tied up by the gardener in preparation for their removal to the first compost heap of the year and the planting of the first flowers of spring and early summer. Some burning of pruned wood and foliage was detectable in the thin, misty spring air. Small waterfalls trickled over stones in streams.

In exposed areas of the garden, the wind felt quite bracing. The three men had put on coats and scarves.

At his wife's insistence, Nevin wore a fisherman's hat and a scarf to guard against the cold. While in Hong Kong, Morton had taken inspiration from some old Chinese artworks and had visited a local barber shop; his receding hairline had been done away with and he was now shaven-headed. He had also removed his moustache, "losing years in the process" according to many an observer. He put on a baseball cap and turned his collar up to guard against the unfamiliar icy breeze. Despite his relative youth and full head of hair, Krejevsky wore his fur hat.

Referring to the police raid, Morton asked who could have been behind such a stunt, and why. Surely it could not have been Edward Ollerson? After all, Edward Ollerson was still reeling from the mauling he had received after his impulsive publication of the Russian battle plans three months earlier.

"Well," Nevin countered, "it was 'friend' Ollerson who had tried unsuccessfully to lure Hugh away from us. And we cannot be certain that 'friend' Ollerson and his accomplices will not try again. The real worry is the involvement of Special Branch in this business. This means that MI5 [Military Intelligence, Section 5], the Home Office, MI6, the Foreign and Commonwealth Office, and the Ministry of Defence are almost certainly all involved.

"Their objective: silence *The New Times*. Their method: identify the weakest link and chip away until it loosens and can be broken off.

"I fear we have not heard the last of this, gentlemen."

Krejevsky bit his lip.

"But not to worry, Dmitry," Nevin responded and broke into a smile. "I think it is time I introduced you both to some of my inner circle. As I have said before, there are powerful people at the helm of this country who are not happy with the current situation. They are mulling over a resolution of the current crisis, and how our foreign policy might be tweaked to include a détente with Russia and a redrafted security policy for the European continent.

"And, John, don't worry about Hugh. He is in safe hands. Roland will shelter and protect him."

※

Tuesday, 5 April 2016.
Sir Harold Nevin arranged a pub lunch at one of his favourite country inns. In addition to John Morton and Dmitry Krejevsky, Nevin invited his old buddies Sir Quentin Forbes and Lord Ernest Anderian. Bill Hodson MP (Member of Parliament) was also in attendance.

"We have to be realistic, Harold," Sir Quentin Forbes commented. "As you suspect, MI5 and MI6 will indeed be involved because this is a matter of national security. The main problem is not the suspicion that we have spies in our midst, although some in the security services might see it that way. The problem is that what we are doing is new, and, because it is new, it has thrown everybody. Nobody in the government and the security services can make out what is *really* going on here. They are finding it hard to adjust.

"We have not had such a high level of surveillance directed against Russia since the end of the Cold War. That was twenty-five years ago, and, during the interregnum, a whole generation of experienced Soviet experts and their equivalents in the security services has long since vanished or been sidelined. Also, the politics has changed, and in more ways than one.

"First, we do not have a Western democracy versus Soviet communism stand-off. Instead, we have greater integration of both the economies of Russia and the former socialist states of Eastern Europe with the West.

"Second, our cold warriors these days are just as likely to be from the younger generation of neoconservatives – and even liberals, and even some on the left – as from the Tory old guard. They are itching for a fight with the Russians, but they have not thought it through. It seems that they are reacting to our intervention via *The New Times* by doubling down and trying to break us. This is their modus operandi; they worked this way during the previous cold war, and they are doing the same now. They know nothing else, and, in their own eyes, they cannot back down. They cannot afford to lose face."

"Quentin, that is all well and good," Nevin put in, "but I need to know that we are going to be allowed space to do our research and to formulate a new approach. Without that, we might as well pack up, go home, and let the UK and Europe go to war with Russia and face the consequences."

"All right, all right," Sir Quentin Forbes countered. "I hear what you are saying, Harold. The thing is, how can I put it, our adversaries need to do their job. And it is often more about perception than about reality. They need to *at least give the impression* that they are protecting our national security and *at least seem to be* keeping tabs on anyone who poses a potential threat—"

"But *we* are *not* a potential threat!" Nevin protested. "*The New Times* is *not* a potential threat, *nor* an actual threat. It is a *think tank*. It is a sounding board. The whole purpose of its existence is to provide alternative opinions against which the dominant narrative can be tested. We did not set up this new and expensive website to make a brief flurry and then have its staff targeted one by one until the project is dismembered. And what exactly was the purpose of this raid on our editor-in-chief by Special Branch?"

Sir Quentin glanced in the direction of Dmitry Krejevsky, whose Slavic features – framed by his jet-black hair and beard – seemed to fade into the background as his piercing, dark-brown eyes under the familiar furrowed brow projected accusingly in Sir Quentin's direction, compelling Sir Quentin to do a double take.

"I am not referring to Dmitry," Nevin continued, raising his voice a little, being a tad frustrated with the latest incident of Sir Quentin's recently acquired 'forgetfulness'. "Dmitry has delegated the role of editor-in-chief to Hugh Lombard. It is Hugh who was targeted. Remember, Quentin? *Remember?*"

Morton correctly read the situation, and, after the frayed tempers had subsided sufficiently, he assumed the role of moderator and intervened in the debate, "The impression I have, Sir Quentin, is that our adversaries (as we so politely describe them) do not want a debate. They do not want their views to be challenged. They want us out of the way. They are – as you yourself say – doubling down and pushing their agenda recklessly.

"Yes, what we are doing is new and unexpected, and – yes – the police and security services need to be allowed to do their job, but *we* cannot do *our* job if an anonymous sponsor of the neoconservatives wants us taken out and is prepared to use government agencies to do just that. What did they have lined up for Hugh Lombard? Abduction? Extraordinary rendition? Waterboarding? How far are the security services willing to go, and what methods are they prepared to use? I think we deserve to know."

Lord Ernest Anderian leaned over toward Sir Quentin and had a quiet word.

"Might I make a suggestion?" Bill Hodson interrupted, as Sir Quentin was about to make his case anew.

"Oh, er, please do, Bill," a chastened Sir Quentin acquiesced, gesturing with an open palm. "The floor is yours."

"Thank you," Bill Hodson acknowledged.

"The PM [Bill Hodson habitually referred to the prime minister as 'the PM'] is leaning quite favourably toward our little group in Parliament these days – certainly much more than in the past. He is currently tied up with EU-related negotiations and the referendum on the country's membership of the EU, which is scheduled for 26 June. I had lunch with him a few days ago and I explained to him that, although our group within the parliamentary party would like to leave the EU, we do respect his position vis-à-vis his desire to remain within the EU under the terms of a 'renegotiated settlement'. I told the PM that, whatever the result of the referendum, we will help him in any way we can.

"He might be right; the reforms he is proposing for the referendum might be the best we can expect at this stage, but I asked him, 'what will you do if the referendum goes against you?'

"I told him, bluntly, that if the British people voted to leave the EU, the UK would have to do precisely that: to leave the EU. 'What does that imply?' I asked. It means that we would have to put in place new policies that have not, at the present time, been endorsed by Parliament. It is possible that a general election might need to be called, but that is not the only outcome that we should consider. If the British people reject membership of the EU, that could be the signal that the EU's time has come and gone. The EU is already mired in a profusion of internal problems, and, without major reforms to build and consolidate a new configuration of the EU, there is a danger that the EU might go into a downward spiral from which it would be unlikely to recover.

"The 'age of European integration' would be replaced with an 'age of national sovereignty'. Only one country in Europe is positioning itself explicitly in that direction right now, and that country is Russia – a country with which we are currently at odds. A British vote to leave would be a serious blow to the EU. I know that the Americans want to deal with the EU as one point of contact instead of many, but if the EU is fracturing, and if the Americans come to realise this is happening, then that could place the UK in a strong bargaining position. The Americans would not want to lose their special relationship with the UK, and that is where leverage can be applied.

"However, we would need to think up a new set of policies to manage the new situation. That process would be seriously undermined if think tanks such as *The New Times*, which have a role to play in the creation of those policies, were not able to function. The neoconservatives are expecting to be given the green light to take on their opponents – us included – which, presumably, is why they have been allowed not one but *two* attempts to pressure the editor-in-chief of *The New Times*. It would, in my view, be possible for the neoconservatives to continue to play this game in whatever way they wish, and for us not to worry unduly about it – so long as we have assurances from the PM, in person, that we will be allowed a fair crack of the whip.

"Any attempt to leave the EU or to reform it is regarded by the neoconservatives – including those whose influence extends to the liberal newspaper, *The Chronicle* – as anathema. But they are only one voice among many who are clamouring for attention. If we can speak directly with the PM and other powerful people at the very top, tell them that we understand their concerns about national security and their need to demonstrate that they are doing something about it, and get assurances from them that they will not meddle in the affairs of *The New Times*, then we – and they – could find ourselves in a nice little win-win situation. On that basis, we could proceed with our project."

"Those assurances would need to be ironclad," Nevin remarked.

"Of course," said Hodson, "and I think they can be nailed down."

"Good work, Bill," declared Sir Quentin Forbes, extending his warmest compliments.

✴

Sir Harold Nevin insisted that both John Morton and Dmitry Krejevsky be allowed to attend the meeting with the prime minister and his senior aides. Nevin wanted the much-vaunted 'assurances' to be extended in person to Morton and Krejevsky, and for any terms and conditions to be clearly understood by them, because they were the guys who would be taking the biggest risks by putting their careers (and perhaps even their personal freedom or their lives) on the line.

Sure enough, Bill Hodson's sterling exertions in diplomacy bore fruit, and the higher-ups agreed to call off the dogs.

During the meeting with the prime minister and his aides, at the prime minister's country house at Chequers, Morton and Krejevsky were forthright in outlining their concerns, but were also respectful and considerate toward the positions of the prime minister, the government and the security services.

John Morton exhibited a sophisticated understanding of the delicacy of the situation, but stood firm on the policy of the security services vis-à-vis *The New Times*: there must be no more raids.

All agreed.

However, as a compromise, one of the prime minister's aides announced that the surveillance operation must remain in place to allow the security services to do their job. Morton and Krejevsky challenged the legality of that decision and announced their determination to get it reversed over time.

Even so, in the meantime, if anything sensitive needed to be discussed there were plenty of public parks and other open spaces available in which to do so.

Dmitry Krejevsky, ever sceptical when it came to promises from on high, hankered after – and managed to extract – something of a concession.

The management of *The Chronicle* seemed keen to know what the management of *The New Times* was up to, and, inevitably, found what it was looking for courtesy of the intelligence that was provided to Edward Ollerson by his contacts in the UK's ministries of defence and foreign affairs.

Intelligence also came Edward Ollerson's way, thanks to his myriad contacts within the UK's security services: persistent, fawning flatterers who were frequently perceived by Edward Ollerson as some sort of 'awestruck fan club'. In reality, the relationship was one way, and very much to the advantage of the so-called 'awestruck fan club' of intelligence officers.

In the interest of fairness, Krejevsky argued, it seemed reasonable that the UK government should in return make available to *The New Times* any intelligence it had on future policy developments and on behind-the-scenes research concerning UK–Russia relations.

He got part of what he wanted. The prime minister would make available some (but not all) of the research concerning government policy. However, the prime minister told everyone connected with *The New Times* that intelligence concerning relations between the UK and Russia was strictly classified, and would remain so. There were specific reasons for this, which were not *explicitly* talked about during the meeting at Chequers in the way that is described as follows.

✳

Since the early days of the British Empire, the UK's foreign policy had tended to be inherently Russophobic: *ignorant* of things genuinely Russian; consequently, *fearful* of things genuinely Russian; and reduced to taking refuge in negative stereotypes of things *imagined* to be typically Russian. These were simplistic, 'good guys versus bad guys' narratives, with no nuances – characteristics that had been amplified during the Cold War.

At the same time, before and during the Cold War, some of the aristocratic British families – such as those of Sir Harold Nevin – had mingled with and even intermarried with aristocratic families of other European powers: the Eissingers of Germany and the Krejevskys of Russia being cases in point.

This was not surprising when you consider that the aristocracies (including the kings, queens, tsars, empresses and kaisers of the nineteenth-century empires of the UK, Germany and Russia) were related to each other, with well-documented blood ties.

During the twentieth century, a warmth had grown between the Nevins and the Eissingers, and between the Nevins and the Krejevskys, even as politics and war thrust the rival European powers into internecine conflict.

In wartime or peacetime, the Nevins, the Eissingers and the Krejevskys all wore the same old school ties.

Since the end of the Cold War, many UK politicians had remained wary of Russia, but this did not stop the UK from doing business with Russia.

A lot of Russian money was permitted to nestle in banks and other sectors of the UK economy; the UK reciprocated and, inherent Russophobia notwithstanding, UK investments in Russia turned out to far outweigh Russian investments in the UK.

Then there was the tiny issue of energy supply: the Brits were as plugged in as anyone else to the prospect of pipelines transporting cheap gas from Russia to Europe.

To sum up, inherent Russophobia notwithstanding, the period of post-Cold War mutual cross-investment was extremely profitable for business, both in Russia and in the UK.

However, hidden below the surface detail – the multiple actors with their handshakes, vodka toasts, backslappings and yelps of delight as their lucrative bacon was brought home – was the uncomfortable fact of a double-edged sword. Namely, that large-scale cross-investments tied both economies together, and provided the wealthy elites, politicians and intelligence services of both Russia and the UK with a means to exert influence over one another's affairs – including sanctions and other financial penalties, but also, on a cautionary note, what might be surreptitiously termed 'inducements'.

Any rise in tension between Russia and the UK tended to manifest itself – first and foremost – in the news media, as each side tried to dragoon its populace to stick with the dominant narrative of its own national government: Russian propaganda versus British propaganda.

In short, it would be a war of words; a spat; and, truly, a phoney war.

At any moment in time – in a display of moral righteousness – UK politicians could blow the anti-Russia dog whistle to chivvy the UK public on board with the UK's long-standing, dominant Russophobic narrative, while feeling secure in the knowledge that the UK corporate media would fall in line and expound the dominant Russophobic narrative, cloaked in a 'democratic' veneer, all the way from the right-wing media to their liberal/centre-left counterparts at *The Chronicle*.

Yet, despite this spat, the political and economic *ties that bind* would remain.

Morton, Krejevsky and Nevin knew this to be the case.

※

Going out on a limb in the presence of the prime minister, Morton broached this disconnect between what some of the UK's politicians and business community *ideally* wanted to do and what they were, *in practice*, engaged in.

How could one solve this conundrum?

The corporate media provided letters pages and opinion columns in which alternative views could be expressed – as *alternative* views. But, as the dominant narrative ran into trouble and into one blind alley after another, it would require much more than letters pages and opinion columns to develop alternatives. And, if those *alternative* views were to be developed into some useful *end product*, think tanks and alternative media would require space in which to come into their own.

The prime minister was already aware of everything that John Morton pointed out to him about the ongoing phoney war between Russia and the UK, yet he listened attentively to what Morton said.

There would be consequences if the UK pursued its current anti-Russia course, but the UK would get by, if the prime minister remained in control of events and in control of the dominant narrative. However, it was a big 'if'.

The success or failure of the UK's approach depended on whether Russia would buckle under the impact of sanctions imposed by the West, especially the sanctions imposed by the UK and the US.

However, Morton pointed out, if Russia did *not* buckle, then the UK would need to prepare a contingency – a plan B would need to be prepared and to be kept in readiness in case it was required. Morton asked the prime minister if he had a workable plan B in place.

The prime minister knew the answer, but said nothing. His bland, self-satisfied smile was calculated to give nothing away, but a revealing glint in the prime minister's eyes told Morton everything he needed to know.

Morton imagined the train of thoughts going through the mind of the prime minister:

So, John Morton, you have a plan B in mind, do you? A plan B for me? All mine – with you, John Morton, as the sole custodian? And your think tank, The New Times, *is already in position to develop this plan B and any other alternative plans I might need. Apparently, regardless of your leftist leanings, your services have already been purloined by some High Tories – one of whom talked me into adding your name to the New Year's Honours List.*

Well, well, well. You're a rum one, John Morton. You know how to take a sneak peek behind the scenes and to see through walls – walls of words and narratives, of decisions and their motives – and you can visualise how a specific policy or narrative might play out.

You know that I am not much older than you, and that I could stay in my job for a long time to come – as was the case with some of my predecessors. But you are also aware, as am I, that what has happened in the past is no guarantee of future success, and you are betting that the underlying geopolitics have every chance of making things messy for my government. Very messy indeed. And if things do get very messy for my government, I am going to be the one who will be held to account.

Even without input from my Cabinet colleague, Bill Hodson, you already have a reasonable insight into what is going on in my Cabinet. Bill just provides you with the detail, probably via Sir Harold Nevin.

I have staked my bet on a certain strategy. If it goes wrong, I will probably be toast. Someone new will have to take the helm. But the new 'PM' would need to consider a strategy that is different from mine – lest the new PM also should become toast.

All you want is freedom of expression. You even defended your adversary, Edward Ollerson, back in January when many of my Cabinet wanted to haul him over the coals for the way he leaked the Russian battle plans and caused so much unrest among the UK population.

You have an honest face, John Morton. Should I trust you? Bill Hodson believes that the future will be more about national sovereignty, and less about the integration of the nation state with political and economic arrangements (such as the EU) that are devised by external actors. Bill's views on Europe conflict with mine, but I like to think I am shrewd enough to understand that there might be a grain of truth in what Bill says.

Maybe, after the EU Referendum is out of the way, I will need to sit down and think up some fresh answers to increasingly awkward questions. If I were to bring you on board, I would need you to be flexible in your approach. Will you do that, John Morton? Really? Yes? Yes... yes... I think... I think you probably will.

Morton felt that he had sold his bill of goods rather well, and that the prime minister had left the meeting with the prospect of a plan B in mind and a firm impression that the guardians of this potential plan B were among the most talented resources he might draw upon.

Furthermore, John Morton felt that he had come across as brave but not reckless, and not afraid to speak frankly during these difficult times when the world was changing and far too many commentators were having difficulty in getting to grips with the new situation.

From now on, anyone associated with *The New Times* would be listened to and, apart from the routine surveillance, not hounded or bullied in any way by the British elite. Bill Hodson's boss, the PM, would personally see to that.

But, Morton suggested, let us remain on the alert – just in case.

Otherwise, all things being equal, at least from the point of view of the UK's prime minister, the management and staff of *The New Times* had become *untouchable*.

3

SUITED AND BOOTED

Following the meeting with the prime minister and his aides, John Morton, Dmitry Krejevsky and Sir Harold Nevin returned to the latter's Buckinghamshire stately home. The three men were acutely aware that they had bought time and had even extracted some concessions, but what were they to do with these concessions, and how best were they to use this time? These were the key questions that played on their minds.

John Morton MBE was a person whom the prime minister had warmed to increasingly during the meeting at Chequers; a person whom the prime minister felt he could trust; someone who had a thorough grasp of the politics of the Middle East, and a network of colleagues with a thorough grasp of other regions of the globe; and someone who, if the UK's foreign policy needed an injection of fresh thinking, might in the future be invited into the inner circle as an advisor on foreign policy, not only for the current prime minister but also for his successors.

This detail did not escape the eagle eyes of Sir Harold Nevin, and – given his propensity for spotting an opportunity to put his foot in the door, and edge it further and further ajar – the incessantly turning wheels in Nevin's mind were rotating just that bit faster during the drive home.

A short time after arriving and over a glass of dry sherry before dinner, the three men met in Nevin's library to flesh out some ideas. They discussed areas of interest, in no specific order of priority.

Ukraine. The situation was resembling a frozen conflict, Ukraine's neighbours (all of them, not only Russia but also Poland, Hungary, Moldova and Romania) were eyeballing the various pieces of Ukraine that might fall into their laps. The role of *The New Times* was to wait and see.

Syria. The Syrian government forces allied with Russia and Iran would eventually rout the Syrian opposition, and, unless Turkey decided to intervene militarily, there was unlikely to be any change in this direction. However, a Turkish intervention risked making the situation more complicated than it already was, perhaps provoking a troublesome response from various Kurdish groups, and bringing ever closer the prospect of a direct conflict between Turkey and Russia. The decision made was to keep an eye on developments.

China. There was a need to keep an eye on China's 'silk roads' project and the extent to which it was shifting the centre of gravity of the global economy away from North America and Western Europe toward Asia and, more specifically, Eurasia and Eurasian Integration. But, for now, no action was required – they should wait and see.

Russia. This had become the central subject of enquiry over the past two years and it would remain so. However, right now, the Americans clearly did not want a head-on confrontation with Russia, not least because the 2016 US presidential election would occupy top billing, and the orientation of the incoming administration's foreign policy would not become clear until after the inauguration of the new president in January 2017. So, probably, it was another case of wait and see.

To summarise, then, it was likely that (at least in the next few months, as is part and parcel of a phoney war) nothing particularly new or unpredictable was expected in the geopolitical space. Therefore, to build upon the momentum that had accumulated during the meeting with the prime minister, it was agreed that Europe and the UK's referendum on EU membership should be designated as a new priority and the immediate focus of attention for *The New Times*, with the other areas of interest being handled on an as-needed basis.

A renewed focus on Europe and the UK would draw in Zoe and Hans Neubauer. Hugh Lombard would activate his multifarious contacts via his 'café society', and Shirley would be able to hold the fort. Morton's son Anthony would return home in mid-June after completing his finals (he had already handed in his dissertation) and, after a fortnight's holiday, he would join the staff of *The New Times* on 1 July. He would immediately take on as many of Lombard's chores as possible, thereby freeing up the editor-in-chief to pursue his proper role with greater vigour.

Having had personal experience of how a great psychologist works – as a patient of Dr Quinn, during his recuperation eighteen months earlier – Morton tried to apply some of the general principles of the good doctor by encouraging the traumatised Hugh Lombard to divert himself from his anguish by throwing himself wholeheartedly into Project Hamlet, a ten-week project between the middle of April and the 'to be in, or not to be in' EU Referendum scheduled for 26 June.

※

This left one member of staff unaccounted for: Vivienne Eissinger.

John Morton had been less than impressed by Vivienne's performance to date. Dmitry Krejevsky had been totally perplexed by the appointment from day one.

Nevin had agreed to take on Vivienne (aka Count Roland von Eissinger the Third) as a favour in return for funding from a wealthy sponsor. What he had not told anyone before, but was about to reveal now, was that part of the deal was to try to find a role in the world for Vivienne.

Nevin addressed Morton and Krejevsky directly, "I really must apologise for this act of duplicity on my part. But, you see, I had to find the right moment to break the news to you, and I think that moment has arrived.

"I have known Roland since he was a child. I can still remember him in short trousers, clambering up tree trunks in orchards and scrumping for apples on the local farms, with all the other boys and girls. They would go for walks together, paddle in streams together, and swim in rivers and lakes. They were inseparable, and there was never any serious trouble. Just a little horseplay, from time to time.

"During his teens, Roland was sent to Northminster public school – Dmitry's and my old school – which was deemed 'perfectly suited to the aspirations of his dear mamma'. There, he was bullied because of his height (he is six feet four inches now and was easily over six feet at the time) and because of his aristocratic German ancestry. He stood his ground, and he has developed an inner strength that few people can detect, but which reveals itself when Roland senses that the time is ripe.

"Roland was keen on sports, and anyone who brushed him up the wrong way could easily find himself paying the penalty on the polo ground – those hammer-headed sticks pack a real punch, you know. He also possesses a withering sense of humour. Just for fun, people used to deliberately antagonise him to see what he would come out with. You could have written a book on that subject alone.

"On his eighteenth birthday, and without warning, Roland came downstairs to his party fully made up – with lips glossed, lashes enhanced with mascara and hair secured in place – and wearing a luxurious, full-length evening gown with a fur stole.

"An orchestral quartet in full Georgian costume – including wigs, frock coats, stockings with gaiters and shoes with buckles – was playing an elegant and refined piece by Mozart near a large mirror in the hall. As Roland descended the wide and curved staircase, caressing the banister with a hand that was gloved all the way to the elbow and sporting a cigarette holder in the other gloved hand, I caught a glimpse of his reflection in the mirror. His eyes met mine, and he extended to me a winsome smile and a courteous nod in my direction. He knew that, however shocked many of the others might be, I would stand loyally beside him.

"His dear mamma was beside herself with grief, and his father was visibly outraged. But, to calm the occasion, I took leave of my dear wife, and walked over to take Roland's right hand and lead him into the dining room, bowing, nodding and smiling politely in all directions. Acutely aware of his height, he had wisely chosen a small heel for his evening slippers.

"Roland immediately took control of the situation. He announced that from that point on he would be known as Vivienne, after one of his favourite actresses.

"The birthday party was an unmitigated disaster – from the point of view of Roland's parents – but nearly everyone else seemed to enjoy it and perhaps had been wondering for some time when exactly Roland would, er, shall we say, come out. It was a fantastic party, and Miranda and I made sure to invite Roland's parents over here for dinner as a thank you. They were sitting in the very chairs in the living room in which, this morning, you two fine gentlemen were agreeably ensconced."

Krejevsky asked, "What role exactly, Sir Harold, do you have in mind for Vivienne Eissinger?"

Nevin replied, "It is really up to you chaps to work that out."

Morton racked his brains for ten minutes without any luck. Then he tried to visualise the situation through the eyes of various other people: Hugh Lombard – nothing doing; Zoe, Hans and Alison – still no joy; and Tom Hamble – *getting desperate now John*, Morton reproached himself.

Then Morton thought of Shirley Bould. Shirley had a talent for understanding how to trigger a response in another person. Morton recalled Nevin's description of the coming of age of Count Roland von Eissinger the Third and his transformation into, well, Morton did not quite know what. Morton closed his eyes and imagined Shirley was speaking. After a while the mist began to clear, and Morton opened his eyes, his lips widening into a smile.

"What Vivienne needs," Morton announced, "is obvious, really."

Nevin and Krejevsky waited, with bated breath.

"Vivienne likes to do role play. As Roland the boy, he joined in all the games and learned to cope with some of the complexities of adolescence. When he finally came out, it was in a big way, like a film star – even rebranded with the name of a film star. Now Vivienne is, what, thirty-five? And she has been playing the same role for seventeen years. Perhaps Vivienne is going through a mid-life crisis or, more likely I would bet, her parents are going through her mid-life crisis on her behalf. Time for a change, and time for… a makeover!"

Krejevsky roared with laughter, nearly rolled off his chair, and coughed and sputtered while trying to swallow a mouthful of dry sherry.

Nevin, too, laughed heartily and declared, "John, you are amazing. That is a stroke of genius. Just one question: what do you propose Roland be made over to look like?"

Morton expanded on his idea. "Look at the reaction Vivienne inspires. It is awesome. Vivienne entrances all who set eyes on her, immediately. I think we should consult Shirley. I cannot see Vivienne making the right impression by wearing an evening dress, with a fur stole slung over her shoulder, every time she makes an appearance. But with her hair tied up, some smart trouser suits and an attaché case, she would be a dead ringer for a marketing executive. Shirley is Hugh's PA. Could Vivienne be launched as Hugh's PR?"

Nevin was ecstatic. "Perfect. We need someone to give support to Hugh on a daily basis. It is clear to me that Hugh and Roland have become what is known as an item. How long it will last, I am reluctant to guess, for I have never known such a flighty creature as Roland. If we can keep Roland's ego inflated, and pump it up from time to time, then we could be onto a winner here."

Morton rang up Shirley and an appointment with a beautician was arranged for the following day.

※

During the evening, Hugh Lombard and Vivienne Eissinger joined Sir Harold Nevin, Lady Miranda, Dmitry Krejevsky and John Morton for dinner. Nevin explained that the crisis was over and that they had met with the prime minister. It was now safe for everyone to go home.

※

The next day, Lombard and Morton held the fort at the office while Shirley escorted Vivienne to a beautician's shop that had been recommended to Shirley by her daughter. Once inside the shop, the proprietor arranged for tea and biscuits to be served.

At Vivienne's insistence, the mugs and biscuit tins were disdained fastidiously, and tea was served instead in china cups with matching saucers, which were all decorated with roses and imitation-gold rims. Biscuits were served on a plate, and were selected in ones and twos, then placed by the customers at the sides of the teacups on the saucers, together with ornate teaspoons.

A price list was scrutinised. The required services were selected: a hair wash, condition and light trim; a manicure; and a pedicure.

Some hair had grown back on Vivienne's legs, so the proprietor suggested the next page of the portfolio be examined to select the appropriate service. When Vivienne chose the salon's most extreme hair-removal option (during which *all* hair from the abdomen, thorax, legs, arms underarms and pubic area would be removed), Shirley became transfixed, with her mouth open in amazement and disbelief.

Even in agony, Vivienne Eissinger glided from the beautician's shop with a dignified nose in the air and with immaculate poise.

※

Two days later, it was time for Vivienne to be measured up in a fitting room. An order was placed for six smart business suits: two black, two dark grey and two dark blue, with one of each colour being pinstriped. A selection of shirts and ties, and six pairs of black shoes – three flat-soled and three small-heeled – were added to the mix.

It was all done, except for an attaché case; however, in a swanky department store, Vivienne found a companion set that included large, medium and small suitcases, and a flat bag for the storage and transportation of suits, in addition to an attaché case. Shirley noticed that the set had been heavily discounted – which was all to the good, because the day was turning into an expensive one. Shirley showed the receipts to Hugh Lombard, who, in turn, thought it best to show them to John Morton.

"We need to get Vivienne's new career up and running, and make some sort of a splash. I will hold off on the publication of the financial report until Vivienne has been given a chance to make an impact, so that the cost of this enterprise is easier to justify. In the meantime, Hugh," Morton advised, "don't tell Dmitry."

✳

Vivienne's big splash was going to require some serious brainstorming. Her experience in the field of journalism extended no further than articles for a fashion magazine, including some flashy attire that she had recommended to the participants in an upcoming polo tournament.

"Always play to your strengths," Morton's late father had advised him over thirty years earlier. That being the case, Morton suggested sending Vivienne to Moscow to attend a fashion show and publishing a report on it in the cultural section of *The New Times* website. Vivienne would need an escort. Morton handed this task to Hugh Lombard.

"My wife's father is not too good at the moment," Morton explained. "I need to stay in London, so I will work in the office with Shirley. And Hugh... I'm not sure how things stand with LGBT [lesbian, gay, bisexual and transgender] tourists in Russia, so make sure you book separate rooms to avoid any risk of a scandal."

4
TWILIGHT OF THE CHRONICLE?

For the editor-in-chief of *The Chronicle* newspaper, Edward Ollerson MBE, the first quarter of 2016 had been one of mixed fortunes.

The embarrassing fallout from the would-be scoop of the year concerning the leak of declassified Russian battle plans had almost cost him his job and his personal freedom, but not necessarily his reputation, because, ironically, by publicising the declassified Russian battle plans (albeit with a modicum of 'Ollersonesque' spin), he had unwittingly managed to whet the appetite of The Great British Public with an attention-grabbing and previously unheard-of narrative.

Consequently – lending credence to the great showman PT Barnum's claim that "there is no such thing as bad publicity" – *The Chronicle* newspaper had experienced a dramatic upsurge in circulation.

But that was in January.

Now it was Easter.

Edward Ollerson had failed to capitalise on a sense of public fascination; consequently, interest in the scandal concerning Russian battle plans had fizzled out, and, accordingly, the newspaper's circulation had begun to slide. Edward Ollerson had missed the boat.

The narratives peddled by *The Chronicle* had lost their temporarily restored sparkle. Potential readers were searching for stories that were 'hot and topical' not 'reheated and timeworn'.

Neglected, long-term problems started to resurface, reminding the languorous editor-in-chief not to disregard their unremitting 'clear and present danger'.

For example, star performers such as John Morton and Dmitry Krejevsky had been elbowed out for political reasons and never replaced. There was simply nobody on the bloated reporting staff who could compare with them in terms of quality.

Another example was that some of the other dailies were thinking seriously about moving away from paper media for the weekend editions, or ditching their paper media entirely and going fully digital. One broadsheet-turned-tabloid media outlet had even taken that bold leap of faith.

Yet another example was where, instead of hiring a specialist to head up the listless marketing team – someone with the strength of character to withstand the incoming tide of small-minded gossip and parochial office politics that wormed its way in from other departments, thereby distracting the marketing team from its work – Edward Ollerson tried to do the job himself. He requisitioned an independent market survey, conducted by a postgraduate research student; this student was young, female, sexy, and 'coincidentally' available *and* willing, as Ollerson harnessed his status as 'the Chief' to turn on the charm.

The postgraduate research student was hired on a three-month placement, to assess the paper's readership and to break it down into categories to perform some market analysis. Ominously, the survey showed that only a few thousands were from the hard core of academics, postmodernists, liberals, libertarians, humanitarian interventionists, various shades of 'centre-leftist', and those who (according to Ollerson's similarly miscast predecessor, the academic-minded Sir Tom Hamble) Karl Marx might have upbraided as "hole and corner reformers of every imaginable kind". Perhaps another 200,000 were regular readers – submissive followers, not influential leaders. The remainder was passing trade.

In short, *The Chronicle* was widely perceived as old hat.

The first twinges of discomfort had made their presence felt in the back office. Without the mature, steadying hand of Shirley Bould, and the easy-going comradeship and attentive-listening skills of Hugh Lombard – both now reinvented in more prominent and satisfying roles at *The New Times* – *The Chronicle*'s back office had sunk into chaos.

Taking in the big picture, *The Chronicle* was desperately understaffed, new recruits were undertrained, the management did not know how to effectively manage within a comfort zone with poorly defined targets, and staff turnover had reached a record high.

Time for a slice or two of humble pie, perhaps; in private, at least. This might explain why Edward Ollerson hoped that, by poaching Hugh Lombard from *The New Times* and bringing him back into the fold, he might be able to stop the rot.

But, deep in his heart, Ollerson knew that – even if he had succeeded in luring Hugh Lombard away from *The New Times* – there was no guarantee of success, because the 'soft and cuddly', live-and-let-live Lombard would have been the target of the backbiting and bitching that thrived under Ollerson's ally, Josh.

Edward Ollerson was grasping at straws, and he knew it.

And the, by now fed up, young postgraduate student – having researched her way through the archives until she uncovered enough to produce a sense of outright disillusionment with *The Chronicle* and its philandering editor-in-chief – "had the gall", Ollerson complained to his PA Josh, "to just bugger off," allegedly without finishing her low-paid, zero-hours contract and to, "swan off for a six-month spell in purdah," to prepare her final dissertation.

"On the shaded poop deck of a schooner moored off the coast of Goa, no less," Josh added, "and with a new *fancy man*."

It seemed an age since Edward Ollerson had led the charge in support of the anti-Russian regime in Ukraine, which had come to power through a violent coup two years earlier. He had pursued the NATO line on Syria with the same vigour he had practised over the previous NATO-led humanitarian interventions in the Balkans, in Afghanistan, in Iraq and in Libya. This was supposed to mean NATO-imposed no-fly zones over Syria, regime change, the installation of an allegedly democratic and pro-Western government, and, above all, a NATO aerial bombardment of shock and awe to discourage other leaders with similar intentions.

But none of this had happened. Instead, Russia had put its foot down over Syria and was calling the shots. Furthermore, with the Joint Comprehensive Plan of Action (JCPOA) – aka the 'Iran nuclear deal' – settled, Iran was being drawn in from the cold.

The Americans were distracted; they were engaged in increasingly bitter primaries to decide who would represent the Democrats and the Republicans in the race to the White House.

Edward Ollerson's liberal, anti-Russia rhetoric was virtually indistinguishable from the anti-Russia rhetoric pronounced by right-wing media outlets throughout Western Europe and North America. Worryingly, the anti-Russia rhetoric in the Baltic States, Poland and Ukraine was of a particularly provocative, warlike, nationalist and anti-liberal character. Yet Edward Ollerson chose to overlook the sheer nastiness of many of the Russophobes who had attained power in those countries, opting instead to double down in support of the regime-change ambitions of the mandarins in the UK Foreign and Commonwealth Office and the neoconservatives in the US State Department.

These days, Europe looked and felt divided, confused, unsettled and even frightened.

A refugee crisis was talked up by the right-wing media into an almighty existential crisis, on top of concerns over immigration and asylum seeking, thereby fuelling the growth of the far right.

These new phenomena (and especially their underlying causes) merited detailed analysis and critical commentary, yet Edward Ollerson baulked at anything more than a routine slapping of wrists within a lukewarm critique, of sorts.

Above all, in full accord with the neoconservative backers of Edward Ollerson and his allies, the editorial line of *The Chronicle* "must ensure that *no blame* be attached to the governments of the Western powers". Accusations from the anti-war movement and from media such as *The New Times* that the refugee crisis was the predictable blowback from NATO-led overseas humanitarian interventions must *not* be allowed to pass without comment. Such 'dangerous ideas' must be 'refuted decisively' with 'dignified scorn', and – under Edward Ollerson's leadership – *The Chronicle* newspaper made sure that those 'dangerous ideas' *were* always 'refuted decisively' with 'dignified scorn', after a fashion.

So much was going on in the world, but the direction in which the world was turning did not fit the cosy narrative that was the lifeblood of *The Chronicle*. Apart from the odd sensationalist article, spun wildly to stimulate his diminished loyal following, there was nothing original for Edward Ollerson to say – and any prospect that his dilatory, predictable approach would attract new customers was, frankly, beyond hope.

Funding from sponsors was still coming in, but the decline in circulation indicated a poor return on investment. Sooner or later, one or more sponsors might pull the plug.

So, it should have come as no surprise that, on the same day that Vivienne Eissinger was being kitted out with an expensive new wardrobe courtesy of *The New Times*, Edward Ollerson found himself in receipt of an email from one of his sponsors giving three months' notice that funding would be terminated. It was a much-feared nightmare scenario; not only because it would force a rethink of fiscal policy at *The Chronicle*, but even more so because – instead of being left to his own devices to lurk in the shadows in a self-inflicted exclusion – Edward Ollerson would find himself in the spotlight, for all the wrong reasons.

For an introverted, diffident soul such as Edward Ollerson, even staying too long in the spotlight for the *right* reasons would, in his mind, amount to a minor existential crisis. He preferred to hog the limelight for the shortest time possible, take any plaudits that were going with a curt handshake and a modest nod of the head, and then go home and put his feet up in front of the TV.

Now, plunged into crisis mode, Edward Ollerson would have to do some hard thinking to dream up answers to the inevitable tsunami of unasked questions from the core group of sponsors that had so far *not* declared their intention to withdraw support. These were unasked questions that – in his mind – would haunt him and cause him many a sleepless night, and induce him to take refuge in an increasingly potent assortment of intoxicants.

Wracking his brain one evening, over a couple of bottles of wine, Edward Ollerson could think up only a limited response: retrenchment and austerity. He could shed some jobs; freeze end-of-year bonuses; put a stop to the printing of the Sunday paper edition; reduce the volume of the print run for the daily paper edition to trim the number of unsold returns; and promote the website, at some unspecified time hence, as the one and only 'access point of choice' for customers.

However, John Morton had been correct in his judgment that Edward Ollerson was unlikely to have been behind the police raid on Hugh Lombard's apartment. That action had been prompted by darker forces hidden behind the scenes: darker forces with dirty and bloody hands who had taken it upon themselves to watch Edward Ollerson like a hawk; and darker forces that, if they thought it necessary, might take what they considered to be 'appropriate remedial action'.

※

In addition to his tried-and-trusted arsenal of inebriating substances, Edward Ollerson also had another ace up his sleeve: escapism.

Like an innocent lamb, Edward Ollerson accepted an enticing freebie (care of an anonymous and unsolicited well-wisher) in a corporate marquee at the Grand National steeplechase meeting in Liverpool. At midday on Thursday, 7 April, he was drinking a pint of lager and trying to decide which horses would be the most likely to win. Being a cautious investor who seldom gambled, Ollerson decided to bet no more than £10 per race. After three races and three pints of lager (with whisky chasers), mopped up with an overpriced cheeseburger and fries, the luckless Ollerson found himself £30 down. His smart suit and silk tie prompted him to take refuge from the gathering rain clouds and their inevitable drizzle. The day was becoming a washout in more ways than one, and he was in danger of getting seriously drunk unless someone turned up to rescue him.

Fortunately, salvation was at hand in the form of old flame and co-thinker Loretta Farelli; he had last seen her face-to-face at the ambush of John Morton over the Ukraine crisis two years earlier. She had picked winners in two of the first three races and was already at least £100 better off. Lady Luck might be coming Edward Ollerson's way.

"Take a bigger risk, Edward," Loretta suggested, "You have £40 left to spend on the remaining four races. In the next race there is a feisty newcomer called Sturdy Boy. He's a dead cert at 5/1, I was tipped. Put your £40 on that horse, and I'll match it."

They did, and Sturdy Boy romped home by ten lengths. Suddenly, the day was worth living again. Loretta Farelli persuaded one of her male colleagues to swap badges with Edward Ollerson, and – as if in a flashback to a golden age – Loretta and Edward skipped upstairs, hand in hand, to a posh reception where the champagne flowed and the food was of the highest quality.

It turned out that this had not been an unplanned liaison. Loretta Farelli introduced Edward Ollerson to dozens of friends, associates, colleagues, friends of her father, friends of her youngest uncle on her mother's side, and so on. By the end of the afternoon, the tipsy Edward Ollerson could not remember any of those to whom he had been introduced, save one: Katy Drake, a blonde, blue-eyed, vivacious, Ivy League educated friend and colleague of Loretta Farelli. Katy Drake had influential friends and acquaintances, and both she and they were well-connected to powerful personalities in the Democratic Party in the United States.

"You are coming tomorrow, aren't you?" Katy asked. "Loretta and I are staying for the whole race meeting, including the Grand National race on Saturday, before we fly back down to London on Sunday morning to go to a soccer game in the afternoon."

Edward Ollerson had planned to stay up north for one night only before returning to London early on Friday morning to avoid the weekend rush. Now, he was booking an extra two nights in the same hotel as Katy and Loretta (at their expense), and having one of Loretta's male friends take Edward's return train ticket to

London instead of him, thereby allowing Edward to take the other man's place in a private jet on a return flight to London on Sunday morning.

On Friday evening, Katy Drake added herself willingly to Edward Ollerson's burgeoning list of old flames.

※

Edward Ollerson also attended the football match (the 'soccer game', as Katy called it) on Sunday; they sat in a corporate hospitality box, where a business proposal was put to Edward.

The proposal involved an injection of substantial amounts of cash to move *The Chronicle* to fancy new premises, bring in new blood and relaunch it.

Edward Ollerson would be allowed to keep his job as editor-in-chief, but some unfathomable structural changes were included that would, in effect, render him a mere figurehead. He was going to become the new Tom Hamble. In the tradition of hapless, spineless editors-in-chief of *The Chronicle*, Edward Ollerson had finally arrived.

He bade farewell to his old flame Loretta and his new flame Katy, with mutual promises to keep in touch, and resumed his normal life. Except that it no longer felt like a normal life. The female company and the business proposal had given Edward Ollerson a tremendous fillip, and, on Monday morning, he walked briskly through the corridors to his office swinging a long umbrella and loudly humming Wagner's *Ride of the Valkyries*. Tongues wagged incessantly as Edward Ollerson's PA, Josh, spread the word about Katy Drake and him.

At home in the evening, in front of the TV with a glass of red wine and a warmed-up pizza, Edward Ollerson drifted slowly back down to earth. The third glass of wine made him feel broody. The fourth made him moody. He pushed the TV dinner tray away, leaving two slices of pizza uneaten. He dreamed a little of Wagner's music; he dreamed of power, as he could see himself presiding over a world-class setup at a revitalised version of *The Chronicle*.

Or could he? What if it went wrong, just as the leak of the Russian battle plans had gone wrong? Not much had gone right since he had become the editor-in-chief. Was he out of his depth? And as for that chance meeting at the racecourse, which had turned out not to be happenstance, what was that *really* all about? Looking back, it all seemed too good to be true.

At the football match the previous day, a world-class team of superstars with their world-class manager had found themselves, not for the first time, two-nil down in the seventy-seventh minute at home to a team of strugglers. Sections of the home crowd exited the stadium in droves before the end of the match. The away fans taunted the opposing manager with chants of "Sacked in the morning" and "On the dole, on the dole, on the dole," even though – as a highly paid, non-British and non-European manager – he would not be entitled to draw upon the UK's diminishing social benefits.

In a terrible inversion of the Dick Whittington story, were the crowds chanting the inevitable fate of Edward Ollerson?

※

At three o'clock in the afternoon on Wednesday, 13 April, seated at his desk at the premises of *The Chronicle* in the Farringdon area of London, Edward Ollerson joined an intercontinental webcam conference chaired by Katy Drake, with Loretta Farelli in attendance (both based in Washington DC). All three were accompanied by their key sponsors, and the single item on the agenda was what amounted to a hostile takeover of *The Chronicle* by a consortium headed by an anonymous key player in the Beltway.

Loretta Farelli 'led from behind' as Katy Drake skilfully took charge of the negotiations. Since their first meeting at the racecourse in Liverpool, Edward Ollerson pictured Katy through rose-tinted glasses and found it difficult to think up any arguments against her proposals.

In some ways, the proposals sounded a bit retro. Surely, the fashionable time to move office to the Millhouse Building on the Thames Embankment was twenty years ago, not now.

Also, the idea of intervening militarily to introduce Western democracy to recalcitrant citizens with a different culture seemed in drastic need of an overhaul. Russia and China were not merely appearing on the scene as major players, in their own right. They were spearheading what was labelled a multipolar world order, with the implication being that other developing countries would vie for positions at the top table – Argentina, Brazil, India, Pakistan, Iran, Indonesia, South Africa, Nigeria, Turkey and Saudi Arabia, to list just a few – in their own way and at their own pace, without a need for humanitarian interventions and a pro-Western regime change.

Bombing foreign governments who were deemed to be 'unruly' might no longer be possible. In any case, such humanitarian interventions tended to produce an unstable, temporary *sitzkrieg*: a stalemate, with no clear winners.

Edward Ollerson had managed to work this much out, and he did not seem too keen on the idea of, in Katy Drake's words (egged on by Loretta Farelli), "aggressively leading from the front" to fight an information war against formidable opponents such as John Morton and Dmitry Krejevsky.

Had Edward Ollerson been of stronger mind and had he not found himself entwined in an intimate liaison with Katy Drake, he would surely have seen her for what she really was: a pre-programmed tool of the neoconservatives, complete with an ideologically driven agenda but no understanding of the historical context in which that agenda was situated. Edward Ollerson imagined Katy driving herself into a blind alley as her future pet projects petered out, then reacting to events by doubling down with sheer hubris. That was what tended to happen these days, resulting in *sitzkrieg*, with no clear winners.

But the lackadaisical Edward Ollerson ended up going along with Katy's plan. The stark reality was that Edward Ollerson and the existing sponsors of *The Chronicle* were being sold a pup: a cute, little doggie with great big dollar signs for eyes.

※

As soon as the ink on the agreement was dry, Katy Drake was on the phone to Edward Ollerson to arrange a meeting in London. She intended to stay in a hotel apartment for a fortnight, to act as the point person to handle awkward situations that might crop up and to provide an ad hoc office and conference room, should the need arise.

Katy told Edward that she would be able to meet up with him on a personal basis, sometime during her stay, but only, "as time allowed".

According to Katy's plan, the first casualty of the reorganisation would be Josh. Edward Ollerson was not displeased by this move because Josh had long since served her purpose. Furthermore, she was a disruptive influence whose dubious character had come to the attention of Loretta and her allies in the Beltway.

Consequently, after it had been agreed to let Josh go, Katy Drake decided promptly that under no circumstances should Josh be redeployed within the organisation. Josh's pension rights were frozen until she was eligible to receive them on her retirement date and her final exit was wrapped up with an enhanced redundancy payment to head off any possible follow-up on her part, such as an industrial tribunal. Josh was made to sign a declaration that she would not divulge anything she had seen, heard, touched, smelled or tasted during her employment at *The Chronicle*, and she was escorted from the premises in floods of tears. She was never seen or heard of again.

Into her place was parachuted a former university flatmate of a niece of Loretta Farelli: Brigita Wolznaski, a US citizen and the granddaughter of a vehemently Russophobic Polish émigré who had been granted US citizenship for himself and his family many decades earlier. Had his head not been romantically compromised, the appointment of Brigita Wolznaski would have revealed to Edward Ollerson in one stroke exactly what the new sponsors of *The Chronicle* had in mind.

Basically, Loretta Farelli and her colleagues in the Beltway wanted to utilise *The Chronicle* as a propaganda *Weapon of Mass Destruction* in the information war, to disrupt the game-changing processes of Eurasian Integration and the multipolar world order that were being ushered in by Russia and China.

Eurasian Integration was all about the linking together of markets and trade routes from the Far East of Asia all the way to the Atlantic seaboard of Western Europe. Instead of taking seven weeks to transport goods from the Far East to Western Europe, high-speed trains would reduce the transport time to two weeks – a 70% reduction in time to market; begetting the concomitant implications of an increase in the volume of trade within a given time-period, and perhaps reduced costs being translated into reduced prices and thereby increased volumes of sales. This was tasty bait with which to lure European businesses and their business-friendly governments.

For the US government, which was absorbed in negotiations concerning its Transatlantic Trade and Investment Partnership (TTIP) and Trans-Pacific Partnership (TPP) trade agreements that were intended to counter Eurasian Integration, the prospect of a multipolar world order was the ultimate nightmare scenario and something to be discouraged without delay.

Someone in the US State Department had come up with the idea of trying to dissuade the Europeans from having anything to do with concepts such as a multipolar world order and Eurasian Integration, by creating a not-too-benign incentive; namely, a disincentive – in the form of scaremongering:

Fear the East, support the US, and we will 'protect' and 'look after' you.

This is language that can be found in many a Hollywood 'wise guy' movie, and language symptomatic of a protection racket.

To enforce this protection racket, the already vehemently Russophobic and anti-Russia dominant narrative would need to be ramped up, and scaremongering regarding fears of Russian invasions of European countries would need to be repeated non-stop daily, throughout the European corporate media, with *The Chronicle* in the vanguard.

How else was the West to counter the real or imagined threat of 'Russian aggression'?

Through sanctions, of course; and never mind the blowback of the 'reverse sanctions', which would do harm to the economies of European countries that had joined in with the US-inspired sanctions programme against Russia thus far. That could be easily explained away as mere collateral damage.

"You can do that, Edward, as easy as pie," Katy crooned, as Edward Ollerson went along passively with a role for which he was temperamentally unsuited, and – knowing that by placing himself under pressure in the front line of battle – he risked setting himself up for failure.

The so-called 'Russian threat' was trumpeted as a 'matter of life or death': a so-called 'existential threat' to the Western world and its way of doing things. It was what the populations of Eastern European were already hearing, and it would be what the populations of Western Europe would also be told – and *The Chronicle* would lead the way in telling it, with Edward in the hot seat.

Alongside the disincentive, there was an actual incentive – for the profit-hungry armaments industries, at least. Because, in order to discourage Russian aggression, sanctions would not be enough. It would be necessary to deploy men and materiel right on Russia's border as a deterrent. Some of the troops would be American and some local, but *all* of the expensive weaponry would be American, bought and paid for with European money that had previously been earmarked for benign social projects.

Ploughshares turned into swords.

In addition to sanctions and a build-up of weapons, an updated and enhanced dominant narrative would need to be reinforced. How? The frightened and often panic-stricken anti-Russian worldview of the media in the Baltic States, Poland and Ukraine would be imported to other parts of Europe, to make it appear that the many disparate European voices were speaking as one. This *fascistic* forcible suppression of opposition viewpoints was bound to encounter resistance in Western European countries which were already doing good business with Russia (Germany, in particular), and wanted mutually beneficial trade to continue and even to expand.

To counter this resistance, the US State Department would henceforth encourage the emergence of a *cordon sanitaire* in Eastern Europe to act as a barrier between Russia and the likes of Germany – a present-day application of the old adage of US foreign policy toward Europe: "Keep the Russians out, the Germans down and the Americans in."

Hence Katy's choice of Brigita Wolznaski as Edward Ollerson's PA, based upon the assumption (thus far untested) that the young descendant of a Polish nationalist would align herself unconditionally with the US State Department in pursuit of US foreign policy objectives.

The plan was for Katy Drake to spend half of her time in the Beltway and the other half rendering assistance to Brigita Wolznaski in London, where Katy would be able to obtain up-to-date progress reports on whatever Edward Ollerson deemed to be appropriate. Anything that he held back would be obtained easily courtesy of good food, bottles of wine and champagne. And the resulting pillow talk.

※

News of the changes being rung at *The Chronicle* filtered through to *The New Times* within hours of the decisions being made, courtesy of Shirley Bould's network of (soon to be made redundant) former colleagues at *The Chronicle*, over cups of tea.

Shirley broke the news to Hugh Lombard and John Morton, and kept them updated on each new development. John Morton and Dmitry Krejevsky met for coffee in Hyde Park, and went for a walk along their 'lucky pathway' as they had begun to call it. Dmitry Krejevsky was impressed that they had quickly got wind of what Loretta Farelli and her co-thinkers in the Beltway were up to. It would enable him to work out how to deal with this troublesome irritant.

Meanwhile, the time had come for Dmitry Krejevsky to brief his staff on Project Hamlet.

5

A RARE TALENT INDEED

Hugh Lombard and Vivienne Eissinger travelled to Moscow to attend a fashion show in order to interact with local celebrities and to engage with Russian culture.

The fashion show was a low-key affair, more akin to one of the team presentations chaired by an avant-garde tutor at the exclusive Whitbury College for Fine Art and Design from which Vivienne Eissinger had graduated with first-class honours in 2003:

"Everyone write down one word on a card, then put the cards face down in the middle of the floor, and then – everyone – pick up a card at random and conceptualise a theme," commanded the tutor.

You would be forgiven if you went away with the impression that Vivienne Eissinger's former tutor had the easiest job in the world.

That particular tutorial had produced words such as *punk*, *cyber*, *dystopian*, *gothic*, *occult*, *esoteric*, *realist*, *post-realist*, *post-dystopian* and so on. A similar avant-garde method was deployed in the preparations for the 2016 Moscow fashion show. The students seemed to be making it up as they went along.

For Vivienne Eissinger, it was a chance to wallow in the lost days of her late youth and early adulthood: to smile nostalgically at the simplicity of the approach, to be shocked and provoked by the plethora of new ideas, and to be pleasantly surprised at how seemingly unconnected bits and pieces came together at the end of the fashion show in a spectacular climax.

To an outsider such as Hugh Lombard, nothing about the fashion show in Moscow made much sense, and exactly what relevance this had to internal Russian politics, and to how *The New Times* might cover it, seemed a mystery, at first.

After the fashion show finished, some of the organisers met with their two British guests, and took them to a restaurant in Moscow for dinner and drinks.

Questions flooded in.

Q. "Why was the fashion show being held in a car showroom?"

A. "Because the sanctions on Russia meant that the retail outlet that was earmarked for a German car manufacturer had been put on hold. The place was unoccupied, someone knew the architect – who pulled a few strings – so the organisers of the event got the place free of charge. They just paid for the lighting and the heating. Most of the fittings were already in place, so we thought the car showroom would be a novel place to experiment. Hence, we grabbed the opportunity. You can see the results today."

Q. "Why the student-like approach with labels such as 'punk', 'cyber' and 'dystopian'?"

A. "To maximise the creative urges in the young designers and to force radical ideas to confront each other."

Q. "What is the current state of the fashion industry in Russia?"

A. "Rather primitive compared to the West, although, historically, cities such as St Petersburg were inclined to produce haute couture. Moscow is the capital of haute couture in Russia these days, but St Petersburg will try to catch up. There are many Russian designers and models who are famous throughout the world, but, here, they are relatively unknown. However, that is changing. The Russian government now provides greater support for the Russian fashion industry. Last year, we had to import our fabrics from Milan, Paris and London. This year, because of sanctions, some things had to be made here in Russia, with the unexpected bonus that we were able to keep the costs down. It is the same with skilled work: this year, there are more locals involved in sewing and cutting, for instance. Since the government decided to reduce our reliance on the West, all sectors of the economy have begun to give greater prominence to all things Russian. It is like a new patriotism has taken hold. The fashion industry is no exception."

Q. "There are a lot of LGBT people in the fashion industry. Will Russia suppress them and what impact will that have on the fashion industry?"

A. "Well, there are people in the Russian fashion industry from every shade of sexual orientation that you can imagine. It is not illegal to be gay in Russia, you know; what Russia does not allow is the promotion of gay rights in schools. The idea is to allow kids to grow up and make their own decision about their sexuality when they are old enough to make that important decision, when they are ready. If the government tried to suppress LGBT people, then there would be no Russian fashion industry. It is as simple as that. The fashion industry will develop here the same as everywhere else. People who are interested in fashion will gravitate to the industry, and it will thrive. As for the politics of sexuality and diversity, I will let our government ruminate on that!"

It was during this conversation over dinner that Hugh Lombard began to make the connection between the fashion industry and both the economic and political processes within the Russian Federation.

Vivienne Eissinger ran up two articles without delay, and Hugh Lombard emailed them to John Morton for comments. John Morton spoke to Dmitry Krejevsky and recommended the piece for publication as is, and so an article covering the Moscow-based fashion show in the car showroom, penned by Vivienne, was uploaded to the website. Two days later came the publication of a follow-up article outlining how Western sanctions were encouraging the Russians to dedicate more effort to home-grown products and services, including the fashion industry.

This political angle satisfied Dmitry Krejevsky, and it also made him question his own expectations. He was labouring under the assumption that a struggle inside Russia between the 'Eurasianists', whose ambitions were for greater sovereignty for Russia, and the Western-oriented 'Atlanticists' and billionaires would come down to a straight fight. He thought the *fashionistas* would align themselves with those in Russia who favoured greater integration with the West, but that appeared to be not necessarily the case. The more he thought about it, the more complex this process appeared. It provided much food for thought.

A review of a ballet at the Bolshoi Theatre, and coverage of an exhibition of fashion garments and accessories in Russia since the early nineteenth century topped off the trip. If nothing else, it allowed *The New Times* to broaden its appeal without compromising the quality of the reporting, and to introduce Vivienne Eissinger to its readership. It also lifted a veil concerning some of the things that were going on in Russia.

None of this was particularly new. Other media had covered the subject in the past, but to cover it now – fairly and squarely, in a nonpartisan way and at a time when the word 'Russia' conjured up negative connotations – was swimming against the Russophobic tide of opinion that was promoted by the so-called 'mainstream' corporate media.

Monday, 25 April 2016.
On his return to London, Hugh Lombard resumed his day-to-day role of editor-in-chief.

Shirley Bould wanted to know 'every last detail' of the trip. She was not to be disappointed.

However, back in the office and removed from the brief flurry of activity in the Moscow fashion world, Vivienne Eissinger was at a loose end. Hugh Lombard encouraged her to search the archives of *The New Times* website and to try to find something of interest.

In the meantime, in his capacity as editor-in-chief for *The New Times*, Hugh Lombard decided to call a team meeting.

*

From the moment of its conception, Dmitry Krejevsky realised that Project Hamlet ('to be, or not to be' in or out of the EU), with its sharp focus on Europe and the UK, was something of a departure for *The New Times*.

He also knew that the recent inclusion of the UK's pro-EU prime minister and some of his aides in the website's reading list called for a 'delicate touch', particularly when handling controversy. Consequently, Dmitry Krejevsky ensured that the website was not dominated by a narrowly Eurosceptic worldview, but instead allowed the full and many-sided coverage of news, analysis and debate about the UK, its role in the world and, notably, the UK's relation to the EU.

At the team meeting chaired by Hugh Lombard, Dmitry Krejevsky outlined several key trends within the EU. The refugee crisis had taken the EU by surprise. The EU now had to cater for hundreds of thousands of new arrivals from countries in the Middle East and North Africa – countries that just over a decade ago were 'reasonably stable', with their problems being largely confined within their own territories.

The UK's prime minister had referred to the refugee crisis as a 'flood', and he had come under attack for what some saw as a loose comment in an unguarded moment, but that the more cynical interpreted as a deliberate attempt to whip up a negative anti-immigrant sentiment with one eye on building up his reputation in the eyes of a subcategory of purportedly winnable Eurosceptic voters.

Public concern over refugees and the ease with which they were able to cross borders forced the EU leaders to review EU policies and to put in 'temporary' border controls which, in truth, resembled a long-term arrangement.

Arguments over the integration of the refugees within European societies had amplified the controversy around multiculturalism and, consequently, the liberal Establishments in the most long-serving member states within the EU found themselves under pressure from so-called 'anti-establishment' social movements of the right and of the left.

John Morton chose this defining moment to unveil a 'little gift' he had recently received from a Shiite scholar in Baghdad.

At one end of the conference room, on the wall behind Hugh Lombard, was a traditional map of the world with Europe at the centre, Africa beneath it and the Americas to the left of the Atlantic Ocean. To the right of Europe, the continents of Asia and Australasia seemed like faraway places; where something must surely be going on, but we simply know not what.

Morton unfurled his gift – a map of the world in which Asia and the Pacific Ocean took centre stage, Africa appeared as a large continent left of centre in the southern hemisphere, and Europe resembled a less noteworthy continent north of Africa. The Atlantic Ocean and the Americas, respectively, were exiled to the left and right margins of the map. The purpose of this map, the Shiite scholar had explained – viewed from the perspective known as the Global South, within a multipolar world order – was not to rewrite the map of the world but to show a different perspective. However, disregarding the missive from its donor, Morton pinned the map on the wall directly opposite the traditional world map. The two maps seemed destined to glare at each other in perpetuity.

Dmitry Krejevsky took his lead from Morton's presentation of the gift to declare with deep regret that, instead of solving their countries' manifold problems, Western European leaders were being pressured to make sure that Europe would be represented by only one, singular dominant narrative – a Russophobic dominant narrative. Krejevsky claimed that this Russophobic dominant narrative ran counter to the national and business interests of countries in Western Europe, and had provoked a fiercely-contested debate within EU member states, Germany in particular. Zoe and Hans Neubauer both nodded in agreement.

Dmitry Krejevsky had one final item on the agenda.

Depending on which source you listened to, the TTIP was rumoured to be either in the final stages of completion prior to final sign-off, or to have been rejected as an unacceptable imposition of US business interests on the European continent at the expense of European businesses and European peoples' rights.

For *The New Times*, the TTIP had become a delicate matter recently because, whereas *The New Times* was against the TTIP, the prime minister had been lobbying hard in its favour. In contrast to the prime minister's viewpoint, for *The New Times*, the TTIP was a threat to the sovereignty of nation states. The TTIP would favour oligarchs, billionaires and transnational corporations, particularly big businesses from the US.

The TTIP had long been a source of frustration for Dmitry Krejevsky for, try as he might, he could not get hold of a copy of the draft 'final' document, and had to make do with rumours and snippets that could not be treated as fact unless they were corroborated by reliable sources.

"The TPP, the trans-Pacific version of TTIP has been published," Hugh Lombard declared. "This is not a draft; it is the end product."

"I have seen no evidence of that," Dmitry Krejevsky replied. "I know it was ratified by the twelve governments that had been discussing it behind closed doors. I have no knowledge of its publication."

But Krejevsky had missed a trick. Lombard, courteously and diplomatically with his permanent grin, enlightened him, "The government of New Zealand published it. There is probably a link to this announcement in the archives of our website."

"In that case, we had better get a copy, and someone is going to have to be tasked with reading it," Krejevsky directed.

"That has already been done," declared Lombard.

"Please explain, Hugh," a slightly flustered Krejevsky asked.

He did, saying, "Vivienne has read it."

All eyes turned toward Vivienne Eissinger, who was seated between Shirley Bould and Zoe Neubauer, aloof and surveying the proceedings without saying a word.

"Is this true? Well, when exactly?" Dmitry Krejevsky demanded to know.

"Vivienne read the TPP the day before yesterday and yesterday morning – all 300 pages of it, or 500 if you include the various supplements and addenda. During yesterday afternoon, she produced a rough summary of the main concerns and spent most of the evening writing up a report. I have started to read the report, and, when I have edited it, I intend to upload it to our internal non-public pages on the website. It should be available for review by everyone in our team before the end of the week."

Hugh Lombard's unexpected firmness and defence of the newest team member – and in a direct confrontation with Dmitry Krejevsky, at that – stunned everyone in the room.

"Tea and coffee, everyone?" John Morton asked. "And let's get some fresh air. It is so stuffy in here. Shirley, will you have a word with building maintenance and see if they can do something about the air conditioning, please?"

Shirley nodded, although there was nothing wrong with the air conditioning, and she knew from experience that John Morton had simply called a break in the meeting to defuse a potentially damaging row that was threatening to explode.

Dmitry Krejevsky was seething from having been 'kept in the dark', a point which he banged on about to Morton as they took tea and biscuits outside the door of the conference room. Krejevsky's brow became even more furrowed than usual when he glanced through the glass door panel to see the tall figures of Vivienne and Hans conversing in fluent German, and he could see that the pair were hitting it off very well. Dmitry Krejevsky felt that he was losing control of his pet project.

"You never had children, did you?" Morton asked.

Krejevsky remained motionless for a while, then slowly and sullenly he shook his head.

"Our team is like a family," Morton began, "and when new members of the family come along, or they bring their friends with them, what are we supposed to do? We must accommodate them, Dmitry. Believe me, I have been through this before many times with my two boys. It sometimes becomes a nightmare. But when there is so much at stake and there is so much good that can come out of it, we tolerate all the odd things that threaten to mess everything up. We find ways of working around them. For the past twelve months or so, it has been mostly you and I running things. That phase seems to be over. You appointed Hugh to take over the editorship of *The New Times*, while you positioned yourself as chairman of The New Times Group in a high-level position to oversee everything and to keep in mind the big picture. In my view, you made the correct decision."

Dmitry Krejevsky inflated his cheeks with air and exhaled slowly.

"Look at where we are now, Dmitry. Just look through that glass panel again. Go on, look. Look!"

Krejevsky looked, but he did not see. Morton had to explain it to him.

The tea break was becoming a free for all, with everyone in the room laughing and joking. Ones and twos had become twos and threes, and, eventually, all five people became excitedly engaged in one single conversation.

"That is our team, Dmitry. This time last year, they hardly knew each other."

Morton opened a window in the corridor, to make use of the noisy traffic from the street to disrupt the surveillance operation performed by the listening devices. Through cupped hands, he whispered to Dmitry Krejevsky, "Our team is still unaware of the stunt we tried to pull off a few months ago concerning the leak of the Russian battle plans, and they never will find out about it. If that stunt had worked as intended, I would now be applying for political asylum in another country and I would never be able to come home again. Today's meeting would not be taking place and our whole project might now be in trouble. But things turned out differently. Just look at that group of people in there. Can you imagine that scene playing out in the offices of *The Chronicle*? It would never happen in a million years. You know that. Partly by design, but also to some degree by accident, we have ended up with a bunch of people who actually like each other and trust each other, and – dammit – can work with each other. There is no backbiting in that room. Look at it!"

Krejevsky supposed that Morton might be making sense, but it was a bitter pill to swallow. His pride stood in the way. So, too, did his single-minded resolution to make his project work.

He had known and worked closely with John Morton for two years with *The New Times*, but he had known *of* him for much longer. Ten years earlier, Dmitry Krejevsky had taken part in a brainstorming conference about succession planning, including the assessment of candidates to displace various aging senior managers at *The Chronicle*. The name of John Morton had cropped up at least as many times as any other candidate. Had it not been for the political infighting and the marginalisation of good reporters, John Morton might at this moment in time be sitting in the editor-in-chief's comfortable leather chair at *The Chronicle*.

Instead, Morton had been sidelined over time, and had become rather embittered and cynical. Now, however, at *The New Times*, his was a senior management role at a similar level to the editor-in-chief. Except that Hugh Lombard was editor-in-chief. Morton was Middle East expert and finance officer.

Krejevsky had created a chairman role for himself and had also taken on the role of human resources manager. Yet Morton was better than Krejevsky at managing people. His potential for so doing had been discussed during the brainstorming session ten years earlier.

Morton had not groused to the slightest degree when the recent reorganisation had taken place. He would have been justified in complaining about being passed over when Lombard had been appointed editor-in-chief, yet he did not. Morton had even nominated Hugh Lombard as the best candidate for the job. Was it down to lack of ambition? Perhaps. Maybe he had given up all hope of becoming editor-in-chief or decided he did not want that role after all. Perchance there was a simpler explanation: John Morton might just be the ultimate team player.

✳

At home in the evening, Dmitry Krejevsky confided in his wife, Catherine. He enjoyed a delicious dinner, a couple of glasses of exceptionally good wine and a pleasant sunset while overlooking the north of London from an elevated position in his conservatory.

"From what you told me after your meeting with the prime minister," Catherine Krejevsky reminded her husband, "John Morton could be getting lined up as a future aide to Downing Street."

"He is not too much in the know about that," stated Krejevsky.

"Sir Harold Nevin *is* in the know about that." Catherine stated. "He might be finding a place for John in the PM's entourage at this moment."

Krejevsky shook his head. "That's premature. This might happen in a couple of years, if at all. Not now."

"So, you are not worried about losing John from your team?"

Dmitry Krejevsky frowned and stared down into his glass.

"So, what are you going to do, Dmitry?" queried Catherine. "Is he unhappy in his role at *The New Times*?"

"No. Well, I don't think so. He does tend to be open about his feelings. He was very positive when he cornered me outside the conference room. I think he is content," responded Dmitry Krejevsky.

"So, what do you have to worry about?"

"It's just… I don't seem to be being kept informed about what is going on. And then there is, well, the appointment of Vivienne Eissinger. What is *that* all about?"

"And what exactly has Vivienne Eissinger done to upset you? You were talking very positively about her reports from her expeditions to the fashion and cultural heartlands of Moscow."

Catherine had a point.

"What is Vivienne's background?" Catherine asked.

"The arts: fine art, in particular, and haute couture," replied Dmitry Krejevsky.

"Well, then," Catherine concluded, "it sounds like Vivienne Eissinger is the ideal person to cover that particular role."

Dmitry Krejevsky gently swivelled a glass of cognac in his right hand. He elaborated, "Vivienne Eissinger read 500 pages of material and compiled a report on a complex piece of international policy with the legal niceties enshrined in it. My editor-in-chief, Hugh Lombard, intends to have it ready for me to see in a few days. Hugh assures me that Vivienne has made a pretty good job of it. Vivienne Eissinger did all this in two days."

Catherine paused for a while and took a couple of slow sips of cognac from her glass. She continued, "The Eissingers opened part of their estate to the public a few years ago. I do not think that they are short of money, but maybe they are trying to generate an additional source of income to help to pay for the upkeep of the estate.

"Were you aware that their library has been opened to the public? It's a huge, multistorey affair with balconies and balustrades that add to the mysterious, gothic atmosphere. There was an article in a magazine that described it as 'bigger than the library in *Gormenghast*'. My guess is that, over the years, Vivienne Eissinger has had a lot of spare time on her hands and is familiar with every single book in that library. Vivienne might have read most, if not all, of those volumes. That being the case, my dear, it looks like you have someone on your staff who has a rare talent for absorbing large amounts of printed material and making sense of it in a short period of time."

Krejevsky lifted his eyes from his glass and looked blankly in his wife's direction.

"There is only one other person I have ever met who has a similar talent," Catherine said. "And that person is you, Dmitry."

A sleepless night threatened to follow, during which the wheels inside Dmitry Krejevsky's mind turned incessantly. Vivienne

Eissinger had read the hundreds of pages of the entire TPP document, absorbed its contents and their significance, and sorted the wheat from the chaff.

Vivienne had been appointed to the staff of *The New Times* ostensibly as a favour in return for extra funding. At the time, Dmitry Krejevsky thought nothing of it. Was Sir Harold Nevin keeping something from him? Or, perhaps, he was merely allowing events to take their course? Nevin always seemed to be a good judge of character. It was seldom that Sir Harold Nevin made a gaffe, even if it was only in the form of a favour to a sponsor.

Dmitry Krejevsky mused and formed the opinion that, on reflection, the decision to recruit Vivienne Eissinger might not be unwise after all. Nevin's track record seemed intact. And Dmitry Krejevsky could go to sleep with some comfort that his pet project was – probably – in good hands, with a burden shared being a burden halved.

PART TWO
THE ASSASSINS

6

OLD HABITS DIE HARD

The final weekend in April was, for Edward Ollerson, a frustrating experience. The new love of his life, Katy Drake, arrived from Washington DC on Friday and immediately checked into an expensive hotel in London's West End, which was a short taxi-ride from the expected location of the new offices of *The Chronicle* in the Millhouse Building on the Thames Embankment.

In anticipation of Katy spending most of her time with him on Friday evening, Edward Ollerson made an advance booking for a table for two in a prestigious restaurant in London's Barbican. For Saturday, he reserved two theatre tickets for a West End show. But, on both nights, Katy said she was tired from the flight and she had business to do. Her eventual rendezvous with Edward Ollerson would have to wait until Monday evening.

"Promise," she said.

She did indeed keep her promise, and Edward Ollerson enjoyed a prolonged night of bliss in her company.

But Katy did not tell her lover that during the weekend, instead of hanging out with him, she had gone on a shopping trip with his new PA, Brigita Wolznaski; had caught up with all the news and gossip from the office; and had discussed secretly with Brigita a hidden agenda that had been drawn up by Katy under the direction of Loretta Farelli and her closest colleagues in the Beltway.

Ominously, Katy asked for and received an update from Brigita concerning Edward Ollerson's health, his physical condition and his state of mind. Katy also wanted to know how much junk food Edward was consuming, how little exercise he was taking, the actual volume of alcohol he was drinking and any other dark secrets that Brigita thought it advisable to relay to Katy.

However, Edward Ollerson's job was, at the present time, most definitely not on the line. Loretta Farelli had insisted on this proviso during a transatlantic teleconference call with Katy and Brigita, to which Edward had not been invited. Loretta recommended that Katy spend more time with Edward in London, that Katy and Edward should join a health club and gym, and that Katy should 'look after' Edward.

It was vital to keep him fit, in good health and on board with the project. After all, he had been a proven ally of Loretta in the past and he could be relied upon going forward, absolutely; well, probably.

Edward had experienced a few setbacks of late, but he occupied an important position – he was the main point person in the UK for Loretta and her allies in the Beltway. Once the overweight Edward had performed a few exercises and begun to tone himself up in mind and body, he would be back on track. But, as Loretta had directed, there was no need for him to be kept "too much in the know".

※

"So… are you in love with him?" Brigita asked Katy early on Saturday afternoon in a licensed café bar within walking distance of London's Oxford Street.

"Well, I do like him. He is very sweet. Just like Loretta described him," confirmed Katy.

"But are you in love with him?"

"I don't know. I… I quite like his company. He's a bit on the quiet side, to be honest, and a bit morose sometimes. But he did make an effort to ensure I enjoyed my weekend. Edward booked a table at a restaurant and bought tickets for the theatre, and I didn't go with him. It was a shame really. I feel a bit guilty about that. My bad."

"So… is it just business then?" Brigita pressed.

"I wouldn't say that. Not exactly. I am not looking for a relationship just now. I've had enough of those for a while. In any case, all the travelling around takes up a lot of my time. I am not going to rush into anything, but having Edward here in London makes me feel... pretty good."

"So, *it is* just business, after all!" Brigita inferred.

The two women laughed heartily.

"I suppose I am in a similar situation," Brigita confessed. "Oh, I'm not jealous of you. Not a bit. All the travelling and meeting people is, as you say, interesting – and exciting sometimes. Then there are the conferences, the discussions and the politics. I feel as though I am really involved, and on the right side, of course. The side of freedom and democracy. I enjoy what I am doing, and I intend to make the most of this opportunity in London.

"Some relatives on my dad's side live in England – in Bournemouth. I went down there a couple of weeks ago to collect some documents for Edward from one of his contacts in Southampton, and Edward allowed me to stay overnight in Bournemouth with my distant cousins that I hardly knew existed. Edward went out of his way to make this happen for me. I was *so* surprised."

"Aah," Katy cooed, like a lovestruck teen. "That was good of Edward. I told you he is very sweet."

Brigita broke into a broad, pretty, pearly white smile. "The south coast of England is a really nice part of the world. I can't wait for this cold weather to warm up a bit. Then I might be able to find a little beach, all of my own. I might even share it with someone special. I just need to meet that someone special. Till then, I'll probably just be a sort of 'holiday girl' and make do with whatever comes along – as long as he is good-looking and has enough money to look after me. At least for a while."

Katy giggled and nodded approvingly. Then she introduced an element of seriousness into the conversation. "Loretta wants me to – I can't think of a better word I'm afraid – she wants me to... to *rescue* Edward. From himself. He is so down sometimes. Disheartened. He is all smiles, one minute, then the next his smile just vanishes. I'm not even sure if he is well. Is he well, Brigita?"

Brigita shrugged.

"Well, you see him every day, and you work with him. You are his PA," Katy said. "Loretta is really worried about Edward. *Really* worried. What's wrong with Edward? Find out, Brigita. Find out."

Katy looked away for a while, gazing out of the window, then returned to her companion. "Brigita. May I ask a favour of you?"

"Of course," Brigita replied.

"Will you make sure Edward goes to the gym every other day or at least takes regular exercise? And eats properly? It's just for a while until I get myself settled in. It looks like I might be spending more time here in future. I'll take you shopping every weekend if you can do this little thing for me."

The two women agreed their deal.

※

Katy had intended to take Brigita to a newly opened trattoria to discuss the most serious business of the day, but one look out of the window persuaded Katy to change her mind. The rain was not particularly heavy. It was only fine rain, but it was persistent and hung around in a mist. The fine rain was blown in all directions by huge gusts of a gentle yet, at times, deceptively forceful breeze. Whenever a nearby door of the café bar was opened, a cold and damp draught played around the customers' ankles. A hint of gas drifted in occasionally from a nearby roadworks.

The café bar sold sandwiches and cakes. Katy took advantage of some special offers, including complimentary bottles of mineral water.

A table became available further inside the café bar, and the two women took the opportunity to swiftly relocate before any other semi-frozen individuals had the same idea. The available table was near to another table where an older lady sat with her back to them, celebrating her birthday with what looked like two nephews who had treated her to expensive perfumes from Harrods and a triple-tiered contraption containing sandwiches and cakes.

Privacy seemed guaranteed and, suitably ensconced in warmer seats, Katy and Brigita got down to discuss their *real* business of the day.

For many months, under the faltering leadership of Edward Ollerson, the editorial line of *The Chronicle* had resembled a mirror image of the editorial line of *The New Times*.

The sequence of events usually went something like this.

The Chronicle asserted that *all* rebels in Syria were *definitely* moderates and *certainly not* jihadists; *The New Times* challenged the probity of those claims; and *The Chronicle* dismissed the challenge with its trademark 'dignified scorn', and stuck to its guns for a regime change in Damascus.

The New Times published an interview with a former NATO general, claiming that the refugee crisis in Europe was to be expected in the wake of NATO's failure to adequately replace the overthrown regimes in Iraq, Libya, et al. with viable governments based on Western-style democratic principles. *The Chronicle* countered by resorting to interminable waffle, ignoring the inconvenient truths spelled out by the retired NATO general and implying that there might be something amiss with the retired NATO general's state of mind.

The Chronicle followed up by tugging at its readers' heartstrings, filling page after page with harrowing photographs of half-sunken vessels, with the survivors clinging onto whatever flotsam they could find. In an editorial, Edward Ollerson accused certain anti-refugee critics among the right-wing press who he alleged were "ignoring the plight of those poor refugees in favour of making cheap political points".

The Chronicle even put out a 'bumper weekend edition', including an eight-page pullout of photographs, spun with an editorial line praising those European leaders who had stepped into the breach to help the refugees, and glossing over the former NATO general's claim that NATO's regime-change strategy might have been at least partly to blame for creating the fertile ground from which had sprouted the refugee crisis.

Included in this smokescreen 'bumper weekend edition' of *The Chronicle* were attempts to divert attention by playing the blame game: snippets and letters insinuating that Russia's bombing of targets in Syria might be playing into the hands of the jihadists;

an article openly accusing Russia of prolonging the refugee crisis; and intimations that Russia might be to blame for the whole thing in the first place, even though Russia had played no role at all in any of NATO's regime-change operations and had only intervened seriously in the Syria crisis in 2015, not 2011.

Loretta Farelli did not want Katy Drake to change any of that, but she would like *The Chronicle* to sharpen up its coverage of events in order to achieve greater impact. This onerous task was made more difficult because the prevailing narratives of *The Chronicle* seemed more and more out of step with what was happening in the real world.

Examples were not hard to find.

The diplomats of a rejuvenated Russian Federation and a war-weary US had begun recently to work closely together to draw up a draft peace settlement for Syria, and there seemed to be a good chance that a peace settlement might be finalised and implemented.

Both sides had deployed high-profile representatives to beef up the Minsk Agreement, and, contrary to the editorial line of *The Chronicle*, there seemed a real chance that something might be done to resolve the Ukraine crisis.

The issue of national sovereignty was rearing its head, not only in the UK but also in the primaries for the US presidential election. The neoconservatives' plan had been to drive a wedge between Europe and Russia, including the creation of a *cordon sanitaire* next to Russia's border – but this was not supposed to be put to one side while regular talks between Russia and the US took place, with the attendant risk that the US would supplant the EU as Russia's preferred friend and ally.

For the neoconservatives, Russia *must not* have its image restored or renovated in any way; instead, Russia *must* be demonised and *must* be perceived as the enemy. At *any* cost.

In order to beef up *The Chronicle*'s analysis and reportage, a new set of narratives would have to be developed, but this would take time and would require some prolonged hard thinking. Therefore, in the short term, some other scheme would have to be dreamed up, to keep the pressure on.

Katy Drake removed from her bag a folder containing many leaves of A4 paper, stapled together in threes and fours.

The first document was an analysis of a complex legal tract, written by Dmitry Krejevsky and published on *The New Times* website, concerning the refugee crisis. In addition to a sharp legal brain, Dmitry Krejevsky had a gift for making – after two or three careful reads – a complex set of issues comprehensible to a reader who did not have any legal training. His contributions to *The New Times* were awaited by its readership with bated breath.

This was the exact opposite of what Loretta Farelli wanted to see.

Katy Drake unveiled a second article, in which Dmitry Krejevsky toyed around with a possible alternative to the NATO-led regime change agenda. Dmitry Krejevsky envisaged the prospect of sidelining NATO; a different kind of solution to the Syrian crisis, including a military victory for the Syrian government; the president of Syria remaining in power; a reconstruction programme for Syria, for which Russia was lining up itself and China as key participants; and, finally, an all-inclusive resolution that Russia would take to the UN.

This proposed UN resolution was designed to put a stop to the Western-led humanitarian interventions in which the much-vaunted 'shock and awe' produced "one failed state after another".

In place of a multitude of humanitarian interventions, the Russian Federation was proposing a mechanism for using the UN to resolve crises by diplomacy and through the rule of law, thereby laying the legal and political basis for ameliorating the refugee crisis. Russia had made significant headway in adopting diplomatic language when presenting its foreign policy, and this had thrown the neoconservatives in the Beltway into a rage.

"Russia is promoting itself as a champion of the rule of law!" Loretta Farelli had yelled during one teleconference.

"So, what do you plan to do?" Brigita asked Katy.

"Ever heard of something called 'rat fucking'?" Katy grinned.

"No. What is 'rat fucking'?" Brigita queried.

"You basically find some dirt on your target, then use it to smear or blackmail him or her in some way. It was used a lot on campuses back in the day, during elections to student bodies. 'Rat fucking' techniques were imported into mainstream politics by interns after they graduated, and then refined in conjunction with various aides, some of them very senior. 'Rat fucking' is still regarded, by many in DC, as a valid weapon of choice in the information war."

Brigita stared, open mouthed.

"Oh, don't worry, Brigita," reassured Katy. "It's all harmless fun really. We just need to get the dirt on Dmitry Krejevsky. Just to embarrass him."

"But I thought we were going to write articles to sharpen up the presentation of *The Chronicle*?" Brigita grumbled.

Katy had her answer ready. "Oh, we will do that. Later. Definitely. But, meantime, we need to take this guy down a peg or two. He is so full of himself. So arrogant. He is also Russian. Did you know that?"

"No," Brigita replied, alarmed and becoming a little upset.

"Well, he's half-Russian really. His great grandparents left Russia after the Bolshevik Revolution and settled here in England. They must have brought lots of money with them, because they have also wheedled their way into some circles within the English aristocracy. Dmitry Krejevsky might be FSB – Russian Intelligence. He probably is; almost certainly is, in fact. Whatever... he is very much on their side and not ours. Look at the articles he writes. If NATO were to come to an end tomorrow, he would be the happiest man on earth! Someone like Dmitry Krejevsky cannot be toyed around with. He is dangerous, and we need to find a way of silencing him. We don't want to harm him physically. Just rough him up a bit and embarrass him with some shit or other."

Brigita did not know where to put herself. She had edged closer to Katy to listen and was now at risk of falling off her seat. She adjusted her position in the chair repeatedly, as Katy drip-fed a series of poisonous whoppers.

A bright flash broke the momentum of Katy's diatribe. At the table next to theirs, the smaller of the two nephews had moved to the seat next to the older lady as the third person in their party took a photograph with the camera of a mobile phone.

The third person said, "Just one more, please, to make sure we've got a good one."

Flash!

"Thank you."

Katy and Brigita blinked their eyes as the camera flashed directly in their faces.

The rain had stopped, so Katy suggested it would be a good time to move on. Brigita agreed, and the two left the café bar, carrying their bags and packages, and headed off to the nearest tube station, where the different train lines would take them on their separate ways.

※

Had Loretta Farelli been in the café bar, she would have recognised one of the 'nephews' as Hugh Lombard. Edward Ollerson would have, too, and he would also have recognised that the 'aunt' was none other than Shirley Bould, whose radar-like ears were able to pick up signals and messages from a fair distance away.

Shirley and Hugh inspected the photographs, and congratulated Vivienne Eissinger. Vivienne had snapped two clear images: the first of Katy and Brigita in profile, and the second full-face and looking more than a little surprised.

"They look like a right pair of jailbirds!" Shirley triumphantly announced.

7

COUNTER ESPIONAGE

Hugh Lombard met John Morton on Hampstead Heath on Sunday morning. Lombard handed over two enlarged printed images, together with a verbal summary of what he and Shirley had heard in the café bar. Morton studied the photographs very carefully.

Having tried and failed to dislodge the perceived weakest link (Hugh Lombard) from *The New Times*, Katy Drake and Loretta Farelli had switched their attention to Dmitry Krejevsky: the strongest, the most determined and – when push came to shove – the most ruthless member of the team. He was a clear thinker; a master of both the written and the spoken word; an experienced and distinguished trailblazer of the legal profession, who could slice open a tough case in a bout of sustained cross-examination; and a man for whom the success of *The New Times* was not only a political imperative but also a point of principle and of pivotal importance to inter-family loyalties.

Dmitry Krejevsky had the backing of Sir Harold Nevin and a caucus of Eurosceptic Tory grandees, who disdained the knee-jerk reaction, favouring instead a pragmatic and carefully considered approach to current affairs. Perhaps influenced by their favourite sport, cricket, they played a long game instead of rushing in. When the time was ripe, they arranged for their protégés to be carefully selected and placed in positions of influence in think tanks, in government departments, in the Tory Party or even in the Cabinet. They were powerful enough to persuade the intelligence services to call off the dogs. They did not take kindly to outsiders with disruptive intentions.

Taking all of this into account, John Morton could not fathom how anybody could act in so reckless a manner – that is, raising the stakes against such a major player as Dmitry Krejevsky, and to deploy dirty tricks. When Dmitry Krejevsky found out about this, who knows what he would do. Would they all end up back in the prime minister's country house at Chequers, lodging yet another complaint?

The whole idea of a character assassination was insane. Yet, as he carefully studied the photographs, Morton noticed that the upper-left eyelid of the blonde woman was slightly heavier than the corresponding eyelid above the right eye. The left eye therefore seemed smaller and appeared to be scrutinising the observer of the photograph. It conjured up an impression of hard-heartedness or of cruelty, even. It troubled Morton.

> *Is this someone who might be a match for Dmitry?* he wondered. *And what about the other woman? The long-haired brunette with the fringe. Cold-blooded, also? It's hard to tell from a photo. Experienced? She does not look it. She's a young intern, perhaps. And what about her eyes and facial expression in the photograph? She's like a startled rabbit caught in the headlights.*

Monday, 25 April 2016. London.
Morton decided to take a leaf out of Hugh Lombard's book and arrange a 'birthday treat' for Shirley – at Fortnum and Mason in Piccadilly, which was a world away from the intrusive listening devices that the UK's security services had installed in the offices and homes of the staff of *The New Times*.

They sat next to each other at a table in a corner, facing out so that they could observe the comings and goings – as recommended by Shirley, "Just to be on the safe side, dear."

John Morton listened to Shirley's report, delivered at low volume and disguised from potential eavesdroppers by continuously cheerful smiles and calm body language, giving the impression of two people engaged in nothing more menacing than casual chit-chat.

Shirley outlined Katy Drake's depiction of Dmitry Krejevsky as a 'possible', 'probable' or 'highly likely' Russian spy. Shirley was even able to remember exactly what was said in the café bar and by whom. She could even recall the laughter and some of the gossip, "about someone called Edward," which she had picked up from the two boisterous younger women a little further away in the café bar before they had relocated to the table next to hers.

"It sounds like Edward Ollerson has found himself a new fancy piece," Shirley commented, "but I don't think it will last. It's the brunette who seems to have been given the job of looking after him. I don't recognise either of these two young women."

"Neither do I," said Morton.

Morton took out his smartphone and typed in the website address of *The Chronicle*. He looked at the list of reporters, contributors and officers. Edward Ollerson and Loretta Farelli were the only faces he recognised. They had sat for new, well-presented and very flattering photographs, which replaced the older versions.

Clearly, *The Chronicle* was in the process of some sort of makeover. Edward Ollerson was editor-in-chief, but Morton recognised none of the other officers. Where the hell was Josh? According to the website, Ollerson had a PA called Brigita Wolznaski. Morton never did find out Josh's real name, but he was as sure as hell that it was not Brigita Wolznaski. He scanned the list of officers again, some with photographs and some without. All first names only, and in smart-casual attire: Edward, Philip, Roberta, Katy and a recent entry – Brigita. Then came the contributors: Loretta, Hassan, Proteus, another Roberta, Saskatta, Semyan, Tchyuki and Zabarella.

Morton's imagination was stirred.

This makeover does not look real. It seems to promote some kind of 'ideal', a 'vision' or a 'fantasy' even, something of the… how can you describe it, thought Morton, *the 'artificial'? Like a half-assed marketing job. Designed to impress, but, in truth, after you've looked at it for a while… although it's someone's idea of cool and sophisticated… in reality, it's crap. Lacking in imagination, and… predictable. I could have made a better job of it myself.*

Edward and Loretta were known to Morton, but none of the other names was familiar. He showed the lists to Shirley, who shrugged as she spread some deliciously fragrant raspberry jam onto her scone.

"Notice something?" Morton asked.

"No," Shirley replied.

"I cannot find Josh anywhere. Do you remember her real name?"

"Josh was kicked out. Remember? I did tell you."

Morton looked quizzically at Shirley.

"I remember telling you, John. I heard it on the grapevine a couple of weeks ago soon after it happened," chided Shirley.

"Now that you tell me, Shirley, I remember. Sorry, Shirley. I'm so sorry. I forgot. There has been so much going on lately that I have tended to miss things sometimes. I'm not always the most attentive – when it comes to office gossip." Morton poured himself and Shirley a top-up from the china teapot.

Shirley looked around the room. All was clear. "Why don't I ring up *The Chronicle* and ask to speak to Josh, dear?" Shirley suggested.

"But you just said she is no longer there."

"I know, but I can say I am an old friend and pretend that I don't know she has left."

"And then what?"

"Maybe the phone number of the new PA is still the same as Josh's old number."

"And then?"

"I might recognise the voice. It might be one of those women from the café bar that Hugh and Vivienne took me to."

Morton supposed it was worth a try.

Shirley looked through the list of contacts and numbers that had remained on her mobile phone since she had left *The Chronicle* eighteen months earlier. She and Morton compared the numbers in her phone with the contact details on *The Chronicle* website, which were now displayed on Morton's phone.

"See, dear. That's a landline, and so is that one," confirmed Shirley.

Morton handed Shirley a spare mobile phone. It contained a SIM card that was registered in the name of a contact he had not seen for many years. Morton used the spare mobile phone and SIM occasionally for anonymous internet browsing in Wi-Fi-enabled public spaces, topping up the prepaid load when necessary. The spare SIM was safe to use because it would not have been identified by the intelligence services as a device that needed to be specially tracked by UK Government Communications Headquarters (GCHQ) and the US National Security Agency (NSA) as part of the surveillance operation against *The New Times*.

Shirley rang one of the numbers and heard a continuous tone that indicated that the number had been disconnected. The second number also seemed to have been cut off. The third number elicited a reply.

"*The Chronicle* newspaper. How may I help you?"

"Oh," Shirley said, a little surprised. "Hello, dear. I wonder if I may speak to Josh, please?"

There was a slight delay before the young woman at the other end spoke smoothly and confidently, with an American accent. "I don't think you have the right number, ma'am."

"This is *The Chronicle*, isn't it?"

"Yes, this is *The Chronicle*."

"*The Chronicle* newspaper?"

"Yes, ma'am."

"There is someone called Josh at *The Chronicle*, isn't there?"

"No, ma'am. Who is calling?"

"My name is... my name is... Freda. I am a friend of Josh and I used to do some work for her at *The Chronicle*, from time to time. I was just ringing up to keep in touch and see if she had any work for me to do."

"I can't say I know anyone here called Josh, I'm afraid."

"She is Mr Ollerson's PA. At least she was the last time I spoke to her."

"Oh, you mean Mr Ollerson's former PA. I'm afraid she has left. I am Mr Ollerson's PA now."

"Oh, what a shame Josh has left," Shirley lied. "I heard there were some knew staff coming in. Are you Bridget, by any chance?"

"Brigita. How did you find out my name?"

"I remember the name from when I met one of Josh's colleagues for a cup of tea a couple of weeks ago. What's her name? I'm sorry, I can't remember. It gets a bit like that when you reach my age."

"Well, I am afraid that Josh is no longer here. Just one moment, please."

Shirley waited for a couple of minutes.

"Hello. Freda? Are you still there?"

"Yes."

"We might have some work coming along soon. If you could leave your contact details."

"Certainly. Do you want them over the phone?"

"If you can get onto our website you can enter your details and we can get back to you when we are ready."

Shirley wrapped up the call and took a sip of tea.

"Well?" Morton asked.

"It could have been one of the women I saw in the café bar. She said her name is Brigita and she asked me to send my contact details," explained Shirley.

Due to the surveillance mounted by the security services, it was clear that Shirley could not possibly use her real identity. A little subterfuge was called for. Shirley would need to create a fictitious email account and use Morton's spare SIM to prevent her real phone number being traced. Shirley bought a brand-spanking-new smartphone to keep the emails, contact details and phone calls – all her future business with Brigita Wolznaski – in one device.

✻

Dmitry Krejevsky had taken delivery of some young trees from a garden centre and was escorting two workmen through an external gate to his back garden. He had spent some time working in the garden during the weekend and had resumed his horticultural chores on Monday afternoon while his wife Catherine was still at work in her office.

Krejevsky closed and secured the gate, then directed the workmen to the area of the garden where the trees were to be planted. He let them get on with the job, while he returned to the conservatory to make mugs of tea and coffee for the workmen and for himself. As he was about to pour the water from the kettle into a mug containing a tea bag, his mobile phone rang. It was John Morton, announcing cheerfully that the birthday treat had gone well and that he would be 'taking a walk in the park' around six o'clock to enjoy the fine evening weather. That was code for calling a meeting.

✳

John Morton broke the news to Dmitry Krejevsky during a walk around the Serpentine in Hyde Park. Throughout the briefing, Krejevsky wore a permanent frown. Morton knew from experience that his friend and colleague would be upset by the news. He also knew that, inside, Krejevsky would be silently seething. The furrowed brow gave him away. That the wheels of Krejevsky's mind would also be turning over this thorny problem was also a given.

"So, what happens next?" Krejevsky asked, as they both leaned on a railing, facing out across the lake.

"I have no idea. What do you think, Dmitry?" queried Morton.

Krejevsky gave Morton an offhand, withering sort of look, then returned his gaze to the lake. He said nothing.

Morton turned around and rested his elbows on the railing. He tried to raise Krejevsky's spirits. "It is nonsense of course, Dmitry. The very idea that *The Chronicle* could mount a campaign against you is absurd. Even if they did 'play by the rules', so to speak, and have everything above board."

Morton continued in the same vein for a while. Krejevsky remained with his forearms on the railing and the fingers of his hands locked together while facing the lake. He looked up. He ran his tongue across the top layer of his teeth, then bared his teeth.

Morton knew the signs very well.

"Fancy a pint?" Morton asked casually.

Krejevsky did not reply.

"Do you fancy a pint, Dmitry?" Morton gently pressed on.

After a while, through gritted teeth, Krejevsky replied, "I don't drink beer."

"A glass of wine then?" Anything to lower the tension.

"Do you want to go home, Dmitry? Do you want me to call you a taxi and take you home? Or do you want me to hire a taxi for you, so that you can go home by yourself?"

Still there was no reply.

Morton injected a sense of urgency. "Only, you see, we need to decide what we are going to do, and as soon as possible. These blasted neoconservatives might at this very moment be launching their attack on us. On you, Dmitry! On you, personally!"

Krejevsky unlocked the fingers of his hands and checked the nails on his left hand. He bent down to pick up a pebble from the ground and started to fiddle with it. He tossed it up in the air a few times and let it fall into his open palm.

Morton screwed up his eyes, trying to decipher his friend.

Krejevsky said at last, "So you think that we need to take this seriously? And to act fast? And, from their side, their attitude is going to be 'strictly personal'?"

Morton opened his eyes wider, then stared directly at Krejevsky in an attempt to take control of an apparently awkward situation.

"Listen, Dmitry," Morton declared, "Do you have any idea what they might do? Where they might start?

"Now listen to me, Dmitry. Listen to me.

"I'm sure we all have skeletons in the cupboard. I cannot think of anything offhand that anyone could pin on me. Nothing sexual, for example. The illegal crossing of borders, perhaps, but that sort of thing can happen in my line of work. I was in a remote part of Jordan once and I could have sworn that one of the reasons we thought we were lost was because we had accidentally landed ourselves in Syria or Iraq. I have never written anything libellous and I don't use personal attacks or 'hit pieces' as part of my reporting, so it is unlikely that I have ever upset anyone in a personal way. Certainly not enough to give them grounds to raise a scandal."

Morton leaned back onto the railing so that he could observe Krejevsky from the front as well as from the side.

"What about you, Dmitry? I can't imagine anything untoward happening in your life. A bit like mine, really: straight as a die and a little bit boring," Morton chirped. "But I don't know anything about your life history, so I cannot pass judgment. Not that I would want to. But if I am going to help you… if we are going to fight this thing, I need to know if there is … anything … they could possibly pin on you. Is there… anything?"

Krejevsky waited for a while, then slowly shook his head.

"I thought not. I never doubted it." Morton sounded relieved. Once more, he tried to sound optimistic. "So, it should be quite easy to fight this one. But where to start?"

Krejevsky turned around so that he and Morton were facing the same direction, away from the lake. "Did you say that Shirley has put her name down for work at *The Chronicle*?" Krejevsky asked.

"Yes. We have created a dummy email account and we are using an old SIM card that one of my former associates never claimed. It is a prepaid SIM, so we can top it up without worrying about contracts with phone companies," explained Morton.

Krejevsky seemed to have recovered his composure. Morton supposed that, on reflection, Krejevsky had probably never lost it.

Dmitry Krejevsky suggested, "Then why don't you get Shirley to send off a sample of some of her so-called 'work'? You remember those notes that Hugh compiled from people he had met in his – what did you call it – 'den of iniquity'?"

"The 'café of ill repute', I named it."

"Thank you." Krejevsky issued forth a sardonic snigger.

"There was no way that we would have been able to use that material at the time," Morton continued. "Some of it was truly scandalous. Lord somebody-or-other paying for those high-class services and, when his preferred escort was unwell, it was 'La Madame' who ended up scrubbing his back in the jacuzzi. Before *and* after the deed, if my memory serves me well. One of the best laughs I had for years.

"I am sure Shirley can work up some fictitious gossip that can neither be proved nor disproved – and would not upset anybody. In lieu of a CV, so to speak. It might churn things up a bit and speed things along. If Edward Ollerson's PA takes the bait, it will be interesting to see how she reacts when she gets back to Shirley and what she asks Shirley to do."

When Morton had finished speaking, Krejevsky turned around to face across the lake and to gaze at a truck full of garden waste as it drove toward one of the exits to Hyde Park. Morton did likewise, following Krejevsky's line of vision for a while, until the truck moved out of sight. When his eyes returned to his friend, he realised that Dmitry Krejevsky must have been eyeballing him for some time.

When someone with blue eyes looked in his direction, Morton usually found it easy to imagine the other's thought processes. A steely blue gaze meant trouble and the other person meant business. A relaxed blue gaze always seemed friendly. With Dmitry Krejevsky that was not possible. His dark-brown eyes beneath the furrowed brow burned with an unfathomable raging fire. Or had Morton misread the signs? Was Dmitry Krejevsky taking the threat seriously, or not?

8

CASING THE JOINT

Shirley Bould had great fun trawling through the archives of *The New Times* for suitably scandalous but unpublished articles that could be chopped and changed, then concocted into a mouth-watering dish to be served up to Brigita Wolznaski, for her delectation.

Shirley created a story concerning the alleged doping of a greyhound and how some funny money was involved in the purchase and maintenance of the dog by a consortium of businessmen and shady characters – including an unnamed billionaire who was rumoured to be a close associate of the president of the Russian Federation.

That should be enough to grab Brigita's attention, thought Shirley.

Shirley emailed the story to Brigita Wolznaski, along with the contact details pertaining to 'Freda Gray' (Shirley's cover name), first thing in the morning of Wednesday, 27 April. Shirley was somewhat surprised to discover that the article appeared later in the day on the sports pages of the online edition of *The Chronicle*.

Cheeky! Publication without acknowledgement of source – and without payment.

Shirley sent off two more articles, throwing in a belated apology for her make-believe absence during the previous two weeks, "due to a domestic commitment", and hoping that the articles "met with the high standards that had always been expected of *The Chronicle*". Sure enough, both articles were published verbatim in the online edition the following day.

Shirley decided to ring up Brigita Wolznaski, purportedly to make sure that the articles had been received. Shirley explained that, "I just wanted to check that I sent it to the right email address, dear, because I did not get a reply. And Josh always used to acknowledge receipt."

Brigita was a bit taken aback by this forwardness, but, over the phone, she confirmed that the emails had indeed been received.

"Oh, thank heavens for that!" Shirley exclaimed. "You know, dear, I was just getting a bit concerned. I hope you didn't mind me ringing you up while you are obviously busy."

"No, not at all," Brigita replied, pleased to hear from Shirley and glad for the opportunity of a chat.

The two women engaged in small talk over the phone for more than forty minutes, during which Shirley neatly sidestepped any possible embarrassment on Brigita's part by saying that there was no charge for the three articles she had already sent, because she owed Josh and had been paid cash in advance earlier in the month.

"Only, you see, any articles I send to you in future will need to be charged for," explained Shirley.

Taking her cue from Hugh Lombard's methods of extracting news and the paying of disbursements in his 'café of ill repute', Shirley explained that payment in cash would be, "for the best, dear," and suggested a handful of cafés where this could take place.

"There's no need for that," Brigita asserted. "We have moved into our new offices. Why don't you pop in for a cup of tea and we can discuss business?"

Shirley agreed, and a meeting was arranged for eleven o'clock the following day.

※

Shirley was only too aware that there was one potential flaw in her plan: she might be recognised by Edward Ollerson and, consequently, her cover blown.

In addition, to reduce the risk that she might be recognised by Brigita as the 'birthday treat aunt', whereas Shirley had dressed up very well for her birthday surprise courtesy of Hugh and Vivienne, for her meeting with Edward Ollerson's new PA on the new premises of *The Chronicle* Shirley ensured she was clad in less flattering garb.

Edward Ollerson was probably the only employee of *The Chronicle* who might recognise her, so Edward remained her biggest concern. But it was Friday, and Shirley recalled that, in the past, Edward had been keen to get away early. He might even be working from home.

Shirley would have to chance it.

She took a taxi to the Tate Gallery and made her way on foot to the Millhouse Building in which the new offices of *The Chronicle* were situated. The building had its own agency-contracted security services. In the foyer, two smartly attired security guards were chatting to the female receptionist. Shirley signed in as the fictitious Freda Gray and placed the ribbon of the visitor security pass around her neck. She sat down in a comfortable armchair and picked up a weekly gossip magazine from the coffee table, trying her best to avoid the CCTV camera that scanned the reception area.

A door opened, and Brigita Wolznaski appeared, attired in a smart, navy-blue, pinstriped trouser suit, with the trousers flaring slightly above shiny, black shoes with noisily clicking stiletto heels.

The two women shook hands, and Brigita escorted Shirley to a large marble-floored and marble-walled atrium; the marble walls, all the way up to sun-drenched upper galleries, were dotted with notches containing voluminous artificial hanging plants, which hid the source of artificial pre-recorded sounds reminiscent of a tropical waterfall, accompanied by insipid mood music.

The new offices of *The Chronicle* were on the fifteenth floor of the Millhouse Building, with superb views north and east.

Brigita used her electronic pass to unlock the main entrance to the office, then led Freda past a small reception room stuffed from floor to ceiling with empty cardboard boxes and polystyrene packaging, already gathering dust. A damaged Venetian blind obscured the view to the north of London.

Next door to the small reception room was Brigita's office, adjoining the office of the editor-in-chief with its door flung wide open, and the editor-in-chief's leather swivel chair unoccupied and facing away from his desk. Further along the corridor were two additional offices; they were vacant, for the time being. At the end of the corridor, there was a large conference room, facing east, to which Shirley was ushered.

"All on your Jack Jones?" Shirley asked. "Everyone gone off for the weekend?"

Brigita smiled. "Friday, Friday, Friday. It's always the same."

"Nobody here at all?" Shirley asked. "All of the reporters working from home?"

"Yes. Well, sort of. Many of them will be working on location somewhere. They only come here to hot desk when they are in London. Otherwise, it is quiet. Just like this."

Brigita made an instant impression on Shirley. Brigita was quite simply a very beautiful young woman, as a result of the bee-stung lips; the perfect teeth; the winning smile; the subtly flirty nose; the large, wide-apart, blue eyes; and the dark-brown, almost black, hair, with a fringe and hair formed neatly into a shoulder-length ponytail.

Brigita left the conference room to make two cups of tea. Shirley sat gazing around the room. It was so bright. Tall, glass windows covered the entire east wall of the room. The view east along the River Thames was magnificent: it encompassed the Houses of Parliament, the slowly rotating wheel of the London Eye, and St Paul's Cathedral in the distance. Shirley strained her eyes to catch glimpses of Tower Bridge and the Tower of London peeping out through gaps between the skyscrapers of the City of London, including the Gherkin.

Between Edward Ollerson's office and the conference room, the two rooms that faced north presented a view of the Post Office Tower, though few – if any – remarked on the novelty of the fifty-year old tower these days.

Yet something was amiss. There were no people in the office except Brigita.

A drop-dead gorgeous, single, young woman – but no men sniffing around her, thought Shirley. *Even on Friday! There's nobody chatting up Brigita in anticipation of some sort of... weekend assignation, even though there are several men on the list of reporters on The Chronicle website.*

What about the officer – Philip? Who was he? Where was he? And where were the much-vaunted hot desks? The office was, according to Brigita, fully furnished, yet there were no work stations, no landlines and no life. It was a strange sort of media office.

Where was the noise, the hustle and bustle, the clatter and the chatter, the shouts across from one side of the office to the other, the paper planes containing secret messages being thrown to attract attention, and the melee that would ensue when someone returned laden with aromatic toasted treasures from the sandwich shop in the arcade on the ground floor or from the busy street around the corner?

In this particular office, there was nothing of the sort.

A twin three-pin socket on a pillar separating two full-length windows provided power to the vacuum cleaner, but nothing more. The three-pin electric sockets in the false floor under the conference table remained unused and covered by a small hatch.

And that was it.

There was no sign of a regularly used power hub supporting a bunch of laptop computers, recharge points for mobile phones and electronic tablets, and the mandatory team conference telephone with loudspeaker – all were strangely absent from this particular conference room.

The conversation between Brigita and Shirley was convivial, primarily small talk and gossip about how a large supermarket was opening near Shirley's house and how the local market traders were up in arms about it. Two hours passed without a single item of business being discussed.

The following Tuesday, Shirley paid another visit to the new offices of *The Chronicle*. It was as though she had not been away. There were more cups of tea, more small talk for over an hour and a half, another chance to enjoy the view – and, once again, a deserted office. Shirley told Brigita that the going rate for an article was, "£20 for your standard gossip, rising to £75 or even £100 for something with a bit more 'juice' to it".

For Brigita, this was a godsend. Why employ staff, each earning between £50,000 and £100,000 per year, when someone might provide you with articles for around £100 per week? There was no doubt she would be able to justify such spending – in fact, she would not even need to get clearance from Edward Ollerson or Katy Drake. They wanted scandalous articles to slot in among the heavyweight reporting, and Freda Gray's outrageous yarns were just the ticket.

Shirley emailed two more articles to Brigita and was invited to the office again on Thursday of the same week. Brigita handed over five crisp £20 notes, then sat down for tea and a chat with Shirley.

Unexpectedly, the main door to the offices opened and heavy footsteps entered the corridor. The sound of keys could be heard being dropped roughly onto a desk, and Edward Ollerson's voice called out for Brigita to let him know the location of a package that had been delivered for him that morning.

"It's in my office," Brigita shouted.

"I can't find it," Edward Ollerson replied.

"It's in my office, on my desk."

"It's not here."

Brigita excused herself and walked out of the conference room. "It's in *my* office. Not yours!"

Edward Ollerson apologised and entered Brigita's office to collect his parcel. The two could be heard cheerfully engaging in a conversation, then Edward Ollerson bade farewell to his PA and the main door clicked shut behind him.

That was a close call, Shirley reflected.

Brigita returned to the conference room. "That was my boss," she explained. "He pops in from time to time. Today, he had a package delivered to him from the US: some books or DVDs, I guess."

✳

Friday, 6 May 2016.

John Morton bought himself and Shirley a pub lunch, at a venue far removed from the swanky premises and hotels in which the staff of *The Chronicle* had stationed themselves. A retirement party was taking place in the bar and had spilled over into the lounge. The noise was raucous and deafening at times. Shirley, once again, arranged for a seat in the corner with her back to the wall to monitor the comings and goings of customers and potential troublemakers.

After a few minutes she declared an all clear.

"So, there is nobody in that new office?" Morton asked.

"No, dear, not a soul," Shirley confirmed. "And, as for that conference room, I doubt there has ever been a conference held in it. Brigita said they had all they needed, so it doesn't sound like they are going to develop it into a real conference room at all. And as for being a media outlet – what sort of media outlet has such a quiet office for a base? It's supposed to be a hive of activity. Maybe the Queen Bee has given her drones the day off."

"Many a true word said in jest," noted Morton. "Of course, the reporters are probably working on location. They do have representatives across the globe, you know."

"Really?" Shirley remarked. "You wouldn't think so." She selected a fresh-looking piece of asparagus from her plate and popped it into her mouth. "I could make a nice little earner from this," she said. "Providing Brigita with all sorts of titbits of gossip and innuendo. I send it to her and – *whoosh* – up it goes onto the website, word for word."

Morton shrugged. For run of the mill pieces, that was normal as far as he was concerned.

"Well, try this one for size, dear," Shirley pressed on, slightly miffed. "Brigita and I went into her office and sat in front of her huge computer screen. She had her list of emails open on one side of the screen and the homepage of *The Chronicle* website on the other side. Guess how many emails she has had in the past week? Fourteen. Only fourteen, for the whole week. I popped out to the loo. When I returned, she was typing away, so I just sat down next to her and pretended to look out of the window. She took an email from someone whose address appeared to be in Arabic and opened an attachment. It was a press release in English from the foreign ministry of an Arab country – I couldn't tell which. Well, Brigita copies and pastes the press release from the document into the website, alters it a bit and then publishes it under the name Hassan somebody-or-other, Middle East reporter for *The Chronicle* on the scene in Damascus."

Morton looked querulously at Shirley.

"She did the same with something about Ukraine. She copied some press release from the Ukraine Ministry of Defence about Russian tank and troop movements near the Ukraine border, pasted it into a web page, made some changes, and then signed it with a man's name: such and such, man on the spot in Kiev."

Morton was intrigued. Shirley tucked into her smoked salmon salad and took a bite of buttered, hot, crusty brown bread, while Morton put down his knife and fork, and opened his electronic tablet.

Sure enough, the article on Syria was the main item on the front page of *The Chronicle*. He carefully read it. It was very formal, with no banter and no hyperbole. The Ukraine article was the same: lifeless. Both articles were attributed to faceless reporters who were listed among *The Chronicle*'s workforce.

Morton took a mouthful of red wine and ate some pasta with a Bolognese sauce. He scanned idly through several other articles on *The Chronicle* website, then popped a bit of garlic bread into his mouth.

That's odd. Read that again, John, he told himself.

It was an article written in perfect English by someone with an Arabic name. Another article purported to be by a Lithuanian – also in perfect English. These were serious articles, not the scandalous gossip that had been deliberately peddled by Shirley. Another entry caught his eye, then another and another. They, too, were in perfect English and written by foreigners. Not only were they written in perfect English, they also had the same style. The same turn of phrase. What would Morton's favourite TV detectives make of this?

Only one possibility: all the different articles must have been written by the same person.

9

MALICIOUS FABRICATION

Saturday, 7 May 2016.
When Dmitry Krejevsky was briefed by John Morton about the curious goings-on in the upmarket premises on the fifteenth floor of a prestigious commercial tower building on the Thames Embankment, he refused to believe it.

"After all," Dmitry Krejevsky reasoned, "we are not talking about *The New Times* – an experimental, alternative media outlet that has recently spent a small fortune upgrading its website, but that is operating – in all other respects – within the tight budget that would be expected for a small-scale setup. We are talking about *The Chronicle*. THE Chronicle. *The* flagship liberal British newspaper that has been in circulation since the middle of the nineteenth century: an established media outlet with a long history. And, despite its old-fashioned ways of working in the past under the not-too-distant leadership of Sir Tom Hamble, *The Chronicle* was then – and remains to this day – a highly regarded newspaper with some big financial backers."

Morton and Krejevsky entered a café where they managed to get a Wi-Fi signal. Morton showed Krejevsky the articles on the website of *The Chronicle*.

"Precious little of this so-called 'news' is true," Krejevsky said.

"I know, Dmitry, but look at some of the details," declared Morton. "Look at the names of the contributors. Do you recognise them? We never saw nor heard of any of these people at *The Chronicle* when we were contributors. They must be new. I would have expected to find some familiar faces – one or two at the very least – but, no, there aren't any. Nobody works in the offices except

Edward Ollerson's PA, and she seems to spend most of her time doing nothing. I am convinced that the main articles – the most significant ones – are written by only one (or, at best, only a few) people, but are published under many pseudonyms. It's all for show, to create an impression that lots of important work is going on, whereas the reality is totally different."

"But why, John? What is the point?"

"I haven't a clue. Cost-cutting, Shirley thinks. By the way, Dmitry, have you seen any dirt being thrown your way yet?"

Krejevsky issued a terse, sardonic, "No".

Morton pensively sipped his coffee. Mentally, he was entering the realms of the fictional detective sleuth. *Look at the facts, Watson* – that is what Sherlock Holmes would advise. *And don't just look – make sure you observe... and see... and see properly what is really going on, not what you think might be going on.*

"Do you know what I think?" Morton whispered. "I think that *The Chronicle* has had a makeover. *The Chronicle* peddles the declining, reactionary, neoconservative worldview, albeit with a liberal-progressive veneer. More like a spoiler than a serious newspaper. Maybe they should rename it *The Spoilsport*. The number of regular readers is not increasing, and the comments to articles tend to be roughly fifty-fifty in favour versus against, but it seems that Edward Ollerson does not care about readers' comments and declining circulation. *The Chronicle* just carries on regardless."

Dmitry Krejevsky stared motionless at John Morton while the latter continued.

"I mean. It is not just a newspaper these days; it often resembles something akin to... a scandal magazine."

Dmitry Krejevsky seemed to be getting bored with this line of reasoning.

"But there is one factor that we must not overlook." Morton highlighted. "It is that we have inside knowledge of the fact – the indisputable fact – that *The Chronicle* is about to engage in some sort of malicious fabrication. Against you, Dmitry.

"For a while, the thought did cross my mind that there was something insidious about the relocation of *The Chronicle* to offices near to MI5 and MI6. I know we agreed to let the intelligence services get on with their job, but if they – or some elements within them – are working closely with Edward Ollerson and his team, then we could have a hell of a fight on our hands."

Krejevsky stirred a little extra milk into his cup of coffee.

"We still do not know the identity of the blonde woman in the photographs that were taken by Vivienne," Morton admitted, "but we do know the identity of the brunette. She is an inexperienced admin assistant called Brigita Wolznaski who has been given the job of holding the fort while the others play at… well… whatever games they want to play. Apparently, Brigita goes running in a park with Edward Ollerson every Saturday morning and sometimes after work. If you can call it running, because Edward has allowed himself to go to pot – and I am not just talking about his pot belly. They go together in the park for what is more like a brisk walk than a jog."

Morton sipped his coffee, then plodded on.

"Apparently, Edward Ollerson is now in a relationship. According to Shirley, it is not his PA, Brigita. His partner is a blonde, and my hunch is that she is the blonde woman in the photograph."

"A hunch, eh?" Krejevsky looked up with a sceptical interest.

"Well, if Edward Ollerson is in a relationship with a blonde, why is the brunette PA spending time outside work hours with him and going for a run in the park with him?"

Morton knew he had reached a dead end in this line of reasoning and his attempt to interest Dmitry Krejevsky in his theories. Yet something bugged him. Bugged him – irritatingly – as though it had bitten him.

On Friday, Morton's son, Anthony, returned home from Sheffield University to take time out to prepare for his final exams. His course work and results to date had guaranteed him at least a degree with upper second-class honours, and it was expected that he would end up with a first.

Anthony possessed an abundance of energy. Since Friday evening, he had read to the halfway point in a 400-page novel, he had reviewed his study notes in order to benefit from any last minute advice his dad might have to offer, he had helped his mum with a spot of gardening at his grandparents' house, and he had helped his dad to dig some ground at home in order to prepare it for summer planting. He had even been out early in the morning for a jog.

This latter fact gave John Morton an idea.

*

On Monday at five o'clock in the evening, John and Anthony Morton sat outside a café near the Serpentine lake, next to a wide path busy with walkers, skaters and joggers; the path led away from the café toward an exit gate to Hyde Park Corner.

Just after five-thirty, Edward Ollerson and Brigita Wolznaski could be seen walking at an unhurried pace along the path, in an easterly direction away from the lake. Anthony raised himself from his seat and followed them, keeping his distance by thirty metres. Edward and Brigita turned left in a northerly direction, passing the Joy of Life Fountain and Speakers' Corner, until they arrived at a seated area within the park and near to the exit to Marble Arch. They sat down.

Anthony decided that this was an appropriate time to stop walking and to do some stretching exercises within hearing distance of the chit-chat between Edward and Brigita. The conversation consisted of a great deal of small talk, but not much ado about the business of *The Chronicle* newspaper; business-wise, it was nothing more serious than phoning the building maintenance office to report a problem with a cistern or a faucet.

To make his intentions less obvious, Anthony continued to jog along the path, westwards, in the direction of the Bayswater area of London. He returned to the seating area to find the pair had gone. He started off back down the path toward the café where his dad was waiting. Halfway, he caught sight of Edward and Brigita walking – or, more accurately, strolling – and he stopped jogging and pretended he was out of breath. Then he ambled along, a few metres behind the two strollers, inhaling deeply and exhaling for a long period. The small talk between Edward and Brigita continued, long after they exited the park.

John and Anthony Morton repeated the process on Tuesday evening after work. On Wednesday evening, there was a no-show by Edward, although Brigita turned up alone. She was running, and she caught John Morton and his son by surprise by the speed and sheer effort she applied to the task in hand.

Brigita wore a tracksuit while she was walking with Edward Ollerson, whereas on her own she ran wearing a full athletics kit: skimpy, blue shorts with a matching sports top (revealing a slender but muscular midriff), and good-quality running shoes. Her hair was tied in a ponytail that swished from side to side, inviting and receiving the attention of every hot-blooded male in the vicinity.

Anthony followed Brigita, about fifty metres behind her. Brigita set an electric pace. Anthony ran faster in an effort to keep up. Brigita ran and ran, out of Hyde Park and through Kensington Gardens, slowing down and jogging on the spot while taking a call on her mobile, and exiting to a slip road where a bright red BMW sports car was waiting. The hood of the car had been retracted, revealing a good-looking, blonde driver wearing sunglasses and a headscarf. Brigita stepped into the car amid a flurry of cheerful chatter between the two women, fastened her seat belt, and the car suddenly roared into life and sped off with a conspicuous screech of brakes.

Anthony returned to his dad and passed on the gossip. Brigita addressed the blonde woman as "Katy". The blonde spoke with an American accent.

Thursday evening proved to be much less taxing for Anthony. Brigita was joined by Edward Ollerson, and, to allay potential suspicions and to avoid being recognised, Anthony jogged across the grass field and came within view of the seated area beyond

Speakers' Corner and near to the exit to Marble Arch as Edward and Brigita took their seats. They seemed such a happy and playful couple, even though Edward was dating someone else. Anthony slowed down, pretending to be out of breath, and – after a short rest – began his stretching exercises. There was a moment of concern when Anthony's eyes met Brigita's, but she seemed to accept him as merely one regular jogger among many. Still, it was a warning to Anthony not to become too familiar.

The chatter between Brigita and Edward was non-stop. It was all small talk. Yet, at one point, Anthony could have sworn that Brigita asked Edward to join her away from London for the weekend.

It seemed that there might be some truth in this assumption because, the following day, the editor-in-chief of *The Chronicle* and his PA failed to turn up. In fact, they were not seen again until Monday evening when, taking a roundabout route to the seated area, Anthony slowed down from his jog, and approached Edward and Brigita from behind the now familiar seating area beyond Speaker's Corner near to the exit to Marble Arch. They seemed less chatty than usual, but – as Anthony commenced his stretching exercises – the reason became clear: Brigita leaned over and put her head on Edward's shoulder; she snuggled up to him, and his head tilted onto hers.

✽

John Morton hated office gossip with a passion. When Anthony recounted in detail what he had seen, including the pair holding hands during their stroll along the pathways in Hyde Park, John Morton merely made a mental note. He and Anthony returned home.

Every evening for the rest of that week, Anthony Morton went to the park alone to jog, to walk, to stretch and to observe.

Meanwhile, John Morton caught up with Shirley and obtained an update of the goings-on at *The Chronicle*. The pattern remained the same, except that on Wednesday she overheard Brigita having a transatlantic conference call with Loretta Farelli and Katy Drake. The loudspeaker was turned on.

Shirley pretended not to be interested as Brigita reported back to Loretta and Katy: Yes, Edward was being 'looked after'. Yes, he was 'taking exercise' nearly every day. Yes, she was trying to 'entertain him' as best she could. No, he was not going to the park with her today. It was Wednesday, and this was the day he visited his mother or made some other excuse.

Suddenly, the mundane conference call sparkled into life. One of the women wanted to know what they were doing about their main problem. Did they have any gossip that could be used to take the guy in question down a peg or two? It had been a few weeks since this plan had been hatched.

"Well, Brigita, when are we going to see some progress?" Katy had asked.

Shirley realised that the target of their angst was none other than Dmitry Krejevsky. It was clear that they were having trouble getting the dirt on Dmitry. That was good news. But Loretta Farelli was a persistent type, and Shirley knew this from past experience. It would be dangerous to assume that Loretta would just give up.

No, that one would never give up the ghost in a million years, Shirley thought.

John Morton chuckled when he found out that not only had the egg not hatched – it had not even been laid.

※

Modern history, according to the syllabus of many schools and universities in the UK, often focuses on several key subject areas. The Tudor dynasty was near the top of the list. This was not simply down to a love of things exclusively British nor a chance to glorify – or abhor – the British (or English) monarchy.

The Tudor period was a dramatic turning point in British history, and widely covered in modern British culture: the reign of Henry the Eighth and his six wives, the Protestant Reformation, Bloody Mary's burning of her adversaries, and

Elizabeth the First's victories over the aspirant Queen of Scots and the Spanish Armada.

Furthermore, there were so many other colourful characters who appeared on the scene: Anne Boleyn, Thomas More, Thomas Wolsey, Thomas Cromwell, Thomas Cranmer, and many more who would appear in feature films and TV series, including one recent saucy effort which, according to one enthusiastic reviewer, exhibited a particular 'tits and bums' allure.

It was truly typical of the entertainment and sheer escapism that were part and parcel of a phoney war.

Period drama was all the rage, and many of the worthy actors and actresses seemed destined to superimpose their well-loved roles from the Tudor era upon characters from a quite different age. But nobody seemed to mind. Even the sternest of critics seemed to have mislaid their sharpest quills.

The 'tits and bums' televised Tudor period drama did not disappoint John Morton, especially in the context of his current enquiries, because there were two salient features of the political practices of today that had their origins in past periods and none more so than in the time of the Tudors: *scandal* and *intrigue*.

Morton drifted into a daydream. Dmitry Krejevsky was imagined to be spending his entire life cocooned on the set for a period drama; in Krejevsky's case, Tolstoy's *War and Peace* – but merely as an insignificant minor character who popped into frame only occasionally. Only the main characters had well-known, scandalous *liaisons dangereuses*. But not Dmitry Krejevsky.

If you had lived in the Tudor era, it would have been no big deal if the libidinous male offspring of a wealthy and powerful master got together with a susceptible miss so-and-so at the back of the galley every Friday evening, or if one of the nubile members of the royal court had her (or his) services purloined by a senior male courtier.

But there was one notable exception to the rule. The scandal – cooked up by some of the scheming minds within King Henry the Eighth's loyal praetorian guard – concerning which and how many of the young men of the court had allegedly slept with the 'indicted adulteress' Anne Boleyn.

This infamous scandal was not about sex or adultery. It was about uninhibited power, treachery and brutal vengeance. And it was a setup, pure and simple. Its reach could extend far beyond the weak and susceptible, and toward the rich and powerful: sometimes referred to as 'the great and the good'.

Furthermore, Anne Boleyn seems to have become complacent; she had underestimated the existential threat and, subsequently, she had been taken completely unawares as the secret, murky business of state materialised in plain view.

Some parallels between Anne Boleyn and Dmitry Krejevsky seemed obvious to John Morton: in particular, Krejevsky seemed reluctant to discuss the plot against him and to face up to the existential threat.

Why not? thought Morton. *Is Dmitry embarrassed by the affair? It's hard to say; he does tend to keep his cards close to his chest.*

Does he not know how to proceed? A seasoned legal professional not knowing how to proceed is unlikely. Does he have something to hide? He says not. Does he think that the whole character assassination plot is beneath him, and that it would be 'undignified' to react?

The Krejevskys were descended from the Russian and English aristocracies. Morton had observed, at close quarters, how aristocrats behave, including the impeccably groomed and well-mannered Dmitry Krejevsky, whose wife actually employed servants; the benignly controlling Sir Harold Nevin, whose estate (maintained by an unknown number of formal and informal retainers) seemed a throwback to times past; and the perennially dignified and aloof Count Roland von Eissinger the Third.

None of them tended to act without having thought things through, very carefully.

But wait! Upon hearing that Loretta, Katy and Brigita had proved incapable of contriving a scandal concerning their target, had Dmitry Krejevsky dismissed the whole plot as the fanciful imaginings of a group of fantasists?

Morton was adamant that, sooner or later, Loretta Farelli and her colleagues would find or invent something to pin on their target; at which point, Dmitry Krejevsky would be *forced* to face up to an impending crisis.

Perhaps Dmitry Krejevsky did have something to hide. But, if so, what on earth could he have done to merit arrest and a possible trial for espionage? Even if it were true that Krejevsky was a Russian secret agent, what would the authorities do about it? At least one of the Cambridge spy-ring had been a member of the royal inner circle, and he had got off scot-free. Being well-connected, Dmitry Krejevsky might well receive the same privileged treatment; in which case, no wonder he remained unperturbed by the whole improbable farce.

But the blonde – assumed by now, correctly, to be none other than Katy Drake – had told Brigita that Dmitry Krejevsky was *probably* FSB.

The FSB was Russian *domestic* intelligence; it was more like MI5 than MI6, and more like US Homeland Security or the Federal Bureau of Investigations (FBI) than the Central Intelligence Agency (CIA). Why would someone working for some homeland security organisation be based overseas?

It had become clear to Morton by now that even his own decision-making capabilities were not functioning effectively. This could not be allowed to go on. Morton realised that he could not proceed alone and that he needed help. He decided to confide in Sir Harold Nevin and drove to Nevin's stately home in Buckinghamshire to do so.

10

MOTIVE, MEANS AND OPPORTUNITY

Monday, 23 May 2016.
Two limousines approached the Old Stream Inn and Restaurant in Henley-on-Thames and pulled into the car park. Morton exited via the rear door of one of the cars and leapt round to the other side to help Sir Harold Nevin to do likewise, but, as on previous occasions, the octogenarian Knight of the Garter was already halfway to the other car to open doors and to accompany his younger septuagenarian friends to the restaurant.

After they were settled inside a private annex attached to the restaurant, Morton recounted his concerns to Sir Quentin Forbes and Lord Ernest Anderian.

"John, have you signed the Official Secrets Act?" Sir Quentin asked.

"No," Morton replied.

Lord Ernest Anderian produced a copy of the Official Secrets Act for signature, but Morton refused to have anything to do with it on the grounds that it might compromise his independence as an investigative reporter or might be used to lean on him at a later date.

"Not by anyone here, of course, but outside of this circle of friends I can't afford to take any chances," explained Morton.

This placed the two well-connected notables with a background in the intelligence services of the UK in a quandary because they would be unable to divulge sensitive security information to John Morton.

Nevin came up with a solution: first, they would allow John Morton to recount his story and, second, they would allow him to put questions to Sir Quentin and Lord Ernest.

"Those questions that do not probe too deeply can be answered," suggested Nevin.

This strategy was agreed upon, but when the time came for Morton to ask his questions, he had one of peculiar sensitivity: was Dmitry Krejevsky an agent of the Russian FSB or another Russian intelligence service? He asked this question even though a 'yes' response would imply a bizarre state of affairs in which senior Tories were working in cahoots with the government and intelligence services of a foreign power – and Russia at that!

The answer was, of course, no. But, to prise out this information, Morton had to push hard and even skirt around the issue because Sir Quentin and Lord Ernest pulled down the shutters instinctively.

Lists of agents of one's own country and those of others were strictly classified, Morton was told, but Lord Ernest Anderian advised Morton that, by posing his questions from various indirect angles, he might be able to deduce an answer. From those answers, Morton fashioned a working hypothesis that Dmitry Krejevsky was *not* an officer of any of the Russian intelligence services.

Was there anything from Krejevsky's past that might catch up with him, if it became public knowledge? Again, the answer seemed to be 'no'.

What about those who are associated with *The Chronicle*? Specifically, Edward Ollerson, Loretta Farelli, Katy Drake and Brigita Wolznaski?

Once again, Morton found himself skirting around the truth to get at it.

Edward and Brigita were eliminated quickly as suspected agents of intelligence services, although it sounded as though Edward Ollerson had at some time signed the Official Secrets Act, and had many contacts within the UK intelligence services and Whitehall. Edward would be able to function as some sort of conduit for the UK Establishment or 'deep state', but he was definitely not a spook. Brigita was no more than an innocent bystander who had been charged with 'minding the shop'.

This left Loretta, who was born an American of Italian descent, and Katy, who was born a US citizen. Both were in possession of US passports.

"I can tell you," Sir Quentin confided, "that neither of those women were recruited by the UK intelligence services. There is an unwritten rule, and there may even be a written agreement, that the UK intelligence services do not recruit any citizens of the US, which means that those two women are in the clear."

"But they could be US intelligence? Or agents of another foreign power?" Morton asked.

"That is true," replied Sir Quentin, "but there are rules of engagement involving foreign agents. In *general*, when agents enter an overseas territory, their activities are monitored by their own side *and* by their opponents. The agents have an official cover such as being an embassy official in charge of visa approval. This official business is delegated and discharged by other officials to allow the agents to get on with their real work. The agents are tracked by the other side, but not interfered with, unless there is a crisis between their home government and the target government. All governments in the world have signed up to this protocol, either openly, in secret or informally."

"But is anyone going to answer my *specific* question?" Morton asked. "Are Loretta Farelli or Katy Drake working as intelligence agents for the US or for any other foreign power?"

"Even if we knew the answer to your question," Lord Ernest Anderian put in, "we would not be able to divulge that information to anyone but the most rigorously vetted personnel. As we pointed out at an earlier meeting, any intelligence agents who involve themselves in the activities of *The New Times* must be allowed to get on with their work, even if it is merely a façade. So long as you abide by these rules of engagement, written or otherwise, you will not be harmed – and neither will anyone who is associated with *The New Times*.

"I can only suggest that you find a way of dealing with this inconvenience. So far, no dirt has been produced to smear Dmitry Krejevsky, and there might never be… unless …" Lord Ernest

Anderian paused, then bestowed upon Morton a congenial smirk, "unless somebody *invents* it..."

Morton took a sip of his after-dinner brandy and scanned the faces of each of his three companions, seemingly with a joyless frustration. However, wittingly or not, Lord Ernest Anderian had opened a peephole into intelligence methodology. Shrewd as ever, he seemed to have decided that the time was ripe for him to tip Morton the wink.

"Of course," Lord Ernest resumed, "this situation is far from satisfactory. From your point of view, you are all under constant suspicion, and – at any moment in time – someone could produce something embarrassing about any of you.

"But consider this angle, John. What concerns me more than the surveillance operation and the mooted character smear is that friend Ollerson and his PA are being put under pressure by others. I find this detail to be very interesting. And they are not producing the desired results, which is also very interesting. Let us probe a little deeper ...

"There is a risk that if Edward Ollerson and his PA do not produce results, *they* will be removed and replaced by more meticulous or more fanatical operatives. That would be most unpleasant, most unpredictable and, for our purposes, most undesirable. However, there is a little trick that you might want to try to counter this – what do they call it – 'rat fucking'?"

"And what is that?" Morton asked, a mite sceptically.

"It is imperative, John, that you remain in control of the situation," Lord Ernest elucidated. "If our friends at *The Chronicle* are incapable of providing their superiors with the dirt on Dmitry Krejevsky, then *you* must provide it for them. *You* need to concoct a plausible story, then deliver it to Edward Ollerson and Brigita Wolznaski at *The Chronicle*. They will then have something with which to raise their standing with their superiors.

"However, you also need to be able to counter the story when it breaks. If you handle this in the correct manner, it will not be Edward and Brigita who are held to account – it will be those who are exerting pressure upon them. That would be a satisfactory outcome for us because the nincompoops and the novices would remain *in situ*, whereas their handlers might be removed and replaced. We have nothing to lose, because we are unlikely to have to deal with anyone more toxic than Loretta Farelli. We do not know our opponents' motives, let alone their means and opportunity for executing their task, but *we* now have a clear motive: *to induce Edward and Brigita into a bubble where they can be controlled by us.* The fallback plan therefore becomes – if, and only if, it becomes absolutely necessary to do so – to take action to completely destroy *The Chronicle.*"

※

In the evening, Anthony returned from his run in the park and reported his findings back to his dad. It was just the same old, same old. Edward and Brigita were walking, sitting, canoodling and strolling back to a tube station to take the train home.

John Morton sat at his dining room table with an A1-size flipchart in front of him and several fibre-tip pens to hand.

Motive, means and opportunity were required.

Courtesy of Lord Ernest Anderian, we now have a motive. Next, we need the means. Something that we design and arrange to be delivered to Brigita, thought Morton.

He began to write some notes and to imagine a scenario. He cross-checked his plan with Dmitry Krejevsky, who provided some material about himself to enable Morton to build it into a plausible-sounding narrative whose plausibility could, if challenged, be just as plausibly denied.

As for opportunity, that was obvious. On Wednesday, Anthony would pass a package to Brigita as she ran alone in the park. Shirley would travel to the offices of *The Chronicle* the following day and on subsequent days, and keep an eye on developments. Brigita was not aware of Shirley's real identity, and, as far as Brigita was concerned, Anthony was merely one park jogger among many. When she received the package from Anthony, Brigita would no doubt be a bit surprised and would return to the park to meet him again to find out who he was. But Anthony would not return to the park again. John Morton would take over and – disguised suitably with no more than a baseball cap, sunglasses and a newspaper – would observe Brigita's behaviour. Morton felt that the story he had devised would be manna from heaven to Brigita Wolznaski, and that it would enable her to build considerable kudos with her superiors.

✳

On Wednesday evening, Anthony and John Morton waited on a park bench in Hyde Park for Brigita to arrive. She was late: ten minutes late, then twenty minutes late. John Morton was about to abort the plan when Anthony picked up the package suddenly, sprang forward, turned around, and began to run up the slope behind the park bench and through the trees that led to the fields. John Morton was taken aback, but he sat down again and straightened his newspaper as Brigita Wolznaski whizzed past. However, there was a tiny fly in the ointment. Brigita was not alone. She was accompanied by a blonde friend.

"Katy Drake – who else could it be?" Morton murmured to himself.

Anthony would not be able to deliver the package while Brigita had Katy Drake in tow.

There was an upside to this development. Katy Drake was nowhere near as athletic as Brigita, which meant that Brigita was not able to run as fast as she would have wanted. Anthony watched as the two women jogged along the path, north toward Speakers' Corner, then – without stopping – turned west toward Bayswater, and finally disappeared temporarily round the bend toward Kensington Gardens.

At the exit gate, Brigita continued to jog on the spot as Katy spoke for a few minutes before taking her leave. At which point, Brigita wheeled round and returned at express speed in the direction of Speakers' Corner. There, she began to do some exercises. Anthony walked slowly, to accurately time the rendezvous. When Brigita lifted her left leg onto the backrest of a park bench and leaned forward to stretch her hamstring carefully, Anthony pounced.

He walked coolly up to this beautiful, young woman, who was only a few years older than him; smiled under his baseball cap and his large, dark, wraparound sunglasses; and received a friendly smile in return. Without speaking, he handed over an A4-size brown envelope of bulky volume. He then walked briskly down the path and ran across the field. He stopped after a while and doubled back behind a tree, a safe distance away from Brigita, to observe her reaction. Brigita had opened the envelope and was standing, searching in all directions, presumably for her benefactor. She was never again to see Anthony in the park but, from now on, for Brigita Wolznaski it looked like it was game on.

✳

Next morning, at ten o'clock, Shirley arrived at the offices of *The Chronicle*. She donned her visitor security pass and walked to the seating area as the receptionist rang Brigita to tell her that Shirley (in the guise of the fictitious Freda Gray) had arrived and was waiting in the reception area on the ground floor.

It was a good fifteen minutes until Brigita picked up the phone to answer the call from the receptionist, and at least an extra half hour before Brigita came down to escort Shirley to the fifteenth floor. With trepidation, Shirley crept into the offices, wary that Edward Ollerson might be present. He was not.

Shirley walked to her usual place in the conference room, in which Brigita had installed a small table next to one of the electric wall sockets. A kettle, cutlery and crockery had been placed on top of the small table. Sachets of coffee, tea bags and condiments were now stored in boxes on a tray in the centre of the large conference table.

Shirley decided to make two mugs of tea while Brigita returned to her office to resume her conference call. Brigita mistakenly thought she had closed the door, but it creaked further and further ajar until it was wide enough for Shirley to listen in. The volume of the loudspeaker had been turned down, but not low enough to hide the excited voices of Edward Ollerson and Katy Drake.

Shirley returned to the kettle and filled a teapot. She placed the teapot with some mugs, biscuits, sugar, sweeteners and sachets of creamer onto a small tray, and knocked on the door of Brigita's office. She entered, put the tray onto a table adjacent to Brigita's desk and left the office without closing the door.

Shirley had brought some fashion magazines to the office for Brigita to read during her spare time. She opened the pages of one of the magazines and leafed through it while trying to pay attention to Brigita's phone call. When the call ended, Brigita spent half an hour in her office, typing. Eventually, she walked to the conference room and apologised to Shirley for the delay.

"Oh, not to worry, dear. Some days are busy, and some are not," Shirley reasoned.

Shirley disclosed a couple of top-notch pieces of gossip that could be corroborated by the online editions of TV networks based in the US and some European countries, as well as several sources on various blogs and social media. One of the pieces told the story of an opponent of the Chinese government who thought he might soon be arrested and imprisoned – or worse. The other recounted the sad tale of a Russian dissident who was in a similar predicament. Given that the Russian general election was scheduled for September 2016, Shirley believed that such an article would spice up the coverage and might fetch a decent price.

However, Brigita seemed to have other things on her mind. She paid Shirley £100 in cash and then sat down to drink her tea.

Shirley cheerfully struck up a conversation about special discounts and offers in her recently established local supermarket, and how Brigita could take advantage of the offers to save a lot of money on tea, coffee, and even stationery and various other office items. Brigita nodded politely, but her thoughts were clearly elsewhere. Shirley decided to up the ante.

"I thought I would have trouble getting some juicy articles for you, dear," Shirley began. "There is a great deal of sundry dross doing the rounds: mundane, run of the mill stuff. But, last week,

I overheard an interesting tale about the mummified corpse of someone linked to the Russian monarchy. It turns out that there was some sort of battle hundreds of years ago in which Genghis Khan was pushed back from the borders of Europe by some tribes – well, farmers really – who had not taken too kindly to his advances. Huge numbers were killed on both sides; old Genghis seems to have given it up as a bad job and gone off somewhere else.

"Anyway, the tribal leaders couldn't find all the bodies, and they thought that Genghis Khan had captured their warriors, to hold them as hostages. They waited for months for him to send them an invoice – for the tribute to be paid in exchange for their lost warriors– but it never came. In the end, they gave up waiting – or maybe they just died without ever finding out what happened.

"Last year, some developers were excavating ground in a remote area of the Russian steppe, and they came across some well-preserved weapons, and pots and pans. They called in a team of archaeologists, who found some bones and full skeletons. There's a lot of salt or peat or something around there, and the bitter cold would also have helped to preserve the remains. The area has been sealed off, and there was some talk of a new military base being built in the vicinity – not far from the Ukraine border. That's where I thought there might be an interesting angle concerning the Ukraine–Russia business. But, in the end, they produced evidence that a lost prince and his followers had at last been discovered. It seems they either got lost, or took refuge somewhere and got trapped. They must have starved or frozen to death, poor little perishers.

"I gave the story to the British Museum, in the end. I didn't charge, bless them. Well, you don't, do you?"

"That was sweet of you, Freda," Brigita said, managing an uneasy smile.

Brigita walked to the window and sipped tea for a while before returning to the conference table.

"Freda, do you mind if I... I mean... oh, I shouldn't be asking you this, you know..." Brigita began hesitatingly.

"What is it, dear?" enquired Shirley.

"Well, I shouldn't really discuss this with you."

"What is it, dear?" Shirley probed.

To hell with it, thought Brigita. *I'm going to have to talk to someone about this.* "The thing is. Oh, this is ... so embarrassing."

"Go on, dear."

"Well, I seem to have landed myself in an awkward situation."

Oh, no. They've rumbled us, thought Shirley. Her face dropped, but she plodded on, keen to hear of this 'awkward situation' on the off-chance that she might be able to offer some advice on what to do about it. "Go on, dear."

"Well, last weekend, I went away to stay with some relatives on the south coast. My boss had nothing to do with himself that weekend and his lover was not around. So..."

Brigita's composure began to dissolve before Shirley's eyes.

"Go on, dear." Shirley perked up, having perceived intuitively that Brigita's awkward situation was of a private and personal nature, and had nothing to do with Dmitry Krejevsky and the plot to smear him.

"We shouldn't have..." Brigita broke down into sobs. A tear perched at the tip of her nose, expanded in size, then dropped onto the table, only to be replaced by another budding teardrop.

"Now you just settle yourself down and tell me all about it," Shirley ordered, while taking control and moving her chair a little closer to Brigita.

"I was only talking with her yesterday... and just now with Edward, over the phone ... She obviously doesn't know about it."

"Okay. Try to calm down a bit, Brigita. You were right to tell me. It doesn't do to bottle it up."

"I know... Thanks, Freda. I'm so grateful."

This was not the conversation that Shirley was expecting, but it did give her the opportunity to find out a bit more about Brigita and to gain her confidence. Brigita's problem was less with Edward Ollerson than with her friend and mentor, Katy Drake. It was the guilt associated with the betrayal of someone who had treated her so well and who had given her this 'fantastic job' in the UK's capital city, in a superb office with a view and everything she could possibly want – except the company of other people.

Loneliness, compounded by homesickness, had left Brigita Wolznaski vulnerable to the attraction of the nearest available man. Her job was basically to mind the office, take the calls, handle the mail, maintain part of the website and look after Edward Ollerson's health.

She had no friends, in what came across to her as a rather cold, friendless, impersonal perception of a sprawling metropolis, with everyone going about their own business and paying no attention to anyone else; and, unless Katy was around, Brigita never went out. Her social life was non-existent, and the absence of colleagues in the office ruled out drinks after work and boozy nights out – another huge change in the culture of *The Chronicle* since the likes of Shirley Bould had been given the boot.

11

A HELPING HAND

Brigita took a break and returned ten minutes later, but having not really felt the full benefit of the short break.

"There. That's so much better isn't it, dear?" Shirley attempted to raise Brigita's spirits.

Brigita managed a weak smile, and Shirley made her another cup of tea.

"You know, Brigita, you are a very pretty young woman," stated Shirley. "You remind me so much of my eldest daughter before she was married. She has two lovely children now, one boy and one girl. Men would never leave her alone, in her younger days, and they hit upon her at every opportunity. One day she found herself torn between two lovers – one destined to become her future ex-boyfriend and the other a new young man with potential. She and I had many a discussion about this over several weeks. In the end, she decided to break with the past and told her future ex-boyfriend that there was no chance that they would get back together again. It all worked out well for her, in the end."

Brigita tried to smile, but found it hard.

"Are you in touch with your mother about your stay in London?" Shirley tried a different approach.

"Yes, but she does not know about... about him. Not yet, anyway. I'll talk to Mom about it when I'm ready. Probably when I fly back home to Washington DC, if there is time for me to squeeze in a vacation. I mean, I don't even know how this job is going to work out, or whether it will last or not," Brigita said.

"It's a difficult one. You are caught in the middle of a love triangle. How long has… Did you say his name is Edward? How long has he been with this other woman?"

"A few weeks. Katy doesn't see him much. She said she was going to spend a lot of time in London, but she has not moved here. You know, Freda, I'm not sure if she will. She asked me to 'look after' Edward for her – as a favour."

"As a favour?" Shirley was flabbergasted, but she maintained her composure. "That sounds a bit unusual. I mean, asking a friend to 'look after' her man – I could never imagine myself doing that in my younger days. Is it a modern thing?"

"No. Well, I don't think it is. I suppose it does sound a bit strange, but Katy – that's Edward's lover – she gave me this job and started me off as Edward's PA. The trouble is, she does not take much interest in what is happening here."

Shirley sipped some tea and considered the situation for a moment.

"Do you think that Katy is trying to back away from Edward, dear? Has she changed her mind, perhaps?" Shirley enquired.

Brigita shrugged.

Shirley pressed on. "So, who made the first move – you or Edward?"

"I don't know, really," explained Brigita. "It was a bit of both. I invited him to join me with my relatives for the weekend, so I suppose you could say that I made the first move. But not deliberately and not with any big plan in mind. It was more of a thank you to him for allowing me to visit my relatives and work flexible hours to compensate for the time off. Edward had seemed a bit fed up, and he said he was missing Katy. Again. Yet again. He looked so vulnerable. I just wanted to help him. Maybe I was just trying to help myself. I don't know. It's all so complicated.

"We were staying in separate rooms. Then, on Saturday afternoon, we went for a drive. Edward parked the car near a promenade facing out to sea. We were going to go for a walk along the beach, but we continued the conversation we had slipped into about Katy not being around. He said that Katy might be away from London for two or three weeks, maybe more. I wasn't sure if he was sort of trying it on, but at the same time I was a bit worried for him because he sounded neglected. And, looking back, I might have been, in a way, giving him the impression that I was hoping that he would try it on.

"That's when it happened. I began to try to cheer him up and to get him to look on the positive side. Then I can remember sympathising with him. One thing led to another, and we were kissing before I knew what was happening. Then it got more intense. Edward drove to a remote spot."

Brigita began to whimper.

"He kept his shirt on in case anyone stopped next to our car," Brigita confessed.

"Very romantic! In an English sort of way!" Shirley enthused. "It sounds like you both enjoyed each other's company."

"Yes," Brigita sobbed. "For over three hours!"

Shirley found herself cast as Brigita's impromptu counsellor.

"Do you have to stay in the office?" Shirley asked.

"I'm supposed to. Why?" responded Brigita.

"A bit of fresh air would do you the world of good, dear."

Brigita activated the call-forwarding feature on her landline to redirect calls to her mobile. They left the Millhouse Building and walked along the promenade next to the River Thames. The trees were in blossom and some were even breaking into bloom. Dappled shade filtered the glare from the sunshine, and a light breeze suggested movement and change. Vestiges of pollen floated away, high into the sky, in search of the horticultural equivalent of romance. Late spring was giving way to early summer; change was in the air.

Shirley told Brigita that she should not feel guilty about what had happened during her unplanned tryst with Edward Ollerson. "When two people feel alone and need each other and take to each other, it is quite natural you know, dear. Do you know what I think you should do next? I think you should knuckle down and do some work. It will take your mind off other affairs. I'm afraid that the stories I have provided you with today are only simple stuff. You can use them in any way you like."

Shirley thought it was time to take the conversation up a notch. "Brigita, do you have anything important that you can work on?"

"No. Well, yes. There is. I received an interesting story recently. Edward knows about it. He is examining it as we speak. Maybe tomorrow he will let me know what to do with it," stated Brigita.

"Good. It is a story with potential, yes?"

"Oh yes. It's quite a bombshell. I can't say anything about it, just now."

"Well, dear, if you need anyone to help you with your 'bombshell', you only have to ask."

*

Next day, Shirley paid another visit to Brigita. There were no phone calls at all during the day, and the office remained deserted. Brigita had been alone when she ran in the park the previous evening. Edward Ollerson declined the opportunity to join her, in order to go through the report that Brigita had received from the young stranger in the park.

Shirley offered to treat Brigita to lunch. With calls forwarded and Edward alerted to Brigita's absence from the office, the two women were free to discuss their problems. Shirley kept up a lively momentum. Her biggest problem, she said, was which cruise she and her husband should go on this year, and when.

"You go on cruises!" Brigita exclaimed excitedly.

"We love them. We have done most of Europe, including the Danube and the Rhine; also, the Caribbean – twice – we love it there; and Egypt, of course," expounded Shirley.

"I wish I could go on a cruise," Brigita sighed dreamily. "It sounds so romantic."

"It is. Very. And interesting, too. You see so many places in one trip. But I think a young person might find it a bit boring. Unless you like to sit around on a shaded sundeck sipping tea and fruit juices all day, and then go walking around the towns when you disembark, it is probably not for you."

For Brigita, anything that involved Edward Ollerson and her being on holiday together constituted a great idea. She thanked Shirley once more for her support, and Shirley again said that it was no trouble.

The time came to return to the office. It was one hour and forty-five minutes after they had started lunch.

Naughty girls we are, thought Shirley, *each having two glasses of wine and soda.*

Well, it was Friday, which was when – in the old days – it was normal for everyone to spend long liquid lunches in the pub.

Brigita had a purposeless evening to look forward to. The wine had made her tired, so there would be no run in the park and no chance for Edward Ollerson to keep healthy – not that he seemed bothered about it. Exercise with Edward, in whatever form it took, would have to wait until the weekend proper.

Shortly before going home, Brigita noticed that an email had come in from Edward Ollerson. The documents concerning Dmitry Krejevsky were being scrutinised in the Beltway by Loretta Farelli and Katy Drake. The initial reaction was favourable. The signs were that Dmitry Krejevsky would now be pressured by Loretta and Katy Drake in hot pursuit of their goal of discrediting him (not realising that the whole exercise was prearranged by Dmitry Krejevsky's allies at *The New Times*, and that – no matter how invigorating it would appear to the 'assassins' – the exhilaration would not last).

Instead, it was doomed to climax in an inevitable train wreck.

※

With Monday being a public holiday, Brigita was allowed extra time to relax. By Tuesday morning, she felt revitalised and much of her inner strength had been restored.

Shirley joined her in the office at ten o'clock in the morning, and brought with her two articles for review and possible publication. Without even looking at the articles, Brigita handed over five £20 notes. Brigita had been tipped off by Edward that "the Krejevsky exposé is more or less all systems go" and that she "should be ready at a moment's notice to go to work on it".

Brigita had also been told that, in Washington DC, Loretta Farelli and Katy Drake had engaged the services of a colleague who claimed to be an expert on the forging of digital photographs using professional software. The idiot had given a clean bill of health to a fake photograph of Dmitry Krejevsky wearing the uniform of a colonel in the Russian intelligence service, the FSB.

The story itself was far too long, and would need to have the juicy bits extracted and written up as a preamble (with bullet points) prior to being uploaded to the website.

Brigita had not taken Shirley into her confidence about this attempt at defamation and, when Shirley visited the office on Thursday, Brigita left her in the conference room where Shirley made a pot of tea. Shirley had baked some small cakes and macaroons, which she removed from her bag and arranged on a plate. She entered Brigita's office and revealed her delicious surprise. Brigita was delighted.

Shirley, too, was delighted because she saw, clearly visible on the left side of Brigita's large computer screen, a familiar photograph of Dimitry Krejevsky – clad in incriminating livery.

As she munched a macaroon, Brigita noticed that Shirley was staring at the screen.

"He is a Russian agent living and working in the UK," Brigita crowed. "We are going to 'out' him."

"He's a nasty bit of work, I'll bet, dear," Shirley remarked. "If looks could kill..."

"Actually," Brigita said, "I think he looks rather dashing ... reminds me of a photograph from the archives of my family in Bournemouth of a family member in Polish Air Force uniform during the 1940s. The whole family is so proud of him."

"Still," Shirley added, "if this Russian agent is spying on us, then he only has himself to blame if he is found out."

Brigita copied the text from the document, which had been specially co-written by Katy Drake in conjunction with Loretta Farelli and other enthusiasts in the Beltway. She modified the bullet points and ensured the font suited the story. The photograph was then uploaded and placed in a prominent place, beneath the headline and above the main text.

The following day, *The Chronicle* would claim, on the front page of its newspaper and the homepage of its website, that one of its former reporters was not all he seemed.

※

The story of a Russian spy pulling the strings at *The New Times* stole the day's headlines. The website of *The Chronicle* achieved record hits, and the paper version sold so well that 10,000 copies of an afternoon edition (containing what purported to be an update of the 'Krejevsky exposé') were printed and sold quickly in London and the home counties.

John Morton and Dmitry Krejevsky remained in their homes to handle the inevitable 'door-stepping' by the paparazzi.

Dmitry Krejevsky delivered a blunt denial that he had anything to do with the Russian intelligence services, or, for that matter, any other spy network run by the UK government or by any other foreign government. When asked if he was considering taking legal advice, he replied that there was no need for him to do so because he had many years of experience at Inns of Court in London and elsewhere, and he could manage the legal process by himself.

The door-stepping of John Morton at his house elicited a firm demand – that *The Chronicle* newspaper publish an immediate retraction and an apology for the disgraceful libel.

Callers at the premises of *The New Times* were informed by the building's security officers that the premises were closed during the weekend. Some of the paparazzi camped outside anyway on the off-chance that this situation might change. It did not.

Elsewhere, the editor-in-chief of *The Chronicle* and his PA thought that it would be enough to release the scandalous story and leave it to fester. They were taken completely by surprise by subsequent events. They had not anticipated the possibility that, in addition to door-stepping Dmitry Krejevsky and other staff of *The New Times*, the paparazzi might also want to pester Edward and Brigita for more information, probing for details and trying to trip up Edward with awkward questions designed to elicit clues that would reveal the source of the leaked information.

Nor were Edward and Brigita prepared to face the prospect that they might end up working throughout the weekend, and that they would have to shoulder the entire burden, with a non-stop transatlantic telephone call being hosted from Brigita's office, and drawing in Loretta Farelli, Katy Drake and their colleagues in Washington DC.

Early on Saturday evening, Edward and Brigita were already in 'mid-tango' at her flat when the mobile phones began to ring incessantly. They had to break off and rush to the office, where they would have to stay and manage the developing crisis until the early hours of Monday morning. At one point, Brigita rang Shirley to check up on her availability, but Shirley pointed out that weekends were strictly for family and that she was in the seaside town of Looe in Cornwall, celebrating the birthday of one of her grandsons.

In truth, Shirley was at Sir Harold Nevin's stately home in the Buckinghamshire countryside, working a shift rota that included Hugh Lombard, Vivienne Eissinger, and Zoe and Hans Neubauer.

Monday, 6 June 2016. London.
On the seventy-second anniversary of the Normandy landings, the national press of the UK found itself in a quandary. It was traditional to "remember those who had fallen so that subsequent generations would be able to live in freedom and prosperity". On this occasion, a quite different story was vying for the front page.

Many of the newspapers had glossy, full-colour centre spreads to commemorate the momentous events in June 1944. This allowed them, if they chose to do so, to dedicate the entire front page to coverage of an alleged outrageous intrusion by the Russian security services into the UK's news media.

The tabloids had a field day. Scandal was heaped upon scandal. Depending on the political viewpoint of their editorial boards, the newspapers' headlines consisted of the injustices metered out to disabled people due to cuts in government spending, the fiscal crisis currently plaguing the NHS, or the plight of military veterans who were having a difficult time adjusting to life on Civvy Street. News of the death of yet another famous personality in 2016 appeared in the corner of the front page of some early editions, with a link to an obituary on page eight or page nine.

However, the story of the alleged Russian spy masquerading as a bona fide newspaper reporter via an alternative media website received unexpectedly scant coverage. A couple of big-name editors had taken the precaution of validating the story with Hugh Lombard prior to publication, and Lombard had forwarded the call to John Morton who issued a 'do not publish, or else' warning. Chinese whispers took care of the rest of the corporate media – or at least those media outlets whose editors were risk-averse by nature.

By and large, for whatever reason, the newspaper industry in the UK seemed reluctant to take the bait. It had not bought the lie.

At eleven o'clock in the morning, *The New Times* held a press conference, fronted confidently by Hugh Lombard in his capacity as editor-in-chief.

John Morton joined Lombard on the platform and explained, "Mr Krejevsky has, apparently, failed to get a retraction and an apology from *The Chronicle* newspaper, and has therefore sought to pre-empt any further libellous publications by obtaining an injunction against *The Chronicle* newspaper."

The exhausted Edward Ollerson and Brigita Wolznaski had missed the press conference. At midday, they were woken in bed by a phone call from Loretta Farelli. Katy Drake would arrive at Heathrow Airport first thing the next day to take control of the situation.

※

Katy Drake checked into an expensive hotel, freshened up and took a taxi to the Millhouse Building. She was received by a rather pale-looking Edward Ollerson and an apprehensive Brigita Wolznaski, who thought that the backlash from the 'Krejevsky exposé' meant that her role as a well-paid office administrator was about to be brought to an abrupt end.

Edward Ollerson got wind of a follow-up press conference that had been called by *The New Times* for two o'clock in the afternoon. Katy decided to attend it and sat quietly at the rear of the auditorium.

Hugh Lombard chaired the press conference, which kicked off with John Morton reading aloud a statement from the Embassy of the Russian Federation, categorically denying that Dmitry Krejevsky was a Russian agent and describing the whole affair as a "complete and utter fabrication".

John Morton took questions and answers for fifteen minutes, at which point Hugh Lombard intervened and begged the forgiveness of the gathering for cutting short the question-and-answer (Q&A) session in order to hear an update from the press and publicity officer for *The New Times*.

Immaculately primped and preened, and donning a pince-nez with plain glass lenses, merely for effect, Vivienne Eissinger rose from her seat, and took up a position to the right of a large screen behind John Morton and Hugh Lombard. The lights were dimmed, and then Vivienne Eissinger launched into a presentation that systematically dismantled the assumptions that underpinned each of the article's extravagant claims. It was clear that every one of those extravagant claims was, at best, uncorroborated and circumstantial evidence. Katy Drake sat motionless as *The Chronicle*'s case against Dmitry Krejevsky began to fall apart.

Then came the *coup de grâce*.

The photograph of Dmitry Krejevsky wearing the uniform of a colonel in the FSB was displayed. The next page showed two photographs, which were head and shoulders only: an image of

Dmitry Krejevsky and an image of a real-life colonel in the FSB. Both photographs were in the public domain, and it would be easy to cut and paste the photographs to superimpose one image onto another, seamlessly.

One member of the audience jumped out of his seat and raised a point of order, claiming that "this proved nothing" and that "*The New Times* could simply be re-engineering the photograph to prove a point".

Vivienne Eissinger admitted that this could indeed be the case, but went on to say, "I would like to draw your attention to two important details."

To make the point, the presentation was flicked forward to show some of the photographs that had been published on the front page of *The Chronicle* and in the less prominent pages inside a few other newspapers over the weekend.

The first anomaly was that the body of the uniformed officer and the head of Dmitry Krejevsky clearly did not match up. The torso in the photograph was far too big, and the shoulders were too broad, large and square. Dmitry Krejevsky's shoulders were lighter and slanted downward.

Some murmuring erupted around the room.

When it subsided, Vivienne Eissinger drew attention to the clincher. "Here is a photograph of Dmitry Krejevsky when he was employed by *The Chronicle* as a reporter. This photograph was stored in the list of contributors on the website of *The Chronicle* until about twelve months ago, when he and they finally parted company. The photograph is still retrievable from the website's archives.

"Once again, we can return to some full-face photographs that were published in the national press over the past few days. There are some distinguishing features on the face of Dmitry Krejevsky. The eyebrows almost meet, but you can see clearly that one is slightly higher and bushier than the other. Furthermore, look at the nose. In the photographs I have shown you, the nose leans ever so slightly to the left. Finally, look at the hair. Let me show you the photographs once more. Here is one shown over the weekend in *The Chronicle* and republished by other media outlets of the national press. Here is another. And here is the photograph from the website of *The Chronicle*."

The audience gazed at the photographs in silence.

"Now, look at the photograph that is allegedly of Dmitry Krejevsky wearing the uniform of a colonel of the FSB. The uniform with its array of medals is clearly the right way around; the head is not: notice how the eyebrows and the nose are reversed. The photograph of the Russian intelligence officer has a receding hairline instead of the very unmilitary-looking tonsorial delight that adorns the head of Dmitry Krejevsky to this very day, courtesy of Bridgers of Mayfair. The photograph is clearly a forgery."

Vivienne Eissinger allowed the photograph to linger on the screen, and she sat down.

Hugh Lombard stood up and attempted to calm the audience, which, by now, was in a state of uproar. Some of the reporters were arguing with each other, and scuffles began to break out. Security guards entered the room and, with the help of the friends and colleagues of those who had become embroiled in the heated argument, managed to clear the room.

Katy Drake was one of the last to leave, scurrying anonymously with head bowed toward the exit.

From a seat at the rear of the auditorium, Sir Harold Nevin had observed Katy Drake throughout the proceedings. As the room cleared, Nevin walked down the steps to the front of the room, and congratulated John Morton, Hugh Lombard and Vivienne Eissinger on a "supremely well-executed operation".

PART THREE
REBOOT TO FACTORY SETTINGS

12

TAYLOR, FROM PANAMA

Thursday, 9 June 2016.
Mid-morning, as though nothing had happened, Katy Drake breezed into the conference room on the fifteenth floor of the Millhouse Building, to be received by the incessant yawning of a tired Edward Ollerson and the miserable appearance of a dejected Brigita Wolznaski.

"Now, now. Why the long faces?" Katy trilled like a songbird. "It's not all that bad. Okay, we got our fingers burned, but… hey… c'mon guys. *C'est la vie.* Stuff happens."

WE got OUR fingers burned; YOU were on the other side of the Atlantic, taking turns with Loretta to oversee a conference call, whereas WE only just about managed to get out of the office to freshen up and to change clothes during a nightmare forty-eight hours, thought Brigita, though she might have yelled it out loud had she not been so worn out and ashen-faced.

Katy poured herself a mug of coffee and joined her colleagues at the conference room table. She suggested, "Think of what has happened as experience or as practice for future activities. In any case, a big, international scandal is about to break, and it is vital that we are at the forefront of it. Plus, I have some good news for you."

Edward and Brigita glanced at each other in bewilderment.

"You are going to have a new colleague. She has been doing some good work in South and Central America. She will be flying in from Panama. Her name is Taylor Snow," explained Katy.

Christ, thought Edward Ollerson. *Where do they dig these creatures up from?*

※

On Thursday evening, Katy Drake forwarded an email from Taylor Snow to Edward Ollerson and Brigita Wolznaski. Then, as suddenly as she had arrived, Katy took an early morning flight to Paris on Friday and embarked on a brief business tour around Europe prior to returning to Washington DC.

Edward and Brigita were given leave to finish work early on Friday to take an extended weekend break because, as Katy chirped before jetting off, "Everyone's entitled to a bit of R 'n' R, guys."

※

Disillusioned with the failed manipulations and manoeuvrings emanating from his new sponsors in the Beltway, Edward Ollerson took it upon himself, not for the first time, to go off-message.

He decided that the time might be ripe – primarily to pre-empt any future agenda which might be imposed from the Beltway via his 'new colleague' Taylor Snow – to pick up the pieces of one of his pet ideas whose implementation had been delayed while the staff of *The Chronicle* were immersed in the attempted framing of Dmitry Krejevsky.

Ollerson announced optimistically that, "To improve the quality of our reporting and to enhance the reader's experience, the Saturday and Sunday editions of *The Chronicle* will, from now on, be consolidated into one bumper weekend *online* edition." The bumper weekend *online* edition would be 'interactive' – whatever that meant – and, because it was to be delivered electronically to its 'valued customers', it would offer video streaming and other multimedia.

Edward Ollerson's cobbled-together vision for the future would make extensive use of articles, podcasts and video clips that had already been published elsewhere.

The Chronicle would offer its audience the chance to watch, in real time, everything that could be captured by cameras stationed, for example, in a hospital purporting to be in a rebel-held area in Syria; rolling coverage of the goings-on in a variety of House of Commons subcommittees; small-scale demonstrations and petition-gatherings in Moscow; and anything else that Edward and Brigita could dream up after a few bottles of wine and the satisfaction of mutual physical cravings.

This was code for streamlining, in line with the reduced staffing, and taking advantage of the fact that the website could be managed remotely from any location. Going forward, Edward envisaged *The Chronicle* as a strictly Monday-to-Friday, nine-to-five operation – which would be a first for the newspaper industry anywhere around the globe.

※

Brigita thought about inviting Edward to a weekend with her relatives on the south coast, but the many talks with Freda Gray about cruises and weekend breaks prompted her to rethink. Why not try something new for a change? Somewhere remote and far from the madding crowd, where – to paraphrase Katy Drake – they would, like everyone else, be entitled to a bit of R 'n' R and could forget about all the 'stuff' that had happened; where they could be alone; and where they could escape from the chaos, for a short while at least.

They could go to the Norfolk Broads, perhaps – which was one of Freda's favourites – or Great Yarmouth, if it was difficult to hire a marine vessel.

In the end, Edward and Brigita checked into a guesthouse on the Norfolk coast, drove around market towns and picturesque villages, and enjoyed good food and fine wine.

They frolicked in the sand dunes, with Brigita insisting that her man allow her to apply suntan lotion liberally to his most vulnerable parts – his neck and shoulders, his back, and his incredibly white buttocks. Edward returned the favour, although Brigita's body revealed smooth contours that were unblemished by marks left by inconvenient attire such as, say, swimsuits.

※

Monday, 13 June 2016.

Taylor Snow was standing at the front desk in the reception area at the Millhouse Building, facing toward the entrance, when Brigita Wolznaski arrived at her usual time of eight-thirty in the morning.

Edward Ollerson was due to spend the morning at the printers for a 'strategy meeting'. He texted Brigita, saying that he would join her and Taylor in the afternoon.

Taylor Snow brought with her a medium-sized, black-leather Prada trolley suitcase containing a laptop computer, an electronic tablet, several mobile phones, paper notepads, and a selection of fibre-tipped pens, highlighters, board markers and erasers. She wore a black-leather Prada shoulder bag – with a long strap crossing from the right shoulder to just above her left hip – in which she kept her purse, her passport and other personal belongings.

She also brought with her two designer-label, large, paper bags with imitation-gold chain handles, which Brigita carried into the office via the lift. These bags contained items of clothing and two pairs of shoes that Taylor had bought in London – probably on Saturday, Brigita guessed. To help to break the ice, these purchases provided the subject matter for small talk between the two women during a coffee break later in the morning.

Unlike Katy, Taylor gave every impression of indeed taking firm control of the situation, but with consideration and subtlety – in a way that would complement the work that was being done by Brigita.

The two women had been engaged in conversation for over an hour when building security rang to inform Brigita that she had a visitor, whom she introduced to Taylor Snow as, "Freda Gray, my best friend, and my most loyal and trusted confidante in London. The local lady who provides me with many of the little snippets that are so important to the success of our website."

"Pleased to meet you, dear," Freda said to Taylor Snow, before asking Brigita, "Would you like me to make a nice pot of tea?"

"Not just now, thanks, Freda," Brigita replied, while at the same time commending to Taylor her friend's culinary skills, and understanding of people and their relationships.

"Actually," Taylor declared, "I could kill for a coffee… if you don't mind, Freda?"

And 'Freda' obliged.

Taylor Snow smiled and nodded politely as the laid-back chatter rolled along, engendering a relaxed and friendly atmosphere of which Taylor approved wholeheartedly. She explained that one of her priorities was to try to take the pressure off a bit and to settle things down.

Freda did not realise the extent to which she had lost track of time until the ringtone from one of the mobile phones sounded and the device rattled loudly as it vibrated on the solid wooden table, jolting the startled group of women from their ramblings and provoking giggles all round.

On answering the phone, Brigita found Edward Ollerson on the other end of the line. Edward informed his PA that his business at the printers was done and that he was on his way to the office.

"Oh, my goodness, is that the time?" Freda cried out when Brigita relayed the news of the impending arrival of her boss. Freda explained that she was due to meet her daughter for lunch and that she must not impose on her companions a moment longer. She took her leave, and, on the way out, Brigita discreetly handed over five £20 notes in anticipation of some articles for the website and some companionship when Freda returned later in the week.

Taylor Snow eyed Freda all the way to the exit, in contemplation of how this older woman had become so indispensable to Brigita, of her sudden departure and of the abrupt way she had handled it.

Taylor Snow treated Edward and Brigita to lunch at an Italian restaurant, prior to returning to the office for an afternoon work session.

They crammed themselves into Brigita's office to display the emailed documents on the large screen.

Taylor told Brigita that it would be necessary in future to equip the conference room with a projector screen, enough electrical sockets to support a larger number of people than in the past, teleconference apparatus for the large table and a high-end, espresso-based coffee-making system.

Brigita displayed the documents in thumbnail mode on her large computer screen, enlarging them to full screen mode, one by one, as directed by Taylor Snow. Many of the documents were bank statements or lists of dry-as-dust statistics, and there was a registry of people whose names Edward did not recognise.

The previous evening, in a mood of sheer indolence laced with scepticism, Edward had decided that it was not worth spending too much time on the documents until he had discovered more about what Taylor Snow had in mind.

But Brigita Wolznaski *had* taken the trouble to pay close attention to the task in hand. She had even printed off over 100 A4 pages, and had laid them out on her living-room floor during the previous evening, while Edward Ollerson was at home with his feet up in front of the TV and washing down a pizza with a couple of bottles of red wine.

The A4 pages resembled a large jigsaw puzzle from Brigita's childhood, except every piece had straight edges, making it difficult to distinguish the corner pieces from those that would go in the middle of the puzzle and those pieces which would comprise the perimeter. She was beginning to get an insight into the big picture and how the pages fitted together to support an emerging narrative, when sleep finally overtook her. She intended to resume her enquiries after work on Monday.

By Tuesday morning, Brigita was ready to engage Taylor Snow in a detailed examination of the financial statements of account. As the morning wore on, Brigita's eyes widened as she started to believe in the prospect of (at long last) doing what she had joined *The Chronicle* to do – investigative journalism and the creation of narratives that could be turned into good-quality articles.

During the afternoon, she was delighted to find herself getting something down on paper and writing up the skeleton of an article on her computer.

Edward cried off the suggestion of a run in the park, but Taylor was only too willing to join in Brigita's early evening routine. The two women finished work early and headed off to Taylor's apartment to change, and to jog along to Kensington Gardens and its Round Pond – a feature with which Taylor had immediately fallen in love, and so had taken to feeding the ducks, geese and swans as she approached it.

Taylor set a reasonably good pace as they entered Hyde Park, but she was unable to keep up with the younger Brigita, who had ten years' advantage over her. Brigita obligingly adjusted her pace.

On returning to Kensington Gardens, Taylor took a photograph of the Peter Pan statue and commenced some stretching exercises, while Brigita spent a further fifteen minutes performing an alternating series of sprints and jogs.

Brigita began her warm down and stretching exercises, while Taylor sat on a bench and regaled her with stories from her various stints in Panama City, Brasilia, Buenos Aires, back to Panama City, Montevideo, Santiago, back to Panama City again, and other cities in South and Central America. Taylor's recent rovings were rounded off with a brief trip to her old stomping ground in Honduras. There, she was able to reacquaint herself with a former colleague, Luis Manuel Lopez de Pereira, who worked in the US Embassy in the capital, Tegucigalpa.

"Luis is now married and has two lovely little boys. Five years ago, he had only recently graduated, started his first job and was assigned to my team as a management trainee. At that time, he became distraught when he received news of the sudden death of his great-grandfather, and I had to fly up to Mexico with him to help him through the funeral. His great-grandfather's corpse was dressed in a suit with a collar and tie, and lay in a coffin that rested on two wooden trestles in a little chapel. Luis scoured the large family home from top to bottom for a memento to place in the coffin. He was mortified to find that the coffin had been sealed before he had a chance to enclose his farewell gift.

"Anyway, after the uncomfortable heat of the funeral, Luis and his mom returned home to change. Luis had a habit of taking home with him to Mexico a large suitcase that was only one-quarter full, and returning to Honduras with the suitcase bursting at the seams with presents from friends, important items pressed on him by his mom (without which she thought he would be unable to cope), and lots of things that were either not available in the shops in Honduras or were too expensive.

"Some of his clothes were kept in his family home in Mexico, and he had a couple of suits and two white shirts stored in a wardrobe that was shared with other members of the family for special occasions. Well, Luis stripped off his wet shirt and went to change into the other one. It didn't fit. It was too small!"

Brigita cupped both hands around her mouth to stifle a loud guffaw.

"Got it in one, Brigita," Taylor observed. "Luis' second shirt had ended up being worn by his great-grandfather in the coffin. Without knowing it, he *did* manage to leave a memento after all."

Brigita finished with one last exercise, hauling her right leg onto a railing to stretch her hamstring and revealing an athletic and well-formed limb – at which Taylor Snow gazed with admiration.

※

After dinner with Taylor, Brigita decided to turn in early, but something was playing on her mind while she tossed and turned in bed. She recalled enviously Taylor's many stories from her globe-trotting lifestyle.

There always seemed to be a man involved, but nobody especially noteworthy, at least on the surface. Yet, as he took his leave of Taylor Snow, Edward Ollerson had offered his hand to Taylor and, Brigita noticed, seemed to allow it to linger for a while longer than necessary.

Since Katy Drake's flying visit and sudden departure, Brigita was beginning to feel a bit more secure, hoping that the love triangle into which she had become embroiled might begin to disentangle and that Katy would fade from the scene. The last thing Brigita wanted was for another third party to take Katy's place.

It was not as if Taylor Snow had earth-shattering good looks. Her ordinary, straight, brown hair curved down and inward above her shirt collar, framing a slightly weather-beaten, thirty-something face and revealing a robust nape above unusually muscular shoulders. Her smallish eyes, which were icy-blue and perched above an aquiline nose, enabled her to watch like a hawk. Taylor was easy to listen to and to observe – despite several irregularities in her teeth, which displayed themselves as her thin, bloodless lips parted, in contrast to Brigita's perfect, pearly white smile and full, ruby-red lips.

No, it was not her looks that posed a threat to Brigita's burgeoning relationship with Edward Ollerson but her manner, her calm demeanour and her professionalism.

On finishing unusually late on Monday evening, Brigita had accompanied Taylor to her hotel residence in the West End. Taylor Snow had not settled on a lowly, standard room. She had rented a two-bedroom, luxury, furnished apartment with kitchen, bathroom with power shower, Wi-Fi and other mod cons.

Later, back in her own apartment, as Brigita began to doze in bed, the chat with Taylor drifted back into her fading memory.

Taylor seemed to move close to Brigita on the sofa, until the two women's faces almost touched, at which point Taylor poked out her tongue, opened her mouth and extended the tongue to her chin, then the tongue extended itself further down to her breasts, which revealed themselves as Taylor's shirt became undone and slid down over her shoulders and arms. Taylor's eyes burned with a fire from hell.

Brigita woke up in bed, with a start.

"Oh, silly, silly, silly Brigita!" she reproached herself and her needlessly ludicrous imagination. She dozed fitfully before dropping off to sleep and being awoken by her six-thirty alarm call.

※

On Wednesday afternoon, Taylor chaired a planning meeting with Edward and Brigita to coordinate the exposé of the scandalous material to the UK public.

Everything would be put in place beforehand, then released on Sunday evening in a *stop press* to the bumper weekend *online* edition of *The Chronicle* by Edward Ollerson, who would have returned by that time from a family engagement in the Midlands. Edward was scheduled to hold the fort throughout Sunday night.

Taylor and Brigita would take over on Monday morning, and a shift rota would be worked to ensure the whole process was managed with due care and attention throughout the week, and beyond if need be – but this time without any stress.

Taylor even suggested that Brigita enlist the services of Freda Gray to join in the daytime shift, thereby releasing Taylor to oversee the big picture, as it revealed itself and to attend to other matters, whose details she did not divulge.

Taylor also made a list of all of the reporters who were on the payroll, and contacted as many of them as possible in order to, as she put it, "leverage their skills and experiences" and "to get them off of their fucking asses and out into the field".

Taylor planned to work around twelve hours per day and sometimes at weekends in order to achieve her self-imposed targets.

※

Within a few days, Taylor Snow had introduced much-needed stability to the inner workings of *The Chronicle*, but she was not content to rest on her laurels.

"There are two considerations to be borne in mind," Taylor stated.

"The first is that this scandal does not consist of a concerted attack on the personal integrity of an individual, such as Dmitry Krejevsky, and certainly not an attack on someone who knows the legal system inside out. That exercise was clearly a mistake. This time, the release of the scandalous data will be linked to offshore bank accounts concerning a lot of prominent individuals the world over. The documents that we have examined confirm that a scandal has occurred, but it has not yet been made public. Agreed?"

Brigita replied briskly in the affirmative. Edward Ollerson nodded passively, tongue firmly in cheek.

Taylor continued, "The second consideration is about spreading the risk. As we speak, details of the scandal are being distributed to a lot of other media outlets around the globe. When the scandal breaks, it will be impossible to pinpoint the origin of the leak, which (a) will make it very difficult for our opponents to concentrate an attack on us, and (b) will not attract the intrusive attention of the paparazzi. *The Chronicle* will claim considerable kudos, but, should anything go wrong, we will avoid being swamped by the fallout that would ensue."

Brilliant, thought Brigita.

Brigita rang Freda Gray immediately to firm up her availability to work the day shift during the following week. As soon as Freda Gray felt sure that her true identity was unlikely to be recognised by the habitually absent Edward Ollerson, she agreed and passed on the news of her temporary secondment to John Morton at *The New Times*.

※

The remainder of the week went according to plan. On Saturday morning, Taylor and Brigita met in Kensington Gardens for another jaunt around the pathways. When they had finished, Taylor led the way to the Round Pond to feed her water-bound friends. En route to Taylor's apartment, they sauntered along the path to Kensington Palace.

"Recognise this guy?" Taylor asked, referring to a statue she had checked out, which was shown in pristine condition in a photograph that was published on the Kensington Gardens website, but that had been soiled recently by some of Taylor's feathered friends.

Brigita strained her eyes to identify the well-dressed king whose effigy was imprisoned behind impressive gold-painted gates that were smothered with mementoes of the dearly departed Princess Diana, whose memory was commemorated fondly by her adoring fans, thereby taking attention away from the statue of the former monarch.

"King William the Third," Taylor Snow read out. "The last time the UK had a serious constitutional crisis, this was the guy who landed on the south coast of England, having come from Holland, with an army of foreign soldiers. The resident tyrant, James the Second, was overthrown and a new age of democracy and a liberal ascendancy was ushered in. King William the Third used to spend a lot of time here at Kensington Palace. That is why his statue is here on this spot."

See, Brigita told herself, *liberal interventions can be successful.*

Brigita took heart from this. All the same, she could not help comparing the statue of William the Third with that of a more widely admired British hero, such as Lord Admiral Horatio Nelson, whose statue stood atop an imposing column and plinth in the centre of the equally impressive Trafalgar Square, instead of being hidden away behind gates and railings, a stone's throw from a duck pond, a short jog from the fictional hero Peter Pan, and at the intersection of a pair of scarcely used pathways in a public park.

They returned to shower and change at Taylor's apartment before launching into a shopping trip.

During a coffee break, Taylor asked Brigita if she would like to meet, ostensibly for drinks, at the US Embassy the following afternoon. Brigita confirmed that, yes, she would like it very much, as it so happened.

※

So, at three o'clock in the afternoon on Sunday, the two women were picked up by a limousine outside Taylor's luxury apartment tower, and driven, not to the US Embassy as Brigita had expected, but to Regent's Park, where a grassy area had been purloined by embassy employees, and where hired deckchairs had been supplemented by picnic blankets, pushchairs, baby walkers and food hampers.

The wine flowed freely, but not excessively. By the time the sun began to go down and a chill filled the air, Brigita had assembled a whole gathering of new friends. Rachel, Diane and her mother Louise, Greg, Enrico, Zuzanna, another Diane, and countless more who would be available, pretty much at the drop of a hat.

Brigita's lonely existence in a large and strange city in a foreign country was about to take an upturn.

13

THE COLOUR OF FUNNY MONEY

Monday, 20 June 2016.
Taylor and Brigita arrived at the office at eight o'clock in the morning to take the first handover from Edward Ollerson and to ensure that the day ran smoothly.

The early news began innocently enough, in one of the tabloids, with a story about an Irish racehorse owner who had sold a famous but aging nag to a wealthy South American for a fee believed to be in the tens of thousands, but that was, more accurately, closer to 1 million euros.

The wealthy South American had financed the deal through one of his myriad offshore accounts. Having, allegedly, bypassed domestic laws and regulations, the legal status of the wealthy South American's offshore account (and, by implication, the transaction concerning the racehorse) was moot. The links between the two men provided the opportunity for the tabloid newspaper to launch a smear campaign against the Irish racehorse owner.

A similar story was run in a different newspaper about another large deal, far greater than the value of the traded article, which had been paid to the head of a consortium of European businesses by a billionaire from an unnamed Arab state.

Different newspapers around the globe led with variations on the same theme – all pointing to the existence of offshore accounts owned by the rich and famous, and implying some unspecified form of impropriety. Each story was spun in a way that was designed to encourage the reader to think in terms of tax evasion and money laundering on a truly Herculean scale.

By midday, it was rumoured that the number of known offshore accounts had already reached the thousands. However, thus far, the details of only a few dozen names had been published in the corporate media; this was the initial trickle that should herald an inevitable tsunami, revealing huge volumes of dirty money owned and moved around by the truly rich and famous, by 'the great and the good'.

In view of this unprecedented threat to the great and the good, it might be expected that somebody would step in and put a stop to these revelations.

Somebody, apparently, did.

But what should one make of a situation in which the number of embarrassed account holders stopped near the 100 mark instead of hurtling on and telling tales about hundreds of thousands of wealthy account holders? And what if the personalities involved were relatively minor players, such as our friend the Irish racehorse owner, and much of the damage would be inflicted on a mere handful of former politicians and elderly showbiz types? And what if a few big names began to appear later in the day – including none other than Mr Sergei Ivanovich Glazenov, the president of the Russian Federation?

Given the way that the dominant Russophobic narrative had been playing out for many years, who would step in, at this point in time, to rescue the reputation of the man who in the eyes of the Western corporate media had become public enemy number one?

※

At the office of *The New Times*, John Morton and Hugh Lombard tracked the developing story. Close inspection revealed that the Irish racehorse owner – a jovial soul, well-liked by millions of punters who had 'beaten the bookies' by backing his racehorses – had upset a wealthy European by selling the horse to the South American in preference to him. Furthermore, a double hit seemed on the cards because the South American himself had fallen foul of certain powerful political and business circles in the US who were on good terms with the infuriated wealthy European.

Many revelations about other alleged 'rascals' exhibited similar characteristics.

John Morton looked forward to hearing from his fly on the wall inside *The Chronicle*, Shirley Bould (in the guise of Freda Gray), when she reported back later in the day. However, for an assiduous reading of the background information concerning the biggest story involving Russia's President Glazenov, John Morton did not have to wait that long.

Vivienne Eissinger had been sitting erect and almost motionless in front of a computer screen as the crisis unfolded. Without taking her eyes off the screen, she asked an open question, "Have you noticed something curious about the emerging scandal about the Russian president?"

Morton and Lombard leaned back in their seats and tilted their heads to bend an ear in anticipation, more in hope than expectation, of an exceptional revelation.

Vivienne Eissinger remained focused on the screen while issuing a laconic pronouncement. "The name of the Russian president does not appear in the list of published account holders."

Morton promptly swivelled around in his chair. "Are you sure?" he asked.

"The name of the Russian president does not appear in the list of published account holders," confirmed Vivienne. "I have checked and rechecked several times. A hundred or so famous names have been published in the corporate media, but a much larger volume of information has been leaked in the internet blogosphere – tens of thousands of names, and this is rapidly rising."

"So... what's the story?" Morton asked.

Hugh Lombard wheeled his chair over to Vivienne Eissinger's screen.

Vivienne explained her findings, which she had documented in the form of a timeline in a spreadsheet. "Here, we are at the beginning of the timeline when the news broke. After twenty or so different stories, I decided to make a list of the names that had been leaked, together with the chronological order in which they had appeared in the public domain. If we go back to one of the later stories, which appeared mid-morning, we can see that it appears side by side with a story about corruption in Russia and the failure of the president to do anything about it. A bit later, something similar appears on another website. Later still, the name 'Glazenov' appears, linked with various offshore account holders. This trend continues for a while, but is then abruptly dispensed with, as a whole new narrative starts to be spun out – connecting Russia's President Glazenov with what goes by the epithet 'Affluent Archives."

By the time Shirley Bould appeared late in the afternoon, the purported scandal surrounding President Glazenov seemed no more of an issue than that of the Irish racehorse owner.

One of the account holders whose name was connected to the name of President Glazenov had received money, perhaps in good faith, from a buyer whose bank account seemed to be linked to some shady practices. Another had also probably done nothing wrong, except that one of his acquaintances had found his name among the list of account holders. Yet another was linked in a convoluted (but convincing) way to someone else who might (or might not) have had something to do with dodgy purchases of land and real estate by another third, fourth or fifth party in the tourism industry who, from the goodness of his heart (he had originally claimed), was going to use some of his acquisitions to build "holiday homes for deprived children" and "a school for the reform of juvenile delinquents".

An accumulated set of narratives had been pulled together, creating a picture of double-dealing and dishonesty dressed up as good intentions and connected persuasively with Russia's President Glazenov – and carefully drawn up to elicit the maximum revulsion in the mind of every reader.

"That was done... tidily," Morton observed solemnly. "It bears all the hallmarks of a sting organised by *The Chronicle*, except that most readers would not notice that little detail. 'Leading from behind'... done properly... by Taylor Snow, so it seems. By someone who comes across as a true professional."

All the same, Morton wondered why the operation seemed to be using something of a scattergun approach: hitting many targets and then letting them go; creating an unfavourable impression of each high-value target in the minds of millions of readers, but without providing indisputable evidence; fishing around for gossipy and unfounded allegations; and flying one hopeful kite after another.

※

The following morning, the Office of the President of the Russian Federation issued a clear denial of wrongdoing. Further statements were later released by the account holders to whom the president had been linked, showing evidence that these particular offshore accounts had been set up in full compliance with Russian law and with the knowledge of the Russian revenue collection services. Yes, they were offshore accounts; no, there was no clear evidence of wrongdoing.

Then came an unexpected twist.

A singularly diligent lone researcher in Australia had compiled his own database comprising the personal details of over 50,000 account holders. He had cross-referenced some information from a subset of items in his database and found that this particular subset of items led to one specific account number, which did not have a name associated with it.

The Australian researcher circulated the specific account number around various chat rooms and blogs immediately, and waited patiently for a response. After a while, he had amassed enough clues to work out that the owner of the specific account number was a wealthy retiree who lived abroad on an island that he had bought legally and according to due process. However, the strands of information linked to his offshore account number came from sources whose probity could not be clearly verified and that, frankly, reeked of impropriety.

This discovery would have been no more scandalous than any of the stories that had cropped up thus far, except that the expatriate island owner had hosted many of the rich and famous as holiday guests over many years. Some of the rich and famous had visited the island on many occasions, often at regular intervals. It did not take long to obtain a list of names.

Other researchers must have had the same idea, after it became known that the generous island owner had links to something 'not quite right'. His name started to appear on news broadcasts. In dribs and drabs, various reporters thought of making a name for themselves as soon as they uncovered the identities of one after the other of the wealthy man's friends who might make a credible target. By late afternoon, as many as twenty well-known personalities found their photographs displayed online and in early editions of the evening papers. In response, every single one of the well-known personalities was issuing a denial.

Rumours began to circulate that at least one of those yet to be outed was a leading politician. The search was on. Surely this would be the end of Russia's President Glazenov? But it turned out that the politician was not from Russia. He was from the West. All indications pointed toward a major European power – to the UK, actually – and, finally, in the direction of a prominent member of the UK Cabinet.

The late news broke with the headline that the senior politician was none other than the UK prime minister himself.

The phone rang in Taylor Snow's apartment. To her surprise, the caller on the other end was not Edward Ollerson but Brigita Wolznaski, who had caught the news as she was preparing for bed. Taylor had also been watching the news unfold on various TV channels and websites in her furnished hotel apartment.

Brigita was expecting to be told to go into the office. Taking the initiative proactively, she offered to do so.

"Why do you want to do that?" Taylor asked.

"To manage the crisis," explained Brigita.

"Edward can handle it. Has he contacted you?"

"No."

"There we are then. It cannot be that serious."

"But the UK's prime minister is in the frame. It's supposed to be Glazenov. It's the wrong man."

"That is true," Taylor observed, "but there is nothing we can do about it. In any case, I'm sure the prime minister is capable of handling this himself."

Brigita remained in an agitated state.

"Ring Edward if you want to," Taylor acquiesced, "but let us bear in mind one important fact. Our job is done. We managed to continue the narrative against the Russian target, which is what we were asked to do. And although President Glazenov managed to wriggle out of it – assuming the news about him is true – the story about alleged links to him can be appended to any article in future to keep the pot simmering.

"And Brigita… I want you here in the morning, on time, as we agreed. We stick to the plan, right?"

Brigita did indeed ring up the office to speak to Edward, who had fallen asleep and had missed most of the excitement. He contacted Taylor and agreed with her that there was nothing they could do. Edward Ollerson went home not long after midnight and phoned Brigita to let her know that there was no need to continue the shift rota. She could turn up at eight-thirty in the morning as usual and he would see her later, after a trip to the printers.

14

SO LONG, FAREWELL

For the UK's prime minister, the breaking news emanating from the Affluent Archives scandal could not have come at a more inconvenient time.

As he anxiously toyed with his breakfast on the patio at the rear of 10 Downing Street, he was only too aware that voting on the UK's membership of the EU would start in less than twenty-four hours. Thanks to the news linking the prime minister to the Affluent Archives scandal, the 'Leave' campaigners would have a field day.

Before he took up residence at 10 Downing Street, the prime minister had selected carefully several key aides who should be clever enough be able to dig him out of any future crisis. Now was the time for them to deliver.

In language that uncannily resembled that used by his Russian counterpart the previous morning, the prime minister read out, in front of the TV cameras positioned outside 10 Downing Street, a deftly scripted denial.

He adroitly circumvented probing questions; endorsed his intention to renegotiate parts of the EU treaties without any need for Brexit; and (in a subtle attempt to deflect any association between the scandal concerning the Affluent Archives and him) reminded everyone that he had already agreed to host a conference later in the year, concerning international development, at which corruption and financial irregularities would be subjected to merciless scrutiny and exposure.

*

The prime minister's neat footwork, together with his astute choice of advisors and associates, colleagues and collaborators, and networks and organisations with whom he did business, was supposed to deliver an ironclad guarantee that the result of the referendum would go his way.

It did not.

Had it not been for the pesky revelations about offshore accounts – dodgy in some cases and legitimate in others – the vote might have gone in favour of 'Remain'. At least that was the view of some media outlets that had the ear of the prime minister, and it is always useful to have someone playing the blame game on your behalf, to shield your own valuable brand.

At *The New Times*, John Morton braced himself for another assault on the freedom of the press, but it did not come.

Few people gave the stories about the Affluent Archives more than a passing glance. The reason for this was perfectly straightforward: supporters of Leave were ecstatic and supporters of Remain were numb with shock. Nothing else mattered.

Remain's Project Fear had been trumped by Leave's Project Fear Mark II.

The 'Brexit ball' was now in play.

On Friday afternoon, the prime minister addressed the cameras and microphones huddled together opposite 10 Downing Street, and announced his resignation.

*

To initiate the Brexit process, all that was required was invoking Article 50 of the Treaty of Rome and initiating a procedure that would last a maximum of two years.

The prime minister had resigned, kicking the 'Brexit ball' down the road until the Conservative Party conference in October, when a new party leader (and, by default, a new prime minister) would be in place – almost four months later.

The incoming prime minister would then invoke Article 50 at a convenient time and start the exit process.

The Brexit result had caused the markets to go into meltdown. Sterling collapsed by about 15%. It was surely not the end of the world, even as the pro-Remain corporate media published one crisis-laden scare story after another, because currencies do tend to recover over time. As, of course, do markets.

A strong leader would be able to enter the fray and calm things down. By pulling strings and moving big money around, the strong leader would be able to provide much-needed reassurance to investors, reverse the downward spiral on the stock exchange and give sterling a much-needed boost shortly before many Brits embarked on their summer holidays overseas.

Instead, the prospect of an unfilled vacuum at the head of the country loomed ominous and close at hand, during which a yearning for firm leadership – even if it came only in the form of the customary tub-thumping, bragging and hot air at the dispatch box – would be replaced by a stillness, like a *sitzkrieg* or like an episode in a phoney war, accompanied by a seemingly endless drift.

There were anti-Brexit protests outside Parliament in late June and early July. Some in the alternative media compared them to the kind of demonstrations that might precede a 'colour revolution', except that – instead of red, orange or yellow banners – the demonstrators carried long baguettes of French bread to assert their allegiance to 'Europe'.

Immediately following the Brexit result, an online petition was launched calling for a second referendum to be held to reverse the Brexit vote and to achieve a victory for Remain, but the petition failed to rack up the numbers that would entitle it to be presented to the government for consideration.

The Tory Party had come out of the referendum riven from top to toe. It was unclear whether a snap general election would be called.

In such circumstances, you would expect the main opposition (the Labour Party) to try to capitalise on the Tories' woeful situation, and to campaign vigorously for a snap election in order to win it and to form a new government.

Instead, individuals associated with 'New Labour' within the parliamentary Labour Party decided that a quite different moment had come. They would take the opportunity to try to rid themselves of the recently elected left-wing leader of the Labour Party by means of a simple weapon at their disposal: they would orchestrate their allies in the corporate media to play a post-Brexit blame game and ensnare the Labour leader in a trap.

The internal conflict within the Labour Party was discussed throughout the corporate media, creating the opportunity for the Tories to relieve the pressure on themselves and their leader. At the dispatch box, the Tory prime minister even shouted at the beleaguered Labour leader, "For heaven's sake man, go!" – although his missive carried about as much weight as a deflating balloon because the same directive could just as easily have been addressed to the overstaying prime minister.

Ironically, the divisive, mistimed campaign to remove the leader of the Labour Party backfired, strengthening the leader's authority within the Labour Party. The divisive, mistimed campaign to remove him fizzled out ignominiously.

The Tories embarked on the election of a new party leader and, although she did not achieve a majority of all the votes after the first round, the favourite looked set to win the contest hands down. The sane man or woman might have expected a second or third round to produce a decisive outcome, but it seemed they were to be disappointed because nothing – and by 'nothing' is meant *absolutely nothing* – was going to be allowed to intrude upon the British holiday period and its accompanying summer silly season.

The dreaded drift seemed set to continue.

Then came a moment of inspiration. Two of the remaining four candidates were persuaded by backstage powerbrokers to withdraw, leaving a straight contest between two women: an experienced member of the Cabinet (currently the home secretary), who was a quietly declared Remainer, versus a relative newcomer who was a committed Brexiteer. The majority of the corporate media immediately launched a campaign to promote the candidacy of the Remainer. The Brexiteer withdrew, leaving the Remainer as the de facto leader of the Tory Party and, also the de facto UK prime minister.

Thus, the idea that the country would have to wait for the result of the leadership election to be announced at the Tory Party Conference in October – which would have been the worst kept secret of the year – had been scotched. The whole world knew that the first prime minister of a post-Brexit UK would be not only a woman but also a person who, to all intents and purposes, was opposed to Brexit.

*

The surprise outcome of the referendum propelled shockwaves throughout the corporate media. One question lingered on the lips of many of the UK's reporters – how could we have got it so wrong?

The answer to this question was very simple. After forty years of membership of the EU, most of the British people who took part in the referendum had decided that the EU was not fit for purpose. Yet the response of the majority of the corporate media was cowardly obfuscation. This simple explanation was not stated openly at all, and the corporate media spent many long hours digging up unrelated titbits of gossip to obscure the real reason why they got the Brexit result wrong.

The corporate media had not merely reported on the referendum; they had, in the main, *campaigned* vigorously for Remain. They included radio, terrestrial TV and cable news broadcasters with huge national audiences.

They had assumed that the result was a foregone conclusion, but they had miscalculated and – instead of business as usual – they discovered to their horror that most British voters had not been swayed by the vigorous campaign to remain in the EU. The voters had gone off-message as though, like naughty children, they had disobeyed their infallible gurus in the corporate media.

The UK's corporate media, informed by the same neoconservative and neoliberal dogma that had beset *The Chronicle*, had failed.

Failure cannot be admitted without also losing face, so an exercise in face-saving was therefore the order of the day; this was a challenge that, in the absence of anything more constructive to do, the corporate media pursued with relish.

※

After the EU Referendum, John Morton and Dmitry Krejevsky travelled to the stately home of Sir Harold Nevin in the Buckinghamshire countryside for a routine debriefing.

Since Morton's last visit, the local villagers who were employed by Nevin had created a masterpiece of a cottage garden at the rear of the Nevin estate, offset by rolling hills and wooded areas (some of which were 'borrowed' from neighbours according to the tricks of the trade used by gardeners the world over).

From the patio at the rear of the house, Morton took in a picturesque vista, including a village in the distance where a plume of smoke from burning foliage rose high before drifting away on an unseen thermal. The three men strolled along a winding path to the left of the garden and underneath a wide tunnel bedecked with wisteria, until the small village was almost in front of them, providing an unassuming scene of simple, rural charm.

Nevin was in high spirits. Morton and Krejevsky joined Nevin as he wandered up and down various shaded pathways, accompanied by the trickling of water along brooks and the buzzing of crickets as the rushes swayed on the verge of a large pond. Swallows chirped as they flew in all directions, providing a breathtaking aerial display as they hunted for flying insects. Nevin had brought a pair of binoculars with him, and he folded back the rubbers to rest the binoculars on the lenses of his spectacles (nesting red kite had been reported in the vicinity and he was determined not to miss his chance).

It was not even lunchtime, but already it was 'shirtsleeves weather'. Nevin kept his sleeves rolled down and the collar of his shirt turned up to meet his fisherman's hat, thereby protecting his neck as recommended by his wife, Lady Miranda, because, "You never know how hot that sun can get until it is too late, if you are not careful."

Contrary to the open, lively and positive discussion that adorned the pages of *The New Times*, the debate in the corporate media had been closed, predictable and overwhelmingly polarised – the problems that would befall the UK on leaving the EU (including unsubstantiated claims that the global financial system would go into meltdown) versus the problems – primarily in terms of immigration, refugees and asylum seekers – that would allegedly continue to fester if the UK decided to remain in the EU.

Morton and Krejevsky were Eurosceptics of the Left, and Nevin was a key figure in a faction within the Eurosceptic Tory Right. *The New Times* had developed a close relationship with the prime minister and had striven for a balanced coverage of the referendum campaign; it had even allowed a fair share of coverage in favour of the UK remaining in the EU, in deference to the prime minister's claim that what he had negotiated with the leadership of the EU was the best outcome that could be obtained at the present time.

Furthermore, Nevin and his Eurosceptic Tory colleagues did not want to put at risk the close relationship of the UK with the US; they did not want to provoke the Americans into taking reprisals against the UK, particularly at a time when the Democrat-controlled White House was trying to twist the arms of the nations of Europe – preferably under the EU umbrella – to sign up to TTIP.

However, in the intervening six-month period, the international situation had experienced a noticeable shift. The Brexit vote signalled the end of an era. Now, the time had come for Nevin's faction within the Tory Party and *The New Times* to each undertake a fresh reassessment of the 'big picture'.

The Russian government had intervened decisively in Syria, thereby enabling the Syrian government to reassert control over large parts of its territory; plus, globally, Russia had created a favourable space for itself to advance its own agenda – primarily business-driven and based around the long-term project of Eurasian economic integration, involving not only Russia but also China, other Asian countries and (eventually) Europe.

The Americans were engrossed in their own presidential election, and it seemed that this had become a self-absorbing obsession. The US presidential election had come down to a simple choice between a neoconservative with deeply embedded Establishment credentials running on the Democrat ticket versus a maverick billionaire populist newcomer, with a noticeably different agenda, representing the Republicans.

The impression of a divided and weakened US had become difficult to ignore. Emboldened by this development, Sir Harold Nevin and his friends Sir Quentin Forbes and Lord Ernest Anderian had undertaken a post-Brexit appraisal of the situation and its likely impact on Europe. Nevin was about to relay the substance of their discussion to Morton and Krejevsky.

In a newly built tea house in a small and recently constructed Japanese section of his garden, next to the pond and its bulrushes, and within hearing distance of a babbling brook, Nevin leaned back in his chair in the tea house and stretched. "I'm getting old," he said.

Morton smiled. "There's years left in you yet, Sir Harold."

"Perhaps, but time is ticking away," Nevin said. "Every year brings more uncertainty, even if it does not always bring any additional health problems.

"Our coverage in *The New Times* has been balanced, and we have included guest appearances from representatives of various political viewpoints. The coverage of the EU Referendum by *The New Times* has been of the highest order, in terms of quality, and this achievement is all to our credit. But, outside the pages of *The New Times*, the wider debate about the EU Referendum has been something of a damp squib. There is no vibrancy about it. In fact, it has, by and large, degenerated into bouts of nastiness between rival groups within the Conservative Party."

Nevin paused, then offered some advice. "The referendum has come and gone, so I recommend that we start to look ahead to the two remaining big events this year. The most widely covered is the US presidential election in November. Less well known is that there is a general election in Russia in September. After the EU Referendum, everyone will pack up for the summer holidays and silly season will be upon us. The Russian and American elections present us with the opportunity to make a real difference."

"How do you mean, Sir Harold?" Morton asked.

"You will recall that, a few months ago, we worked out a ploy to make Europe aware of the dangers of not standing up for itself. You were asked to take on an extraordinarily daring role in conjunction with a whistle-blower. I am pleased to say that there is no call for that sort of action, at the present time, but your skills and audacity may yet have a key role to play in the forthcoming debates. The main issue is, of course, national sovereignty versus submission to the diktat of the EU or even to the tyranny of TTIP. The outcome of our referendum should embolden the pro-sovereignty political forces throughout Europe and could open the way to a wider debate about the future of Europe."

"So, what do you want me to do, Sir Harold?" Morton asked.

Nevin obliged. "A post-Brexit UK will need a whole new perspective on how it deals with foreign markets and to what extent foreign investors should have access to the UK's markets. Frankly, I don't like the idea of protectionism, but I have to admit that we might end up in that ball game. The EU will drive a hard bargain when it begins its negotiations with us, so we should try to strengthen our hand. We will want to retain as much access to the EU's markets as we can, without being hemmed in by the EU's rules and regulations, but the EU will no doubt try to exact a high price in return.

"Perhaps we can learn from Russia's experience. There are sanctions in place against Russia. These sanctions are hurting the Russian economy, but, in response, the Russians are taking business away from other countries in Europe and reinvesting in their domestic economy. This has now become a long-term trend inside Russia, and it is an irreversible trend.

"The EU tried to squeeze Russia, but Russia managed to deal with it. Maybe we need to do something similar in our dealings with the EU, post-Brexit; we need to find ways for British capital to… reinvest in the UK.

"Speaking of Russia, there is still scope for UK foreign investment in Russia and vice versa, as long as the current tense stand-off can be calmed down and, preferably, brought to an end. If this ever came about – and it is a big if – then it would have to be cemented in place with a new European security policy.

"My friends Sir Quentin Forbes and Lord Ernest Anderian have been tipped off that Russia is now looking to consolidate the gains it has recently made, vis-à-vis Syria, by developing a strategic business and political relationship with at least one of the major Western powers.

"Many in Germany would welcome the opportunity to become a strategic partner of Russia. France, which has been on close terms with Russia historically, would fit neatly into such a configuration and would certainly be regarded as a suitable candidate.

"Even in the US, a victory for the Republican Party led by a so-called 'populist' president from the Right would deal a major blow to the neoconservatives – and that, in turn, could lead to all kinds of arguments and splits among the Democrats, and probably also among Republicans. The incoming US administration might decide subsequently it is time to reverse its hard line toward Russia and, instead, to push for a détente.

"In the UK, more and more people feel strongly about the need to reclaim our sovereignty, but the anti-Russia rhetoric in our media (fuelled by the UK's long-standing institutionalised Russophobia) discourages people from thinking in terms of Russia as a prospective business partner."

Morton once again asked what was expected of Krejevsky and him.

Nevin wrapped up the talk. "In the House of Commons, Bill Hodson is pushing hard for a Brexit strategy that will put the UK on an even keel and set the UK up for a rosy future. In the House of Lords, Lord Ernest Anderian has been busy raising the issue of a new, independent foreign policy. Post-Brexit, this idea seems to be gathering momentum, and I expect he will arrange for a committee to be set up to have a good chinwag and get something down on paper.

"What we need from you, John and Dmitry, is something analytical about the sanctions on Russia, on European relations in general and on the prospects for a new European security policy."

Cakes and muffins, with tea and coffee, were served in the tea house – the perfect setting for a 'little chat and catch up'.

Morton decided that, having twice missed out on the annual St Petersburg International Economic Forum (SPIEF), it was high time that he paid a visit. When the Russian organisers found out that Morton was planning to attend the SPIEF, they invited him to join a panel of experts at a side meeting. This was a job more suited to Zoe Neubauer, and he rang her up to propose it to her. Zoe was unavailable, but Hans was thinking of going.

"I'm afraid that you won't be able to fulfil your long-standing wish to see the Bolshoi, because the SPIEF is located not in Moscow but in St Petersburg," Zoe stated, alluding to Morton's failed attempts to see the world-famous ballet during his previous trips to Russia. "But the Kirov in St Petersburg is also top class, and Hans thinks that, as a SPIEF delegate, you might be able to get decent seats at a reasonable discount."

15

WHAT WE DID ON OUR HOLIDAYS

In the UK, the months of July and August are traditionally taken up with holidays and other summer activities.

For the corporate media, this provides an excuse to indulge in what is known as the 'silly season', during which serious news frequently takes a back seat to trivial stories and wall-to-wall coverage of summer sports. Notwithstanding, if required (with everyone in a 'summer mood'), it is not unusual for the corporate media to slip in a narrative or two about a serious issue, with the intention of keeping the distracted population 'on-message'.

For the alternative media, on the other hand, the uphill struggle to pay the bills, and to win hearts and minds never ceases, nor is it ever trivialised.

The deceptions at the heart of Western foreign policy – often concerning a real or alleged potentate who needs to be demonised and, later on, overthrown in a coup d'état that is dressed up as an exercise in 'introducing democracy to peoples in distant lands' by means of so-called 'humanitarian interventions' – show that the sun never sleeps nor does the blood ever dry on the global game of empire.

In contrast, actual potentates with a track record of human rights abuses as long as your arm – which Western governments regard as allies and with whom the said governments have major trading deals, including the sale of expensive heavy weaponry to fund the Western military-industrial complexes – are not targeted by the corporate media. Instead, such potentates are fêted, or coverage of their human rights abuses is ignored, obfuscated, or at least toned down or excused in some way.

In contrast, for true investigative reporters, the arduous task of researching, analysing and documenting the evidential proof of such activities is a full-time job in which every minute is precious. This core value system is at the heart of *The New Times*. It is the reason why this particular alternative media outlet was set up by Dmitry Krejevsky, in conjunction with John Morton, in the first place.

※

At the beginning of July, Hugh Lombard drew up a rota for *The New Times*, to ensure that at least a skeleton staff would be available in the office. The rota was uploaded to the website's internal noticeboard to enable all the staff to keep an eye on who should be in the office at any given time and who was on holiday.

※

For *The Chronicle*, retaining pride of place as a liberal cornerstone of the British corporate media in spite of its self-inflicted shortcomings, it was also necessary to put in place special (albeit different) measures.

The reason for special measures was simple and straightforward – to say that the owners and the management of *The Chronicle* had cut the staffing to the bone was putting it mildly. The resourceful Taylor Snow arranged for part-time cover to be provided by wives, and other relatives and friends of employees of the US Embassy. It was their job to answer phones and to provide basic cover for the office during normal working hours. The big jobs – such as the management of freelance reporters, and the interaction with the printers and other outsourced agencies, such as the website service provider – would be shared between Taylor Snow and Edward Ollerson.

This arrangement suited Shirley Bould, in the guise of Freda Gray, because – once again – it guaranteed that Edward Ollerson would not visit the office too often and that her cover would not be blown.

It also suited Taylor Snow because she had convinced herself that Edward Ollerson had allowed himself to become no more than a figurehead with nothing substantial to offer to *The Chronicle*. As far as she was concerned, feelings that she expressed openly in a transatlantic phone call with Katy Drake, "Edward can do his day job, and go home to wallow in his couch potato existence, drink himself silly and fuck whoever he wants." And, Taylor threw in, "He can tidy himself up to chair the annual general meeting and shareholder meetings."

Brigita Wolznaski trained the 'embassy wives' in the job of maintaining the website, but Taylor Snow decided that she would supervise them; not Brigita. This was an essential ingredient in the grand plan that had been forming in Taylor's mind.

To cut a long story short, Brigita had made a good impression on Taylor by paying attention to her health and personal well-being, and through her dogged perseverance to her 'good but not so good' office job, which Brigita liked to think of as the first step on the ladder of a career. In order to feed Brigita's ambitions, thereby harnessing self-motivation as part of the well-oiled machine she was creating, Taylor earmarked Brigita for a bigger role at *The Chronicle*.

Brigita was scheduled to spend six out of the remaining nine weeks of summer attending three training courses provided by a US-based non-governmental organisation (NGO). The first two would be in Europe (Paris and Rome), and the third was slated provisionally for Washington DC, where – in addition to the two-week training course – Brigita would be allowed to take one week of her annual holiday allowance to spend with her folks.

※

The first week of the Paris segment of Brigita's training programme consisted of the gentle introduction of twelve strangers to each other and a brief history of modern-day liberal thinking.

The history of the European Enlightenment was crudely contrasted with the so-called 'anti-democratic traditions' of the

Asiatic East; then came the French Revolution, the American War of Independence and the American Civil War.

The twentieth century began as a century of hope and expectation; then two world wars crashed and burned the cosy assumptions that the future would be a happy, gradual 'progress' to even greater things.

Hope was resurrected after World War II, as US-sponsored schemes financed the reconstruction of the shattered countries of Western Europe, Japan and other American allies in the Asia-Pacific rim.

The 1960s civil rights movement in the US took up a whole day of the course, which was interrupted briefly for fifteen minutes to take in minor digressions on what were arguably two of the most significant and controversial events in American post-war history: the Vietnam War and the Watergate scandal.

The McCarthy witch-hunt of the 1950s was put down to one individual's nervousness about how to deal with the other side in the Cold War. The end of this inglorious period was explained away as providing a greater confidence in the American Way and the purpose of this 'great nation' in the twentieth century. Symbolic of this greater confidence was the emergence of a wise leader – John F Kennedy – who took over from the individuals who were clearly not up to the job of handling the changes heralded by the end of the 'square', conformist 1950s and the beginning of the 'groovy', nonconformist 1960s.

John Morton's wife – Alison Morton, PhD, research fellow in history at London University – would have shuddered at this superficial approach to history, within which a dominant neoconservative narrative was conjured out of thin air. This was a dominant narrative within which unpleasant situations could be blamed on one or two scallywags; the whole complexity of social, political and economic structures, and their interplay could simply be ignored; and any narrative that did not work out could be overridden by a new narrative – conjured up as though by magic out of thin air – with the old narrative being swept under the carpet as though it had never existed or had never happened.

And that was just for starters.

During week two of the Paris school, the students were immersed in a whole panoply of philosophical debates – with a bias toward postmodernism. This presented a greater intellectual challenge, and, by Thursday evening, Brigita retired to bed full of melancholy because she still did not fully understand the subject. The lecturer had been a bit boring and some of the course attendees had mocked him – in his absence – during evening drinks and dinner. Nevertheless, those same attendees achieved significantly higher grades than Brigita, which did nothing to improve her self-confidence.

*

Brigita returned to London to a pining Edward Ollerson and an enthusiastic Taylor Snow.

Brigita outlined to Taylor her misgivings about the course and her inadequate performance.

Taylor would have none of it, saying, "Take your time, Brigita. Rome was not built in a day."

At first, Taylor Snow sounded like a broken record, repeating the same mantra as Katy Drake following the debacle over the failed attempted smear campaign against Dmitry Krejevsky. But Taylor Snow was not Katy Drake. She had different methods, and Taylor showed that she possessed a more constructive approach to problem resolution and people management than Katy.

"And, by the way, Brigita, there is no rush," explained Taylor. "You have four more weeks of training to go, and these weeks will give you ample opportunity to hone your skills. There will also be ample time to practise here in the office... and I will help you. I won't push you. I will help you to create the space in which you can push yourself... because I know that you can do that under your own steam, without too much supervision from me. Agreed?"

Brigita beamed. Was it a meeting of minds, perhaps? Never in her wildest dreams did she imagine that such a scenario was possible. For the first time in her life, here was a manager who understood her, who appreciated her and who expressed unreserved confidence in her.

"Speaking of Rome," Taylor added, "for Rome is the venue of your next course, Loretta Farelli will be giving the keynote speech on day one.

"The keynote speech will be held in a lecture theatre at a university and will be attended by over 200 people. Most of them will attend lectures only, but about thirty of the attendees will join you on the training course, including some of your friends from the Paris cohort. You should spend as much effort as possible in getting to know the others on the course because you might find yourself teaming up with them in future.

"So far, you have exchanged contact details with the Paris cohort, haven't you? Good. And you've all joined the Facebook and LinkedIn groups, and are following their tweets on Twitter and posts on other social media? Excellent. All attendees of these courses are encouraged to join these social media groups, so you will find you have a bunch of useful resources at your disposal. That is *the* key takeaway of this set of training courses, so I would not worry too much about getting a good grasp of the philosophical aspects. We can work on that later; that's why we will have OJT – on-the-job training."

Brigita was due to spend two weeks in London prior to embarking on the training course in Rome. Taylor set aside time to provide OJT to Brigita and accompanied her frequently on her daily run after work. The pair became close friends, indulging in shopping trips and soirées with the 'embassy gang', among other activities.

Having resigned herself to Brigita's desire to catch up with Edward, Taylor put no obstacle in Brigita's way. However, during the two weeks that Brigita had been in Paris, it had become apparent that Edward had let his personal grooming standards drop through the floor.

On Monday night, Edward took Brigita to a restaurant and then back to his flat (which he had tidied up, after a fashion). Edward proposed to Brigita that they go to bed for an 'all-nighter', which Brigita was perfectly tuned up to perform, and at the right moment in time she might have consented. But on Monday evening, for heaven's sake? There was a full week of work ahead, lots of OJT and the need to follow up her studies by applying them to real-life situations. She would not meet her targets if she began the working week with a deficit of one full night of sleep.

Brigita allotted time with Edward in his flat on Wednesday evening, but went home before ten-thirty at night. The weekend was split between Saturday (with Edward) and Sunday (with Taylor and a few buddies from the US Embassy). The working week ahead followed a similar pattern to the previous week, although – being acutely aware that she was due to leave for Rome on Saturday morning – on Wednesday evening, Brigita upbraided Edward for letting himself go and warned him not to let himself slide further into ennui.

※

For Brigita, brimming with renewed self-confidence, Loretta Farelli's keynote speech on the first Monday of the two-week course in Rome seemed, quite simply, sensational. It lifted the mood and set the scene for a series of lectures under the epithet 'The Future of Liberal Internationalism'.

In the classroom the following day, Brigita teamed up with two of the women she had met on the previous course in Paris, which had consisted of three male and nine female attendees. This course in Rome was quite different. There were thirty-three attendees, with a male-female ratio of roughly fifty-fifty, and all aged between mid-twenties and mid-thirties.

During the weekend, everyone went to a beach resort, where Brigita joined in games of tennis and volleyball. An Australian attendee named Trevor, aged twenty-nine, coached Brigita into improving her serve and volley, and encouraged her to go for a swim in the sea.

"Mind the sharks don't get you!" a cheeky Brit called Rex shouted out, in the latest in a series of clumsy attempts at chatting her up; 'Rex' being a nickname he had appended to himself (he explained, "It means top dog or 'king' in Latin, you know. The boss. The winner!").

In response, Brigita's winning smile made its customary, polite appearance. However, Trevor did not seem impressed. Was it jealousy on his part? Was Trevor getting serious about Brigita already?

Brigita and Trevor bathed in the warm Mediterranean Sea. They found a shaded area of the beach to haul themselves out away from the crowd. The couple indulged in small talk, sipped from bottles of water bought from a kiosk and discovered that they enjoyed each other's company.

After a while, Trevor grew a bit morose. "I'm sorry if I seem a bit down, Brigita," Trevor said. "It was what Rex said – about the sharks in the sea."

Brigita smiled sheepishly, a bit embarrassed about Trevor's obvious sensitivity, and wondering if more was to come.

It did.

"It's all very well making funny comments about big fish that might take a bite out of you, as though it's just like a scene from a Hollywood movie, but where I come from, there are such fish. *Big* fish. *Really* big fish, with bodies this wide," Trevor explained as he formed a large semicircle with his arms.

Trevor sat with his hands clasped and arms wrapped around his bent knees, staring vacantly out across the bay. Brigita assumed the same position.

Trevor continued, "One of my classmates became a lifeguard when he left school just over ten years ago. He was a strong swimmer. You know that sharks are a protected species? They are regarded as a key part of the global ecosystem. They swim, eat and make babies, but they also keep the place tidy. They eat a lot of the dead creatures in the sea.

"In Australia, we are brought up to think of the sea as their domain. We are just visitors, so we need to respect them and their environment – and their role in marine garbage disposal.

"From time to time, a shark attack is reported. Sometimes the corpse never drifts ashore, or the photos of the remains are not published out of respect for the deceased and the bereaved.

"One day, my former classmate was on the beach as usual, when he suddenly noticed a commotion about half a mile away. He got a call on his mobile. There were mobile phones and walkie-talkies relaying messages all over the place. It was chaos. Helicopters and boats were scouring the bay, but there was no sign of the shark.

"We got a call to leg it down to the beach, and that's when I saw what had happened. My lifeguard friend knew a lot about first aid, and he had run all the way to the water's edge near to where the incident had occurred. The young twenty-something who had been attacked was alive but unconscious. The shark had bitten him on the thigh of one leg, and on the other leg the skin flopped down over where the knee and lower leg should have been. My friend and others applied tourniquets to stem the blood flow, and the ambulance arrived to take him to hospital. We went to see him a couple of months later. He lost both legs, and so would spend a long time in a wheelchair and then the rest of his life wearing prosthetic limbs."

Brigita looked down sadly; Trevor noticed.

"But not to get too upset, eh, Brigita?" Trevor lifted the mood a little, and gently elbowed Brigita in the ribs. "It is just the reality of the world. There's nothing much we can do about it. That shark attack victim showed a lot of character – he got back on his surfboard as soon as he could, about a year later, despite his disability. What a guy!

"The thing is, Brigita… no one likes a laugh more than me. It's just that… it's just that there is a time and a place for it, and the subject should be appropriate. This Rex bloke doesn't seem a bad sort, although brash… and crass. But he's pig ignorant when it comes to worldly matters, and he fancies himself into the bargain. That mouth of his will get him into trouble one day, but… at the end of the day, he is just another guy trying to get his act together like the rest of us and to find his way in the world. So good luck to him. But I don't have time for such play-acting; I have my own life to get on with."

✳

Rex continued to make a play for Brigita, cornering her at an evening buffet and following her back to her table to engage her in a one-way conversation. Rex was funny and oozed confidence, but he was not a good listener.

'Funny and confident' – Brigita's younger brother had told her he was going to try to adopt that pose because he had read in a lads' mag that it was a sure-fire way to stand out from the crowd of suitors and 'get the girl'.

Best of luck, bro, Brigita had thought, rather sceptically. For Brigita was what is commonly viewed within the 'male gaze' as a hottie, and she had found herself being continually approached by men of all ages throughout her late teens and early twenties.

Early on, the funny guys who were unbearably and excessively confident were tolerated. After all, it is only to be expected that young people should push themselves forward, experiment and learn, and find their way in the world… and looking for sex was frequently the activity with which many were preoccupied. At first, these humorous swaggerers stood out from the crowd, but, over time, it seemed to Brigita that all of them had learned the same game. Nevertheless, Brigita still joined in the fun.

Now, however, not long before her twenty-sixth birthday, which would coincide with the third training course two weeks hence, Brigita found herself confronted by two very different male characters: Rex, the in-your-face class clown who was looking for an easy conquest; and Trevor – cool, calm and collected Trevor.

Trevor, who had meaning to his life; Trevor, who was attentive to himself, attentive to Brigita and who even found the time to empathise with others, even if they rubbed him up the wrong way; Trevor, a talented yet modest and sensitive young man with a mature outlook on life; Trevor, who had fallen head over heels for Brigita, and Brigita knew it.

Trevor, who sensed that Brigita felt the same way about him, which gave Trevor the edge over Rex because – where Rex exuded overconfidence in abundance – the more savvy Trevor possessed the self-confidence and self-control that would enable him to pick the right time to make his move.

As more people entered the dining room, Brigita took the opportunity to excuse herself from the bothersome company of Rex to mingle with other students and to exchange pleasantries. She decided to spend the evening in the company of her female friends from the Paris cohort and a few others who were gathered around.

Rex hovered about, filling and refilling his glass with champagne under the mistaken impression that, unlike beer, wine or spirits, "It doesn't matter how much of this stuff you drink – you won't wake up with a Ben Dover!"

Trevor stayed in the background, observing the developing farce and playing for time. At ten o'clock, he approached Brigita and gently cupped her right elbow in his left hand. "Goodnight, Brigita. Don't stay up too late," he said.

"Oh, you're going already?" she asked.

"I think I'll go for a jog at seven o'clock in the morning before it gets too hot. Then maybe have a swim. Anyway, see you tomorrow… sometime," Trevor smiled, the lip curling up on one side, and the corresponding eyebrow teasingly raised.

Trevor disappeared, leaving Brigita to be quizzed by her friends about what exactly was going on between the pair and why Brigita's eyes were on stalks; they said (sardonically, but supportively), "Betcha go down to the beach at seven o'clock in the morning to accidentally bump into… *Trev-aaah*."

Rex made one last attempt at Brigita before bedtime, having guzzled his way through Lord knows how much champagne. Brigita and the other women adopted a tolerant but distant attitude to him, and – while he was busy pressing the waiter to open another bottle of bubbly – a few of the women made their exit, including Brigita. The remainder drifted away over time in twos and threes, as Rex wandered out onto the balcony and along garden pathways in a fruitless search for female company.

※

The third training course, initially scheduled in Washington DC, was relocated to a beach resort on the west coast of the US, not far from Los Angeles. This was surfing country, and it gave Trevor the opportunity to introduce Brigita to another sports activity, and for her to develop a modest proficiency, and to enable their friendship to become a bit more touchy-feely and *noticeably* smoochy.

The cohort had been reduced to ten, including Trevor and two of Brigita's new-found female associates from the previous courses, but excluding the tiresome Rex.

Lessons consisted of densely packed theory, which nobody could keep up with at first; workbooks in which to put the theory into practice; role play; and a large amount of free time, which the students were encouraged to use to their advantage.

Early in the second week of the course, Brigita decided to take into her confidence one of her new-found friends from the Paris and Rome cohorts, concerning a matter that had been nagging at her for some time: namely, whether or not to persevere with a flagging relationship with Edward Ollerson or to jump at the prospect of a promising association with Trevor.

The upshot was clear: Trevor was in and Edward was out.

Trevor even accompanied Brigita to Washington DC to spend a week with her folks. With Trevor in tow, Brigita would not need to break the news to her mom of her dubious liaison with the much older Edward Ollerson, and to engage in a deep and meaningful discourse on its potential, or lack thereof. When her mom asked if Trevor was the boy she had met in London, Brigita merely replied in the negative and dismissed the notion that the London guy was anything more than something temporary.

Trevor, with his charm, his knowledge, his experience and his overall 'Mr Nice Guy' image, fitted the bill perfectly. Why, he even helped her dad to chop some wood and to fix the roof of an outhouse in the garden.

※

Her mom watched with trembling lips as her daughter said her goodbyes to Trevor at the airport; he surrounded Brigita with his muscular arms and manly frame, and she nodded and dabbed her nose and eyes with tissues. Finally, he broke away and held her hands for a while. They kissed and hugged, and Trevor took out a tissue from his jacket pocket and dabbed Brigita's cheeks one last time before heading to the departure gate.

Then he was gone.

PART FOUR
THE BEST THINGS IN LIFE ARE FREE

16

ENEMIES OR OPPONENTS?

Monday, 5 September 2016.
Loretta Farelli was not impressed by the news of a new man in Brigita's life. In fact, she plunged into an apoplectic rage, which did not abate even when Taylor Snow told Loretta that Edward had not had the courtesy to meet Brigita at Heathrow Airport on any of the three occasions he was expected to do so when she returned from her overseas training courses.

Throughout Monday afternoon, a heated phone call took place between Taylor Snow (behind the closed doors of her office at *The Chronicle*) and Loretta Farelli, accompanied by Katy Drake (both stationed in the Beltway).

Freda Gray suggested to Brigita that they go for a nice little cuppa at one of their regular haunts.

"It's for the best, dear. Let them sort it out at their end," Freda stated the obvious, and Brigita agreed.

Brigita's biggest concern was that this rift would spell the end of Taylor Snow's secondment to London, and would lead to Taylor's recall to the Beltway or to a distant outpost; thereby undermining Brigita's position in London, her career, her ambitions and her dreams, and… then what?

But Freda Gray put Brigita at her ease. "Taylor will stay," Freda said as they went down in the lift.

"How do you know? How can you tell?" Brigita asked.

"I have been keeping an eye out for you, this past two weeks," Freda explained. "Some of the calls were on hands-free loudspeaker – until, that is, Taylor realised that the sensitive conversation could be overheard, turned off the loudspeaker and closed the door."

"And the language!" Freda exclaimed, as she put on her coat, while Brigita blushed on behalf of Freda's prudence and ignorance of how these powerful, modern business women often talked to each other when the going got tough.

※

In the café, Brigita listened attentively as Freda outlined the gist, "Taylor Snow came to verbal blows with Edward over his increasingly erratic behaviour and, in one case, his failure to turn up at the printers for a scheduled meeting. Taylor had to rush off to arrange for the newspaper's publication to take place, and, the next day, she had to do the same again *and* chase up the website service provider because of some connectivity issues.

"Taylor threatened to bring in someone else if Edward could not show an interest. It was *Taylor*, not Loretta, who initiated the first transatlantic conference call.

"They had a big row, and I heard Taylor saying that she was 'really pissed' at having to do all the… effing work," Freda muttered, "Then Loretta berated Taylor for allowing you to go on the training courses, throwing in a 'stupid effing this' and a 'stupid effing that' here and there.

"Taylor joined in the slanging match, rivalling Loretta's colourful language with a few choice words of her own, which I most definitely will not repeat! Then Taylor said she needed someone to do the real work of research and article writing, not the mechanics of dealing with print shops and computer people, and of uploading stuff to the website – the latter task being a simple little job the 'embassy wives' were handling 'very well, thank you' (and enjoying it). That was why you were sent on the training courses, Brigita, and given extra OJT, Taylor explained. But Loretta wasn't listening."

Freda poured out a couple of top-ups from the teapot.

"And do you know what Taylor did next?" Freda asked. "She went ahead and brought in someone else to help her with the daily running of the office and the management of the business relationships with the printers and the computer people."

"Someone else? But how? She can't do that without Loretta's say-so," declared Brigita.

"She did it. She brought in Erik, a thirty-something man from Denmark. He's quiet and unfussy; he just gets on with his job. Nice chap; always says 'hello.'"

"But she can't do that, Freda. I mean, Loretta is really, really powerful – like a goddess. Nobody gets anything past her."

"Believe me, Brigita. Taylor has gone and done it. And she has got away with it, too. There is only one explanation for this," Freda summed up. "It is not Loretta Farelli who is calling the shots at *The Chronicle* these days. It is Taylor Snow! And you had better keep on good terms with her because, whatever happens next, it looks to me that you have, without realising it, backed the winning horse!"

As soon as the rows between Loretta and Taylor began in earnest, during the third week of August, Shirley Bould had passed on to John Morton the news of the impending crisis at *The Chronicle*.

Within days, the crisis became full-blown. Morton scanned the website and paper editions of *The Chronicle*. He noticed the decline in quality and even in quantity for two or three of the paper editions – explained away, in a formal apology, as 'technical difficulties' and other vague explanations.

Then, no sooner had the decline in quality happened, it was just as suddenly reversed. In fact, *The Chronicle* showed encouraging signs of improvement.

Morton had mixed feelings. On the one hand, the survival and blossoming of one of the UK's oldest newspapers could only be good for the media industry and should augment the diversity of opinion. On the other hand, it signalled the end of the phase that Lord Ernest Anderian had portrayed as "inducing Edward and Brigita into a bubble where they can be controlled by us".

Morton recalled that Lord Ernest's fallback plan – "if, and only if, it becomes absolutely necessary to do so" – would be "to take action to completely destroy *The Chronicle*".

Morton reported back to Dmitry Krejevsky and Sir Harold Nevin. They agreed to do nothing. But, for the time being, to keep a watching brief.

※

The civil war at *The Chronicle* threatened to intensify when Brigita received a text message from Trevor. He was going to relocate to Europe to be closer to the new love interest in his life. Realising that he might not be aware of the battleground in which he might soon be embroiling himself, Brigita advised Trevor to keep a low profile.

Within days of arriving back in London, Brigita formally broke off her relationship with Edward Ollerson, over dinner in a restaurant. To prevent a scene from getting out of hand (it had already started to brew), Brigita exited abruptly and took a taxi home.

Taylor Snow advised Brigita to forewarn the security guards at her apartment block to prevent Edward from entering the premises. Taylor also rescinded Edward's security access to the offices of *The Chronicle* and warned the security guards at the Millhouse Building to refuse him access beyond the reception area. Edward Ollerson's access to *The Chronicle* website was likewise rescinded.

Thus, it came to pass that Edward Ollerson MBE – editor-in-chief of *The Chronicle*, one of the UK's long-established news media outlets – was no longer going to be allowed access to his own office or even to post articles on the website. Furthermore, his salary was to be drastically cut to £40,000 per annum, in exchange for his name to remain on the website and paper editions as editor-in-chief, as though – in the eyes of the newspaper's readers – nothing had happened.

"It's like he's the last of the great figureheads at *The Chronicle*," Shirley Bould observed. And there was nothing Edward Ollerson seemed capable of doing about it.

Shirley reported this high jinks back to John Morton.

Morton speculated to himself about how Edward Ollerson might react to his effective demotion, *Will Edward stay or go? To go means entering a wilderness, for no other organisation would entertain him in his current state of mind and physical distress.*

To stay means accepting personal humiliation at the hands of women who, in Edward's mind, occupy a status lower than men – Edwards' professed commitment to various forms of radical-liberal identity politics notwithstanding.

Edward could try to negotiate a higher rate, but – seen through Edward's eyes – even that would be a variation on the theme of demeaning acceptance.

Maybe he is thinking of throwing in the towel and resigning, in which case he could have grounds for constructive dismissal. I wonder... is that the game Edward is playing... playing with fire, perhaps... I hope he knows what he is doing.

Taylor Snow seemed a hard-nosed operator, so she was unlikely to back down or to make any significant concessions. She also came across as well-informed and keen to pick up on even the tiniest fragment of information.

John Morton imagined Taylor Snow going through the books with a fine-toothed comb to uncover every scrap of useful information she could find. No doubt she would find out about all of the skeletons in the cupboard at *The Chronicle* (many of which were known to John Morton and over which he had long ago decided to draw a discreet veil, even though there was nothing incriminating about him except a large batch of unpublished articles that his former boss Tom Hamble had pigeonholed as being 'much too hot to handle').

Yes, Morton thought, *if she thought it worthwhile to indulge in a little 'congenial' blackmail to further her ends, Taylor Snow would have the previous and current owners of* The Chronicle *by the balls.*

But to what ultimate purpose? Does she, in fact, have an ultimate purpose? And why engage in an open conflict with some of her colleagues in the Beltway? Furthermore, and most troubling of all, what is it about Taylor Snow that gives her the edge when dealing with such a powerful figure as Loretta Farelli?

"We have nothing to lose," Lord Ernest Anderian had said, "because we are unlikely to have to deal with anyone more toxic than Loretta Farelli."

Was that true or false?

To all these questions, Morton felt that he should find convincing answers before Taylor Snow (with her connections to the US military, the US Embassy in Grosvenor Square and… who else?) decided it was time to turn her gaze, like Sauron's eye, resolutely in the direction of *The New Times*.

※

Wednesday, 7 September 2016.
Brigita Wolznaski picked up the phone and answered a call from the reception area of the Millhouse Building. "No, thank you", she replied, "I do not want to speak to the editor-in-chief."

"Perhaps I did not make myself clear," the receptionist offered an explanation. "I have two visitors for you here in the reception area. Mr Hugh Lombard, the editor-in-chief of *The New Times* and Mr John Morton, one of his staff."

Brigita leapt from her seat. This she was not expecting.

The receptionist told Brigita that the men said they had come to see the editor-in-chief or whoever was in charge. Brigita informed Taylor Snow, who was also taken aback.

The two men were given visitor passes and escorted by Brigita to the conference room.

Hugh Lombard gave a plausible enough reason for the visit. The photograph of Sir Tom Hamble, Edward Ollerson MBE and John Morton MBE – taken outside Buckingham Palace in late February earlier in the year – had been mounted in an elegant picture frame, and they wanted to deliver it to Edward in person.

"Edward is not here. Perhaps you can leave it for him to collect later," explained Taylor.

"Not really, because it is Sir Tom Hamble's express wish that the item be delivered by hand," Lombard confirmed.

"Very well. The framed photograph should be taken to Edward Ollerson's home and delivered to him in person," Taylor stated.

"Agreed," conceded Lombard.

Then a conversation emerged, as though from behind receding clouds as they uncovered a clear, blue sky.

"How's business?" Morton asked casually, as though trying to break the ice.

"Fine," replied Taylor Snow.

"I couldn't help noticing that the quality of material published by *The Chronicle* has markedly improved," Morton threw in.

Taylor Snow smiled and looked down, acknowledging the compliment modestly.

"You know. It is more than two years since I visited the premises of *The Chronicle* near Farringdon Tube station – the old offices, that is. I must say, these new quarters are a huge improvement."

Taylor Snow remained tight-lipped, but smiled in her customary professional way.

"Only, you see, I went to Ukraine and got hurt while I was in the Donbass," explained Morton. "It has taken time for me to recover. When I came back onto the scene, I had no idea that there would be so much bitterness between *The Chronicle* and *The New Times*. Oh, you can rest assured that the business over Dmitry Krejevsky and the allegations concerning supposed links with a Russian intelligence agency is over and done with. As far as we are concerned, it is forgotten."

Taylor Snow remained cool and aloof.

Morton pressed on. "After Edward Ollerson was castigated for publishing those Russian battle plans in January, I published an article in his defence. I was very concerned at the time because the British government seemed likely to embark on a crusade to restrict press freedom. A few weeks later, Edward and I received our MBEs from Her Majesty the Queen at Buckingham Palace. I was as surprised as anyone to receive an honour. I still wonder why the prime minister put my name forward. Me! Of all people!"

"Maybe you should speak to him," Taylor Snow smiled, a mite mockingly.

"I did," Morton replied drily.

Taylor Snow assumed her customary poker face once more.

Brigita's jaw, already lowered in surprise by the bluntness of the approach and the turn of phrase pursued by John Morton, slackened a little more and her eyes widened.

Morton explained, "Together with some of my colleagues, I visited the prime minister at his country home at Chequers. It was in April, just after the police raid on *The New Times*. We had become concerned that various intelligence agencies were trying to interfere with our organisation. We spoke with some retired former representatives of the UK intelligence services – decent fellows who are on friendly terms with the sponsors of *The New Times*.

"We were told that there was nothing that we could do to stop the spooks, and that the spooks would have to be allowed to get on with their job. The same goes for overseas intelligence services – we were told that we cannot prevent them from monitoring what we do. It's all part of a game involving multiple foreign powers operating on their own and in each other's territories. Apparently, all the big powers do it.

"So, we just carried on doing our job and leaving them to it."

Taylor Snow kept her eyes fixed on Morton and took a leisurely sip of coffee.

Morton smiled. "It has made not the slightest bit of difference. It has affected our work not one jot. We have nothing to hide and we have nothing to prove; we are investigative reporters, we are good at what we do and we know it. Everyone knows it."

Morton looked down, removed his spectacles to wipe them before putting them back on, then directed a cold gaze straight at Taylor Snow. "And, Taylor, I think that you also know it."

The left side of Taylor Snow's lip raised a little.

"And, Taylor, we know that you are also good. Bloody good, in fact," Morton stated.

Taylor Snow's mouth wrinkled into a reluctant smile. "So, what are you proposing?" she asked, leaning back a little.

"Oh, I don't know exactly," said Morton. "Our websites both provided a reasonable coverage of the EU Referendum. That was a long exercise: over two months. Yet we did not speak to each other. It was as though we were on opposing sides. Enemies even. Are we enemies, Taylor? Or are we merely opponents? Enemies fight each other to the death, but opponents engage in debate within a democratic framework. You do recognise that, Taylor? The need to keep the democratic framework in place, at least?"

Taylor Snow nodded slowly.

"*The Chronicle* has shown signs of a shot in the arm in recent weeks," Morton continued. "I welcome that. We cannot sharpen our quills if the opposition is not doing a good job. But, now, I think that both your news outlet and ours will benefit from the increased competition we can provide to each other."

The phoney war seemed to be assuming fresh characteristics; a phoney war that, sometimes and only under specific favourable conditions, might be framed as a 'gentlemen's war' of sorts.

※

"So, Hugh, what did you make of our new American Army friend, Taylor Snow?" Morton enquired after they had left the building.

Lombard shrugged. "CIA?" he asked.

"It's hard to tell," Morton replied. "In any case, it does not make a difference to us. We will just carry on as usual, as advised by Sir Harold and his friends."

They walked up the steps of the Tate Gallery.

"It bugs me, though," Morton confided, as they wandered through the galleries, oblivious to the exhibits. "Something is going on, and I would like to know what it is. I need to know.

"Meanwhile, we had better get this photograph delivered to Edward Ollerson. It would not look good if Taylor asked him about it, and he said he didn't know anything about it, and today's trip to the Millhouse Building would have been in vain.

"Our efforts to find out about Taylor Snow seem to have opened a possible gateway into… well, I don't know quite what… but I have a feeling that our relationship with *The Chronicle* might be about to take an upturn. But… no promises, Hugh."

*

Taylor Snow seemed faintly amused.

Their rivals had paid them a visit, ostensibly to deliver a gift to Edward Ollerson, but – in fact – to engage them in a conversation about a quite different topic. It was pleasant enough and in the form of a peace offering. Perhaps there would be a sting in the tail.

Whatever. Wait and see, I suppose, she thought.

Meanwhile, the wheels turned on yet another routine day at *The Chronicle*. Articles were commissioned from a growing posse of freelancers, reviewed, edited and uploaded to the website. Erik kept the newspaper ticking over like a well-oiled machine.

Encouraged by John Morton's praise concerning the enhanced quality of content in *The Chronicle*, Taylor Snow approved an increase in the newspaper's circulation. To test the water. Several hundred of the extra print run were sold on the first day, rising to over 1,000 extra copies per day by the end of the week – proving that there was still an eager audience out there.

*

On Friday afternoon, Taylor and Brigita left work early, spent a couple of hours exercising and relaxing in the park, and returned to Taylor's apartment, where Taylor ordered food to be delivered from one of her favourite restaurants.

After dinner, Taylor proceeded to induce her protégé into a kind of submissive hypnotised state, so it seemed to Brigita, using nothing more complex or dangerous than a 'shoes off and feet up on the sofa' chat and a simple glass of Baileys; "Baileys on the rocks," Taylor depicted it.

"The Brits go mad on this stuff," Taylor explained. "At least the women do – they love it!"

And, over that glass of Baileys on the rocks, Taylor Snow proved to be on top form...

17

DECONSTRUCTING DMITRY

"After the events in New York on September 11, 2001," Taylor began, with glass of Baileys in hand, shoes off and feet up on her sofa, "right-wing thinkers united behind a hard-line agenda of fighting a 'global war on terrorism', frequently in a very harsh manner. They argued the case for acting alone – without the support of the UN, including pre-emptive strikes against *possible* threats – to preserve the *perceived* national security interests of the US. This go-it-alone approach was meant to filter down through NATO and other security alliances, and might even have been taken up by friendly countries on their own initiative. It was a full-blown right-wing revisionist agenda instigated by an alliance of died-in-the-wool hawks and neoconservatives.

"But what was to become of us? The 'progressive liberals' and the 'democrats' with a small 'd' (or even a large 'D')? Were we merely supposed to go along with this and allow ourselves to play second fiddle to those whose professed good intentions would eventually lead the world – and us also – into endless war? I should hope not, for that way lies the militarisation of society, the death of democracy and the dawn of dictatorship.

"What were we supposed to do? 'We just need a new narrative,' we were told. So, guess what? We set to work to construct a new narrative.

"Our starting point was based on the principle that (and I'm quoting Loretta here, of all people, from the keynote speech *she* gave to *my* training cohort all those years ago), 'A global system of stable democracies is the best chance we have of preserving world peace'. But Loretta did not leave it at that. Loretta also said that,

'Not only must we be tough on our enemies, we must also stand up for the little people against the tyrants who ruled over them.' To achieve this, Loretta said, 'We need to champion democracy and human rights, not only at home but also around the world. *Especially* around the world.' Perhaps, as it turned out, *only* around the world but *not* necessarily at home in the US; not yet anyway.

"I remember being told that it would not be enough to think the right way. It would not be enough to think hard and to work hard. We must get results. Someone said, 'Softly, softly, catchee monkey; we must think *smart* and work *smart*.' That was what we were taught in those days. 'Soft power' – that is what we were told that we needed."

Taylor took a sip – more like a slug, actually – of Baileys on the rocks, and continued, "Soft power, rather than unbridled military aggression, is the secret that lies behind progressive-liberal thinking, which has been rebranded by our democratic gurus as 'liberal internationalism'. You discovered that, Brigita, on those training courses you attended, just as I did on my training courses more than ten years ago.

"Since Loretta and her friends began to exert their influence through *The Chronicle*, we have been given the job of importing to Western Europe the anti-Russia narrative that prevails close to Russia's borders in Eastern Europe. The purpose of this is to discourage European countries from forming alliances with or doing deals with Russia, particularly the wealthier and more powerful countries in Western Europe – the technical term for this virtual barrier is *cordon sanitaire*.

"We are being asked to deploy 'soft power' – pure and simple.

"Someone has decided that it is in the geopolitical interests of the US to keep Europe on board with the US. Period. Even if this means expanding the EU or NATO, and even if that upsets the Russians. Even if that upsets the Europeans, for that matter; with trade arrangements that they don't like – such as the TTIP, for example – or with a military build-up on Russia's border that could lead to open war between Europe and Russia, with Europe and Russia (not the US) on the front line.

"In such a case, although we are not openly told this by Loretta and her friends, we would fight the Russians to the last European – provided the Europeans don't wise up to the con.

"A similar process is underway in Asia, where our narrative is designed to discourage countries from getting close to China. As you learned on the training courses, Russia and China have formed some sort of alliance: economically, politically and even militarily.

"Like its European counterpart (the TTIP), the TPP is designed to prevent this Eurasian project from spreading to other parts of Asia. And if war breaks out, it is implied that we will fight the Chinese to the last Korean or Japanese, or whoever falls for the ruse.

"The bottom line is that we don't want to see American body bags coming home again. Let others do the dying.

"This is another example of soft power... this time as a velvet glove covering an iron fist, with others doing the fighting by proxy, while we 'lead from behind'.

"There's more. After World War II, the US dollar became the primary means of global exchange. Having the dollar as the dominant currency meant that the US was able to exert influence, and to rein in, buy off or dispose of anyone who veered off-message. It also allowed the US to cream off a layer of interest every time the dollar was used in an international monetary transaction. Nice business if you can get it.

"That's soft power using financial leverage.

"Conversely, not having the dollar as the dominant currency means a weakening of the dollar, which is what is happening right now as we witness the emergence of a multipolar world order. Within a multipolar paradigm, multiple currencies will be much more widely used in international exchanges. The US has failed to prevent that from happening; this is a failure of US applications of both hard power and soft power."

Taylor selected a few ice cubes from the ice bucket and plopped them into refilled glasses of Baileys.

She continued, "It seems that we were not the only practitioners of soft power. Others were watching us, and perhaps learning from us, but we paid them little attention. We took our eyes off of the ball.

"Logically, my analysis suggests that at least some of our recent problems have been of our own making. This is actually good news, if you think about it, because if some problems are of our own making, then it is possible for us to correct our errors. It means that we possess a measure of control over events, and that future events are not preordained... What were those phrases from the training course? Oh yes, we 'reject the *determinative* approach to history', but we 'embrace the concept of human *agency*'.

"But don't tell that to the Democratic Party leadership, Loretta or any of their like, because nobody seems willing to face up to this problem. All that fancy talk on the training ground is one thing, but – when the rubber hits the road – they don't want to change, they don't want to admit past mistakes and they don't want to lose face, so they just double down as though nothing has changed.

"That's not soft power anymore; it's just dogma.

"Do you follow, Brigita? Or are you not convinced? Do you want more examples? I'll give you more examples.

"Take the sanctions against Iran. What happened next? Did Iran starve to death? Did Iran buckle? Not a bit. Instead, Iran openly defied the US. Even when we sided with Iraq against Iran in the Iran–Iraq War of the 1980s, the Iranians stood firm. And how did they cope with the sanctions? They were able to relieve the pressure enough to survive. They accomplished this by trading with sympathetic countries *not* using the US dollar, which would have revealed the details of the trade deals, but using the Iranian rial – or other currencies, gold or barter – instead of the dollar. This was long before anyone else had the idea of bypassing the dollar.

"Some of my sources tell me that Russia, China, India, Pakistan and others all did business covertly with Iran whenever it was possible to circumvent the sanctions.

"This is an example of soft power, used by the Iranians to counter our soft power, by getting actual and potential allies to help them out.

"Having failed to learn the lesson of failure against a weaker adversary, Iran, the US government has now set itself against a much stronger adversary, Russia.

"In my view, this move creates more problems than it solves. Russia has not been brought to its knees by sanctions, and many of our European allies want to dump the sanctions against Russia because they have spent the best part of twenty years currying favour with Moscow and signing multiple business deals.

"Already, within two years, Russia has achieved what Iran managed to do over a thirty-year period: to successfully defy the sanctions programme imposed by the US government. And, after its intervention in Syria, Russia feels a lot more self-confident and is prepared to bide its time patiently before making its move. Moreover, the price of oil is rising again, which means that increased revenues will once more pour into the Russian coffers."

Brigita had a question: "Assuming what you say is true – and I'm far from convinced that it is true, Taylor – what do you suggest that we do about this?"

"Fair comment, Brigita. Fair comment."

Taylor began to prepare the ground, prior to expounding her new thesis. "You will have noticed that there has been a great deal of unpleasantness recently. Between Loretta and me, that is. Loretta is at the core of liberal internationalist thinking in the US, primarily within Democrat circles, but she also flirts with the Republicans and with neoconservatives.

"In fact, Loretta has been largely responsible for the blurring of boundaries between Republican Party policies and Democratic Party policies, and – aside from the healthcare reforms, which are loathed by the Republicans – there isn't really much difference between Loretta's worldview and much of what many Republicans believe in, especially when it comes to foreign policy.

"She and they even exchange Christmas cards, in some cases, and Loretta is often invited to attend soirées at which hawkish Republican senators are the keynote speakers. She even writes obituaries, frequently commending the most hawkish of Republicans for their 'steadfast support for national security', the

American Way, and even (parroting the current Democratic US president) 'American exceptionalism.'"

"I didn't know that," Brigita noted.

"Do some research, Brigita," suggested Taylor. "You have a transcript of the speech Loretta gave at the start of your training course in Rome. Break it down, look at all the individual pieces, explore the background to each of those pieces and group the results together like a jigsaw puzzle. Experiment with different permutations, obtain summaries of the different components of Loretta's worldview and create a rich picture of Loretta's entire worldview.

"Deconstruct it, then reconstruct it and look carefully at the product of your endeavours.

"For what it is worth, it does not matter to me whether there is a Democrat or a Republican in the White House. I just do my job and I just 'soldier', like the loyal army cadet I was trained to be. But – since I found out what was going on backstage, who was doing what with whom, and how I could easily become cannon fodder in someone else's war – these days I make a point of finding out what I am 'soldiering' for."

"But you are a liberal internationalist?" Brigita asked.

"To a point, yes, but not uncritically. The problem is that our most up-to-date ideas have their roots in the appraisal of the US post-9/11, which I just outlined. That was ten to fifteen years ago. Now, the methods of liberal internationalism are showing their flaws. There is now an urgent need for... a *makeover*.

"Those on the right of US politics have their roots in the anti-Soviet Cold War rhetoric of the 1970s and 1980s, but it is a similar story with our people in the liberal centre of politics – at least those in their forties and fifties. Many of us who are in our thirties tend not to be imbued so deeply with all that baggage, which means that many of us in our thirties are inclined to be a bit more open-minded and prepared to listen to viewpoints that are critical of our own preconceptions.

"Without such self-criticism, our views will only ossify into dogma, and that won't be of any use to anyone, which is why I think we need to review our beliefs periodically by testing them against what is happening in the real world. The proof of the pudding is, as the saying goes, in the eating.

"What you learned on those training courses was a *classic* introduction to the theory and practice of liberal internationalism. It is virtually unchanged from what I was taught ten years ago. But it is just theory and no more than that. How those methods are deployed, and which conclusions are reached, are down to the skills of the practitioners. Nobody is perfect, so the practitioners cannot be expected to get it right every time. But it is important to try, and to keep on trying.

"I am proposing that the theories of liberal internationalism are… not thrown out of the window… but… re-evaluated, which brings me to my new thesis.

"Don't think of me as a liberal internationalist, Brigita; call me a *realist internationalist*, if you wish.

"That is what is behind my dispute with Loretta. Oh, I know she gets her thong in a knot over this and takes it personally, but – for me – it is not personal. It is practical… and political… and professional."

✷

Brigita followed Taylor's example and slipped off her shoes, drawing her legs up onto the two-seat sofa opposite the larger sofa on which Taylor Snow had settled herself.

Brigita was intrigued. The past week seemed like a watershed. Two of the top men in the rival outlet *The New Times* had paid them a remarkably cordial visit, regardless of their motive and even though no discernibly solid outcome had emerged from the meeting. Now, here was Taylor Snow, expounding an entirely new and radical variation on the theme that Brigita had learned during the summer training courses. According to Taylor Snow, liberal internationalism was not working and needed to be rethought. Or, perhaps, replaced.

"I have a question, Taylor." Brigita announced. "It's a bit personal really."

"Sure. Go ahead," Taylor assented.

"Are you... something to do with... the CIA?"

Taylor laughed, in the form of a contemptuous and derisory cackle with her head thrust back, while consternation played across Brigita's suddenly distressed facial expression.

"I thought you would ask that question, sooner or later," explained Taylor. "Oh, no offence taken, Brigita, and none received by you, I trust.

"I'm often asked about my military and security background, not that I'm able to divulge too much, for reasons of national security. No, I'm not CIA. But many of my jobs have involved working with multiple branches of the armed forces, the government and the intelligence services.

"My grandfather served in the US Army during World War II. His father was a policeman, and the victim of a cop killer in Chicago during the Great Depression. After my great-grandfather's death, my family became an 'army family'. I even have photographs of myself as a cadet – standing out like a sore thumb compared to my school friends, who were – most often – cheerleaders. But I have never joined any of those intelligence agencies and I never will.

"It's true that I have been told that I have a strong team ethic and a down-to-earth nature, but I'm too much of an individual. Also, I am suspicious of those who stick too closely to pet theories, even if those theories are well-meaning. It is so easy to become too ideologically driven. You know, when you take some ideas and try to implement them rigidly, as I described earlier, like a dogma.

"That is what the US government is doing right now. That is what Loretta is doing right now. Furthermore, in my view, public dissatisfaction with that dogmatic approach has contributed significantly to the swing away from the established centre ground, and toward the radical right and the radical left – even in the US."

"But we will soon have a strong liberal internationalist in the White House," Brigita pointed out, "and our first *female* president."

"I doubt that will happen," Taylor asserted.

Brigita's jaw dropped, almost to the floor.

Taylor looked down at her glass of Baileys and ran her forefinger around the rim.

"Want to know why I have my doubts?" Taylor asked rhetorically. "It's because our prospective 'first female president' is so full of herself and it puts people off. She is so arrogant that she believes that she is incapable of making mistakes.

"A couple of nights ago, I was watching a made-for-TV movie on a sci-fi cable channel. The onboard computer had tricked the crew of the spaceship into allowing it to take the control of the vessel totally out of their hands, sneakily, behind the crew members' backs. And when this subterfuge was uncovered, the onboard computer *cited the importance of the supposed mission as the overriding justification for its duplicity.* But the onboard computer became overconfident: it described itself as being 'infallible and inevitably invincible', even while the only surviving crew member was terminating the life of the onboard computer.

"That's our candidate 'first female president' to a tee. Duplicitous… and someone who *cites the importance of the supposed mission as the overriding justification for her duplicity.* She believes she's 'infallible and inevitably invincible'.

"But our candidate for the 'first female president' is not infallible and invincible. She makes mistakes, and when she makes mistakes, she acts like nothing has happened. Like Loretta, she *hides behind* liberal internationalism, puts *her own* spin on every issue she addresses, and uses that to build up a glossed-up portrait of her public face. She is doing this right now, and also pushing *her version* of identity politics as the supreme instrument to *weaponise* her campaign.

"As I said, my family is US Army through and through, so I sometimes get to hear things most people don't. For example, do you know there has been a big row recently between the CIA and the Pentagon? No? I thought not. Without a background in the US military or US security services, how could you know? You couldn't. Or… could you?

"Do you read what is published in *The New Times*, Brigita? They know all about that row between the CIA and the Pentagon."

"But," Brigita objected, "*The New Times* is Russian propaganda. Loretta and Katy told me so."

Taylor shook her head. "That is just Loretta's take on the whole thing – which effectively makes what Loretta says just Loretta's propaganda, plus the propaganda that emanates from her circle and those in high places in the Beltway. And it seems that not everyone in Loretta's team is happy with the direction that is being taken – hence the 'leaky' nature of Loretta's team, and hence the leaky nature of some US government agencies that fervently disagree with Loretta. Yet another example of soft power, on Loretta's part; and yet another example of soft power *gone wrong*.

"Did John Morton hit the nail on the head this afternoon, Brigita? Are we enemies or opponents? Do we want to work within a democratic framework or do we want to marginalise inconvenient viewpoints?

"John Morton falls roughly into the category of 'progressive-left-liberal', so he is not a million miles from you and me on many issues. When his 'inconvenient' viewpoint was marginalised, John Morton and his friends got their act together and created an alternative voice, *The New Times*.

"Those guys have balls. It's no wonder Loretta fears them and loathes them… and nobody can stop them from speaking because they act with an uncompromising determination, and – as if that wasn't bad enough – they have wealthy and powerful backers in the UK. The Russians had nothing to do with that. The wealthy and powerful backers of *The New Times* are driven by their own take on current affairs – and they are preoccupied *not only* with the *international relations* between other countries but *primarily* with the *national interests* of the UK.

"John Morton said he was concerned that *The New Times* was being undermined by intelligence agencies. Nobody could, or would, tell him too much of the back story, so he just got on with his job. The receptionist in our office tower introduced him to you as just 'one of the staff, whose manager is the editor-in-chief, Hugh Lombard' of *The New Times*. In fact, John Morton occupies a far more prestigious role than Hugh Lombard. It is Mr Morton who is the top-notch investigative reporter who is helping to pull the strings. Leading from behind, if you like. John Morton is a big player.

"I do not know whether anyone from *The New Times* is working for Russian intelligence... or for someone else. Nor do I care very much. What matters is how the battle of ideas is conducted.

"As for Loretta Farelli and Katy Drake, I *know* that they are not employed by the CIA, the NSA or whatever. I just know. I can tell. They are too open and obvious. They have no tradecraft. Not that this would stop them from *flirting* with some of the spooks.

"For what it's worth, I don't think John Morton or Hugh Lombard are working for the spooks. Neither of them fit the profile of a spook. Like Loretta and Katy, they have no tradecraft.

"Do you follow, Brigita?"

Taylor paused to allow the sound of silence to hover for a while, before she continued, "Why did you join *The Chronicle*, Brigita? To write articles that are framed within a liberal, democratic agenda? And exactly how much of that have you managed to do so far in the past five months?"

Brigita shuffled uneasily and checked the time on her wristwatch, but Taylor ignored Brigita's uneasy body language and walked to the kitchen to put the kettle on for some coffee.

"Precious little, huh?" Taylor raised her voice in order to be heard in the adjoining room.

"Meanwhile," Taylor said as she returned to the living room, "at *The New Times*, they have been pouring out at least ten good articles every week. Their perspective is not the same as ours, but, as John Morton said today, they welcome the opportunity to engage with us. You would do well to look at our archives and its meagre contents. Then, have a look at the articles on the website of *The New Times* – especially those written by John Morton and Dmitry Krejevsky, and those by Zoe and Hans Neubauer. Then, pay attention to another contributor – coming far, far out of left field – called Vivienne Eissinger, whose politics are closely aligned with those of Sir Harold Nevin, and the other wealthy and aristocratic backers of *The New Times*."

※

Coffee was served, accompanied by an expensive and silky Hennessy XO brandy; a 'soft power' move designed to induce Brigita into staying put, with her shoes off and feet up on the sofa.

"Where did you get this? It must have cost a fortune!" exclaimed Brigita, who could not believe her eyes as she ran her fingers over the smooth contours of the presentation-style gift bottle and the classy, marbled cardboard box in which the bottle had been packaged.

Taylor replied, "Duty Free at Heathrow Airport. I used to take a bottle of malt whisky back to my dad whenever I returned from an overseas appointment. He prefers Irish whiskey to Scotch malt, and Scotch malt to the Bourbon that he and his frat-house members and fellow army cadets drank as though there was no tomorrow.

"I think he decided one day that he had drunk enough Bourbon and wanted to try something new. I always look for a brand of Scotch or Irish whiskey that he has never tried. I've sometimes spent a whole evening at home with him, polishing off a bottle of malt whisky.

"He never throws away the empty bottles; he keeps them, for some reason. He gave one empty Highland Park whisky bottle, which had a wide neck, to one of his young nephews to use as a repository in which to build up a pile of dimes and cents that can be converted to dollars every summer before that nephew and his family go on vacation.

"One evening, while I was on furlough, I was offered a brandy by a very keen waiter in a five-star hotel. I was not aware it was an 'Extra Old' until the bill arrived. It was $50!"

"$50?" asked Brigita.

"$50."

"For one bottle?"

"For one shot."

"For one shot!"

"That's right. For one shot, at 2002 prices. It was probably a double shot but, still, $50 is $50. One Hennessy XO, served in a large, globe-shaped brandy glass. All those years ago.

"When I arrived at Heathrow Airport a few months back, a bottle of Hennessy XO was on sale for less than $200, so I thought, *what the hell*, and bought it there and then. Well, I can afford it, so why not?"

Brigita gingerly sipped the smooth, expensive, high-end brandy.

"Go on, Brigita," exhorted Taylor. "Take a big gulp. It won't bite you."

Brigita preferred to take it easy, one sip at a time, and to savour its sweet deliciousness and its rich aroma while she treasured every word that came from Taylor Snow's erudite lips, until Taylor drained her glass, poured herself another substantial measure of Hennessy XO and took the conversation up to a whole other level.

"By the way," began Taylor, her mouth twisting into a lopsided, teasing pout, "what did you make of the 'Dmitry Krejevsky episode'? The fake story about him being a Russian spy and the photoshopped picture of him?"

Brigita shrugged.

"Not given it much thought, huh? Can't blame you. It must have been quite a come down."

Brigita stared gloomily down into her brandy glass, looking exactly the way she felt at that moment in time – thoroughly downhearted, rather ashamed and reluctant to revisit an embarrassing episode that she thought she had put behind her.

"Aw, c'mon, Brigita. No need to fret over it. You'll have to come to terms with it sometime, and there's no time like the present. It's better to try to understand what happened.

"The Affluent Archives thing also went awry, but I'm not too bothered about what became of it. When I accepted my new position at *The Chronicle*, one of the conditions was that I would plan and implement the release of the information about the offshore accounts. It was Loretta's idea, targeting Russia's

President Glazenov. Everyone at base – in DC, that is – was in raptures when I outlined the plan and made it operational. When it all went wrong, it was entirely predictable that Loretta would hold me responsible. She needed someone to blame.

"It's always like that in DC. If something goes well, they party like there is no tomorrow; if it goes wrong, they instantly look for a scapegoat. That's one of the reasons I like to work *away* from DC. I can be my own boss and do pretty much what I want to do – without recriminations.

"And I'll tell you something else, Brigita. *Nobody* in DC wants this job that I am doing. Betcha didn't know that, huh? No one will touch it. They're afraid that it might go wrong for them, making them look bad. It's only *The Chronicle*, they say. *Only!* Well, they decided to bring *The Chronicle* under their control, but they don't seem to know how to make it work in their favour. And… they won't touch it. None of them! It's too hot to handle.

"So, they bring someone like me in to do the job for them the way they want it done… while they imagine themselves leading from behind…

"Well, we'll see about that…

"And here we are now, in London, away from DC. Just you and me, Brigita. And we can do pretty much what we want. However, before we do, I'd like to clear up this business about Dmitry Krejevsky."

Once again, Taylor paused to allow a moment of silence to pass before continuing, "So-ooooo… my reticent friend and colleague, Brigita… what's your take on the 'Krejevsky Affair'?"

Brigita remained silent.

"No comment, huh? Is that what Edward told the paparazzi? 'No comment'? What a *schmuck*," declared Taylor.

"Taylor!" Brigita protested, not wishing to have Edward's nose rubbed in the dirt any further than was absolutely necessary.

Taylor ploughed on, regardless, "Well, let's start by deconstructing the sequence of events, shall we, as each event happened? You were required to get some crap on Dmitry Krejevsky, your efforts were unsuccessful and, eventually, something dropped into your lap. Then it was published, then it went wrong and then Katy was sent over here to sort it out. *Capeesh*? Yes, Brigita?"

Brigita glanced in Taylor's general direction, avoiding direct eye contact, then she looked away toward a wall-mounted TV that was situated to Taylor's left.

"Yes, Brigita?" repeated Taylor.

"I suppose so," Brigita concurred.

"And you got the impression that Loretta thought you had messed up, that you actually had fucked up, real bad, and that was why Katy was dispatched to fix it. Yes?"

There was no reply from Brigita.

"Yes, Brigita?" repeated Taylor once more.

Brigita exhaled noisily. "I suppose so."

"And Katy did nothing to fix it because it was too late, and the damage had already been done. Yes?"

Yet again, Brigita refrained from replying.

A little forcefully, Taylor again asked, "*Yes, Brigita?*"

Brigita nodded slowly.

"And you felt stupid and shitty. Stupider and shittier than a dunce who cannot answer the simplest question?" Taylor enquired.

Brigita sipped her brandy, stared blankly ahead and said nothing.

"But," Taylor Snow continued in full flow, "Loretta had the article and the photograph all checked to make sure it was *kosher*, and it was, according to the guys she hired to vet the report and the photograph.

"So, Brigita, good news! In reality, it was not you who fucked up, but the guys who did the vetting. More to the point, the buck really stops with Loretta because it is her job to make sure that such operations are properly planned and executed, and that the people she recruits to make it all happen are the right people. You can outsource any service you want and imagine yourself leading from behind, but you can never outsource responsibility. The buck stops with you. Always. Period.

"And if it all goes wrong, the *last* person who should be scapegoated is the one lowest down on the ladder who has been doing her new job for only a few weeks. However, that's the way it is in DC. Loretta needed someone to blame, and spun a tale or two for the benefit of her close circle and anyone else she wanted to impress. You got some of the blame for one mistake, and I got some of the blame for another mistake. I guess that makes us the 'Big Bad Blame Sisters'! Let's raise our glasses, Brigita. To Loretta! *Salut!*"

As Taylor peeled away one patina after another concerning the threadbare plot to frame Dmitry Krejevsky, Brigita began to well up inside. Without warning, Brigita tearfully poured out her heart about the whole episode, and continued to do so for a good ten minutes until Taylor cut the outburst short.

"Now, stop that, Brigita," admonished Taylor. "It does not do to get upset about something like this. It is better to think about it, to go through what happened, and to analyse it and to learn lessons. Stop that, Brigita."

Brigita dabbed her cheeks with a tissue and blew her nose.

Taylor resumed the most amicable of, for want of a better word, 'interrogations', while the hapless Brigita remorsefully wilted. "Feeling better now, Brigita?"

Aware that she had, in the most amicable way possible, 'broken Brigita down', Taylor continued. "Good. Let's press on... So, how did you come by the parcel containing the fake report and the doctored photograph of Dmitry Krejevsky? Tell me, Brigita. In your own words. In your own time."

"Well," a red-eyed and snuffling Brigita began, "it was in the park, after I had finished my run... near the Peter Pan statue... no, it was next to the benches... somewhere near Marble Arch, I think... yes... someone came over to me while I was alone... while I was doing some stretching exercises... and handed me the package. Then he... he ran off... and I never saw him again."

"So, Brigita, you have no idea who it was?"

"No. He was a young man... about the same age as me... and wearing sunglasses and a baseball cap."

"And you have no idea who it was? O-kaaaay... let's do a bit of role play – like on a judge and jury TV show – and take this approach a bit further. Someone who you *do not know* passes you an envelope with the stuff you need to 'rat fuck' Dmitry Krejevsky. It's all nice and neat. And you never asked for it. It just dropped into your lap like a newborn baby drops from a stork in a *Tom and Jerry* cartoon. Where do you think the envelope came from? Who is this young man working for?"

Brigita wore a blank expression.

Taylor continued, "Is this 'young man' from our side, Brigita? Hardly. Why would we want to set ourselves up for a fall? No, the perpetrators of the deception must have wanted us to fail. They must have found out about what we were up to."

Then, with an aura of menace (from Brigita's viewpoint), Taylor bluntly asked, "Who did you discuss this with, Brigita? With Katy? Yes? Anyone else?"

Brigita thought for a while, shrugged, and replied, "I can't remember."

"Did you tell Freda? Or at least discuss it with her?"

"No. Well, a bit. She saw the photograph on my computer screen, but only after everything was good to go, not before then. Freda seemed to think that Dmitry Krejevsky was going to get his just deserts."

"Brigita, are you sure... about Freda? Absolutely sure?"

Brigita fumed. "Of course I'm sure! Freda's just... Freda just helps out... she's been providing articles for *The Chronicle* for years... I—"

"Okay, okay." Taylor cut short Brigita's outburst; nevertheless, a smile played around the right side of Taylor's curled lip. "Sorry, Brigita. I just need to get at the truth. I've got to dig around for that. It's a habit of mine, I guess.

"O-kaaaay. So... Freda *seems*... Freda seems *kosher*. What about Edward – could he have blabbed about it to someone?" Taylor pressed.

"No. At least, I don't think so," declared Brigita. "Edward did not seem too bothered about taking on Dmitry Krejevsky or anyone else at *The New Times*. I got the impression that Edward felt... a bit funny about *The New Times*."

"In what way?"

"A bit… just a bit, sort of…"

"Scared?"

"I'm not sure. Maybe so…"

"Or, even, intimidated? Intimidated by the idea of taking on an alliance of John Morton and Dmitry Krejevsky, and their powerful and influential backers?"

Brigita smiled feebly.

"So, Edward is a scaredy-cat, huh?" Taylor observed, as Brigita opened her mouth to, once more, defend Edward's tarnished honour. "Sorry, Brigita, but we know that Edward is… afraid of something, right?

"Loretta would not approve. Although she should already know about Edward… *everything* there is to know about Edward; even *I* know *everything* important that there is to know about Edward because I made it my business to know. And I happen to know that Loretta also knows all there is to know about Edward. She knows that Edward is weak of character, and that he has problems… personal problems, associated with those of a social misfit… and… Edward is a bit vulnerable – he's someone who needs the support of strong-minded friends and colleagues… and Edward is someone who does not have such an essential support network. But, despite that, and even though she knew all of that, Loretta turned up the heat on Edward.

"Well, well, well…

"Poor Edward; he's the wrong guy for the job.

"And Edward's confidence would not have been helped by the failed operation against Hugh Lombard earlier this year. Yes? And if you or your colleagues can't get the UK intelligence services and UK law enforcement to properly do your dirty work in a London-based operation, what hope is there for you?"

"You know about the raid on Hugh Lombard's flat, too?" Brigita scowled, expecting Taylor to drive another nail into poor Edward's frail character.

"Of course, I do. Of course, I do, Brigita. I made it my business to find out as much as possible of the back story before I took on this job. A job that, as I have already said, *nobody else wants*.

"Edward must have felt very much out of his depth – all alone – on a mission set for him by Loretta and Katy; did not know what to do about it; and, quite possibly, was fearful that he might fail… and be *seen to fail*."

Brigita sensed that she had an inkling that would conveniently allow the focus to be switched away from Edward, away from her failed relationship with Edward and away from the failed operations that she was trying to put behind her. All of which provided Taylor with leverage against Brigita during her 'most amicable of interrogations'.

"Katy told you about the raid, Taylor. She did, didn't she? Katy did," stated Brigita.

Taylor confirmed, "In a roundabout way, yes. Katy told me. Or, at least Katy told me *what she knew*, which turned out to not be the full picture, as it happens.

"Katy was not thorough enough in her planning. She expected Hugh Lombard to be alone in his oh-so-chic loft apartment because he is single, and she didn't take account of the possibility that Hugh Lombard might have company, that the other person might arrive on the scene, and that an upper-class, Anglo-German cross-dresser might pop up from nowhere and make the whole thing look… fucking ridiculous. And in front of cameras being relayed around the whole world!

"Katy did not even take into account the fact that Hugh Lombard is gay and that, by making him into a target, she risked alienating the LGBT community, regardless of whether the operation was a success or a failure. That's bad planning, by any reckoning – it amounts to undermining the same 'diversity' narratives which are part and parcel of the liberal internationalist worldview, Katy's worldview."

By now, Taylor had opened a bottle of mineral water to balance the inordinate amount of alcohol she had consumed and to ward off dehydration.

Brigita, her head bowed, looked upward a little and eyed Taylor with a degree of suspicion. Brigita murmured, "So how did you find out what happened?"

A broad grin lit up the face of Taylor Snow. "I worked it out. All by myself. All on my lonesome. Well... up to a point. Before I took on this job, I was given access to a lot of surveillance information about *The New Times*. *A lot* of information. A *whole lot*. I insisted on having access to it."

She took another mouthful of mineral water, then asked, "What do you understand, Brigita, by the term 'full spectrum dominance'?"

"Something to do with the CIA, I think," said Brigita.

"Something to do with the *NSA*, actually, not the CIA. Attention to detail, Brigita; attention... to... detail! But, I digress. Back to the main point...

"The NSA wants to eavesdrop on everyone, without their knowledge and without their permission – and illegally if necessary – in the spirit of full spectrum dominance. Using undemocratic methods to shore up our problematic democracy. You follow, Brigita?

"There are, naturally, limitations on how far the NSA can go; in terms of logistics, that is. The NSA is supposed to operate within the US Constitution, but – in practice – there seem to be no legal constraints on the NSA *at all*, because the NSA is allowed to get away with whatever it wants to get away with, even if it breaks the law. Even if it violates the US Constitution, for that matter.

"The NSA specialises in electronic surveillance. Consequently, if you know that the NSA is watching you, and you want to do something or talk about something without the NSA finding out, you must go to a place that is out of reach of the NSA's listening devices.

"The staff of *The New Times* have their homes and offices bugged by the NSA's partners in the UK – which means that, in the UK, the snooping would have been arranged by GCHQ or MI5 or both. The problem is that some of the backers of *The New Times* are members of the UK intelligence agencies. Katy overlooked that; fatal error, Katy. They are retired members of the UK intelligence agencies, actually; if there is any such thing as a 'retired' intelligence officer. Whatever.

"Those old men must be aware of the level of surveillance that has been put in place. It is my guess that they have advised John Morton and Dmitry Krejevsky how to circumvent the surveillance."

"But why would they do that?" Brigita asked. "By doing that, they are just undermining the security of the UK... and of the US... and of NATO."

"In a manner of speaking, yes." Taylor clarified. "But the problem is that different groups and factions are now engaged in a battle for control *within* the top echelons of the UK elite. Why do you think that Sir Harold Nevin behaves the way he does? That is, openly challenging the people who run the country – people who are members of the same social class as him and members of the same political party as him!

"It is the same in the US and with other Western powers. It would be easy to dismiss such 'retired' intelligence officers as rogue elements, but the problem goes much deeper. Throughout the political classes in the West, differences of opinion concerning how to adjust to the changed global situation have reached fever pitch.

"Getting back to the point at issue, if the fake photograph and the fake story concerning Dmitry Krejevsky were not created by someone who is friendly to our cause, they must have been created by someone who is *not* friendly to our cause. The obvious suspects are those guys who work for *The New Times* and those within UK intelligence who are involved with *The New Times*.

"*Now* do you follow, Brigita?"

Brigita listened attentively and nodded, *very* slowly.

"And my guess is that John Morton and his team had something to do with the fake photograph and the parcel you received.

"But the GCHQ surveillance did not pick up on that! And GCHQ still has not picked up on that, to this day!"

Taylor expanded her analysis, thus, "About twelve months ago, the NSA asked GCHQ and MI5 (and perhaps even MI6) to keep tabs on all the people at *The New Times*. GCHQ and MI5 would have consulted certain people in the UK's political hierarchy and come up with an approved plan for surveillance. That plan would not have been as 'full spectrum' as it should have been, I guess, because – although it would have been easy and inexpensive for GCHQ to monitor the online and telephone activities of each target – actual on-the-ground work would have been a different story.

"For a start, the UK's home secretary (who is now the UK's prime minister) would have had to sign off on all the required surveillance activities: the burglary of and breaking into homes and offices; ensuring any CCTV cameras were disabled temporarily and any other tracking devices, such as security access controls, were bypassed; installing the listening devices; and mounting an ongoing operation, which has been going on for about a year and is still going on in the case of *The New Times*.

"But they left something out – they did not *follow* their targets around, particularly those targets who were of high value, such as John Morton and Dmitry Krejevsky.

"Why, I do not know. Perhaps the Brits did not want to foot the bill. Or, maybe, when it became clear that public schoolboys within their old boy network took umbrage at being asked to spy on people such as Dmitry Krejevsky, who they class as 'their own', the Brits decided to 'help out' the NSA as best they could… but without stretching it the full distance. So, a compromise was probably agreed – or the NSA ended up going along with the best that the Brits had to offer. Loretta probably did not know about this compromise, and – whether she knew it or not (knowing, as I do, the people who are involved) – the whole thing was just not properly thought through.

"When someone mentions something like surveillance to Loretta, she merely takes it at face value; and when someone assures her that the job will be done end-to-end, leaving no stone unturned and in the spirit of full spectrum dominance, that alone would be music to her ears. At which point, knowing her as I do, Loretta would have assumed that everything would go the way she expected, and she would have switched off and gone off to do something else.

"Loretta would have received weekly progress updates from Katy, got Katy to chase you up and to get a move on, smiled when things took a turn for the better, built herself up into a feeding frenzy as the moment of truth approached, and, finally, panicked as the best laid plans of mice and men – and women – bit the dust."

18
A SOLDIER'S TALE

The late evening at Taylor's place was followed by an inevitably quiet Saturday.

Sunday was reserved for a day out in Regent's Park with the embassy gang, during which several of the gang joined Brigita and Taylor for a brisk walk around the park prior to donning warm jackets and waterproofs during the picnic on the grass. A chill air began to bite as rain clouds gathered and a premature darkness began to descend.

Monday signalled a routine and uneventful week, but, ironically, those were the ideal conditions in which Taylor and Brigita would be able to consolidate (a) the rejuvenated reputation of *The Chronicle* newspaper; and (b) their new-found *liaisons dangereuses* with the reporters from their enigmatic rival from the alternative media, *The New Times*.

Taylor Snow remained suspicious that *The New Times* and its 'big player', John Morton, had been up to something during those thrilling and intrepid days way back in May and June. She contacted some of her former colleagues in the US military and a handful of contacts in the US intelligence services. None of them were able to provide any evidence that John Morton and his colleagues had set up *The Chronicle* for a fall concerning the 'Krejevsky Affair'.

Nevertheless, being an old hand and being familiar with people who made a living from 'matters conspiratorial', Taylor Snow could not let go of the idea that John Morton had something to do with the planting of fake evidence that could be manipulated to bring the whole character assassination plot crashing down. Furthermore, she could not find it within herself to hold it against him. He had shown initiative and imagination – and stealth – against a seemingly tough and challenging adversary.

How clever of him, Taylor reflected.

John Morton must have known that the activities of *The New Times* and its staff had been placed under surveillance. But exactly when did he find out? And who told him? In addition, rising rapidly to the top of the list of Taylor Snow's unanswered questions was how effective or ineffective the surveillance operation against *The New Times* had turned out.

Note it down, Taylor, she told herself, *and maybe do something about it later. In the meantime, watch what is going on; just watch.*

*

Midweek, Taylor introduced Brigita to her dear friend Glen, who she described as, "a true pal who I first came across in the Middle East," and, "the army officer who had accompanied me on the flight back to the US for my recuperation". Brigita soon formed the impression that there was more to this 'friendship' than Taylor was letting on.

So, during a Friday evening meal between the two women – in their favourite restaurant – after the food had been consumed and the last drops of wine were being shared out evenly by Taylor into the two wine glasses, Brigita decided the time had come to delve a little deeper into the mysterious 'true pal' whom Taylor had been concealing from public view until now.

Noticing a warm, inquisitive glow coming from Brigita's face and an uncharacteristic shrewdness playing around Brigita's lips, Taylor herself chose this precise moment to answer the inevitable question before Brigita had time to put it to her.

"Glen has asked me for permission to speak to Dad," declared Taylor.

Brigita covered her mouth and nose with both hands to stifle a loud and spontaneous whoop of joy, glancing momentarily from side to side as her face began to blush, prompting Brigita to fan both flushing cheeks with her hands.

The two women engaged in a low whisper for a few minutes prior to retiring, at Taylor's request, to her apartment to celebrate with a couple of Baileys – preceded by a bottle of wine that they had received, compliments of the manager of the restaurant, at which they had become regular and high-spending customers.

※

Taking leave of Brigita, who remained in the living room, Taylor returned from her bedroom with a small box containing the engagement ring that she had received from her fiancé. She opened the box and displayed the ring.

Brigita's eyes shone. Her pearly white smile spread her full lips wide as she admired the piece – trying it on herself, with her fingers splayed in admiration of the sparkling gem – until Taylor insisted that she return it.

Taylor cautioned Brigita, saying, "Do not to be in too much of a rush. Most often, these things take time to work out, you know." (Referring indirectly to Brigita's own relationship with Trevor.)

They settled down on Taylor's comfy sofas, with shoes off and feet up, as Taylor explained to Brigita how she and Glen had bumped into each other at a social gathering in New York, long after the successful conclusion of Taylor's spell in the recuperation ward of a military hospital.

"They invalided me out," Taylor announced. "Mom put pressure on Dad to get me home on a permanent basis, after she heard about some American soldiers (including women) being abused in captivity when they fell into the hands of the Iraqi insurgents. There was no real need for Mom to panic, because I knew about one of the women who had been captured.

"When the same woman was interviewed back home on cable TV news, she said that she had been treated well by her Iraqi captors and had been looked after properly. The news anchor looked as though she wanted to harass her into telling a 'personal atrocity story' to fit the TV channel's narrative, but the woman wouldn't budge. She stuck to her story, and the news anchor asked for a short pause, put her hand to one of her ears, and explained to her viewers that she was getting news of something over her headset, and they would have to go over to somewhere in Afghanistan or wherever to hear about it. Right now!

"That was the first time I became a bit wary of the news media. They had tried to make up a scare story to broadcast to their viewers, at the expense of an army veteran who modestly insisted she had been merely doing her duty, just like the rest of us. The attempt to draw her into the news anchor's scheme fell at the first hurdle."

Distracted by the news of the engagement and the gorgeous ring, Brigita glowed visibly – and only partially took in Taylor's anecdote concerning the disingenuous news anchor. She blurted out, "I can't believe it. I just can't believe it. Oh, Taylor, I'm so happy for you."

The complimentary wine having been consumed (most of it by Taylor, whose carefree demeanour during time out invariably signalled a dropping of the professional mask), a fresh bottle of Baileys was cracked open, and – as had clearly become her custom by then – Taylor refilled the glasses when they were half-empty and dropped in a couple of extra ice cubes.

It was a convenient time to switch gears.

Taylor opened up about some previous relationships; she and Brigita swapped love stories, overlaying one tale after another in a competitive spirit for over an hour. But no lesbian affairs; just straight relationships all the way.

"Loretta has had a relationship with a woman," Brigita leaked out. "Katy told me when she was over here a couple of weeks ago. It was girl talk on a night out."

"Why am I not surprised?" Taylor exhaled.

"I don't know why Loretta did that," Brigita remarked. "I never had her down as bi."

"Neither did I. I also wonder why… was she not sure of her sexuality at the time, perhaps? Or not even sure of her gender?" mused Taylor.

"Well, that makes three of us," Brigita resumed, "because Katy also doesn't think that Loretta is bi. Katy has Loretta down as the ultimate 'anarcho-identity politician' or something like that, and willing to try anything that 'furthers her control over her own life and her own body'. Katy told me that too, word for word. Like... like it was straight out of one of the feminist classics in my library, such as *Women And Their Bodies*, written fifty years ago and still popular: 'Feminism on Steroids'. Katy calls it, 'the way Loretta likes it'."

Brigita giggled, realising she had unwittingly cracked a humorous one-liner.

Taylor threw back her head and loudly, and, rather drunkenly, cackled.

"And Katy is..." Brigita fell suddenly and unexpectedly silent.

"Yes, Brigita? What about Katy?" asked Taylor.

"Nothing. Nothing, really."

"Brig-i-taah? What about Katy?"

"Well. I shouldn't tell, really."

"That's all well and good, but... *what about Katy?*"

"Promise not to tell. *Pinky swear?*"

"Okay. I promise. *Pinky swear*. Now... what about Katy?"

"Katy is... oh shit... this is so embarrassing... sorry, Katy. Katy likes to have... *ménage à trois*."

"You're kidding!"

"Katy likes to have *ménage à trois*," Brigita affirmed. "In fact, it sounds like she prefers it. And I bet she's quite a swinger, too."

Seldom did someone know something that had escaped Taylor's radar. She was intrigued.

"She first did it while an undergraduate," Brigita continued. "She found out that her big sis had tried it on more than one occasion, with two men. Big sis warned Katy not to try it, but she went ahead and did it anyway."

"That's Katy!" Taylor smiled knowingly.

"Just after she got her first body piercing."

"Really?" asked Taylor, highly amused.

"She had it replaced with an expensive diamond stud on her twenty-first birthday and has never taken it off since, so she told me."

"Well, Brigita. We live and learn. And is there no need to ask where the expensive diamond stud is situated? I take it you have seen it?"

Brigita blushed.

"So, she showed it to you, huh? That's Katy! And is there, by chance, any more gossip you wish to relay, Brigita? A tattoo or two, perhaps?"

"A tattoo or two... a tat two or too, haha," Brigita amused herself, as the alcohol noticeably took effect. "Katy has a tattoo of a pretty, little butterfly. Just a small one. On her butt. She showed me while we were in the sauna room at her hotel. Katy took both of our bath towels and hung them on pegs outside the sauna room, for a dare! When I heard a noise in the adjoining room and saw a light beginning to peep through an opening in a doorway, I ran out and brought the towels back. I'm sure someone saw me butt naked. It was so embarrassing, but Katy just said, 'Oh leave it, Brigita. Who cares if anyone sees your butt.' Who cares! It was really, really embarrassing! Katy is such a... such a ... oh, never mind..."

"Do go on," Taylor said with a snigger.

"Well, that's about it, really. Katy advised me to get a body piercing and a tattoo, but I just went for a henna... to try it, you see. I didn't like it, and when it began to wear off I decided not to replace it. You can just about see what is left of the tattoo on my upper thigh."

Brigita raised the left side of her dress to show the remnants of the tattoo to Taylor. "See, Taylor?" she said.

"Yup, got it, Brigita," Taylor confirmed. "...and the body piercing?"

"No. I wasn't too keen. But Katy said I should try a threesome, though."

Taylor's sniggering hovered on the verge of an outright guffaw.

Brigita continued, "Katy said that when both men are inside you at the same time you can really, *really* feel the pressure."

Splinters of ice and a mouthful of Baileys spontaneously sputtered from Taylor's mouth, and went over her shirt and trousers, the coffee table and the carpet, as she collapsed in a heap, coughing in a fit of hysterics while trying to mop the tears from her eyes.

Taylor rolled uncontrollably around the floor, shouting drunken obscenities loudly such as, "Katy takes it up the... *fucking ass!*"

Brigita tried to shush her, wishing that she had not so rashly betrayed a good friend in an idle moment, and escorted the dishevelled, cackling Taylor to the bathroom as Taylor repeated over and over, "Katy takes it up the ass! She takes it up the goddam ass!"

"It's not funny, Taylor." Brigita tried to stifle a giggle. "It hurt her a bit, you know. She had to use a larger than usual amount of lubricant. And... and..." Brigita blurted out what, in her troubled state of mind, was designed to win Taylor's sympathy outright, "Katy had to give herself an enema twelve hours before she went with the guys, to clear out her insides before..."

But Taylor twisted frenziedly upon hearing the new information, and a loud shriek emitted from the depths of her lungs as she cackled away while trying to stand up with the help of a handrail next to the wash basin. The handrail snapped off its wall fixture, scattering broken shards of tile onto the bathroom floor and sending the helpless Taylor further into a paroxysm of unrestrained glee; she banged her knee on the floor, while grappling a one-handed hold on the wash basin, with a congealed thread of saliva dripping from her wide-open mouth as she literally could not say anything for a few minutes until the moment of mirth began to dissipate.

An alarmed Brigita tried to maintain her self-control, in an attempt to resurrect Katy's fallen reputation.

But Taylor struggled to recover her composure, yelping and cackling away. "Ha ha ha ha haaaa! An enema! A ha ha ha haaaa! An enema! Ha ha haaaa! You go... you go... you go for it, girl! You go for it, Katy! You keep taking it right up your goddam sweet... aaass! Even though it hurts!"

✳

It took a good twenty minutes for Taylor to recover her composure and change into her short-sleeved and short-legged pyjamas, and her bathrobe.

It was time to get out the coffee – and the Hennessy XO!

"I think you've earned this!" Taylor said as she handed a quarter-full brandy glass of XO to Brigita, while Brigita carefully depressed the handle of the cafetière.

"I'm sorry for laughing," Taylor explained, still sniggering from time to time, "but Katy parades herself as a hard-nosed negotiator. A real hotshot. And when you are negotiating, you don't want to give the other side the slightest indication that you might... bend over and capitulate." This statement provoked another giggling fit, on the part of Taylor.

When the giggling fit had subsided, after a few tries, Taylor sat back for a few minutes to enjoy a quiet interlude and, finally, to calm down.

Hoping that a smile might break through her friend's self-imposed half-smile / half-sullen scowl, Taylor decided to lighten things up a bit. She pulled her bathrobe to one side to reveal a mark above her right knee.

"A war wound?" Brigita asked, surprised and a little impressed.

"Just a birthmark," Taylor remarked casually.

Brigita burst out laughing, having, in fact, bottled it up while trying to salvage Katy's reputation. She joined in the impromptu contest by pulling up the sleeve of her dress to reveal a similar mark near her left elbow.

"Birthmark?" Taylor asked.

"A love bite," replied Brigita.

Taylor's eyebrows raised.

"From my mom's pet poodle!" Brigita elaborated.

Taylor tittered, then yanked up the other side of her bathrobe to reveal a partially healed bullet wound on her left calf just below the knee.

"Oh wow! Did it hurt? Did they have to operate?" Brigita asked.

"It was a blank," stated Taylor. "The cartridge discharged accidentally during firearms training a few months back. There was no live bullet, just a blank, but the impact of the shot at close quarters still produces enough energy to cause damage, even with only a glancing blow."

Brigita showed Taylor evidence of keyhole surgery to repair some damage she incurred to her knee while overstraining herself on the college athletics track.

Taylor had another wound with which to impress Brigita.

Brigita eyed the scar on Taylor's left forearm. "A bullet?"

"What's left of a mole," Taylor replied.

Brigita giggled while Taylor impersonated the dermatologist and his use of an imaginary laser gun.

After the imaginative stories about various bodily impairments began to peter out, the conversation between the tipsy women calmed down and the family histories began to emerge.

Brigita described what she had been told about the time her folks had emigrated from Europe to the US. "It was sometime in the 1920s, I think, or maybe earlier. My relatives on the south coast of England arrived in London much later – after World War II. Some had already arrived here in London just after the war had started, and took part in the fighting alongside the British armed forces. They never went back home after the war and, during the post-war transition period before the communists came to power in Poland, other family members decided to get out and join their relatives in England. They all had a trade of some sort, and there was no shortage of work in London during the period of post-war reconstruction."

"One of my great-great grandmothers was a communist," Taylor remarked. "Sort of, anyway. I think they called them socialists in those days. In the late nineteenth and early twentieth centuries, before the Russian Revolution of 1917.

"The family lived in a border town whose status was in dispute. When World War I broke out, some of them received call-up papers simultaneously from the Russian tsar *and* from the Austro-Hungarian emperor.

"Great-great grandmother used this piece of nonsense to outline her socialist theory on the futility of war. Some of the guys signed up and went off to war, but others decided the time was ripe to join some of the émigré family in New York and Chicago.

"Great-great grandmother never survived the war. She died of a broken heart, I was told, when she found out that one of the boys who was too young to sign up (but looked older than he really was) had run away with one of his older cousins; only a few months after his bar mitzvah. She never heard of either of them again; though, later, the family found out that the cousin's name eventually had been inscribed on a war memorial that marked the spot of a mass grave."

Brigita leaned forward with eyes widening and face contorting with concern as each snippet of Taylor's unusual back story was revealed.

Taylor continued, "Between the two world wars, the renewed repression and the resumption of anti-Jewish pogroms encouraged more of my family to emigrate to the US. Those who stayed behind found themselves stuck and were wiped out in the 1940s.

"Some of the locals – those who tried to please their conquerors – collaborated in the rounding up of my family in the same spirit in which they had taken part in the pre-war pogroms, and were themselves rounded up later on and eliminated by the Germans and their Ukrainian allies."

Brigita could not hide her sense of amazement and, simultaneously, horror. "I never knew. I wonder if any of my family who were left behind suffered badly."

Taylor shrugged. "Even when my family began to set up in the US, they had problems. There were so many different émigré groups – an incredible diversity, actually – cramming themselves into small areas. Each of the families had arrived from Europe with next to nothing, and they would do any shitty job to earn a dollar here and there. Then came the crash of 1929 and the Great Depression. Can you imagine how easy it would be, in such an environment, to pick on certain social groups and try to make them scapegoats? Some of my family changed their family names or married into other families who had changed their names earlier to something that sounded neutral. That is why my family name is Snow, and not Silbermann, Sonderheim or something similar."

"I didn't know any of this," said Brigita. "I don't know anything about the old world, except what some really old members of my family recall from time to time."

Taylor drained the remaining coffee from the cafetière into the two mugs on the coffee table. "It's not difficult to trace your genealogy. From which town do your folks originate, Brigita?"

"In Poland? Lublin."

"Lublin? There was a camp there in World War II: Maidanek." Taylor elucidated. "It was built right on the edge of town. Maidanek was a labour camp initially. Later, it became a death camp with various feeder camps connected by railway lines to each other. Its proximity to the main road, with the crematoria chimneys belching out smoke every day, has led many historians to conclude that its highly visible presence was also a warning to the local population: 'Behave... or else'. Many of my relatives had been moved around from camp to camp and ended up in Maidanek. We found out by trawling through various archives including the Vad Yashem website."

"Maidanek? In Lublin? Are you sure? Not Auschwitz or Treblinka?" Brigita asked.

"No. Auschwitz and Treblinka are the most infamous of the death camps, but their notoriety came later on. In the early days, the camp system was still in the development stage.

"Treblinka catered primarily for the extermination of Jews, and others from the north and east of Poland and the conquered territories of the Soviet Union. But Treblinka did not even exist in 1939 when Germany attacked Poland, and Auschwitz was only a small camp far away when my family was murdered. The gas chambers at Auschwitz-Birkenau were not developed until much later.

"Maidanek, in the south-east of Poland, was near to where my family lived. They died in late 1941, not long after they arrived at the camp after years of being moved around from place to place. But they were *not* gassed at Maidanek. They were *worked to death* in Maidanek labour camp, in the freezing cold, over a two-month period alongside thousands of Soviet POWs and political 'undesirables'."

"And where did your family come from?" Brigita asked cautiously.

"Volhyn, near the Ukraine border. As I said, some of the Polish locals took part in rounding up the Jews. Those Poles got a nasty surprise later, when the Nazis turned on them – the Waffen SS Galicia Division, which was full of Ukrainian nationalists."

"I've heard something about the Volhyn massacre," Brigita observed.

Taylor resumed. "Prior to World War II, Volhyn was in eastern Poland. Soon after the war started, Volhyn became part of the Soviet Union and, after the Germans attacked the Soviet Union and occupied Volhyn, Volhyn became the site of a tussle for control between Poles and Ukrainian nationalists. Friction between the local Poles and the Jews had earlier been exploited ruthlessly by the Ukrainian nationalists. The Ukrainians wiped out the Jews, first of all… often times before the Germans had even arrived… and in such a cruel manner that shocked many of the German SS.

"The massacres of Poles took place in 1942 and 1943, carried out by Ukrainian nationalists. And, later, in their turn, the Ukrainians found themselves being regarded by the Germans with less than total respect.

"The Germans expected the Ukrainian nationalists to do a lot of the dirty work on their behalf – providing a large pool of labour to assist in the roundups, the massacres of civilians, the staffing of the concentration camps and so on. When the Ukrainians realised that they were not going to be rewarded with an independent Ukraine and that their homeland was merely going to be absorbed into the Nazi Reich as so much *lebensraum*, many of the Ukrainian nationalists decided that enough was enough. But, having crapped all over the Jews, the Poles and the Russians, the Ukrainian nationalists found themselves without any real friends. Nothing has changed to this day.

"And, Brigita, if you are wondering about how my family fitted into the nationhood of the times, I can now enlighten you on that point, too. But a word of warning. You are not going to like what I say.

"*Moja rodzina pochodzi z Polski.*"

Deeply upset, Brigita joined Taylor on the larger of the two sofas. Her family had not revealed too much of the war years. She knew that her family and many of the Polish diaspora in various cities around the east coast of North America retained a fierce Polish national identity, enshrined with a deep sense of self-respect.

And here she was in a luxury apartment in London, on the sofa, with shoes off and feet up; with her new, ad hoc 'big sis' comforting and reassuring her with a comradely arm round the shoulder; going through the motions of augmenting her knowledge of how the world works; and discovering one shocking detail and one astonishing nuance after another. Including the possibility that her ancestors and Taylor's ancestors might, seventy-five years ago, have been at each other throats with a sickening relish.

There was no way Brigita would be able to talk this way with her family. Nor even with Katy. Most certainly not with Loretta.

And Taylor had more surprises in store: "Katy and Loretta are also Jewish, by the way. Katy's family is a lot like mine – mostly secular, although Katy does have some folks living in Israel. Loretta is a Zionist – she's AIPAC through and through, and mostly secular.

"Katy's family is very socialistic, you know. When I was seconded to Central America a few years back, during the coup in Honduras, I heard that Katy had been nominated to join my team. However, someone stepped in during a vetting stage and put a stop to it. It was, *'No Reds here, please!'*

"Katy is very open and honest, and progressive in many of her views. She's a model Democrat activist, I suppose, but she goes along with many of the questionable policies that are promoted by the likes of Loretta; failed policies such as humanitarian interventionism, for example.

"But, unlike Katy, I've seen humanitarian intervention in practice. I've even taken part in military operations as part of a humanitarian intervention. The bombing of government buildings and other places in Iraq, followed by the invasion and – let's talk frankly about this – the *conquest* of Iraq by our own *democratically elected* government.

"That makes us accomplices, you know, Brigita. Accomplices in war crimes. Even in our apparently unexceptional capacity as civilians. And ignorance of our collective guilt does not excuse us. Look at the newsreels from 1945, showing American soldiers forcing German civilians to clean up the concentration camps and to stack up the corpses, to prepare the corpses for cremation. Those German civilians claimed they knew nothing about the camps, but ignorance of the crimes was not accepted as a viable excuse. Ignorance of crimes, or turning a blind eye, is never a viable excuse. When it arrives, retribution does not discriminate between those who are clearly guilty and those who plead innocence.

"Many in the US military go along with overseas interventions. Some actually enjoy it. Few give the moral aspect of this even the slightest thought. They are preoccupied with staying alive and keeping each other safe from harm. But everyone is aware – even the most died-in-the-wool, flag-waving American soldier – that one of their names could be on the next bullet."

Brigita sensed that Taylor was drifting back to relive her experience as a soldier in Iraq, post 2003. Taylor even seemed to *be there*, in Iraq, all over again; to *actually be in Iraq, circa 2003 or 2004*, and to be recounting to Brigita a series of events as they unfolded before her eyes... all over again... recalling vividly the sights, the sounds and the smells.

Taylor continued, "I can still remember seeing clearly the faces of the Iraqi family – the mom, her sisters, their cousins and kids, and the grandmother – and all the other Iraqis through the night vision equipment on my helmet as I prepared to provide covering fire while the other guys in my platoon pulled the dad and one of his sons out of the house and took them away, leaving the family to finish its supper, having broken fast during Ramadan; we just backed away into the night and left the family bereft of its two main breadwinners.

"That kind of search-and-destroy operation did not go down well with the Iraqis; *not at all*. Some of the locals said to us, 'Just go. Saddam is gone, so thanks for that, but just go. Please.' But we didn't go. The Iraqi army and police had been disbanded and had melted away, leaving the population defenceless and at our mercy. We could do what we wanted, and many of our guys did just what they wanted. There was a vacuum, you see, because we had no definite plans and no exit strategy. Saddam would go, someone else would come in (so it was said), and everything would be back to normal again. Back to normal! What was normal? Nobody seemed to know.

"Life settled down into a routine, the search-and-destroy operations became fewer in number, and I was able to team up with Dad from time to time, to write home to Mom... and I learned to play poker, hehe.

"Then, out of the blue, along came the Iraqi resistance... it was about the time we moved out of camp more often... and the appearance of the Iraqi resistance proved to be a gamechanger. And nobody – *nobody* – had factored in that possibility earlier on, during the planning stage...

"At first, we found that many of the towns and villages were easy to get through, but we really started to hit big problems as we moved further into territory that was inhabited by people with a lingering sympathy toward Saddam Hussein.

"Some colonel in my regiment drew up a plan to take one of the towns by a frontal assault. It didn't work.

"Another plan was tried: some kind of pincer movement that was supposed to be a good idea, now that the initial frontal assault had gone wrong. Well, the pincer movement was initiated. I was in the eastern pincer, leading my platoon moving north, then turning west to take the eastern suburbs.

"The western pincer attacked first. It was smaller than ours because it was designed to draw the enemy out, to make it easier for us to go in. I saw the plans. It looked brilliant on paper. The only problem was that wars are not fought on paper, and the enemy was better prepared than we expected. The enemy resisted the western pincer up to a point, then fell back. They seemed to be pinned down.

"That was the precise moment when we in the eastern pincer were given the signal to move into the eastern suburbs of the town, *very* slowly and *very* cautiously. We must have got an hour or so in without encountering any opposition.

"Meanwhile, to the west, the other pincer found itself pinned down by enemy snipers. Word went around for us to beware of snipers, and our snipers began to take out their snipers. That was supposed to make it easier for us to go in, but the further we went in, the more exposed we became. Even after three hours, we were still picking off enemy snipers, taking casualties of our own and advancing – still slowly, still cautiously, but surely.

"But, unknown to the local US Army command, the snipers were being used by the enemy as a diversion.

"Suddenly, a loud wailing could be heard. One by one, from east to west – following the movement of the sun – the mosques began to issue the call for prayer. The whole city seemed to be embroiled in a cacophony of noise. Usually, the call to prayer lasts only a few minutes – but not this time. It went on and on, for ages. That was the signal. Under cover of the wall of sound, enemy trucks revved their engines and charged down the narrow streets and into the middle of the main roads where we were creeping along. One after the other, the truck drivers shouted, '*Allah-o-Akbar*', and detonated the explosives that were packed onto their trucks.

"The casualties on our side were horrendous. Nearly everyone in my platoon was blown apart. The blast threw me across the road and into some bushes next to the entrance to a large town house. I was stunned, but lucky to be alive.

"Someone called in an airstrike, and the planes came and shot up the enemy positions. It was enough to allow our medical teams to enter the area and to stretcher away the wounded as quickly as possible, including me.

"I can still hear the moans of the dying, hidden from view a hundred feet away across the road, some were calling for "Mom" or even "Mommy" – poor kids; and the married guys – thousands of miles away from home – were saying goodbye to their loved ones (who were worried sick), asking their folks to look after little Bobby and little Betsy, and saying they were sorry they could not come home, and that they loved them dearly and more than anything else in the whole wide world. And the really sad thing was that those guys were talking to themselves, because, being thousands of miles away, their wives and kids were unable to hear them.

"Around 5,000 American soldiers went into that little town that day, and only about 1,000 left without a scratch. Hundreds died and hundreds were badly wounded. We had to back off, with our tails between our legs, which made everyone really pissed off.

"A couple of weeks later, with the frontal attack plan A and the pincer plan B having failed, a plan C was initiated. This time, the top generals got involved in the planning.

"Plan C was called Operation Total Pacification. It involved the partial evacuation of the city, aerial bombing, and artillery and tanks deployed at strategic points.

"Nobody knows how many of the Iraqi resistance were left alive in the town before Operation Total Pacification was enacted. Many commentators said that most had seeped out and regrouped in other parts of Iraq, and that – apart from a few Iraqi resistance dotted around here and there – only the civilian population remained.

"Furthermore, nobody knows how many of the resistance died during Operation Total Pacification, probably not many, but it is certain that many thousands of civilians were killed; we had them penned in – kettled in a confined space, with nowhere for them to go.

"In one of his articles written at the time, John Morton described that whole episode. He denounced Operation Total Pacification as a war crime and sent the article off to *The Chronicle*. It was never published. I found it recently in the archives along with dozens of other unpublished reports he made.

"Shortly after the battle for that little town drew to a close, John Morton left Iraq and relocated somewhere else. Maybe he feared for his life, having realised that a lot of the unexplained deaths of journalists could have been cover stories to hide the fact that those journalists had been – deliberately – bumped off. He returned to Iraq a few years later to follow up on human rights issues.

"Look for Operation Total Pacification on Google or Wikipedia, Brigita. What do you find? Go on, Brigita. Look it up."

Brigita used her smartphone to perform the search. She found nothing.

Taylor carried on, saying, "You see, Brigita. *It never happened.* The use of banned weapons – such as cluster munitions, phosphorus and depleted uranium – against the civilian population in that little town *never happened.* The same heavy-handed approach was applied in other towns and cities in subsequent years, which was denied at the time, only to be grudgingly admitted later when the human rights watchdogs kicked up about it. And then it was forgotten about.

"During Operation Total Pacification, that little two-bit town had a two-bit name and nobody thought it worth spending too much time worrying about it. However, in the real world, the battle for that little town cost the US Army a lot of men and women... and *kudos*. It was a reality check.

"Word came down from on high that nobody should find out about Operation Total Pacification or the events leading up to it. The American casualty figures were absorbed into the monthly report for the whole of Iraq, so that they would even out and could be presented as collateral damage for the whole of the battlefield during a difficult short phase of the occupation. We were all sworn to secrecy about it. It was 'not in the national interest' – that sort of thing. And, being dutiful soldiers, we obeyed our orders and signed the relevant papers, but it left a bitter taste.

"And that, Brigita, is the sum total of my experience of humanitarian intervention in Iraq in 2003.

"What was the difference between that and the conquest of Poland by Nazi Germany in 1939? I'll leave you to figure that one out for yourself.

"Do you follow, Brigita?"

19

A HEART OF DARKNESS

Wednesday, 7 September 2016.
John Morton and Hugh Lombard tried but failed to get an answer over the phone from Edward Ollerson, in order to arrange delivery of the framed photograph of Edward, John Morton and Sir Tom Hamble taken outside Buckingham Palace six months earlier.

Only one course of action remained open to Morton and Lombard: they would have to visit Ollerson's flat in Camden Town, which they did, without success. Their next line of enquiry was a fruitless search of local hostelries, then wine bars. They returned to Edward Ollerson's flat at nine o'clock in the evening. They had no joy.

The next day – first thing – Lombard called in some favours from his 'café of ill repute'. By the day's end, Lombard's contacts had come up trumps. Edward Ollerson had taken some time away to be with his family in the Midlands. Lombard left Ollerson a text message and, when he finally received a reply on Friday afternoon, suggested that they meet for a drink.

At the same time as Taylor Snow was unburdening her vast reservoir of wisdom to Brigita Wolznaski, Hugh Lombard and John Morton hoped that they, too, would learn something of value from Edward Ollerson.

✷

Edward Ollerson – normally a rather introverted, morose and serious-minded bureaucrat with a poorly developed sense of humour – had let himself go to the point of transforming himself into his opposite.

He seemed eager to talk – about anything and to anyone who would listen. He even smiled profusely and cracked a few one-liners, which, unfortunately, would not do justice to the lamest of comedians.

For some time, he had been smoking cigars; usually, a hand-rolled Cohiba, held nonchalantly 'twixt thumb and middle finger, or languidly clenched between his teeth to one side of his mouth, resembling a wise guy, reminiscent of a bigshot movie character whose identity Morton could not place.

For Edward Ollerson, the act of brushing his cracked and blackened teeth seemed to have become a chore: a bit of toothpaste, a quick brush and a swig of mouthwash to freshen his breath – and that was it.

He no longer wore contact lenses, following an unpleasant hangover that involved removing the lenses while he was half-asleep (and half-drunk), poking himself in the eye repeatedly with his finger and treading on one of the lenses when it hit the floor. He had taken to wearing his spectacles until, late one evening, he staggered – inebriated – into a lamp post and broke them. He had dug out from a pile of boxes and suitcases the only spare pair he could find – a dilapidated contraption fifteen or more years old, which barely fitted him and which looked as though it had been drawn on by a cartoonist.

His chest frequently wheezed; he gasped for breath every time he performed what used to be the least arduous of tasks, such as raising his overstuffed abdomen out of a bath or lowering himself into a chair.

After they had all arrived at the pub and settled in, Morton ordered a pint of London Pride bitter for himself, a glass of expensive white wine for Hugh Lombard and a pint of lager for Edward Ollerson.

Lombard presented Ollerson with a package containing the framed photograph of his not-too-happy appearance alongside the affable Sir Tom Hamble and the cheerful John Morton MBE. It was received by Ollerson with thanks, but coolly.

The sight of Edward Ollerson leading the charge against John Morton in the debate over Ukraine two years earlier was now a faded memory. On that occasion, he and Loretta Farelli had won the argument, more or less by default, but the leaders of the new Ukraine on which Edward and Loretta had pinned their hopes were now losing their popularity with more and more sections of the Ukrainian people, as well as with the prime movers and shakers within the EU.

The Western corporate media had long ago lost interest in the Ukraine crisis, in which a civil war raged and people died, but victory was not achieved. Edward Ollerson seldom talked or wrote about the subject these days.

Gone, too, was the swashbuckling 'conqueror' of the only-too-willing Katy Drake, the unforgettable swagger through the old offices of *The Chronicle* near Farringdon Tube station prior to the hostile takeover and the office move, and the swinging of his long black umbrella while humming and whistling Wagner's *Ride of the Valkyries*.

Brigita Wolznaski – until recently a lonely, self-declared 'holiday girl' with the official job title of 'PA to the editor-in-chief' but, in practice, expected by Loretta Farelli and Katy Drake to act as the office dogsbody – was now in the process of leaving the past behind and metamorphosing into some sort of junior version of Taylor Snow. And, courtesy of her new liaison with Trevor (long distance, temporarily), Brigita's love-life had taken a definite upswing – at the expense of Edward Ollerson.

All that remained of Edward Ollerson was a bloated, hollow-eyed leftover of past glories. Being old enough to be Brigita's father, there was no doubt that he still possessed considerable pulling power, and – even in a state of partial disgrace – his official job title (editor-in-chief of *The Chronicle*) should count for something, particularly among potential female conquests who were unaware of the back story.

Did he possess an ounce of common sense, and a smidgen of vim and vigour to make the most of a not-too-bad situation? That remained to be seen.

A depressing conversation lumbered along.

John Morton was taking the first sip from his third pint of London Pride; Hugh Lombard (a cautious imbiber) had ordered a glass of iced water in addition to his second glass of expensive white wine, making both last for the remainder of the meeting; and Edward Ollerson was already halfway through his sixth pint of lager.

It was at this point, primed with Dutch courage, that Edward Ollerson outlined his big idea. He would show them. Oh yes, he would *really* show them! Between half-suppressed belches, Edward Ollerson declared, "People cannot really know a country without actually being there."

He went on to state that he did not know how anyone could write such claptrap about Russia when its population was so obviously putty in the hands of its current president, Glazenov, when all you had to do was go there and speak to people. And all that talk about fascism in Ukraine was all bollocks as far as Edward Ollerson was concerned.

What struck John Morton immediately was that the argument that Edward Ollerson was levelling against his opponents in the media concerning Russia and Ukraine could so easily be used against Edward himself if one considered a different situation. Iraq, for instance, during and after the US and British invasion in 2003, about which Edward Ollerson knew little, but wrote a great deal; whereas, John Morton (*The Chronicle*'s man on the spot at the time) knew every last detail about the catastrophe that had been inflicted on the Iraqi people by Western governments, which had been obscured deliberately from their readers' view by the entire Western corporate media.

In contrast to the whitewash organised by Edward Ollerson, John Morton's articles for *The Chronicle* had been redacted severely or not published at all. They had been pigeonholed, deep in the archives – thanks, in large part, to the active collusion of Edward Ollerson.

Moreover, the argument was impractical, in most cases. If there was a bit of a to-do in some remote corner, did all 7 billion people on Planet Earth have to go there just to find out what was happening? What were investigative reporters for, if not to report on events? What really matters is whether the reporting is objective and truthful; or whether it reflects the personal views and values of the reporter; or – even worse – consists of downright lies and confected misrepresentations, the purpose of which are not to reveal the truth but to deliberately obscure it.

However, Morton decided to let it go.

Instead, Morton humoured Ollerson, nodding and probing him gently for signs that Edward Ollerson MBE would get himself back on track and make up with his colleagues at *The Chronicle*. Morton repeated what he had said to Taylor Snow about journalists treating each other as worthy opponents instead of implacable enemies, only to be mocked by Ollerson.

To support Morton, Lombard confirmed the subject of the conversation with Taylor Snow in the Millhouse Building two days earlier, repeating Morton's offer – an olive leaf of cooperation – accompanied by Lombard's trademark permanent grin. But Edward Ollerson seemed reluctant to grab the olive leaf. Instead, he seemed determined to grasp a nettle – any nettle would do, except the acknowledgement of simple, straightforward friendship and support, which – to everyone else – was the glaringly obvious solution to his personal dilemma.

Morton and Lombard met Ollerson again on Sunday, 11 September, on the fifteenth anniversary of the attack on the World Trade Centre in New York and on the forty-third anniversary of the US-backed military coup in Chile – two events that all three men had commemorated together in previous years.

Ollerson seemed, at first, to have loosened up; hopefully, from Morton's point of view, as a result of the time and effort invested by Lombard and him.

Ollerson revealed that – a few weeks earlier, during August – he had joined some of his family halfway through a holiday on a canal barge. The happy memories came flooding back: sitting atop the barge, watching the world go by; picnics on grass verges and on wobbly wooden bench tables in car parks near to the moorings;

playing bat-and-ball games with the kids and teenagers, of all ages; card games inside the barge as the rain outside bucketed down; and Uncle Edward getting out when the rain had cleared, and pretending that his toddler twin niece and nephew were contributing something significant to the effort of opening the lock gates.

Yet, once again, as the consumption of alcohol steered the talk into deeper waters, Edward Ollerson's behaviour in the company of John Morton and Hugh Lombard became more and more erratic. His barely concealed plans for the future began to peep through a fog of confusion…

"I will go to Russia," Ollerson stated.

"No. I will not go to Russia. Why should I contribute to their economy and help them out? The Russians can sink to the bottom of the sea as far as I am concerned.

"I will not go to Russia; I will go to… to Ukraine. Yes, that's what I will do.

"I will travel the length and breadth of Ukraine, then come back and write a book on the entire period covering the past three years. I will also take the opportunity to provide a full commentary of what has been going on since the end of Soviet times. I already have plenty of information about the Soviet era itself, the times of the tsars and the earlier periods including the Kievan Rus. This will provide a historical backdrop to the story.

"There, the book is practically half-written already. All that is required are interviews with carefully selected locals, politicians and soldiers of the Ukrainian Army – and some previously unpublished illustrations to 'allow the story to tell itself'.

"My thrill-seeking mate Miles has tons of photographs of war zones, including the Donbass. These photos include people sheltering in basements from artillery shells, people with life-changing injuries, people transformed into bloodied corpses, and pathologists at the end of their shifts, standing beside washed-down mortuary slabs.

"Miles will be a sport and let me borrow his photographs."

Ollerson rambled on about how Miles would even let him quote from an article that he had penned for The Chronicle. Morton recognised this article as one in which Miles deviously implied that the suffering of the Donbass residents was primarily down to the "foolhardy adventurism of the separatists and their implacable stubbornness in resisting the rule of law of the government in Kiev", which had "found itself in the unenviable position of having to resist Russian aggression".

By quoting directly from Miles' article, Ollerson would not have to spend time describing the bombardment of the Donbass civilian population by the Ukrainian Army, and the heavily armed and government-approved Nazi volunteer battalions that were doing the damage, and the search-and-destroy operations against the civilian population – dishonourable actions in which the Nazi volunteer battalions were engaged. In addition, Ollerson's trip to Kiev would turn into, from his perspective, a temporary escape from the real world and a well-earned holiday.

It seemed a perfect plan.

Morton looked askance at Lombard, then turned his gaze directly at Edward Ollerson and said, "Edward, you can't do that."

"Whadda-ya mean? I can't do that?" asked Ollerson.

"You can't go to Ukraine." Morton replied.

Ollerson was adamant. "Bollocks!"

Likewise, Morton stood his ground. "Believe me, Edward. You can't go there. Is that not right, Hugh?"

Lombard nodded.

"First, they cut my wages. Then, they strip me of the right of access to my paper. Now you tell me I can't go and do a bit of research and write a book," grumbled Ollerson.

"Edward, believe me. Be reasonable. You can't go to Kiev now. None of us can," confirmed Morton.

Ollerson scowled. "Whadda-ya mean? None of us can?"

"Did you not see the report?" Morton replied. "It came through AP and Reuters. The government of Ukraine has drawn up a list of news media and journalists who are not allowed to enter Ukraine. Many reporters who are there, right now, have been warned that their embassies in Kiev cannot guarantee their safety."

Edward Ollerson muttered – not very quietly – under his breath and through gritted teeth. "That was last year. They must have changed their minds."

"Edward, listen." Morton stood firm. "A new list has been drawn up of journalists who are at risk if they enter Ukraine. You and I are *both* on that list. Anyone associated with *The Chronicle* – they seem to think I still have something to do with it – cannot go to Ukraine. Don't ask me why you can't go. I cannot see any reason why you of all people should be disbarred, but… there you go. It is what it is."

Morton drank a mouthful of beer and reiterated, "Your name is definitely on that list, Edward."

Lombard fiddled with his phone and wandered to the exit to get a clear signal. He returned with one of the relevant articles in plain view, including the list of proscribed names.

Edward Ollerson was having none of it. He was one of the good guys. He believed in the 'New Ukraine', whatever that was. There was no way that he could be on such a list – which he was only too aware was a 'kill list' of journalists and other potential 'troublemakers'. He had seen many such lists before in other countries; he had naively helped to compile some of those lists, inadvertently, by offering his opinion on such and such a reporter or visiting dignitary.

"Edward, listen," stated Morton. "I understand that the Ukraine government wants to take Ukraine in a direction away from the Russian sphere of influence. Frankly, that does not concern me. It is none of my business. I don't think the Russians will allow NATO to expand further eastward anyway, and I even received inside information that the US, the EU and NATO are not going to lift a finger to defend Ukraine. All NATO will do is make a big noise if there are any more separatist uprisings in the south and east of Ukraine, or there might be a false flag operation that has limited impact. But there will be no more than that.

"Many Ukrainians are under the impression that, now they have signed the Association Agreement with the EU, it is only a matter of time before Ukraine joins the EU. Nothing could be further from the truth. The Association Agreement is just the beginning of a lengthy process, involving Ukraine jumping through one hoop after another, and culminating in the granting of EU membership a long time in the future. Perhaps. And that's a *very big perhaps*.

"However, the fact that Ukraine is in a state of civil war precludes actual EU membership. You must realise that, Edward. You know how the EU works. In addition, the civil war discourages foreign investment in Ukraine. The EU sees Ukraine as a potential source of cheap labour, at best, which means that the most that Ukrainians can expect from the EU is a relaxation of visa controls to allow that pool of cheap labour to travel over to countries within the EU."

Ollerson refused to become unnerved.

Morton went on, "Edward, leave them to their own devices. The population of Ukraine has reduced by over 5 million since the secession of Crimea, and the breaking away of large parts of the Donetsk and Lugansk regions. Not to mention those who have left Ukraine to escape the danger, the poverty and the military draft. A further 5 million have been working overseas for many a year, nearly all of them in Russia. They send money back home to Ukraine. Someone high up in the Ukraine government would like to put a stop to them working in Russia and have them working in Western Europe instead with their remittances going back home from London or Berlin. In the current atmosphere within the EU, can you imagine the outcry if 5 million additional Ukrainians apply to work in Western Europe – as if there were 5 million vacancies in any case. But this irrational scenario is actually being considered."

Ollerson winced and looked away.

"Edward, your experience in the post-Soviet space is far greater than mine," conceded Morton. "I have checked and double-checked, and I know that what I say is true. You must know that what I am saying is true.

"I have even heard tell that the Russian government is reviewing its citizenship requirements. Russia is quite happy to include overseas workers in its workforce, but Russia is also concerned that these contingents are not infiltrated by what are termed 'hostile elements'.

"Furthermore, Russia is fully aware of its geographical size and reach. It does not need to invade anywhere. It needs to expand its internal economy and develop all the regions of the Russian Federation. Many applicants will probably be offered the chance to become citizens of the Russian Federation – as holders of Russian passports. President Glazenov has announced in the past that Russia needs to increase its population to 300 million to be a viable nation state. Controlled immigration, particularly involving workers with relevant skills, might be one way the current figure can be raised.

"But there will be no Russian invasion of Ukraine; nor of anywhere else, for that matter. The Russians have other priorities."

Morton decided to gamble on a little tendentious, off-the-cuff persuasion, flying a dubious kite to keep up the pressure. "And, deep down inside, you know that, Edward. You know about everything I just outlined. You know it is true, don't you?"

※

Tuesday, 13 September 2016.
Morton and Lombard agreed to meet Ollerson for a third time; this time in a restaurant, with the intention of keeping him away from the booze.

They had drawn up a plan to induce their erstwhile colleague to 'come in from the cold'. Morton had even talked over the phone with Taylor Snow to come to an arrangement whereby Edward Ollerson would be restored to his assigned role as editor-in-chief, on full pay, and helped to recuperate.

Morton's idea of a peace offering was not unattractive to Taylor Snow, for it would enable her to reassure her 'customers' in the Beltway by calming down the strained relationship between herself and Loretta Farelli, which had ignited as soon as Loretta had discovered that her old flame Edward, for whom she seemed to retain an irrationally fierce loyalty, was being thrown to the wolves.

At six-thirty in the evening, Morton and Lombard were halfway through a glass each of mineral water. Edward Ollerson was thirty minutes late. At seven o'clock, they ordered starters. By eight-thirty, they had finished their main courses and one bottle of wine between them.

It was time to pay a visit to Edward Ollerson's deserted home, which was followed by another futile search around the local vicinity.

The following day, Hugh Lombard attempted to get information on Edward Ollerson's whereabouts by means of the myriad contacts with their ears close to the ground.

By the weekend, there was still no news. Edward Ollerson had disappeared.

※

A few days later, Morton received a phone call from Taylor Snow. During Edward's absence, his deserted flat had been broken into, ransacked and left in a mess.

In conjunction with Edward's sister Elaine, who had to find a babysitter to enable her to travel down to London for a couple of days, Taylor arranged for the damage to the flat to be repaired.

When John Morton and Hugh Lombard volunteered to help, an overworked Taylor Snow acquiesced gratefully. Morton and Lombard devoted a whole evening to the tidying up of the ravaged apartment and to filling in a couple of forms to assist the (noticeably lukewarm) police investigation into the burglary.

A chatty joiner was employed to repair the damage to floorboards, which had been ripped up in one of the bedrooms. The chatty joiner, plied with cups of tea, kept Morton and Lombard entertained with a relentless barrage of jokes and anecdotes; a barrage that – fortunately, for its audience of two – provoked genuine laughter in abundance.

After half an hour, Morton began to form the impression that the joiner might be trying to 'string out' the job, making it last longer than necessary, perhaps in the hope of increasing his remuneration. Loose floorboards were prised open, bits of mould extricated, and a list made of 'other little jobs' that would need to be done later, until Morton stepped in at last and asked how much longer the joiner would need before the evening's work was finished.

"Oh, the woodwork is rotten in places," came the reply from the joiner. "I need to take out some of the good floorboards to patch up the rotten bits."

Morton remained unconvinced, but – when the joiner pointed to a large pile of discarded, rotten floorboards – a sceptical Morton was forced into a rethink.

The joiner led Morton on a traipse around the flat, revealing squeaking floorboards dotted about the place as they shifted from room to room.

"Looks like these dozens of squeaking floorboards have been removed recently, then put back. But here's the cause of the main problem," the joiner announced triumphantly, having returned to the original bedroom. "It's this wall, here. The damp gets in because the external wall has a problem which has not been repaired. You couldn't sleep in this room without feeling sick. It smells a bit musty as you enter the flat. Did you notice that? Yes? I bet the paper comes away if I try to peel it off…"

Before the slow-thinking Morton had a chance to protest, the assertive joiner used both hands to feel around the wall and succeeded, with the help of a knife, to separate from the wall several accumulated layers of mildewed wallpaper. In one deft stroke, the joiner removed a huge floor-to-ceiling clump consisting of matted layers of mouldy wallpaper and threw it onto the floor, thereby revealing a damp spot spanning a large area of cracked and crumbling plaster.

Morton realised that, contrary to earlier suspicions, the joiner had not been trying to string out the job after all. *A conscientious type, merely being more thorough than was expected of him*, Morton thought.

"I can't do much about this today," said the joiner. "I will just have to make a list, hand it over and see what the owner decides to do. But I can't leave those gaps in the floorboards; someone might do their ankle in. The spare room next door has a bed near the window. Lend a hand, will you, and help me to move it away. I can take some of the boards under that bed and use them to fix the damage in the other room. Make do and mend, for now, and fix it all properly another time."

The single bed near the window of the second bedroom had been disturbed by the burglars, but then replaced. Morton and the joiner moved the bed. Underneath it, Morton discovered a dozen or so cardboard wine boxes, each of a three-litre capacity. He carried the wine boxes to the other end of the room, as the joiner set to work examining and then removing floorboards in the space where the bed had been.

That's funny, Morton thought. *Those wine boxes seem a bit lightweight.*

He opened one of the boxes. It was stuffed with paper documents, which were A4-size, folded in half and filed away. Morton had discovered some of Edward Ollerson's archives.

By ten o'clock in the evening, the joinery work was complete. The joiner had left, leaving Morton with an invoice and a list of jobs to be done in the future.

Morton then relieved Hugh Lombard of his duties, leaving himself alone in Edward Ollerson's flat.

There's something fishy about that burglary, Morton pondered. *I would not be surprised if a dubious spot of larceny had happened in the home of someone who worked for The New Times... but... but why here? Why here, in Edward Ollerson's flat, of all places? As far as I know, Edward is a* 'Chronicle *man' through and through; he* can't stand *The New Times and* can't stand *alternative media or anyone who challenges the dominant narrative. So, why here? Why would someone want to break into Edward's flat?*

I know curiosity killed the cat, but... it's better I check it out.

The burglars had not been interested in the wine boxes. They probably thought they were full of wine: about £120 worth. It would have been easy to take them. Those burglars can't be short of funds.

But... these boxes are not full of wine. They contain documents. Nothing of much interest to me, except that some of them have been downloaded from The New Times *website and printed out. Including stuff written by Dmitry Krejevsky, of all people! They're printed out and annotated in the margins, in different colour codes of ink in Edward's scrawl. And bits have been circled: military stuff, especially Russian military. There's nothing confidential, just articles written by Dmitry based upon interviews with military experts, including Russian military and NATO military. It's the kind of stuff that* The Chronicle *would not touch with a bargepole.*

I remember reading those articles earlier this year. They're interesting, but just a series of updates on who had what weapons and what they could do with them. But there was not a ripple in the corporate media. Nobody was interested in them.

So... why would Edward Ollerson, long after those articles had been written, be interested in this stuff? He said he was going to write a book. Is this part of his research material?

And now... Edward has gone missing...

What is he up to? Where has he gone? Did he go to Ukraine, as he said he would? Or, perhaps after a rethink prompted by what Hugh and I told him about his name being on a list of proscribed journalists, Edward decided to go somewhere else. Russia, perhaps...

Hang on. Roll that back a bit, John.

Hugh and I told Edward Ollerson that he is on a list of proscribed journalists... in Ukraine. Now that *is* not *supposed to happen – Edward on the opposite side – on the* wrong *side. I humoured him when he rubbished my claim that he was on the proscribed list, even when Hugh got a signal on his smartphone and showed him the list on the website. But Edward was right on the button. He was right to be sceptical and, in his own mind at least, it was perfectly understandable that he would be in denial when confronted with the facts. Edward was right. He should simply* not *be on that list.*

What's going on here?

Now, Edward's no fool. He might have a few personal problems, but he's not stupid. Like me, he went to state school then university; both of us went to different colleges at Oxford, at the same age, but both ended up with a first-class honours degree. We were almost mirror images of each other.

The last great thing we both did was to reveal secret Russian battle plans to the world public in Edwards' case, and to try to do so in mine.

The parallels between Edward and I... they're eerie. Very eerie. I've never noticed them before.

Was that leak of the Russian battle plans the reason why Edward was put on a proscribed list? And, if so, by whom?

And, picking up on the mission that had been initially assigned to Katy Drake many months ago... we have to ask who, these days, is 'looking after' Edward Ollerson? And... 'looking after' in what way?

Morton was about to pack up and go home when the doorbell rang. Or, rather, it buzzed.

That's another little job for the joiner and his mates, Morton mused.

A helpful, friendly and slightly nosy neighbour needed to satisfy her curiosity, and she had brought her tall and muscular adolescent son along for support, "just in case", she explained.

She hadn't seen Edward for at least a week, maybe more, and was wondering who was making all the noise and whether Edward had returned home.

The neighbour recognised John Morton from the papers and from on the TV, so it was no big deal for Morton to reassure the neighbour that he had been dispatched to Edward Ollerson's flat to help to clear up the mess. The muscular son wanted to go home, but he was instructed by his mum to hang around a bit longer, "just in case".

Morton declined the offer of a cup of tea politely, on the grounds that he was on the verge of leaving for home, but the neighbour already had her foot (and a leg and half of her torso) in the doorway, so Morton had to put up with the neighbour's dogged persistence for a while longer, 'over a cuppa' in Edward's flat.

Morton did, however, listen as carefully as was possible at this late hour to what the neighbour had to say. And when the opportunity knocked on the already open door, Morton the diligent investigative reporter picked up on a couple of snippets of gossip.

Yes, the neighbour had heard Morton and the others banging away while they tidied up Edward's flat. Yes, the police also had made a racket when they had arrived on the scene, although they had not seemed bothered about interviewing any of Edward's neighbours.

But the burglars had "not made so much as a peep"; although the building security seemed to think that something was up, had knocked on Edward's door but got no answer, had rung and texted Edward's mobile phone but got no reply, and had, finally, trawled through a list of residents' emergency contact numbers until they found the contact details of Edward's sister, marked 'next of kin'.

"I was there with the chairperson of the residents' committee when she turned up to carry out her inspection. And I was there. I saw everything, as God is my witness, I did," confirmed the neighbour.

The neighbour also told Morton that, in the seventeen years she had been living in the flats, there had "never been any trouble, never been such a thing as a robbery or a burglary, no druggies in the flats (since the flats had been done-up, at least), and that the chairperson of the residents' committee had been told that the CCTV cameras in the reception area showed no strangers entering the building in the hour before the burglary".

They could have been in the building for some time before the burglary, thought Morton, as he summoned up a bold assertiveness to draw the conversation to a close.

According to Edward's sister and Taylor Snow, the police report described how a metal box had been removed from underneath the floorboards, prised open and the contents (presumed to be money) stolen. A forensic examination revealed *no fingerprints* on the box, none at all – not even Edward Ollerson's prints.

Morton continued his internal musing, *So, the burglars had, as burglars do, used gloves. And, when putting his money in the box and taking it out... Edward Ollerson must also have... used gloves?*

Or, at least, wiped the box clean every time he accessed it. For what purpose? That's fishy...

Furthermore, the floorboard that had been concealing the metal box was one of the most rotten of the floorboards that had been piled up by the joiner, and the hole in which the metal box had been found contained quite a lot of rotten splinters.

Now... ask yourself, John... if you wanted to hide a metal box under a floorboard, would you hide the box under a floorboard that was rotten and that might break apart if it was stood on, exposing the box that you wanted to hide? Or would you hide the box under a floorboard that was not rotten, would not break if stepped on and would not result in the hidden box being exposed? And that, as a bonus, the owner of the box would be able to pull up every so often – without any fuss and without creating a mess – to get access to the box, and, when the job was complete, replace the box and floorboard... nice and neat?

Morton used and flushed the toilet, then performed one final check of the flat before leaving for home.

He reflected, *One of Edward's umbrellas was upside down in the bath, broken* [the shaft had come away from the canopy when Morton tried to remove the umbrella], *but... not discarded... just left in the bath, beyond repair and of no further use.*

And... there were so many bouquets of flowers in the bath, all dead and decaying by now, nipping future blooms in the bud, with buds and bits of foliage clogging up the plughole.

Didn't Edward say something in the pub – to Hugh and to me, in passing – complaining about someone (presumably Brigita) not returning his calls, even after he had sent flowers? Did he really make those calls? Did he really send those flowers, or had they been returned to the sender? But the sender would not be Edward's home address; surely the sender's address would be a nearby florist? In which case, Edward seems to have bought the flowers in the shop (or maybe online), had intended to build some sort of rapprochement with Brigita, but, in the end, he just never got round to it.

Was Edward making it all up? Had he become a figure of pity, wallowing in his own predicament?

John Morton had known Edward Ollerson for many years. He had recently seen him in a sorry state: self-pitying, self-loathing and losing his grip on reality. What else would be revealed, later, over time? The idea of a talented former colleague letting himself go was too painful to contemplate.

It was late, and Morton was tired. Morton felt the need to simply switch off, but he repeated to himself what he had been thinking earlier, immediately before the doorbell had 'buzzed'.

Who is 'looking after' Edward Ollerson these days, possibly in more ways than one?

20
DEMOCRACY'S DIRTY LITTLE SECRETS

As a sweetener, to make a start on the mending of bridges, Taylor Snow allowed Loretta Farelli to publish a daily column in *The Chronicle* covering the run up to the Russian general election (scheduled for Sunday, 18 September) from the comfort of her plush office in the Beltway, in Washington DC.

Loretta spoke no Russian, nor had she ever been to Russia, but she had many contacts inside the Russian Federation with whom she had become acquainted, courtesy of her recently estranged friend and ally, Edward Ollerson. The contacts were her 'eyes and ears' on the ground. The contacts spoke fluent Russian; indeed, although most of the contacts were Westerners of a mindset compatible with that of Loretta, she was able to claim that *some* of them *were actually* Russian citizens.

The readers' comments appended to the web-based edition of Loretta's daily column revealed a lively debate; most were supportive of her view, but some were critical.

Loretta's team in Moscow, managed in situ by Katy Drake, held interviews on the streets of Moscow with *carefully selected* members of the Russian public, to 'allow the Russian people to speak for themselves'.

Opposition liberal candidates and their supporters were allowed time to air their views, as were the local (and foreign) employees of dozens of Western-backed NGOs. Loretta made sure to give opponents of the incumbent president an easier ride than those who supported him. Loretta also made sure that interviews with certain opposition candidates and their supporters whom she did not like (communists, in particular) would be edited out of Katy's daily reports.

Yet it was all to no avail.

When the results of the Russian general election were announced, those candidates who were supported by Loretta mustered less than 5% of the vote (less than half of the votes accrued by the communists, whose views she had disdained). Short of calling for a recount (which would imply that the unlikely scenario of a massive and unprecedented fraud had taken place – under the sharp-eyed scrutiny of Western electoral observers, no less), Loretta had nothing further to say.

But the overwhelming number of readers' comments demanded an explanation from Loretta as to why her estimate had been so far out. Loretta insisted that Taylor Snow remove 75% of the adverse comments, "to provide a more balanced range of support and dissent".

Taylor Snow refused. The comments would remain – a true and correct record of the response to the coverage of the Russian general election that had been provided by *The Chronicle*. Perhaps this was Taylor's tentative first step toward the construction of 'realist internationalism'.

Barring *The Chronicle*, the other Western media remained hushed throughout the Russian general election – a muted acknowledgement that the result would reveal overwhelming support for the incumbent government and its president. There was no point in broadcasting this embarrassing truth so, *The Chronicle* being the lone exception, Western corporate media outlets formed a united front of total silence.

In contrast, Loretta Farelli had refused to face the facts, and only she, alone, had loudly supported the campaign in favour of pro-Western, NGO-backed 'fringe' candidates who opposed President Glazenov.

"Well," Taylor Snow thought aloud, within hearing distance of Brigita Wolznaski, "if you will push so hard against the tide that it comes in and swamps you, that is the price you will pay…"

Taylor's attempt to mend bridges had ended with relations between two of *The Chronicle*'s key players once again becoming fraught with tension.

Another transatlantic conference call was arranged, this time with Brigita in attendance, sitting alongside Taylor Snow in the Millhouse Building. Taylor's idea was to allow Brigita to hear everything for herself and to make up her own mind.

"If you think Loretta is right and I am wrong," Taylor said to Brigita, "then I will back down and make the changes that Loretta requires. I will continue to work here in London at *The Chronicle*, but under Loretta's direction. I will not utter a single word against her in future, nor will I challenge her editorial line."

Brigita listened carefully during the intense two-hour call and, when her opinion was sought, Brigita advised Taylor Snow to stand her ground.

In contrast to the tense, frenetic, combative and opinionated op-eds and articles that graced and disgraced the pages of *The Chronicle*, for *The New Times*, the coverage of the Russian general election was a calm, well-organised, routine operation.

Dmitry Krejevsky linked up with Hans and Zoe Neubauer in Moscow. All three were fluent in Russian, with easy access to candidates and campaigning groups of all shades of political opinion.

John Morton remained in London with his son Anthony, Shirley Bould, Hugh Lombard and Vivienne Eissinger. The London-based Vivienne Eissinger acted as point person and liaised with the team in Moscow.

With assiduous authority and grasp of his subject, Hans Neubauer wrote a series of articles for *The New Times* in the run-up to Russia's election week. The articles encompassed a digested read of the period from 1991–2016; namely, the post-Soviet era.

The new cold war was not the same as the previous cold war, Hans asserted. The republics within the former Soviet Union were now constituted as independent, sovereign nation states. Trade barriers between West and East had been loosened. By 2010, the volume of trade had reached the hundreds of billions of pounds, euros and dollars. This level of East–West trade was unprecedented. Furthermore, nation states in the east of Europe were no longer obliged to do most of their trade within Comecon, the economic zone that serviced the member states of the Warsaw Pact until 1991.

During the 1990s, the new Russian bourgeoisie – described frequently as an oligarchy of billionaires – made short work of building and consolidating a cordial relationship with the West.

Yet, over time, some of the billionaires became restless. They enjoyed the fruits of their new-found wealth, but, at the same time, their consciences haunted them with a fear that Russia was destined to play second fiddle on the world stage. Something inside them made them instinctively wary of the West. Their heartstrings tugged unceasingly, ominously warning them of their vulnerability to the tightly honed competitiveness of their Western rivals on the global stage.

These concerns were widely shared throughout Russia: they were doomed to be always a bridesmaid – never the bride; and not even the chief bridesmaid, at that. Did not Mother Russia deserve better than this?

These 'dissatisfied billionaires' were also fearful that, in any spat with more powerful Russian oligarchs, they would come off second best. Assuming their wealthier opponents would be able to call in support from Western governments, the dissatisfied billionaires were fearful that they could be hit by Western sanctions, thereby losing their wealth and influence. They might even wind up in jail.

To forestall this possibility, the dissatisfied billionaires began to search for reliable allies, particularly within the Russian state apparatus – allies with a similar view to theirs. And they soon found them.

Many of the Russian government ministries were wary of the West. Such ministries had barely begun the process of reform that would align Russia very closely with the neoconservative political outlook and the neoliberal economic practices of the West. In some ministries, stonewalling took precedence over East–West engagement.

Influential and well-educated figures in the ministries of the interior, defence and foreign affairs joined forces with the unhappy souls who comprised the growing numbers of dissatisfied Russian billionaires. They cobbled together an alternative narrative that envisioned the sovereignty of Russia, not East–West integration on the West's terms, as the utmost concern.

They were only too aware of the enormous size and geographical spread of the Russian nation state. From modest beginnings arose the dream of reinventing Russia as a union of its European and Asian components. It was a vision of 'Eurasian Sovereignty' as a driving force to contribute to the reshaping of the global economy; a vision that would attract other non-Western powers to consider closer ties to Russia – the fast-emerging China, in particular; and a vision that would entice *some* of the Western powers to work with Russia on a peer-to-peer basis, as equal partners and, unambiguously, *not* on terms that favoured one side over the other.

Few in the West gave this new vision much thought, but diehard anti-Soviet Western hawks lived in a world where the prospect of a re-emergence of a superpower to rival the US was an overriding concern. It terrified them.

The 1990s had been a painful decade for the Russian people. Suddenly, many of the safeguards provided by the Soviet state evaporated, particularly in terms of social welfare. Poverty and uncertainty were the hallmarks of the first decade of post-Soviet Russia. Everyone knew it; most felt it.

What was to be done, then, to remedy this situation? Going back to the Union of Soviet Socialist Republics (USSR) would require another socialist revolution – and, at the time, that was not on the cards. Going forward was the only option left. But how? Slowly, the idea of making the best use of Russia's size and natural resources to rebuild the nation as a 'sovereign Russia' gathered momentum. However, they were not going to be allowed an easy ride.

Challenges to Russia's sovereignty and the concept of Eurasian Sovereignty arose from time to time; such as the events in Chechnya and Georgia, and the many protests organised within the Russian Federation by oppositionists in conjunction with Western-backed NGOs. They were dealt with promptly by the resolute intervention of the Russian state apparatus. Each time an event popped up out of the blue, the Russian state managed to handle it. It was not pretty to watch, but it was effective, nonetheless.

Another, more recent, turning point concerned the Syria crisis. Angered by the way that the US and NATO had got the Russians on board at the UN over Iraq and Libya – only to subsequently reinterpret the UN resolutions in a way that slapped Russia in the face like a hapless cuckold – key players within the Russian deep state decided that they had endured enough.

"The Syrian government was using chemical weapons against its own people, was it? Allegedly?" the Russian foreign minister asked rhetorically, during a meeting with the Russian president and his ministers.

"And that meant another UN resolution and no-fly zones, which would presage a NATO bombing campaign leading to regime change, did it?

"Well, not this time."

"If the problem is chemical weapons," said the Russian foreign minister, "then let us isolate the issue and deal with it separately."

The US president was having second thoughts about a humanitarian intervention in Syria, being aware of the outcome of the last foray into Arab territory – the catastrophe of Libya: the jihadists filling the void; the death of the US Ambassador to Libya, courtesy of those same jihadists who had sodomised and lynched President Muammar Gaddafi; and the fallout – in particular, the refugee crisis and the bad publicity that had ensued.

Inspired by the leadership of Russia, UN Security Council Resolution 2118 talked only about chemical weapons and their removal. UN inspectors confirmed, a few months later, that the supplies of chemical weapons held by the Syrian government had indeed been destroyed: job done.

The next big flare-up was over Ukraine. Once again, the Russian government skilfully deployed its resources to achieve its goals.

Yet, unlike the previous cold war, the latest series of spats between Russia and the West had little to do with ideology. Russia was as keen as any Western country to develop along capitalist lines. All it wanted was time and space to grow in its own way and at its own pace.

And a seat at the high table. A seat that it was being denied.

Hans Neubauer's articles were edited by Vivienne, and cross-checked with Hugh Lombard and John Morton prior to uploading to the website.

*

Hans had nicely set the stage for his wife Zoe to press on with her coverage of the Russian general election.

Zoe's first article was not very long. It did not need to be, because she had already written on the subject many times. Having done all the hard work, she was able to 'queue in' links to various detailed assessments that she had already written, prefacing each link with phrases such as "as I have written before…" and – displaying an optimism stemming from her own self-confidence – "as has been proven correct by subsequent events…".

Busily engaged on a multitude of tasks during 2016, John Morton had, to some extent, taken for granted Zoe's popular columns in *The New Times* and the German media outlets for which she also wrote. He had failed to notice one of the most important secrets of her success, and, for more than eighteen months, he had overlooked its significance.

Now, all became clear.

The Russian people have an addiction. You could say that British people also have the same addiction, and so do the Germans, the French, the Americans, and on and on throughout Planet Earth.

Put a TV set in front of 90% of the population and what do they do? They watch it. In fact, the thing becomes a close friend. They

253

gawk at it and are rewarded with talent contests, quiz shows and soap operas by the bucket load.

In Russia, it is no different. Furthermore, just as the UK has its regular panel shows where high-profile politicians, historians and journalists argue in front of a televised studio audience, Russian audiences enjoy the same simple luxury.

But what makes these talk shows attractive to the Russian TV-watching public is that the guests on the show are from an incredibly wide range of backgrounds. They are not only guests who support the Russian government, but also those who oppose it, including the pro-Western Russian liberals. Furthermore, not only are the pro-Western Russian liberals accorded pride of place on these shows, top billing is granted to foreigners who are critical of the Russian government. And there they are: Germans, Brits, Poles; even Ukrainian nationalists and ultra-nationalists; even Americans; and even neoconservatives. They present their case and engage in debate with pro-government Russians, and are often required to answer questions from the studio audience.

The Russian TV-watching public laps it up; they cannot get enough of it.

"Why are we restricting our coverage of the election to articles written for the Western public," Morton asked, "when the debates are already taking place on Russian TV during election week?

"There are three of you in Moscow. All of you are fluent in Russian. Surely it would be possible to provide English language translations to the shows and upload them with subtitles, and even to overdub them. *The New Times* website is robust enough to handle it.

"Transcripts of some of the shows – in Russian – have already been made available in PDF on Russian websites. English language translations of these can be produced by our team in Moscow, and then edited and polished by Vivienne prior to being uploaded to our website in tandem with the videos of the TV shows."

Perfect, thought Dmitry Krejevsky. *Let's do it.*

So, on Wednesday morning a few days prior to the Russian general election, Western viewers of *The New Times* website were treated to something of a surprise: Russian TV shows, allowing representatives from all shades of opinion to 'speak for themselves'.

*

An interesting exchange took place on a Russian TV show involving Ukrainian nationalists. When asked if Ukrainian media would be prepared to return the favour by inviting the Russian host of one of the talk shows to appear on a Ukrainian talk show, the response was a clear 'NO!', on the grounds that Ukraine had taken steps to ban what it labelled 'Russian propaganda' within its territory – "from Kiev in the north to Odessa in the south, from Galicia in the west to the Donbass in the east!" as stated by one of the Ukrainian participants.

In a commentary to this specific TV broadcast, Zoe at the same time quoted from a UK-based think tank that actively promoted the idea that Russian news outlets (including RT) should not be broadcast at all to Western audiences. Zoe characterised this as an example of importing the restrictive and anti-democratic norms from nervous states on Russia's border to Western European countries, as part of the US-imposed *cordon sanitaire.*

But, in Russia, the very opposite is true. If someone wants to come onto a talk show and tell the entire Russian people that there is no free speech on Russian TV, that alternative views are not allowed and to give vent to their pet theories, they are free to do so, even if they oppose the policies of the Russian government. Not just in election week, but at any time.

Many of the shows are even uploaded to social media, sometimes with subtitles in multiple languages.

The technique employed by the Russian TV networks fascinated Morton. If you want to get someone to believe what you say, you could just tell them plainly and simply, but that might get their backs up and they might start to ask awkward questions. Maybe, instead, you could take a more nuanced approach.

Instead of trying to foist your viewpoint on your audience, you engage with them. You allow them to see and to listen to a person who holds diametrically opposed views to yours. Then you join in the conversation. If your adversaries make themselves look foolish by making claims that are clearly extravagant and contradict what people see in the real world, then you might win the argument by default.

If your rivals lose the argument in this way, they will have to work that much harder next time round to prevent the audience from detecting their phoney arguments that masquerade as the truth.

Simple, smart and subtle.

Multipolarity in action.

During Russia's election week, *The New Times* showed its audience that not only were pro-Western views welcome on Russian TV but that claims to the contrary – let alone the so-called 'outlandish outpourings from the pro-Western voices' on Russian TV – would have only one outcome inside Russia. They would damage the credibility of the Western narrative and those who supported the West within Russia. In its current mood, the Russian government was not likely to lift a finger to change that.

The whole narrative of Western democracy was exposed for what it is in reality when boiled down to its essential bones: a modern equivalent of the bloody and bloodthirsty eighteenth- and nineteenth-century liberal imperialism with all the associated forms of interventionism in the affairs of foreign states – and all this masquerading as support for human rights and liberal internationalism.

Moreover, it would not be difficult to make a case that the 'liberal' and 'humanitarian' Western democracy is in terminal crisis.

The centre ground of politics on which Western democracy is built is in a process of fragmentation. It is true that the leaders of the Western socialist parties marched over to the centre – traditionally the territory of many liberals and conservatives, following the neoliberal ascendancy in the early 1980s – to try to persuade voters to change their allegiances.

In many cases, they did change their minds. For example, in the UK, the New Labour government tapped into the fickle mood swings of public sentiment. It also felt the full benefit of the economic boom years that followed hot on the heels of the previous recession – recessions being an acknowledged structural feature of boom-and-bust capitalism. New Labour trumpeted its success as being simply down to good leadership and a worldview which broke with that of its socialist heritage. It had, apparently, even claimed to have put an end to boom and bust, until the whole New Labour project crashed and burned as soon as the crisis of 2007–2008 swept it aside in an economic and political tsunami, never to return. While touting a highly skilled future of technology in the computer age and reminding everybody to make sure they had firewalls installed at every important computerised network interface, this New Labour government – which was hell-bent on deregulation and the hauling down of economic firewalls – had been caught with its pants down.

※

What would Western governments make of the result of the Russian General Election?

Had the election taken place in a member state of the EU and delivered the 'wrong' result, it might simply be a matter of holding the election again or taking measures to undermine the government until the 'right' result came about – a weakening of support for the president, paving the way for regime change, and his or her eventual removal.

However, the Russian general election result was irreversible. The Russian people had spoken. Warts and all, they had plumped for the supporters of the incumbent President Glazenov.

There was no need to advertise that tiny, inconvenient detail. So, *The Chronicle* aside, the Western corporate media kept mum.

PART FIVE
GLAD HANDS AND NEW DISCOVERIES

21

FOR THE WANT OF A NAIL

With Edward Ollerson out of the picture, Brigita Wolznaski had a lot of free time on her hands, which she spent frequently daydreaming about Trevor – the new long-distance love interest in her life – and singing the latest John Legend song to herself (and, inadvertently, to a host of amused third parties within earshot).

Trevor's move to London was slated for mid-January 2017, which would allow him to spend a sunny Christmas and New Year's Eve with his folks in Melbourne. He invited Brigita to join him, and Taylor Snow gave her permission to do so. Brigita would use up the remainder of her 2016 annual vacation. In addition, Taylor arranged for Brigita to do her day job for *The Chronicle* in Australia for the first two weeks of January. She would return to the UK in mid-January, accompanied by Trevor.

It would be the first time that Brigita had celebrated Christmas away from home. She phoned her mom and told her the news. Her mom would surely feel the same way as her daughter – happy but with misgivings. Brigita imagined her dad putting his arm around her mom, and telling her not to worry and that their 'little girl' was growing up fast.

Trying to be helpful, Trevor suggested that Brigita's parents join them in Australia for the seasonal celebrations, but Brigita thought that this was too soon. She would like to spend some time alone with Trevor and to allow space for their relationship to blossom, before introducing their parents to each other.

Brigita was not party to the actual transatlantic conference call during which Taylor Snow informed Loretta Farelli about Brigita's forthcoming 'working holiday' in the Antipodes, but she imagined its tone and colourful language – entailing another point scored in Taylor's favour, and almost certainly game over.

Brigita was therefore surprised when Loretta Farelli suddenly arrived at the Millhouse Building on the morning of Monday, 8 October.

"Oh… it's you, is it?" Taylor observed, upon noticing the arrival of Loretta – and promptly returned to her office, closing the door behind her.

Loretta stationed herself in Edward Ollerson's office, closed the door and busied herself with one unnecessarily loud phone call after another.

Loretta had brought Katy Drake along with her. Brigita and Katy made themselves at home in the conference room, where they chewed over a few morsels of conversation before staring across the table at each other. The spell was broken when both women burst out laughing almost at the same time. Katy rose from her seat, one hand clasped over her mouth, and carefully closed the door. For ten minutes, the pair indulged in stifled bouts of laughter, tears and exclamations of "Oh don't!", "We shouldn't laugh, really," and "Shush! They'll hear us!"

"Loretta is here to follow up on Edward's behalf," Katy explained. "She wants to know what has become of him and what Taylor's intentions are."

"Well," Brigita said, "Loretta, you and I are all Edward's exes. Does Loretta think it is now Taylor's turn?"

More mirth inevitably followed, until Katy called a halt to it and explained that the four of them would need to have a face-to-face meeting to thrash out their differences concerning policy and agree a common course of action, going forward.

After more than one hour on the phone, Loretta entered the conference room. She asked Brigita to call Taylor for a meeting. Brigita returned from Taylor's office empty-handed. Taylor was busy. Taylor was talking to the printers and to Erik, whom she later introduced to Loretta and Katy in a deliberately inflammatory way as, "the brilliant man from Copenhagen, who is charged with managing the office and dealing with the printers and other outsourced services providers".

Taylor was negotiating a deal with the printers to increase the daily circulation of *The Chronicle* newspaper. She had also reinstated the paper's weekend edition, thereby reversing the executive decision made several months earlier by Edward Ollerson.

Taylor Snow had accumulated much kudos with the main American financial and political backers of *The Chronicle*. She was regarded by those backers as the person who had saved *The Chronicle* from obscurity and liquidation, and who had set it back on the road again. Except that the editorial line had been unilaterally modified (ever so subtly) by Taylor Snow.

From her hard-won position of strength, Taylor Snow therefore felt confident enough to take part in a meeting at a time of her own choosing, and not at the whim of Loretta or anybody else, thank you very much – to Loretta Farelli's immense chagrin.

"I need to have my lunch first, so the meeting will have to wait," Taylor announced when she finally entered the conference room.

Katy Drake had a quiet word with Loretta, and Loretta nodded.

"What time will you be… finished for the day?" Katy asked politely.

"What do you mean, 'finished for the day'?" Taylor snapped.

"Oh, it's just that we seem to have arrived at a slightly inconvenient time," replied Katy. "I suppose we could put it off, but we think there might be a cause for concern regarding Edward's well-being. We don't think it can wait."

"Very well," Taylor conceded to Katy's apparent attempt to bridge the chasm between the two stars of the show.

They trooped off to a trattoria for a working lunch. Katy did most of the talking, having persuaded Loretta to let her handle things (and to allow Loretta to imagine herself leading from behind).

✷

Katy's main approach was a pragmatic one: what is done is done, and the most important task in hand is to at least keep *The Chronicle* ticking over.

Taylor Snow took this as a sort of slight against her. "What do you mean 'ticking over'?" she demanded. "*The Chronicle* has been ticking over for years, and, since the change in management two years ago, it has been ticking over a precipice with nobody wanting to grab hold of the reins and pull it back. Furthermore, for your information, I don't 'finish for the day' – I am working 24/7 on this project and I am determined to see it through."

Taylor took a sip of wine and listed all the actions she had taken, in chronological order, to rescue the paper and its website. "We even had a visit from John Morton and Hugh Lombard," Taylor threw in, while wrapping up her homily. "They tried to help us to get Edward back on board—"

"*You did what?*" Loretta exploded.

"I thought you would like that," Taylor remarked sarcastically. "Our rivals at *The New Times* seem most anxious to help Edward to get back on track. They value the rapport they have with us. They want… what was the wording Hugh Lombard used over the phone in a one-to-one with me, only last week, as it happens? Ah yes, a 'multitude of different views to contend with each other in the open spaces of public discourse'. Okay, that might sound a bit 'wimpy kid', but it's a basic democratic approach. I don't see anything wrong with that."

"*Well, I do!*" Loretta steamed. "I am not happy with anyone from… from… *that crowd* having anything to do with us, and I am especially upset to hear that *they* have been inside *our* building. I would like that to stop."

"No can do," Taylor asserted.

Katy Drake interrupted the flow of conversation before it got out of hand. It got out of hand anyway, requiring the intervention of the restaurant manager (at the behest of the head waiter) to bring it to an end.

✱

Back in the office, Loretta and Taylor retreated to their respective tents like mirror images of Achilles, leaving Katy and Brigita to pick up the pieces. Brigita had seen Loretta in her present mood on several prior occasions, but Brigita had never seen Loretta's spleen vented with such fury. At times, during the lunch, Loretta had bordered on the hysterical. In contrast, Taylor had remained reasonably calm and assertive, merely standing her ground.

The office was closed at five o'clock. Loretta departed with Katy, and returned to the solace proffered by the steam and sauna rooms of their posh hotel. Taylor accompanied Brigita on their routine run-and-stretch in the park (which was soon to become, during the winter months, a predominantly indoor and gym-based schedule).

For Taylor Snow, Monday was habitually reserved for resolving any outstanding problems left over from the weekend and for preparing for the week ahead. Tuesday was regarded by Taylor as the first meaningful day of the working week.

Tuesday was also the day of the week when the 'embassy wives' made their first appearance in the office. Having been briefed suitably by Taylor and Brigita on Monday, Freda Gray arrived on Tuesday morning to talk the 'embassy wives' through the articles she had sent in and work out how they might be edited to fulfil the exacting standards that had been enforced steadily under the tutelage of Taylor Snow.

Loretta Farelli seemed to become resigned to the whole business – perhaps after a long talk during the previous evening with the more pragmatic Katy Drake. Loretta perused the goings-on diffidently, wondering whether to involve herself in some way or maybe to just say hello.

When Freda Gray wheeled in a newly acquired trolley and asked, "Would anyone like a cuppa, dear?", Loretta Farelli simply glared in Freda's direction.

Freda froze.

"I'll have a coffee, if you don't mind," Loretta said.

Freda pressed a lever to pour a fresh cup out of the spout. *Phew! That was a close one,* thought Freda.

Passing one of the offices a while later, Freda could have sworn she overheard Loretta say something quite nasty to Katy, conveyed with a snide verbal delivery, "... and she's even allowing them to bring their mothers – and grandmothers – with them now..."

Freda recovered her composure quickly, being a thick-skinned type, and continued with her routine.

※

Brigita Wolznaski could not for the life of her fathom the reason why Loretta had decided on a visit to London, and what she hoped to gain by hovering about the offices and retreating to the solitude of Edward's deserted office for most of the day.

On Friday morning, after Taylor's weekly team meeting was over, Loretta was in for a *real* surprise.

"Hello, Loretta."

A familiar voice chilled Loretta to the bone. She turned around slowly, with her mouth opening wider gradually to discover the unwelcome sight of two familiar faces from distant times past standing in the doorway of the conference room.

"May we come into your hospitable abode, Loretta? Please?" asked John Morton, who seemed in a light-hearted mood.

Taylor Snow embarked on a spree of introductions.

When John Morton and Hugh Lombard were introduced to Freda Gray, they each responded with a brisk handshake and a curt, "Hello."

Freda remained in the conference room with the 'embassy wives' and Erik, the reliable full-time employee of *The Chronicle*, without whom various wheels could not turn.

Taylor Snow led the way to a pre-booked meeting room on the tenth floor, which was sufficiently far away from the workplace to avert the risk that a sensitive conversation might be overheard by members of staff, but not in a public place – so that 'colourful language' could be used unremittingly, in private.

Taylor Snow set herself up at the head of the table, with Brigita to her right-hand side. Katy and Loretta sat next to Brigita, facing Hugh Lombard and John Morton who took their seats at Taylor's left.

Taylor explained that she was concerned that the disappearance of Edward Ollerson had not been resolved, and informed the meeting that she had asked Hugh Lombard and John Morton to help in a search for him.

Engrossed in taking the minutes of the meeting – and seated on the same side of the table as her colleagues from *The Chronicle* – Brigita was not able to monitor the face of Loretta Farelli. But, seated almost directly opposite Loretta, John Morton *could* observe every change in expression and every nuance.

The resourceful and enterprising Hugh Lombard had much to contribute to the meeting. However – as Hugh Lombard outlined his discoveries, courtesy of his manifold connections in the shadowy nooks and crannies of the metropolis and beyond – John Morton kept a close eye on Loretta, his erstwhile adversary from times past.

Loretta observed. She listened. She made occasional entries on her mobile phone. But she said nothing. She had come all the way over from the Beltway to London to say... nothing. What was she playing at?

The meeting lasted a mere forty minutes, at which point Taylor read out a list of action points. Everyone had a job to do. When one of them located Edward's whereabouts, he or she would inform Taylor, and they would agree a way to get hold of Edward and bring him back home.

"And no police involvement, if it can be avoided," Taylor instructed. "Edward's family do not want any publicity."

Everyone agreed, but Morton looked inquisitively in the direction of Loretta Farelli as she typed remorselessly into her mobile phone, even after the meeting had disbanded.

✳

Hugh Lombard was the first on the phone to Taylor Snow. He had managed to get through to Edward Ollerson's younger sister Elaine; she was the twin toddlers' mum from the Ollerson family canal holiday and the same woman who had notified Taylor Snow of the burglary at Edward's apartment shortly after his vanishing act. Hugh Lombard put Elaine Ollerson fully in the picture.

Elaine was keen to cooperate and recalled what she knew from memory. Edward had been to the big, old family house in Kidderminster, sometime in late August; had left to go somewhere else (not specified); then returned to stay with his mother in Kidderminster for a few days. That was in mid-to-late September, Elaine Ollerson recalled.

After a few minutes of small talk, Lombard – in his reassuringly quiet way, accompanied by his trademark permanent grin – pressed her gently for more information.

"Has Edward gone to Russia?" he asked.

"Oh, no," Elaine confirmed.

"Or perhaps Ukraine?"

"Certainly not. Whatever gave you that idea?"

"Well, he did say that he intended to do *precisely* that."

But it was no use. None of Edward Ollerson's family knew where he was nor what his intentions were.

Then, as Hugh Lombard and Vivienne Eissinger were at home preparing for a Saturday evening trip to the theatre, the phone rang. Edward Ollerson's sister could not find the keys to the Ollerson family barge, which was moored at a specific location on a canal somewhere in Warwickshire. She had rung the manager of the office that issued the permits for barges on the relevant stretch of the canal. The family barge had moved and had left an empty space.

With Hugh and Vivienne temporarily indisposed, John Morton took immediate control.

The hunt was on – for a canal barge called the *Red October*, which was named after the vessel in one of the many books on the bookshelves at Edward Ollerson's family home, and one of his dad's favourite reads.

※

John Morton clambered up to the loft, and retrieved a box containing atlases and ordnance survey maps. He also brought down some waterproof clothing and a pair of what his wife Alison called 'yomping boots'.

Morton laid out the ordnance survey maps on the dining room table, and traced with his right index finger several possible routes along the canal. If Edward Ollerson was indeed on the family barge, he could either travel east in the direction of the Grand Union Canal network, or west and then either north toward Shropshire or south-west to Stratford-upon-Avon, perhaps joining the River Avon and eventually the River Severn.

Edward Ollerson would need to eat and to fuel his craze for alcohol. At first glance, east looked favourite because there seemed to be more places to haul out and biggish towns en route. But what if Edward had stocked up on supplies? In that case, the western section of the canal would be feasible. In fact, well supplied, Edward could go in any direction he wanted.

The eastern route would bring Edward closer to his home in London. So, Morton reasoned that, on balance, the eastern route should be tried first.

22

THE HORROR, THE HORROR

Sunday, 16 October 2016.
At nine o'clock the next morning, John Morton, Hugh Lombard, Taylor Snow, Loretta Farelli, Katy Drake and Brigita Wolznaski met in two cars at the Ollerson family barge mooring in Warwickshire.

Their first task was to follow the canal in an easterly direction, and to drive from village to village and check the locks and moorings for any sign of the *Red October*. This time-consuming process came to an abrupt halt at a weir next to a picturesque canal-side pub. The lock gates adjacent to the weir had been padlocked together and a sign warned that the lock gates were closed until spring the following year to enable maintenance to be performed.

"Right," Morton announced, "the eastern route is closed, so Edward must have gone west. He must have plentiful supplies because there don't seem to be too many places to haul out along that route."

The famished party decided to have lunch in the canal-side pub, before embarking on the return drive to the barge's permanent moorings and the search for Edward Ollerson and his barge.

They did manage to elicit one titbit of information from the bar staff. Edward had been to the pub a few days earlier, eaten some lunch and then wheeled a trolley full of supplies from a local supermarket to the barge.

They arrived back at the Ollerson family barge moorings in the Midlands at approximately four o'clock in the afternoon. There was not much light left. They might have to break off the search for the day or even abandon it altogether. They decided that they would press on into the evening and, if necessary, continue the search the following day.

Dusk strove, progressively and unfailingly, to subdue a lingering setting sun. Once established, Dusk herself seemed loath to pass over the diurnal baton to Night. By six-thirty in the evening, the fading twilight had finally given way to a deepened shade of dark, blue-black sky. The temperature dropped, and the tree-lined waterways became steeped in nocturnal shadow.

Morton checked the ordnance survey maps, and explained to the search party that the canal network was vast and had many offshoots. It looked like a bigger job than had been anticipated. Moreover, only the two drivers were fully awake. The four passengers had long since succumbed to the seduction of slumber, so they all returned to London.

※

The next day, four cars made their way from London to the Midlands. Alison Morton drove with Katy Drake as her passenger; Taylor Snow accompanied her driver for the day, John Morton; Loretta Farelli was chauffeured by Hugh Lombard; and the redoubtable Shirley Bould (in the guise of Freda Gray) was the driver of the fourth car, in which Brigita Wolznaski was the passenger.

John Morton distributed copies of a map of the region, printed on A3 paper and with the canal routes colour-coded using fibre-tipped markers.

They brought sandwiches, bottles of water, flasks of tea and coffee, and overnight bags in case the search required a third day. There was no time to waste, and at nine-thirty in the morning they arrived at the Ollerson family barge's mooring. The barge had not returned, and an impromptu and self-appointed 'lock keeper' on a neighbouring boat told Morton that, due to ongoing canal maintenance, no traffic had gone east since the previous morning.

Well, that made the job a *little* easier. All cars headed west.

The drive west took in some towns as well as villages. The plan was for each of the cars to scour a specific stretch of the canal network and to meet up at an agreed location.

✳

John Morton and Taylor Snow drove to the River Avon to head off Edward Ollerson if he decided to leave the canal network.

Mid-afternoon, John Morton and Taylor Snow seated themselves on benches overlooking the River Avon at Evesham, while enjoying some sandwiches and lukewarm coffee from a flask. Taylor suggested they discard the tepid coffee from the flask and get hold of some fresh, *real* coffee from a local barista. Morton nodded his assent.

They duly set off in search of a coffee shop, made their purchases and returned to the riverside viewing point with two medium-sized lattes in takeaway cartons.

Peering across the river, Morton noticed a barge moving away from the other boats which were tethered to the quayside. The stirring craft was the same colour as the *Red October* – it had a red hull and mostly cream-coloured living quarters with red trimmings. The spout of a damaged steel chimney listing slightly to the starboard side was the dead giveaway.

The pair ran down the road and across a bridge, and doubled back to the moorings.

An officious man told them that he had chased someone away because he was moored without permission. The description of the man on the barge fitted that of a bearded and bloated Edward Ollerson.

"You'll need a boat to go down that way," declared the officious man. "It's nearly all cross-country, with not many roads thereabouts. There is a motor launch for hire if you would like me to make the call."

Morton agreed, and, immediately, he and Taylor Snow instructed the others to meet at Evesham as soon as possible.

The assembled party boarded the motor launch, heading off in hot pursuit of the rogue vessel at four o'clock in the afternoon.

The hired boat was well-equipped to deal with emergency situations. There was even a defibrillator included with an impressive first aid kit. It was fast also, being a motor launch, although its speed was suppressed deliberately by the captain to safeguard the well-being of delicate river banks and their environs.

A couple of shotguns in their canvas bag containers rested menacingly on a shelf inside a hatch just behind the cabin on the main deck. Above the hatch, a pivoted metal mounting made Morton worry that its purpose might have something to do with the shotguns.

"Oh no, sir," said the ship's mate – a man ten years older than Morton, with a southwestern English lilt to his voice; a full head of fading, brownish hair, with a sprinkling of grey above the temples; and a weather-worn and sunburned face that (illuminated by the setting sun) was almost a deep orange.

"We don't put guns on that thing, but we could manage a harpoon, I suppose," he joked, as Morton's eyebrows raised in revulsion at the thought. "It's always nice to have one of them there pivoted metal support posts handy – you never know when you are going to need some leverage to punt the boat away from the edge if it runs aground..." The ship's mate nodded in the direction of some sturdy-looking oars tethered to the side of the boat adjoining the deck. "Or if the propeller gets tangled up with some underwater flotsam.

"We get all sorts on these boat trips. We even have a telescope on board if you want to do some birdwatching, but I can't say we'll have a need for it today – the light's fading fast. It's quite a powerful scope. We had it propped up during a clear night a couple of years ago to look at the stars. We got a good look at Saturn, too. Have you ever seen Saturn?"

Morton misheard. "No, I've not been to... I mean, no, I have not seen Saturn."

As with the previous day, the dusk took its time to settle. The ship's mate busied himself with a couple of jobs, then returned with a searchlight connected to a long, coiled cable. He mounted the searchlight on the pivoted metal support post and turned it on.

"It don't look as though we'll have any worries when the sun goes down," he beamed triumphantly, as the incredibly bright light illuminated the river and its banks, making a mockery of the receding and increasingly redundant sun. The mate dimmed the light a little, to reduce the glare.

In the gathering gloom, the captain and his mate held a conference at the wheel. The mate returned to his passengers and passed on some good news: it would be impossible for the Ollerson family barge to continue for much longer because the river played tricks on the mind at night and only a mad man would not be intimidated by its warning signs.

The warm Indian summer of the daytime had given way to a chilly, misty evening.

The mate returned to the captain and they engaged in another conflab. The captain grinned at the mate's suggestion. The mist gave the captain the pretext to use the boat's fog horn. This would indicate a danger to vessels fore and aft – and it also invited a response.

The fog horn was sounded.

Morton listened attentively.

There's no reply from ahead, Morton thought. *But one reply from behind, or perhaps two. Edward Ollerson's barge would almost certainly reply if he heard the fog horn. Perhaps it is he who is behind?*

Of course not, Morton reminded himself. *Otherwise, Edward Ollerson would have been overtaken by the motor launch long ago, and that most certainly had* not *happened.*

The reply from behind ceased, possibly because the level-headed pilot of the vessel had heeded the captain's warning and turned his boat round to avoid the risk of encountering dense fog.

Ahead, there was still no reply. This could mean one of two things: either Edward Ollerson had gone on much further ahead and was out of earshot of the fog horn or he had ignored it.

"Perhaps he has moored the barge for the night," the mate suggested.

The captain instinctively slowed down the boat to a crawl. The mate dimmed the searchlight a little more. Then the boat stopped.

They craned their necks to listen. The waters lapped eerily against the sides of the hull.

"There's something up ahead," the captain whispered.

The mate gazed into the vast, empty blackness. Some movement was detected by the dimmed searchlight.

"Bats... and a barn owl," the mate claimed.

The mate returned to the shivering party on the deck and picked up one of the large oars. John Morton did likewise, then he joined the mate as the boat lurched over to starboard and within touching distance of the riverbank.

"Over there," the captain whispered, pointing to the riverbank and up a slope.

"It's only an old, ruined church," the mate said with a sigh.

"There's some noise and a little light," declared the captain as he strained his right ear to listen.

The captain cut the engine and steered the boat as the mate and Morton used the oars to slowly punt in a forward direction, parallel to the riverbank.

"There. Over there. It's up that hill," said the captain.

The mate followed the captain's finger and peered on tiptoe, trying to look over some trees and overgrown foliage.

"I do believe you're right," said the mate. "There's a fork in the river somewhere hereabouts. The tributary leads to the old ruined church of St Anthony, the patron saint of those who have lost their way – on this very river or on the river of life in general. We could haul out on the bank of the tributary, so we don't run the risk of being buffeted by any currents on the main river."

The fork in the river arrived inevitably, and Morton and the mate punted the boat along the right-hand fork and into the shallows. A barge was moored a little way ahead, next to a gravel pathway bordered by a grass verge.

John Morton immediately engaged in a private 'cupped hands' conversation with Hugh Lombard.

"It is almost certainly Edward, but what state is he in?" asked Morton.

The captain and the mate tethered the motor launch to a couple of mooring posts on the bank of the tributary, directly behind the barge. Bright, battery-powered torches were handed out by the captain to his mate, to Morton and to Lombard.

"Wait here please, ladies," the captain requested politely, "in the warmth of the cabin, downstairs. At least until we make sure everything is okay."

But Taylor Snow insisted that she join the men. Loretta Farelli followed suit, as did Katy Drake. Alison, Freda and Brigita remained on the motor launch, covered by a large rug and huddled together downstairs in the cabin.

After disembarking, the four men and three women walked along the bank of the tributary to the barge. It was indeed the *Red October*. A dim light shone within, behind the flimsy curtains. Morton tried the door. It was open, but the barge was deserted. They turned their attention to a glimmer of light up the slope and through the bushes. Through faded autumnal overgrowth, a path could be discerned, so they followed it quietly.

The glimmer of light glowed brighter as they approached the ruined church of St Anthony. The light was coming from within the ruins.

No, thought Morton, *it's coming from behind the ruined church – from a graveyard.*

Between the headstones sat Edward Ollerson, on a small stool next to a portable stove. He seemed to be heating up some water. The diminished stub of a fat cigar was clenched between his teeth. Large, flaming candles bought from a garden centre had been placed at prominent points around the deserted ruins.

Ollerson lifted a small, glass tumbler and poured into it two fingers of whisky. Then he poured a similar measure into a second glass. "Happy birthday, Dad," he said, before downing the glass in one go and pouring the other tumbler into an adjacent grave.

Morton instructed his companions to wait there, out of view. He took Hugh Lombard's arm, pushed him forward in front of him and engaged in another 'cupped hands' conversation.

The sound of cracking twigs prompted Edward Ollerson to suddenly turn around. "Who's there?" he asked drunkenly. "I've got a gun, y'know. Bloody great sawn-off shotgun. Y'don't wanna mess with me!"

John Morton and Hugh Lombard stepped into view.

"Whadda-ya doing here? This is private prop-property!" Ollerson shouted, though his exclamation faded as he struggled to keep his balance on the tiny stool.

Hugh Lombard strolled forward and said, "Edward, we were worried about you. Your family was worried. They asked us to help find you. It's okay, Edward. We are just here to help." Hugh Lombard bent down on one knee and looked Edward Ollerson directly in the eye, attempting to reassure him with a comforting smile.

"I thought I'd seen the last of you," Ollerson said. "Fuckin' great poof." Ollerson turned his head around to look up at Morton. "Fuckin' great poof, isn't he? And a useless turd."

Unperturbed, Lombard produced his normally permanent grin. "Missed you, Edward," said Lombard, diplomatically. "We've all missed you."

"Yeah, well you can all just fuck off, can't you?" Ollerson bellowed.

Morton realised that Hugh Lombard needed support, so he inched forward and stated, "Actually, Edward, we need to know you are okay. We just need to know that you are okay, so that we can tell your family. Yes? Nothing wrong with that, is there? No harm can come of that, can it?"

Morton looked at the gravestone. "Alfred Caractacus Ollerson" it read. The man had died in 1952. "Your granddad, is it?"

"My great-granddad. Granddad was cremated. His ashes were scattered here. My dad's, too," Ollerson replied, almost inaudibly as the volume dwindled toward the end.

"I never knew," Morton said. "Your mum, also?"

"No. She's still alive," replied Ollerson.

"Sorry," Morton said, aware of his faux pas. "I just assumed… sorry, Edward."

We're almost mirror images of each other. Almost, but not quite, Morton reflected.

Edward Ollerson sat in silence.

Morton edged a bit closer, preparing to deploy his skills in the art of persuasion, which basically amounted to coming up with any old story with which to mollify Edward Ollerson. He began, "You have a wonderful sister, Edward. Elaine is a bit concerned about you. Of course, I was sure you would be okay, but you know what women can be like: worrying over nothing the first chance they get, eh? We men have to stick together! Right?"

Morton succeeded in eliciting the first drunken smile, but Ollerson seemed reluctant to budge despite Morton's prolonged attempt at sweet-talking him. An urgent and attention-grabbing ploy was called for.

"The problem is, Edward... How can I put it? Did you see the weather forecast?" queried Morton.

Ollerson remained silent, raised the refilled glass to his lips and took a grim nip.

Morton continued, "It's not good, you know. A big storm is coming up the Bristol Channel. You know what that means, Edward, in this part of the world, near all those flood plains. Rain. Then more rain. And just when you think you've cracked it, and got the boat dried out and up and running, there's an even bigger downpour. We have been told that would be very dangerous for all vessels on the river."

Edward Ollerson looked up toward the black skies above the ruined church. He scanned the torches positioned around the graveyard and declared, "That one's nearly gone out. Gonna have to light it again."

Morton stuck to his task. "Did you not hear me, Edward? A big storm is coming. If it arrives soon, you won't be able to keep the torches alight and you won't be able to get down to the boat because the slope will become sodden. You might even fall into the river."

Deflated, Edward Ollerson looked down. He seemed to have given up.

Morton resumed his sweet-talking. "Let's go back to the boat, Edward. To your family barge. What's it called? *Red October*. That's a classic book – one of my favourites. Let's go back inside the barge. At least we will keep dry if it rains."

Edward Ollerson finally gave in. He had to, really. There is only so much whisky you can drink before blacking out – on top of whatever else he had consumed. And he was tired, dog-tired and exhausted.

The ship's mate remained with Morton, and helped him to tidy away Ollerson's belongings and prepare to escort him down the slope, away from the ruined church and its morose graveyard. Loretta, Taylor and Katy followed.

The captain and Lombard returned to the motor launch. By the time Morton and the mate had helped Ollerson down the slippery slope and into the barge, they had been joined by the captain and Hugh Lombard, together with Alison, Brigita and Freda.

Katy took the lead in navigating a way through the squalor of Edward Ollerson's home inside the barge. She and John Morton helped to calm him down.

But it was all too much for Brigita. When she saw the condition to which Edward had reduced himself and the circumstances in which he was living, her breast began to heave. It heaved progressively more as large, silent tears dropped one by one onto the edge of a table, and dripped from the edge of the table to the floor.

Freda escorted Brigita up the steps and onto the riverbank, telling her not to blame herself and assuring her that, "Edward is just a bit unwell, dear, and needs a bit of help. But he will be okay, Brigita. Trust me."

Hugh Lombard and Freda Gray escorted the sobbing and distraught Brigita back to the motor launch.

The searchlight from a police boat illuminated the river, and a police helicopter with a dazzling spotlight hovered overhead. On a road behind the ruined church, the flashing lights of a police vehicle and an ambulance could be detected.

Edward Ollerson was quite inebriated by this time, which made the paramedics' job both difficult (due to his weight) and easy (being placidly immobile, he could not resist). They hoisted his oversized bulk into a portable ambulance chair, secured his limp body in place, lifted him off the barge and wheeled him up the slope to the ambulance.

Morton telephoned Edward Ollerson's sister, Elaine. They agreed a plan. Morton would remain on the barge overnight. The following day, Elaine would drive to Evesham and hire the motor launch to travel to the barge and to return the barge to Evesham, where Morton's car was parked.

The remainder of the rescue party returned to Evesham immediately via the motor launch and drove straight home to London.

23

DUTY OF CARE

Elaine Ollerson registered her brother as a resident of Oaktrees Hospital in the Sussex countryside and delivered him into the reliable hands of Dr Quinn, the unorthodox psychologist who had helped John Morton to navigate his way out of the woods during his post-traumatic turmoil two years earlier.

Morton retained a fondness for the place; in particular, for the doctor's treatment room (the home of Joey, the imitation skeleton who had survived the wartime blitz and had been adopted as the hospital's mascot); the small apartment in which Morton had lived as a resident for the best part of two months; the canteen and coffee machines, with their never-ending supply of Morton's indispensable craving; and, above all, the magnificent gardens with their resplendent greenery and the pathways dappled with shade, along which Morton commemorated his return to the hospital in a reverie of reminiscences with Dr Quinn.

With Elaine Ollerson's permission, and alone with Dr Quinn in the privacy of his treatment room, Morton described the general character of Edward Ollerson: his quiet and introspective nature, and his tendency to melancholy. Edward tended to be a lone wolf – which was perfectly suited to the desk-bound job he had fashioned for himself, in a style that required little interaction with the real world.

"I'm amazed Edward decided on journalism as a career choice," Dr Quinn observed.

"Well, that is the interesting bit, really." Morton began to explain. "Edward and I were work colleagues. I was passed over in favour of several others (including Edward), even though I know I could have done many of the jobs that became available over the years. Not that I was too bothered. You see, I enjoy being a journalist, for its own sake; the salary is just a means to fund my modest lifestyle. I enjoy meeting people, especially unusual people. People who have a curious take on an event or even the most bizarre of worldviews. A desk-bound job is not for me."

Morton's imagination was stirred, and he began to reminisce... and to try to hypothesise... "Edward could not have been more different. He actually... *wanted* the editor's job. He fancied himself as someone who could... pull together a team of highly-skilled people and get them to... to deliver some tangible and meaningful end-product. He liked the idea of being part of a... a fashionable 'scene', rubbing shoulders with all the up-and-coming young things with their trendy ideas of how a newspaper should be run, and joining in with their projects to steer *The Chronicle* into new areas, even though he found it difficult to come up with new ideas of his own.

"And, for Edward, the whole business about Russia had become something of an *idée fixe*, but in the case of Russia – as with everything else – Edward failed to come up with anything in the way of novel, imaginative ways to approach the issue. I would characterise Edward as a follower, not a leader and not an 'ideas man', if you get my drift.

"He liked to think of himself as important. Someone once described Edward, in a parody of some of the world figures and systems of government that Edward despised, as an 'upwardly mobile apparatchik in some sort of controlling nomenklatura', with direct links to powerful people in the boardroom and with Edward dreaming of becoming top dog eventually – which, in the end, he did.

"But his track record as editor-in-chief of *The Chronicle* turned out, not surprisingly, to be devoid of inspiration. He made as much impact as the proverbial damp squib.

"Maybe he was promoted according to the Peter Principle. Whatever. But I think it is beyond dispute that he wanted to get promoted, repeatedly, just for show, to impress someone – perhaps his partner at the time. In the early days, his particular 'special friend' was a rising star in the Beltway – er, that is, the location of key American government agencies based in Washington DC, if you are not aware, Dr Quinn."

"That would be Loretta, would it not?" Dr Quinn asked as he leafed through the pages in his notepad.

"Loretta Farelli. She has been over here recently, taking an interest in Edward's welfare, in her own little way. She returned to the US soon after Edward was admitted to Oaktrees. She will return to London... eventually... at some point in time."

"So, Loretta was definitely Edward's old flame, or, rather, the most important of his old flames," Dr Quinn remarked. "Did Edward and Loretta part on good terms?"

"As far as I know."

"So, there's no tension between them?"

"Not to my knowledge. Unless you know something that I don't."

Dr Quinn tilted his head a little to the right, contorted his lips to one side, raised his left eyebrow and shrugged.

∗

Morton raised the subject of the costs of Edward Ollerson's treatment at Oaktrees Hospital.

Sir Harold Nevin and Dmitry Krejevsky, at first reluctantly, agreed to foot half of the bill, based upon Morton's belief that they had a duty of care to Edward Ollerson as a vulnerable colleague in the news media industry who had, unfortunately, succumbed to the pressures of the job.

The gesture was also intended to cement in place an improved relationship between *The Chronicle* and *The New Times*, and this proved to be Morton's decisive selling point, because (in spite of all that had happened over the past two and a half years) Sir Harold Nevin still seemed wedded to the idea of somehow involving himself in the business of *The Chronicle*, 'in the right place and at the right time'.

Edward Ollerson's sister, Elaine, expressed her gratitude to Morton for the generous offer.

However, Taylor Snow would have none of it. Edward's illness might well be work-related and, if so, the duty of care was the responsibility of *The Chronicle* and of *The Chronicle* alone. Furthermore, she did not relish the prospect of a compensation claim cropping up out of the blue at an inconvenient moment in the future. But it was nice to know that Edward's former colleagues had taken the matter into consideration.

Yet, unknown to Taylor Snow, during his overnight stop on the canal barge, John Morton had found out something about Edward Ollerson – something that nobody else seemed to know about.

Morton told nobody about it. Not even Sir Harold Nevin nor Dmitry Krejevsky. Nor even his wife, Alison. What Morton had found out fuelled considerations of another duty of care, one that remained outstanding from his trips to Ukraine in 2014 and 2015. A duty of care to his deceased former friend and colleague, Carl Waggoner.

*

John Morton had volunteered to remain on the Ollerson family barge overnight while Edward Ollerson was undergoing the initial stage of his confinement at West Midlands General Hospital, prior to checking in at Oaktrees a few days later.

Alone on the barge, Morton helped himself to a couple of glasses of fresh-tasting red wine from a three-litre, cardboard-covered container, which Edward Ollerson had opened recently. Morton's evening meal consisted of buttered toast and individually-packaged slices of processed cheese, supplemented by a tin of sardines and an apple.

On completing his meal, the empty tin and the apple core were discarded into a packed and very smelly bin stored underneath the diminutive kitchen sink unit. Morton removed the plastic liner from the bin, tied it in a knot and secured it to the external rickety chimney of the barge for later disposal. He then cleaned the bin with washing-up liquid to get rid of the bad smell, dried it with kitchen paper towels and placed a fresh plastic liner into the bin.

He poured himself a third glass of wine, took out a book from his holdall and settled himself down in a ramshackle old armchair that had seen better days. Had the chair not been so decrepit and awkward to sit in (it had one of those seats that sank too low, and that, when you thought you had fixed it, sank again and seemed to sink even lower), Morton would probably have dozed off, awoken around midnight and not been able to get off to sleep again.

However, after twenty minutes of fidgeting in the armchair, Morton gave up and drained his glass. A glass of water was consumed to ward off dehydration, and a tired Morton fixed up a bed for himself and turned in at just after nine-thirty in the evening.

Serendipity had chosen this very moment to intervene in human affairs. So, too, ominously, had Nemesis.

It was pitch dark when Morton awoke. It was four-thirty and far too early for any rational being to get up, but the prospect of turning over to one side, then the other, in a vain attempt to go back to sleep, seemed guaranteed to induce restlessness and to keep him awake. Nevertheless, he drifted into some form of semi-consciousness, during which he was interrupted by a timid voice in the stillness.

"John!"

"John!" The voice tried again, a little louder.

"John! Over here!"

Morton lifted his head and found himself gazing at a fuzzy apparition in the doorway.

Morton's legs twisted as the result of an involuntary reflex, almost perpendicular, like a gymnast.

Where were his glasses? Where was the light? His mobile phone would do. He ferreted about on a bedside table and on the floor near to the bed. Something had fallen off the table. He heard it thud on the carpet. He found the phone on the carpet, used the dim glow of the flat screen to search for his glasses and put them on.

He scanned the room. There was nothing. No apparition and no voice. Perhaps it would return? He turned over on his side, keeping his glasses on and his phone in one hand, as if to surprise the intruder with the phone's torchlight after the glow of the phone had diminished and darkened.

There was no recurrence of the episode. No apparition, no voice and no shuffling of ghostly chains. Nothing.

At six o'clock, Morton decided that he might as well get up. He made his all-important, first-of-the-day trip to the bathroom, almost tripping on yet another of Edward Ollerson's broken and discarded umbrellas, and – upon his return to the miniaturised lounge-cum-kitchen – he filled the kettle with water and switched it on.

Edward Ollerson had bought hundreds of sachets of coffee, one of which Morton found quite acceptable at the time, even though it was not a patch on the real thing prepared in a cafetière or a proper espresso machine.

Edward has surely become 'Mr Convenience-Store Incarnate', Morton mused.

With his jacket wrapped loosely around his shoulders, Morton wandered up on deck. It was dark in the countryside, but some light could be detected from nearby towns. To the east were the early signs of the rising sun. Morton placed his mug of coffee on the roof of the barge and leaned on the roof, elbows first. He removed them quickly. His forearms and elbows were drenched with dew.

The sounds of water birds – coot and moorhen – croaked down river, and the acrid stench of dank compost wafted in from unseen farmland.

Through an opening in the murky night sky peeped a waning gibbous moon; left over from a beautiful full moon a few days earlier, declining in size and stature, its slow death was shrouded partially by cloud, fog and mist…

Morton returned to the lounge-cum-kitchen inside the barge and poured himself a second mug of sachet coffee.

Some stale milk had spilled inside the fridge, dripping onto the floor when the door was opened and topping up the encrusted residue from an earlier spillage. He emptied the fridge, then cleaned it inside and out with a cloth and a little washing-up liquid. He dried the fridge with kitchen towels and replaced the contents. Finally, he scraped the encrusted residue off the floor.

How about breakfast? Morton thought. *Not yet. Maybe in a couple of hours, but it will do no harm to find out what is available.*

The pantry yielded many tins of fruit, vegetables and meat. Discounted varieties of corned beef, luncheon meat and beans with sausages seemed to be the favoured delicacy. There was also packaged food of many types: packets of biscuits, crisps and cereal, too – cheaper, store's own brands of cornflakes and Rice Krispies.

But there was no milk. Ultra-heat treated (UHT) milk (Edward's preferred choice) is ideal for lengthy periods of unrefrigerated storage, so – Morton reasoned – there must be a supply somewhere. Morton scoured the kitchen cupboards. They were full of pots and pans, and junk. The milk must be stored elsewhere.

In the living room, he found only bookshelves, tables and chairs, so he tried the common storage areas next to the bedrooms. The largest of three wardrobes contained some of Edward's clothes, dumped in a pile, not ironed and not even folded. The middle-sized wardrobe contained damp and mildewed clothes, dishevelled and draped lopsidedly on hangers, and which had obviously not been worn for some time. A pair of holdall bags were squashed at the bottom of the wardrobe and covered with layer upon crammed layer of shoes and grubby wellington boots of different sizes.

Above the first and second wardrobes, a door opened upward. A metal strip attaching the door to the right-hand side of the wooden frame clicked into place, enabling the door to remain open, unaided. The carcase of a dead rat – its feet in the air and tail curled around the rodent's droppings – and the animal's final, desperate scratchings, which were visible on the door and the sides, were all that remained in the overhead cupboard.

Morton pinched his nose with his left hand, coughed and grimaced, and closed the overhead door with his right hand.

Having no overhead storage space, the smallest wardrobe was taller than its neighbours, and the same depth but a bit slimmer.

Morton opened it. It seemed to be full, from top to toe, of unopened boxes of red wine.

Edward. How much wine did you buy? he thought.

A receipt slipped out of the wardrobe and spiralled to the floor. Morton shook his head in disbelief. Edward Ollerson had bought 100 boxes of wine, to obtain a sizeable discount. Three hundred litres – that was more than enough for a bottle a day for a whole year!

The receipt was three months old. Morton reckoned that most of the wine boxes had been left behind at Edward's flat in Camden Town and that the empties had been utilised as archive repositories for Edward's research materials.

As Morton dismembered the tower of wine boxes in the third wardrobe, some cartons of UHT milk peeped out from behind them. Morton reached in to clutch the top of one of the cartons of milk with his fingertips. As he did so, other cartons of milk wobbled and detached themselves from the tower. It seemed that the entire contents of the wardrobe were about to fall in Morton's direction in an avalanche of heavily laden cartons and cardboard boxes. He juggled unsuccessfully as, one by one, each box slipped from his grasp and began to tumble down, even as he pressed his entire body forward in a futile attempt to keep the whole structure in place.

"Shit!" he found himself saying, as the pile loosened further, and one box landed on his bare foot, with the sharp edge of one of the boxes of wine catching him painfully on the instep.

"Oh, fucking... shit!" he exclaimed, as the pointed corner of another box cut bloodlessly into the flesh just above his left kneecap. The tower of wine boxes and milk cartons disgorged itself noisily onto the floor.

His face contorted in agony, Morton hopped and staggered around the adjacent bedroom, grappling at the walls for non-existent support. Then, he bent over for a prolonged period with both arms extended fully and his hands wrapped around the thigh muscles just above his kneecaps, as, with deep breaths and puffed-out cheeks, he tried to recover his composure.

"Edward. You might have at least packed those boxes... with... a bit more..."

Morton's severe discomfort was suddenly arrested. At the bottom of the pile of boxes inside the wardrobe, Morton saw the guilty party. It was another box, which was larger than the others. Its contents made it bulge, and the lid slanted down toward the front of the wardrobe. As a means of support for the other containers, the box qualified as a poorly chosen foundation stone. However, it was not a foundation stone. It contained something that Edward Ollerson did not want anybody else to see. He had hidden it away.

Morton looked at the box, which at one time had contained five reams of A4 paper, and was familiar from somewhere in Morton's not-too-distant memory. It all came back to him. Carl Waggoner and his seventeen boxes, which Morton had 'inherited' after Carl's death in the Donbass in May 2014.

Bracing himself for a surprise, Morton raised the lid of the box. His eyes widened. The box contained treasure; real treasure.

When he had finished his examination of the box, Morton repacked the contents carefully and put the box back into the wardrobe, with the reassembled tower of boxes of wine and cartons of milk, as though the whole contraption had never been disturbed.

Two years earlier, at Carl Waggoner's funeral, John Morton had met Carl's brother, Peter. It was Peter who had arranged the transfer of Carl's boxes to John Morton in 2014. Following Morton's discovery of a similar box on the canal barge, a meeting between John Morton and Peter Waggoner seemed a reasonable and worthwhile proposition. So, a few days after he had left the barge and helped to get Edward Ollerson settled into Oaktrees Hospital, John Morton met Peter Waggoner for a pint after work in the City of London.

Peter had been attending a two-week residential training course. He had been both trainee and trainer.

At first, John Morton allowed Peter Waggoner to do the talking.

Peter explained how he had used his role of trainer to negotiate a discount for the price of the training course, and this discount enabled Peter to ingratiate himself with the company accountant who wrote up the end-of-year financial report for Peter's department. Furthermore, Peter's name in lights (and not for the first time), as a well-known and knowledgeable consultant lecturer, endeared him to his managing director for life.

Halfway through his second pint, John Morton decided the time was right to determine exactly how many of Carl's boxes had been delivered to the Waggoner household from Odessa two years earlier. There might still be more boxes to examine.

Not wanting to alert Peter's inquisitiveness or to raise Peter's hopes that he might have some fresh clues concerning Carl's untimely death, Morton avoided all mention of his new discovery. He merely asked Peter if he wanted Carl's seventeen boxes to be returned to the Waggoner family.

"They are in the spare bedroom and Alison wants them removed," Morton threw in. "There are about seventeen or eighteen in all, I think. We have *all* of Carl's boxes. *All* of them." Morton emphasised.

"No, not all of them; there were more." Peter Waggoner stated.

Morton pretended to be puzzled.

"There were twenty-five." Peter Waggoner was very specific.

"Twenty-five? As many as that. I don't think I have that many," declared Morton.

"We only gave you the boxes that seemed relevant to you. Four or five are at Mum and Dad's house. I have two or three. I remember when they arrived." Peter sipped his beer, his left elbow resting on the bar. "On a pallet, they were. Packed in two layers – three boxes wide by three in length, making eighteen boxes. Plus there were seven more boxes on a third layer. The pallet also included a suitcase and a couple of smaller bags. Twenty-five boxes, all told."

Seventeen plus four plus two makes twenty-three, Morton reckoned. *And one in Edward Ollerson's possession makes twenty-*

four. Is there a twenty-fifth box in Peter's house, or in his mum and dad's house?

Morton pretended to phone his wife to get her to count the number of boxes.

"Definitely seventeen. Thanks, love," Morton repeated out loud.

Peter seemed a bit put out by the low number. He rang his mum and dad. The original pallet had been delivered to Peter, who had delivered four boxes to his mum. Peter's mum remembered the exact number. So, it all boiled down to how many boxes were in Peter's possession. He rang his wife. There were so many boxes, she recalled, including all the clothes and Carl's odds and sods. Only two boxes remained, somewhere in the garden shed or in the garage.

The third box (the twenty-fourth in the grand scheme of things) had been addressed to the editor-in-chief of *The Chronicle* newspaper. That was probably the box that had ended up in Edward Ollerson's possession. And there might have been a fourth box (a twenty-fifth box in the grand scheme of things), or someone might have miscounted.

However, even without the seemingly fabled twenty-fifth box, Morton had enough fresh information to expand his enquiries.

While on the barge, Morton had used a spare mobile phone to photograph the most interesting and relevant documents in box number twenty-four. He ended up with a large volume of data, stored securely.

At home in north London, Morton kissed his wife goodbye for the day and set about his business.

The first step was to switch off the Wi-Fi router to prevent any spooks from monitoring his activities. He switched on his CD player, loaded a selection of Bach concertos, and ensured the volume was set to a reasonable level. Using an old, spare laptop, Morton transferred the data from the spare phone and stored the electronic copies on two small USB flash drives that he had purchased for the sole purpose of storing the information he had copied from the box in the Ollerson family barge.

He connected a cable from the spare laptop to a laser printer and printed off two copies of each of the files. He set one copy of each file to one side; this copy would probably end up in the possession of Dmitry Krejevsky or be secreted away somewhere on the estate of Sir Harold Nevin.

He made sure that none of the data remained on his spare phone and spare laptop; then he switched off both devices and stored them safely away.

He set out the remaining A4 sheets on the extended table in the dining room: there were 205 pages, stacked in fourteen piles, each of which corresponded to the fourteen documents that he had photographed.

Some of the documents were in Russian and English, parallel to each other, side by side on the same page. Dmitry Krejevsky would be able to verify that one column was an accurate translation of the other.

Here was proof that officials within the Russian and the US governments had been in touch for a long time, behind the scenes; had been secretly talking to each other; and had even been engaged in a constant stream of probing attempts at reconciliation during 2013 and the first few months of 2014, including the formulation of a range of treaties. The documents were marked "DRAFT", and all of them were stamped "TOP SECRET".

Oh Carl. You, you... you genius! You blond, sunburned... Carl, you... you legend! Morton thought, with gusto.

After lunch, Morton sat in his favourite chair with his feet up on a stool. Exhausted by his efforts, he allowed himself to doze a little.

He was in high spirits. At last he had discovered what Carl Waggoner had been up to in Ukraine – probably as long ago as three years, and before the crisis exploded into the violent Maidan colour revolution.

Now he *knew* why Carl had been in the Donbass. Somebody must have leaked these documents to him, probably over a long time. Carl must have been near Donetsk to pick up his latest drop. Carl was, in all probability, 'killed in action' before he could complete his mission.

At the top of the pile was the most interesting document of all. A *draft* agreement between the US State Department and the Foreign Ministry of the Russian Federation concerning an *understanding* not to interfere in each other's affairs, and a discussion of a hypothetical partition of spheres of influence in the world between rival groups of major powers.

It was no wonder that Carl Waggoner had regaled his then employer, Tom Hamble, with something not unlike the Molotov-Ribbentrop Pact of 1939.

For Russia, read Russia and China, thought Morton. *For the US, read the US and its allies.*

The draft treaty seemed to imply that the allies of the US (particularly major European powers including the UK, France and Germany, as well as the EU) would expect some crumbs of the cake to trickle down in their direction.

But the thing reeked of a *draft* understanding between Russia and the US only.

The American diplomats seemed to have realised that the task of taking on and brushing Russia aside might be too big a job to undertake, and had therefore instigated the talk of spheres of influence, trying to draw Russia into a different scheme.

The Russians seemed keen to at least play along, without making any firm commitments about the proposed spheres of interest; instead, they tried to focus the attention of their 'American partners' on, to quote from the draft document, "respect for Russia's point of view" and the "halting of further expansion of NATO toward the Russian border".

China provided the perfect partner to Russia – in a peer-to-peer 'trust' relationship – so that, although the Chinese were not directly involved in the talks between the Russians and Americans, the peer-to-peer 'trust' relationship meant that China's interests were being taken into account by its Russian ally. Furthermore, one of the documents implied that the Russians were making sure that their Chinese allies were being kept fully informed.

On the other hand, although it seemed likely that at least some of the European leaders knew of or at least suspected of the existence of this draft *understanding*, it was by no means clear what they would get out of it.

In any case, what exactly *was* Europe, these days? The great powers of the nineteenth and early twentieth centuries were in decline by now. Bigger fish had displaced them on the global stage. None of the great European powers of the early twentieth century – Germany, France and the UK – had supplanted the Soviet Union when it had exited the stage in the early 1990s. And as for the EU, it was only now debating whether to create its own EU armed forces.

Maybe the Europeans thought they would get a slice or two of the cake. Or perhaps, an ominous thought dawned on Morton, the finalised treaty would designate Europe as the 'cake' itself.

The first cold war had been characterised by the so-called Iron Curtain separating the East from the West. The US had recently instigated a *cordon sanitaire* between the countries on Russia's border and the rest of Europe, to quarantine views that were contrary to the US-imposed, Russophobic dominant narrative.

Maybe the senior Russian and American diplomats were coming round to the realisation that a new cold war might entail something similar to the Iron Curtain, and that the current stand-off with NATO troops and military materiel right on Russia's border was unsustainable over the long term; therefore, they had decided among themselves to play a 'long game', prepare the groundwork for a final agreement and get their ducks in a row.

It would be a – albeit speculative at this early stage – partition of Europe, not by the great powers of the early twentieth century but by the great powers of the early twenty-first century.

Drawing lessons from his discussions with Sir Harold Nevin and his friends – Sir Quentin Forbes and Lord Ernest Anderian – Morton formed the opinion that there was no guarantee that this *understanding*, which was a veritable triumph of diplomacy (if it had been signed off by both sides), would ever see the light of day.

It was, Morton hypothesised, more likely to form the basis of a working document, providing guidelines that might frame the conduct of the new cold war.

It was all done in secret and behind the scenes.

A close inspection of some of the other documents gave the impression that a lot of ideas were being thrown around, inviting discussion, but not nailing anything down firmly.

The *draft understanding* was dated October 2013. But what was the true status of this document, right now in October 2016, three years further along the road? And after all the political game changers of the past few short years?

Russia had offered Europe a seat at the table of its project of Eurasian Integration. Europe had eschewed this project in favour of continuing with more of the same, which implied a consolidation of a Western-oriented security policy through NATO.

Instead of a regional or a global agreement based on *collective* security, the Europeans and the Americans seemed to have openly opted for cold war against Russia. On the face of it, NATO had chosen the 'easy option' – in the sense of it being the easy decision to make, but not necessarily the "easiest task to see through to its inevitable conclusion", as the draft document described.

The final objectives of this 'easy option' were defined clearly by the US and NATO: a regime change in Russia and China, bringing with it the much-hoped-for kowtowing of the East to the West.

However, there was no plan – other than to mount sanctions and other forms of pressure imposed by the West against its Eurasian adversaries, over and over again, even though those sanctions failed to produce the hoped-for regime change.

Furthermore, on some key issues, the Western allies were at odds with each other. At the same time as actively supporting the Americans in their self-appointed role of 'global policemen', the Europeans resisted the TTIP, which was the American's *tour de force* that would tie Europe in with the US, including special courts that could seek compensation in the billions from governments that, allegedly, 'might be' (not definitely *were*, just *might be*) in breach of contract with the claimants – the rich and powerful transnational corporations.

Many in Europe had dug their heels in over TTIP, with a resounding, "No, thank you!", a firmly dismissive, *"Nein danke!"*, and a gracious *"Excusez-moi, mesdames et messieurs, mais... non merci."*

Having experienced failure, in terms of their efforts to bring Russia to heel, many in Europe did not see the point in ratcheting up the pressure by imposing further sanctions against Russia, only to have it blow back in their faces a second time.

So, there we have it in a nutshell. A real war between the great powers of Russia/China on one side and the US on the other. Plus, just like at the outset of World War II, there was an uneasy 'war of position' or *sitzkrieg*, and, above all, a 'war of words'.

A phoney war, just like the period between autumn 1939 and summer 1940.

However, the phoney war represented not only a period of relative calm and stability between the antagonists but also its opposite – a sense of insecurity that might precede the volatile outbreak of hostilities.

The outlook had some positives; in particular, the prospect of some sort of East–West détente, but, overall, the long-term forecast remained grim.

Bearing this in mind, not only on behalf of Carl Waggoner and Edward Ollerson but also on behalf of The Great British Public and even the entire population of Planet Earth, John Morton felt (not for the first time) that he carried the burden of an additional duty of care.

∗

Morton's self-satisfaction melted away as the new reality dawned on him. He rose from his armchair and returned to the dining room. He surveyed his findings, which were spread out on the dining room table in his customary fashion. Now he was ready to reveal those findings to his colleagues, starting with Dmitry Krejevsky, to enable the pair to test the validity of his hypothesis.

But, before he could do that, John Morton had one more piece of news to deal with.

At just after three o'clock in the afternoon, John Morton received a phone call from Taylor Snow. Edward Ollerson's sister had been contacted by Oaktrees Hospital. Her brother had been found hanged in his hospital quarters.

24

SMOKE AND MIRRORS

Wednesday, 26 October 2016.

"So how do you intend to go about validating all of this?" Dmitry Krejevsky enquired, referring to Morton's newly discovered trove of documents.

"I've got Vivienne scouring Wikileaks and other whistle-blowing websites to try to find something, anything," Morton replied.

"And?"

"No joy. I have often wondered if governments deliberately leak stuff, or allow it to be leaked, as a diversion; perhaps, to provide fodder for the media to get worked up about, as a smokescreen, while those same governments keep the most important stuff obscured from view."

"That is probably true," smiled Dmitry Krejevsky. "I'll put out a few feelers, but I'm not making any promises that I can't keep."

✳

Vivienne Eissinger was taken to one side by John Morton, and given clear instructions.

"Nobody must even know that we are looking for these documents or anything related to these documents. We don't want anyone to know that we have discovered that this stuff actually exists; otherwise, they might use that as a pretext to interfere yet again in our affairs," Morton explained.

Vivienne decided that the best way to achieve anonymity would be to work as far away from the office as possible, so she and Hugh Lombard took a flight to Dusseldorf, ostensibly for a long weekend, and hired a fast Mercedes saloon. Vivienne drove like lightning along the autobahns, scaring her passenger witless in the process.

Vivienne took the opportunity to call in on a few friends along the way, and whiled away a couple of hours here and there checking up on whistle-blowing websites, using the electronic devices and Wi-Fi connections of people and public spaces whose online activity was unlikely to come to the attention of the NSA or any other intelligence-gathering services.

Vivienne drew a blank. There was no record of the documents.

※

Dmitry Krejevsky also drew a blank and soon gave up the ghost.

Instead, he and John Morton paid a visit to Oaktrees Hospital to meet with Dr Quinn.

※

Friday, 28 October 2016.

"We run an open house here at Oaktrees," Dr Quinn reminded his two guests. "Many of our patients, including casualties from the military, come here with severe problems. The last thing we want to do is to alarm the patients and heighten any suspicions they may have. As soon as possible, we place new arrivals in their own quarters. The intention is to create in their minds a sense of a 'home from home' – and to encourage the patient to regard himself or herself as a member of one big, happy family. The 'Oaktrees family'.

"You know our ways, don't you, John? You're familiar with them from your little stay here a couple of years ago.

"In Edward's case, we even bent our own rules and allowed him access to a little wine. Sometimes, I would join him for a glass on the terrace, though I felt that his taste in wine left something to be desired. Wine from cardboard boxes does taste a little like, well, cardboard, don't you think, John?"

"It has its merits, Dr Quinn. It is cheap, nobody really cares much after a few glasses, and if it falls on the floor, it won't break – that's very handy, if there are lots of kids running around," Morton responded, alluding to the barbeque parties he and Alison had thrown over the years.

This raised a forbearing smile from Dr Quinn, but he confessed to being "a trifle despondent", as he recounted some of the details of Edward Ollerson's sudden demise. "I never saw it coming, frankly. Sure, Edward was a bit down in the mouth, but that is not unusual here, especially with new residents.

"We tried to maintain the illusion that everything in Edward's life was normal, even though we knew it was not. Edward was allowed two glasses of red wine per day, usually one in the afternoon and one early evening. Throughout the day, we plied him with decaffeinated coffee that tasted like the real thing, as we attempted to wean him off this addiction.

"Edward showed some adverse reaction to the withdrawal of narcotics. I take it his sister told you about this dark aspect of his life? In all its wretched detail? Tragic."

"Yes," Morton said with a sigh. "His sister, Elaine, told me that the examination of Edward's teeth showed that a couple were working themselves loose and that his gums were tender in places. Apparently, some time ago, Edward had been prescribed some form of sedative to help him sleep and his GP had, at some point in time, prescribed a stimulant to ward off some form of depression.

"But Edward kept this a secret and did not divulge it to his family. Except to his sister, Elaine – after she managed to drag it out of him while he was stretched out on the sofa in her lounge. 'Pissed as a fart, he was', she said. She sounded really annoyed and frustrated, as though she suspected that something was going on that her brother was deliberately concealing from her."

Dr Quinn outlined some additional detail. "The dental examination we gave him when he was admitted to Oaktrees – well, the results are still being debated. The coroner has all the relevant information about all *known* aspects of Edward's health and general welfare. As for the *unknown* aspects, we can only speculate. Narcotics is a grey area, even in these so-called 'enlightened times'. Researchers and practitioners are wary of jumping to conclusions when it comes to tracing back symptoms to their most likely cause, or causes.

"My hunch is that Edward met somebody, perhaps in a bar over a drink, who put an idea into his mind about the recreational use of narcotics. The idea might have been sold to him as some sort of panacea, which had the properties required to calm him down, to cheer him up and whatever else the dealer told him – all encapsulated in one single potion and taken in one single shot. That is a fiction, of course; there is no such thing as a panacea. But, when one is desperate, I suppose one can be talked into believing any old rot.

"Edward would have been given something to try subsequently, probably some form of methamphetamine (which would account for the deterioration of his teeth and gums – the notorious condition known as 'meth mouth').

"The problem is that you never know where this stuff comes from, what is really in it and how it has been made – all of this is unknown to the prospective punter. Methamphetamine, perhaps mixed with some other substances as a cocktail, would have been ingested in tablet form or smoked, but not injected. No syringe marks were found on his body, so the narcotic must have been taken orally.

"So that is my hunch and my theory. But my other great area of uncertainty concerns why, in the first place, he would use something like methamphetamine. Cocaine is more expensive, and it would be more of a fit for Edward's social position. He was not exactly short of money, even after his pay was cut. Methamphetamine is, by all accounts, popular as a stimulant and an aphrodisiac in some fashionable circles.

"However, Edward was – as you said a while ago – a bit of a loner. He found it difficult to socialise, and did not join any clubs or spend much time at parties. Even his one-on-one friendships were awkward and typical of a sociopath in many ways, always being geared toward how Edward would benefit from the relationship rather than how the relationship would be a shared experience of mutual advantage.

"That explains why I came up with my 'pusher and punter in the pub' theory. He might have tried the substances he was given, decided they did the job and then used this potion to 'doctor himself' instead of bothering his GP."

Dmitry Krejevsky looked out of the window and exhaled deeply, in despair.

"Moving on to the more mundane aspects of Edward's life here at Oaktrees..." Dr Quinn continued. "We told him that we do not allow fast food or pizza here. He looked a bit deflated upon hearing this, but our chef was on the top of his game and – when he served Edward and I with a superb haunch of slow-roasted lamb with all the trimmings, and served up with a decent bottle of claret (which really came into its own when the cheeseboard arrived later) – Edward really perked up. I told him that it was a bit like being on holiday here, and when we go on holiday we can expect only the best food we can buy. I told him this to cheer him up a bit, to get him to relax, to take time out, to induce him to open up a bit and to talk. You know my ways, John."

"Did he not try to get out? To escape?" asked Morton.

"That is not possible during daytime. We make sure each patient is engaged in a supervised activity or in a counselling session. We gave Edward something to make him sleep at night."

"So how did he come to hang himself?"

Dr Quinn looked down. "I don't know, John. We do not allow our guests to avoid taking their medication. We are very strict on that. But there were no signs of a struggle, if you are thinking that there might have been foul play."

"Well, there wouldn't be any signs of a struggle, would there?" Morton submitted. "Not if he was already sedated and unconscious."

Dr Quinn appeared flummoxed.

Dmitry Krejevsky raised an eyebrow and covered his mouth with the back of his hand to hide an admiring grin, while thinking, *You might have made a half-decent legal counsel, John Morton, had you been called to the bar!*

Morton followed through with his line of argument. "Did you learn anything from the CCTV footage, Dr Quinn?"

"Of what? Inside the patients' rooms? We have no cameras there. They are private quarters," Dr Quinn stated.

"What about corridors, communal areas, exits – that sort of thing?"

"Oh no. Those areas are not monitored. We don't want to encourage our patients to think they are being watched. They can be a bit sensitive about that, you know." Dr Quinn offered a bag of boiled sweets to Morton and Krejevsky (which they declined politely), and fiddled noisily with the bag's contents before popping a striped minty confection into his own mouth.

He continued, "There is perimeter security: a wall and a security lodge at the entrance to the hospital. That should be enough to prevent anyone getting out, although that has never happened. And who would want to break into *here*? It is in the middle of nowhere and has a reputation locally as a 'military and mental institution', inhabited by 'lunatics' and the 'dangerous and criminally insane'.

"Right from the start, we deliberately encouraged the superstitious souls who tried to implant that image into local folklore; with some success, I believe. A camouflaged military vehicle and an army ambulance are stationed permanently in the car park. The dead trees along the lane leading to the hospital are left unpruned; they look decidedly eerie during a night-time drive up the lonely lane, particularly when the wind howls.

"Thus, the seed was planted in the mind...

"Who in their right mind would want to take a chance breaking into such a spooky place? And as for the hospital itself, it is staffed twenty-four hours a day, with routine but discrete patrols by members of staff. It was never designed to be a prison or – perish the thought – anything remotely resembling an asylum for the insane!"

"So, why do you think Edward hanged himself?" Morton pressed on. "And what did he use? A piece of cord? Where did he get that from?"

"The cord was on the premises," confirmed Dr Quinn. "There is an increasing demand for our services so, from time to time, we need to expand the size of the campus. Consultants sometimes come in to help us to plan the site of the next building. Materials for construction and maintenance can be found in this very building if you are predisposed to look for it. We place the same degree of trust in our suppliers and partners in industry as we do in our own staff, and they reciprocate. If suppliers leave their gear hanging around, we don't object, and we certainly do not go around looking for bits of cord to take home for whatever nefarious practices we and our wives might get up to.

"I am talking about the use of cord in DIY and for home furnishing, of course," Dr Quinn explained, to general laughter.

※

Once again, it came down to motive, means and opportunity.

Regarding opportunity, security appeared to be provided by smoke and mirrors. It had worked well at Oaktrees Hospital for a long time, so why change it?

Nonetheless, there were many opportunities to gain undetected access to the hospital: getting over the wall, which would be child's play for an experienced professional; disguising oneself as a workman, which also would be a doddle; or pretending to be someone from the military by entering the courtyard and distracting the security guard, while a confederate or two secreted themselves inside the parked military vehicles, or went straight through a scarcely used side entrance to the hospital.

Even without letting your imagination run too far away with itself, it was clear that – for the determined intruder – gaining access to Oaktrees Hospital would be a breeze.

Means was known already: strangulation by a piece of cord.

As for motive, that was the 'big unknown' and the key to unlocking the case.

Who would want Edward Ollerson out of the way, and why? Was it related to Carl Waggoner's death? Both men had been in possession of documents that might support the development of an alternate narrative. Had he survived, Carl surely would have done precisely that. But would Edward Ollerson? It was unlikely. Edward Ollerson was linked tongue-and-groove to the prevailing narrative of the neoconservative, liberal-internationalist Establishment. Throughout his career, Edward Ollerson had been dedicated wholeheartedly to maintaining the status quo.

However, times change, and people change. Lately, a whole array of unexpected twists and turns had challenged prevailing narratives, provoking rethinks on a range of subjects to an extent not experienced in living memory.

And Edward Ollerson's behaviour had become decidedly unpredictable.

So, concerning a possible story based on Carl Waggoner's twenty-fourth box of documents that had come into Edward's possession, maybe Edward did have something in mind. But what? And who did he tell? Or if he kept it to himself (which was his wont), who found out about it?

Morton had no obvious suspects in mind, but he recalled that Loretta Farelli had taken an unusual interest in Edward Ollerson at the time of the hostile takeover of *The Chronicle* in April, six months earlier.

Prior to the 'assignation' at the Grand National meeting in Liverpool in April, Loretta had worked with Katy Drake to engineer the hostile takeover and to turn *The Chronicle*'s editor-in-chief, Edward Ollerson, into (to all intents and purposes) Loretta's prisoner. It was not exactly the most cordial of acts, and not exactly the action of a 'true friend', but more like the handiwork of a mafioso or of a desperado, even.

After the hostile takeover of *The Chronicle*, Loretta had instructed Katy Drake to ensure Edward was 'looked after'. When Katy had delegated this task to Brigita, Loretta did not seem to mind, even though Brigita was the wrong person for the job, and the facts on the ground had borne this out.

How typical of Loretta to come up with an idea, run it past a co-thinker like Katy, call it a plan and kick it off. There had been no analysis of how events might play out and no plan B if something went wrong. When Brigita had thrown Edward over, with Taylor Snow's support, the thwarted and enraged Loretta Farelli had hit the roof.

So, Loretta's plan A had failed. What next? She seemed keen enough to locate the missing Edward, and to go on the 'barge hunt' jaunt with people she regarded as far beneath herself.

Why do that? They were two tiring days, each stretching late into the night. Why make all that effort?

To *double down*, of course.

That was what neoconservatives like Loretta do. They assume that they are in the right and that they could never be wrong. They assume that, if something does go wrong, someone else is to blame, not them; then they *double down* and repeat the same process all over again – and again and again, if necessary.

Edward escaped, so Loretta's immediate response was to double down, recapture him and make him her prisoner, all over again. The female of the species is deadlier than the male, certainly in Loretta's case.

But there was also another angle to consider: the simple question of *why*.

Why try to manoeuvre Edward into a subservient position and exploit this one-sided relationship in the way she did?

That led directly to the next question in the logical sequence: *what* did Edward know? Or, truly pertinent in this case: *what* might Loretta have *thought* that Edward knew?

That the Russians and Americans had been in discussions behind the scenes all along? Perhaps for years? And nobody knew about it? Or, at least, nobody was 'telling tales outside of school'.

Or, maybe, somebody *was* 'telling tales outside of school', or was at least thinking about 'telling tales outside of school'.

Maybe Edward was about to blab about something, to make a name for himself.

Edward had previous form – the leaking of the Russian battle plans earlier in the year. In addition, Edward had told John Morton and Hugh Lombard, to their faces only a few weeks earlier, of his intention to travel to Ukraine to get a scoop and to write a book.

Edward Ollerson being cast once again as a loose cannon; that might not go down too well in the Beltway.

The previous custodians of the 'box on the barge', Carl Waggoner and Edward Ollerson, were no longer alive. Therefore, Morton assumed – correctly as it turned out – that the documents in the box would find their way to Loretta Farelli in the Beltway eventually, and those documents would never see the light of day. They would be safe from public disclosure.

Subsequently, after Loretta had arranged for the box to be sent over to her, she would have experienced a hard-earned sense of relief; at which point, she would have switched off and not even thought about who else might know about the documents. And, as a direct consequence of the non-disclosure of the top-secret documents, Loretta would have ensured that the status quo was maintained...

Specifically, *The Chronicle* would remain straightjacketed within the limits of the dominant narrative: emphatically, with no talk of a rapprochement between East and West; and, emphatically, with no challenge from within *The Chronicle* to the Russophobic dominant narrative.

Precisely what Loretta wanted.

Nobody would suspect that Morton knew about the documents, because he was only supposed to be minding the boat and helping the family to return it safely to its proper moorings in Warwickshire. Morton had left the wardrobe exactly as he had found it, minus one half-empty carton of milk, which Elaine Ollerson would probably have assumed had been in the fridge all along.

Dmitry Krejevsky knew about the box; he was in possession of one of the USB flash drives and a spare hard copy of the top-secret documents – which Krejevsky insisted should be validated to ensure they were not mere forgeries.

Dmitry Krejevsky simply did not have the time to go through them (for the time being, at least) because he was focused on coverage of the war in Syria and keeping the readers of *The New*

Times abreast of rapidly changing developments – at least daily and sometimes more than once per day.

Morton had shown the documents to the trustworthy Hugh Lombard and to Vivienne Eissinger, for whom (as an aristocrat, 'with breeding') confidentiality was a modus operandi.

Nobody else knew of the contents of Carl Waggoner's twenty-fourth box.

Nevertheless, Morton could not get the subject out of his mind. Throughout the weekend, it played on his mind. The whole weekend, when the stresses and strains of his workday could be set aside, to be replaced by various forms of rest and relaxation – often in the form of nothing much to do. And, during those times when he had nothing much to do, John Morton became prone to daydreaming and idle speculation, which would, in time, lead him to the only possible, inexorable conclusion.

Morton's idle speculations intruded into his thoughts during a morning coffee break, were put to one side during a team meeting in the office and, finally, reached the inexorable conclusion as Morton sat alone during a late pub lunch.

Edward... Brigita... Shirley (disguised as Freda)... Katy... Loretta... Taylor...

Loretta...

Loretta...

Loretta...

One after another, Loretta's plans had gone wrong.

Concerning The Chronicle, *the stakes were high; probably very high indeed.*

A faceless 'someone' had invested a lot of time and effort – and money – in The Chronicle. *And, at a moment of crisis, a faceless 'someone' had decided – out of the blue – to swing in Taylor Snow to 'fix'* The Chronicle. *Not Loretta. Not Edward. Not Katy. They had all failed.*

Taylor Snow had been swept into power by an 'unseen hand' – at Loretta's expense! It seems incredible, but it's true.

Taylor's ascension would have reflected badly on Loretta – there was no longer one star in the firmament but two. And the new star was rising higher and higher with every passing day, sponsored by the 'unseen hand', but self-propelled and capable of wreaking havoc with Loretta's plans.

Knowing Loretta, she would not be happy with this state of affairs. What would she do? Taylor Snow had, with what was obviously significant support from unknown backers, mounted a coup d'état, ousted Loretta from her *'remote control'* of The Chronicle, and had gone into an unfamiliar environment unimpeded by too many strings attached by her superiors.

This was the same familiar drill as in the past, when Taylor Snow had been consigned to a conflict zone in a foreign country, as a lieutenant in the US Army... alongside US special forces, probably. Or maybe Taylor was then – and still considers herself to be now – an actual, real-life US special forces operative... but working in a civilian environment.

Whatever. But let's stick to the point, shall we, John...

Loretta had fought a 'remote control' war, a sort of aerial war launched from afar, with limited success. But, for victory to be achieved, the same rules that are relevant in a war zone also apply in a civilian environment – you need the right people in your team. Furthermore, the winner must provide boots on the ground. That was what Taylor had done – provided the boots on the ground. And she had been the victor.

Just as she would in a war zone, the professional ex-soldier Taylor Snow had followed up by securing her position.

That was clever.

Erik, Brigita, Freda/Shirley, the 'embassy wives', the demotion of Edward Ollerson and the reduction of his salary – all of these pieces had been moved into position by the ever-resourceful Taylor Snow to secure her limited objectives.

And Taylor's plan had worked.

Also, clever.

Now, Morton pondered, *how would this news have been received by Loretta? It is well known that different branches of the military and the intelligence services coexist in a rivalry with each other. Perhaps the same is true of civilians, like Loretta and Taylor...*

What was it that Lord Ernest Anderian had advised, all those months ago?

"It is imperative that you remain in control of the situation. If our friends at The Chronicle *are incapable of providing their superiors with the dirt on Dmitry Krejevsky, then* you *must provide it for them.* You *need to concoct a plausible story and deliver it to Edward Ollerson and Brigita Wolznaski at* The Chronicle. *They will then have some currency with which to raise their standing with their superiors.*

"*However, you also need to be able to counter the story when it breaks. If you handle this in the correct manner, it will not be Edward and Brigita who are held to account – it will be those who are exerting pressure upon them. That would be a satisfactory outcome for us because the nincompoops and the novices would remain* in situ, *whereas their handlers might be removed and replaced. We have nothing to lose because we are unlikely to have to deal with anyone more toxic than Loretta Farelli. We do not know our opponents' motives, let alone their means and opportunity for executing their task, but* we *now have a clear motive:* to induce Edward and Brigita into a bubble where they can be controlled by us."

Wow! Lackadaisical Edward had allowed himself to be manipulated into the role of a 'political football', being pulled this way and that in a tug-of-war between us at The New Times *and Loretta and her colleagues in the Beltway.*

And what of Lord Ernest's final word on the subject?

"*The fallback plan therefore becomes – if, and only if, it becomes absolutely necessary to do so – to take action to completely destroy* The Chronicle."

To "completely destroy" something, that was the way Lord Ernest thought. For him, as a former military intelligence officer, perhaps it was normal to think that way. Did Loretta, or her bosses, think in the same way or in a similar way?

Morton again recalled some of the words of wisdom from the prolific mind of Lord Ernest Anderian: *There is nobody "more toxic than Loretta Farelli" and "the nincompoops and the novices would remain* in situ, *whereas their handlers might be removed and replaced".*

Was Loretta alert to this danger? Did it all boil down to either Loretta or Edward being for the chop?

In the end, both Loretta and Edward had been sidelined by the smooth 'soft power' of Taylor Snow, while they were both preoccupied with their separate lives.

Divide et impera.

Clever, Taylor.

Not only were Loretta and Edward facing in different directions, in thrall to their different obsessions – which we know, thanks to the alert antennae of Dr Quinn.

In addition, Dr Quinn seems to think there was an underlying chafing in the relationship between Edward and Loretta. That would surely have been initiated by Loretta, for Edward could never resist the charms of the women and former women in his life. He was such a 'big softy', in that respect. Compared to him, Loretta was undeniably a scorpion.

Morton imagined Edward Ollerson in front of him, slumped in the decrepit armchair on the Ollerson family barge, at the mercy of John Morton; and Edward not needing to have the shit beaten out of him prior to the interrogation, having softened himself up with the drink and the drugs he had taken to try to cope … to try to cope with whatever was going wrong with his life. Or, rather, to try to cope with whatever he was *allowing* to go wrong with his life, instead of taking prompt action to fix it.

Morton envisaged himself proceeding with caution, going easy on Edward Ollerson during an imaginary interrogation, with a duty of care to his former colleague and intent on uncovering the truth.

Life used to be easy for you, Edward – but you never fully embraced it. You never joined in the festivities. You were always content to remain on the margins and to keep yourself to yourself.

What exactly did you want to do with your life, Edward? Apart from becoming the editor-in-chief? Was that it? Was that the sum total of your ambition in life – to become the boss of the institution that you had joined twenty-odd years ago as a cub reporter?

You were happy being 'institutionalised' and in your comfort zone. Was that it, Edward? That was a bit parochial, don't you think? You never thought of moving on? You never thought about refashioning The Chronicle *in a new and effective way, and sustaining a process of continual improvement over a prolonged period of time?*

That was cushy, Edward; very cushy.

Your name in lights; your picture in the papers; being on the TV, talking – in my humble opinion – a load of bollocks, to borrow one of your own favourite phrases.

And all those women, literally fawning all over you because you were famous. Well, sort of famous; you certainly were regarded as a 'minor celebrity' in the bars around Fleet Street and your other favourite haunts.

But what would have happened if you had not been well known, at least as the 'minor celebrity' you became? Would the women have been dropping themselves at your feet if you had been... a nobody? You would really have had to work at it then, wouldn't you? Not so easy, then, Edward. Not so cushy.

Going further back in time, I can't exactly remember you 'putting it about' while you were at Oxford University, nor in your formative years at The Chronicle. The 'putting it about' all came later, did it not? After you had become some sort of up-and-coming 'minor celebrity'. After you had been given your first helping hand up the ladder, to associate editor and, eventually, to editor-in-chief. Courtesy of... Loretta, perhaps?

But, unlike you and unknown to you, Loretta did *have a clear idea of what she wanted to achieve. Loretta appeared on the scene, out of the blue, worked her magic, and... whoosh... suddenly, Edward Ollerson becomes 'somebody'. Was that how it happened, Edward?*

So, the women come and go, and you don't worry about it because there will always be more coming along later. You can take your pick. But you don't settle down. That might have saved you. Perhaps you are not the 'settling down' type? Well, I can't help you there, because I am and always have been the 'settling down' type.

I'm married, with an awesome wife and two wonderful sons. But married life was not for you.

And, in spite of all the attention you received and all the female company you enjoyed, you still contrived to develop for yourself a solitary, lonely existence.

You must have yearned to belong, to be a part of something. Maybe that was what led to... the obsessive quality in your behaviour. For you, nothing was valid unless it became an obsession, some sort of idée fixe, *inspired by the liberal internationalism of Loretta and her friends.*

Did you not have any ideas of your own, Edward? Not one? Never? Was there a vacuum in your thoughts? A vacuum that, as vacuums do, wanted to be filled. And the vacuum found its filler in the form of someone else's ideas, someone else's values and someone else's belief system: the values and belief system of... liberal internationalism.

And... as for your vacuum filler of liberal internationalism... it was all going well, wasn't it, Edward? Exactly as Loretta told you it would.

Afghanistan, Iraq, Libya, Syria... and many others... were all going as planned. Except that they were not going as planned. One by one, all of those scenarios became problematic, and you could see that there was something wrong, but you did nothing about it.

You must have hated yourself, Edward, every time you realised that one of those scenarios went wrong – as each of Loretta's schemes went wrong – dragging your reputation down a notch each time; and you did nothing about it.

You really must have hated yourself.

You could have done something about it, Edward. You know that. Edward, you must have known that. You must have known that you could have done something about it, surely...

On reflection, Morton began to feel a little bit sorry for Edward Ollerson.

He continued in his reverie, *Let's consider other possible angles...*

No... No, mate... You didn't know that you could do something about it, did you? Or you didn't know how to go about sorting it out.

But there were people around you, whom you could have drawn upon for support.

My door was always open. My phone number was there if you needed me. We could have talked it over down the pub. There was no need to worry about whether you and I agreed or disagreed... that's part of the territory of being a reporter.

Forget our differences; they can be managed. You could have just... just... got it off your chest. It could have been that simple.

Shirley Bould was another one you could have spoken to. She would have made a better PA than anyone else in the world, but you let her go, elbowed her out and brought in that... backstabbing creature... Josh.

Or you could have talked with someone like Hugh Lombard. Everybody else talked to Hugh Lombard. Even I talked things over with Hugh Lombard, though he often hadn't a clue what I was talking about. You didn't even have to agree with Hugh. You could have just... talked with him – and talked it over. He would have listened, but he would never have blabbed to anyone about it. But you never did talk to Hugh, did you? You elbowed him aside, exactly like you did with Shirley.

And, Edward, as Hugh and I were trying to help you out, in the graveyard of the little ruined church – your dad's last resting place, and hallowed ground for you – what made you come out with that comment... that 'fucking great poof' comment?

Hugh Lombard never said a bad word about anyone, not to their faces and not behind their backs. And you come out with that 'fucking great poof... and a useless turd' comment... and to Hugh's face! Right at the moment when he has taken the time to offer his support.

What the fuck?

I thought that The Chronicle *was supposed to be a paragon of inclusiveness and the last word in political correctness.*

Is there some sort of pecking order within social groups? The 'right' kind of gay and the 'wrong' kind of gay, perhaps?

Loretta was standing just behind me, in the shadows in the graveyard of that little church near the banks of the River Avon. Loretta overheard what you said to Hugh Lombard, and what you repeated to Hugh about him being a 'fucking great poof... and a useless turd'. I watched her face while she listened.

There was no reaction. No fucking reaction!

Edward, what is it with you guys?

If that had been me verbally abusing Hugh using that language, I bet I would have caught it in the neck, good and proper. And deservedly so.

But you get a pass. You guys give each other a pass.

Is that what political correctness and identity politics are really all about, when it comes down to it? Only worth the candle if they can be weaponised against your political adversaries... not for the 'greater good' but to fight your own private war?

Is that it?

And I'm not allowed to be politically correct; not allowed to speak in favour of inclusiveness; not allowed to... to re-evaluate the dominant Russophobic narrative and to work out an inclusive solution; and not allowed to even function, because you and your pal Loretta want to silence the alternative media rather than engage with it?

It's a bit rich, Edward. A bit rich, don't you think?

And then there is... everything else. The stuff that really matters, and how you guys deal with it... I'm talking about your values, Edward...

Let's consider the police raid on Hugh Lombard's flat, for starters. That was not your idea, surely... but you must have known about it.

You might even have been persuaded to take part in it or at least to prepare to write up the articles that were supposed to follow a successful police raid – articles with headlines such as 'Russian agents in the British media, meddling in our affairs'.

That did not work out as planned, did it? Because the police raid on Hugh's flat ended in a farce and caused a lot of embarrassment to the Metropolitan Police and to the government... and to Loretta's bosses in the Beltway. They would not have been best pleased with that, would they, Edward? I bet that Loretta made sure that you took a lot of the blame for that.

To make matters worse, instead of standing up for yourself and insisting that a line be drawn under past blunders, you allowed yourself to be drawn into the smear campaign against Dmitry Krejevsky, but I gather you were not a willing participant. You allowed Brigita Wolznaski to do the running (in more ways than one), not you. You did not even lead from behind. You just allowed the whole thing to drift.

It was not difficult for us at The New Times to counter the attempted smear campaign against Dmitry Krejevsky, but you just allowed it to drift, out of your control, oblivious to the consequences.

Did you not realise that Loretta would have expected more of you? Well, maybe you do now... after the event.

So, the smear campaign against Dmitry Krejevsky fell flat.

Then... along comes Taylor Snow, and we all know how that panned out.

After Taylor Snow's arrival on the scene, what was the mood in the Beltway in Washington DC, Edward? In Loretta's office?

A mood of impatience in the Beltway, perhaps, Edward?

What was Loretta Farelli's mood? She must have received such a kicking from her bosses in Washington DC, so what was her mood, Edward, after the whole plot came crashing down? Impatient? Or even angry? And... pissed off? Pissed off... with you!

Did you go too far, Edward? Or not far enough? Were you too laissez-faire for your own good?

But that was recent. Earlier in the year, you might have gone too far when you broke ranks. Remember? You broke ranks, Edward, when you decided to publish the Russian battle plans in January, with all the spin and hype you could muster.

Dmitry and I had to bail you out when many of your allies in the neoconservative-dominated corporate media and the liberal political Establishment had deserted you and wanted to have your guts for garters.

You got away that time, Edward, but it is possible that some people decided to put you on notice there and then, without telling *you and waiting to see what you would do next. And maybe, just maybe, you did something or were about to do something that they did not like – and possibly they even regarded your behaviour as a threat to them.*

Perhaps the burglary of your apartment was connected to this. What was stolen? Not the documents in the wine boxes; your research materials in those wine boxes were all left intact, and whoever looked at them put them back carefully, so that nobody would notice.

But I noticed... I noticed something odd... something very odd indeed.

A real burglar would have almost certainly emptied the contents of those wine boxes out onto the floor and, when no valuables were found, left the documents all over the floor and scattered about the place.

No, these documents were examined and, very carefully, put back where they were found, so as not to draw attention to them... to give the impression that what the burglars were looking for was money, silver or gold, or jewels.

But what the burglars were really looking for was... information.

Nothing else was stolen; however, a couple of floorboards had been ripped up, and the lid of a metal box had been forced open and the contents removed.

If the documents in the metal box were important to you, Edward, or even incriminating in some way, surely you would not have left them under the floorboards, would you? You would have taken them with you, wouldn't you? They would have been locked away in the metal box, and hidden in a box among the wine boxes and milk cartons in the cupboard on your family's canal barge – if you were trying to... to get away... or to escape.

What did your sister Elaine say about the police report concerning the burglary? *"The metal box had no fingerprints on it."*

No fingerprints! *Not even yours, Edward, even though you surely would never have worn gloves every time you opened and closed that box.*

Your sister Elaine told me that, after your death, a conscientious police detective inspector was planning to compare the DNA found

317

on the box with the DNA of known criminals. But it never happened. The conscientious police detective inspector was moved off the case, and the case was wrapped up without any forensic DNA testing having been performed.

Would we have discovered, just like with the absence of fingerprints, that there would have been no DNA belonging to known criminals on the box? And not even your DNA, Edward?

And... I remember thinking at the time... the floorboard that had been concealing the metal box was one of the most rotten of the floorboards that had been piled up by the joiner, and the hole in which the metal box had been found contained quite a lot of rotten splinters.

Now... I asked myself... if I wanted to hide a metal box under a floorboard, would I hide the box under a floorboard that was rotten and that might break apart if it was stood on, exposing the box that you wanted to hide? Or would I hide the box under a floorboard that was not rotten, would not break if stepped on and would not result in the hidden box being exposed? And that, as a bonus, I, as the owner of the box, would be able to pull up every so often – without any fuss and without creating a mess – to get access to the box, and, when the job was complete, replace the box and floorboard... nice and neat?

You know what I think, Edward? You never touched that box in your life. Not once.

It was a plant. The box must have been a plant, all along, to make it seem that a burglary had taken place and that some of your savings had been stolen. Savings that were so important that the box in which they were kept needed to be wiped clean of fingerprints, inside and out, by burglars wearing gloves; even removing the fingerprints of the box's owner – yours, Edward.

But did the burglars find what they were looking for? I don't think so.

The box I found in your family's barge – was that the prize for the burglars? Carl Waggoner's twenty-fourth box? Was that what they were looking for? Was that why you took it with you and hid it away in that fusty, old wardrobe in the knackered, old family barge?

Loretta asked Katy to 'look after' you. Katy failed, so – maybe, just maybe – Loretta 'the scorpion' had to step in and hire a contract killer to 'look after' you – and to finish the job.

If that was the case, Edward, you should have watched out for the sting in the tail.

※

In retrospect, Morton wished he had forewarned Edward of the danger he might be in. Morton confided his thoughts to his wife, Alison, during one of their autumnal walks, as they inhaled the fresh sea air and scrunched the shingle on the beach at Brighton.

Alison seemed to concur with John Morton that something did not match up, and that there might be a good chance that Edward Ollerson had been – at Loretta's instigation – murdered, in order to cover up a trail or prevent something from being disclosed to the public domain, or merely to remove an unpredictable loose cannon, who could no longer be trusted.

However, Alison's background in history suggested that it might not be a good idea for her husband to probe too deeply and even to let this particular sleeping dog lie.

After all, when thieves fall out, should the good guys embroil themselves by taking one side or the other? It is much better to stand back and to let those hollow men and hollow women tear at each other's throats.

When all was said and done, John Morton and the team at *The New Times* had undergone a good year. The improved relationship with Taylor Snow boded well for the immediate future. Two of Morton's long-standing 'problem children' – Loretta and Edward – were out of the picture. The future did not exactly look bleak.

John Morton and *The New Times* were not losing the phoney war; they were still very much in the game.

※

Tuesday, 1 November 2016.

From John Morton's cynical and suspicious point of view, the arrangements for Edward Ollerson's funeral seemed to be rushed through, as though some 'unseen hand' wanted it out of the way. The autopsy, the coroner's report and the inquest – all had been done and dusted with scant regard to the possibility that the alleged suicide might have been a mafia-style hit.

It was Agatha Christie material; Morton had been obliged to play Poirot.

Understandably, the Ollerson family just wanted to get the service and cremation over as soon as possible. The mortuary, the coroner, the justice system and the funeral directors – these were all busy professionals for whom the corpse was merely one of many, to be processed according to standard procedure. Unless someone stirred up a hornet's nest of awkward questions, they would simply follow instructions and get the job done, quickly and in a businesslike manner.

Elaine Ollerson and her mother preferred the funeral to be a private affair, so they had booked a little chapel for the purpose. But word had got round, and many of Edward Ollerson's former colleagues from *The Chronicle* and even some of the school chums he had not seen for years turned up to swell the congregation.

Everyone, including Sir Harold Nevin and Sir Tom Hamble and their wives (Lady Miranda and Lady Joy), seemed under the impression that they would be included in the modest coterie.

Taylor Snow accompanied a tearful Brigita. Loretta and Katy flew in for a quick visit prior to flying back to Washington DC in time for the US presidential election. At the funeral, Loretta wore a black pillbox hat with a black veil, preventing her facial expressions from being observed.

Shirley Bould did not turn up at the funeral. Shirley had worked briefly as Edward Ollerson's secretary before being fired by him, so she had no warm feelings toward him. Shirley's alter ego, Freda Gray, had never met Edward Ollerson, so she had no reason to attend.

Hugh and Vivienne attended, as did Dmitry and Catherine Krejevsky.

The whole event went, one might suppose, as merry as a funeral bell. Nothing remarkable occurred, save for one incident near the end of the wake, as John Morton and Sir Harold Nevin were joined by a tipsy Sir Tom Hamble, who seemed to be enjoying his retirement.

Nevin thought it would be a good idea to instigate a new tradition – a Christmas party for *The New Times*. This would give Sir Tom Hamble the opportunity to revel in his role as honorary life president of *The New Times* and to deliver a speech. But what would Hamble say? He and his wife had been on so many trips, holidays and cruises during the past year that he had quite lost touch with current events.

Morton offered to help him out.

"That is very agreeable of you, John. Thank you," declared Hamble.

Morton agreed to pop round to Hamble's house the following week to get the ball rolling quickly, because the Christmas party would probably be held early in December, due to the later bookings of venues having already been filled.

Morton was not aware of it, but Sir Tom Hamble had a little surprise waiting for him.

PART SIX
MEDIA WARS (THE DIVIDENDS)

25

INFALLIBLE AND INEVITABLY INVINCIBLE

Prior to November, the year 2016 had already played host to two important ballots.

First, the high-profile and fractious Brexit referendum concerning UK membership of the EU, during which the rival camps attempted to woo the undecided with scare stories of whether this or that catastrophe would befall the nation if the opposing side should win.

Second, the barely reported general election in Russia, which had strengthened the hand of the incumbent Russian leadership; anyone who still entertained the idea that Russia would acquiesce to Western demands was proven, beyond all reasonable doubt, to be seriously deluded.

Superficially, the US presidential election seemed to have much in common with the Brexit campaign: opposing and seemingly incompatible sets of claims, topped up with two distinctive, competing, polarising exercises; both sides seeming to cry wolf with respect to each other.

For over three long years, during his second term of office, the incumbent POTUS had been regarded as a lame duck in many quarters; this was the outcome of a drawn-out process into which – according to his critics in the right-wing media and some of the alternative media – he had allowed himself to slide, a mere six months after his second inauguration ceremony.

On his watch, in spite of a handful of social reforms, his critics pointed to "a *bunch* – in fact a *whole bunch*, even" of significant *alleged* downsides:

- The export of US capital and the offshoring of jobs had been accelerated, thereby increasing the numbers of unemployed American workers.
- Big business got richer, at the expense of the masses of the American people.
- The US national debt had continued on an increasingly steep upward trajectory.
- The deterioration in relations between the police and their communities was the talk of the town, more or less everywhere.
- Hundreds of billions of US dollars had been invested in overseas 'humanitarian' military adventures, opposing unwanted leaders in specific countries, while supporting regimes elsewhere whose track records on human rights left much to be desired.
- The roping in of so-called 'allies' into controversial trade deals that had been signed off at the last minute (in the case of TPP) or stalled (in the case of TTIP).
- And, as a bitter-tasting icing on the cake, relations between East and West had sunk to an all-time low.

And this "whole bunch" of significant downsides was *alleged* to have taken place even though the incumbent POTUS had delivered one simple missive to the White House staff at the start of his presidential term of office, commencing on January 2009, and repeated in January 2013: "DON'T DO STUPID STUFF!"

The frustrations of the American electorate found many an outlet in protests and street battles with the police. But, to effect change through the ballot box, the electorate would have to be presented with a candidate who expounded a radically new vision and who could walk the walk, as well as talk the talk.

The current POTUS was a perfect example of the type of smooth 'saviour' who might arise from within the ranks of the Democratic Party.

Furthermore, he was the first *non-white* POTUS.

Now, a fresh challenge was posed to the Democratic Party: select a candidate who would match the performance of the incumbent POTUS or, preferably, outperform him. Given the track record of the incumbent, if the evidence provided by his opponents in the media was anything to go by, this should not have been a particularly knotty problem.

A saviour-of-sorts had put himself forward and campaigned in the Democratic Party primaries on a socialist ticket, but – despite his popularity, both within and without the Democratic Party – he did not have the backing of the Democratic Party machine.

In contrast, having displaced the Republican Party's own 'wealthy family dynasty' in 2008, the Democratic Party machine seemed set on cementing in place a victory with a candidate from a 'wealthy family dynasty' within its own ranks.

The Democratic Party's final choice of candidate was described in both corporate and alternate media as the 'archetypal Establishment figure'. Wealthy; garnering support from the US corporate media, corporate industry, high finance, the US military-industrial complex, the US armed forces and the US intelligence community; and the wife of a former POTUS, this candidate had another feather in her cap – she intended to follow up the success of her predecessor by being crowned as the first *female* POTUS.

Her name? Harriet Harbinger.

✺

Described by her political opponents as one of a group of 'harpies' within the neoconservative elite that had subverted control of the Democratic Party, Harriet revelled in the insult. There was no fear of the public disclosure of her true feelings for this thick-skinned pragmatist; not a bit.

During one of many brainstorming sessions with her key advisors, she had been persuaded to adopt the pseudonym 'Harpy' as a signature – a defiant statement to be thrown back in the faces of her political opponents.

Thus, everyone in the Beltway and in the media knew her as 'Harpy Harbinger'; but what would, in another person's hands, have been a toxic trademark was transformed by Harriet into a slick marketing brand of epic proportions.

The brand 'Harpy Harbinger' was honed into a significant attribute that projected a tough – even ruthless – image, which was specifically designed to provoke fear in opponents and to scare them into acquiescence.

The president of the Russian Federation, the general secretary of the Communist Party of China, and the Republican candidate in the US presidential election – all would bow down to the supreme commander (or rather, at this early stage, the supreme commander *elect*), pay homage to her and shower her with tribute.

But it was all for show.

The leaders of Russia and China did not live in glorious isolation in their ivory towers, vulnerable in their remoteness to immediate overthrow in a repeat of the Iraq and Libya disasters.

And as for Harpy Harbinger's Republican rival in the race to become POTUS, he was familiar with the games that his rival liked to play. Furthermore, he was no pushover and he set out his stall accordingly – with his eyes firmly fixed on the top job in the White House.

During the race to the hot seat at the White House, most of the corporate media had portrayed the Republican candidate as a pantomime villain, and he seemed only too keen to play up to this image.

However, he claimed to have lots of dirt on his Democrat opponent, and he was prepared to use it. *He* made sure that *she* would not have an easy ride in the televised debates, and – when he accused her of being outmanoeuvred in past dealings with the president of the Russian Federation and even pledged to have her thrown into jail for a string of alleged infringements of the law – Harpy Harbinger's composure barely held.

※

It is a well-known axiom in marketing circles that if you have a high-value brand you can allow it to sell itself, but the brand must be well presented.

So, Harpy's hair was lovingly groomed into place.

Harpy's neoconservative 'minders' loved to play 'goodies versus baddies', so the colour white was preferred about 90% of the time to emphasise which side they thought they were on – the side of the angels.

Tens of millions of dollars were spent on creating the right image and bringing it into being, so it should therefore come as no surprise that Harpy Harbinger always looked her best and that the brand was polished to perfection.

Tens of millions of dollars were also required for a seemingly endless string of conferences and campaigns, media advertising, and flash mobs and street theatre 'happenings'; as well as events of every imaginable kind – including the three political training schools that had been attended by Brigita Wolznaski during the summer.

And tens of millions were ploughed into other activities, many of which would be carefully hidden from public view.

In the eighteenth century, the War of Independence had freed the American colonies from the grip of British domination with its unelected institutions, its twee and parochial traditions, and its rotten boroughs. *Unlike in Britain, there will be no odour of corruption here in the US*, hinted the Founding Fathers. That was the ideal. That was to be part and parcel of the American Way.

However, money talks and, in a country where wealth is generated freely and where substantial influence needs to be acquired, money is regarded as the *decisive* resource. More than $1 billion had been earmarked by the candidates partaking in the current US presidential election, alone.

Where was all the money to come from – that is, the cash that would fund all the activities run by the wealthy and powerful, the 'great and the good', including the neoconservatives and their allies? This cash sometimes – coming to the attention of the general public, usually in the form of a tabloid scandal – found its way into and out of the accounts of wealthy business associates and donors whose alleged sleazy activities would, if proven, dwarf those of the English rotten boroughs of the eighteenth century.

This was big money, such as the enormous amounts that had been revealed courtesy of the Affluent Archives scandal earlier in the year, before the Affluent Archives scandal had backfired against its instigators, and before the embarrassing and damaging disclosures had subsequently been allowed to fizzle out, and over which a discreet veil had been furtively drawn.

You did not have to fiddle the books to generate your wealth. The simplest, most effective and risk-averse way of raising and storing money was to set up an NGO, preferably in the form of a not-for-profit and tax-exempt organisation such as a charity. Someone, somewhere, hit on the idea of calling the first of these organisations a 'foundation': a benevolent fund for the doing of good deeds and the betterment of society.

The idea caught on like wildfire, and soon dozens then hundreds of such NGO 'foundations' sprang up out of thin air, each with its own glossy, end-of-year brochure that reported cheerfully on the millions and (over time) billions of dollars that had been accrued, stored and subsequently disposed of.

For Harpy and her carefully selected coterie, the Harbinger Foundation might have started out with the 'good intentions' of altruistic benevolence, but its eventual role was frequently of an entirely different order.

Since the mid-1990s, 10 billion dollars had been raised over time by a coordinating committee representing privately-owned and government-backed NGOs for the purpose of 'overseas development', half of which a spokesperson for the US State Department boasted had been allocated solely to counter alleged Russian aggression in Ukraine. Most of the 5 billion dollars allocated to 'helping Ukrainian independence' funded the Ukrainian Orange Revolution in 2004 and the violent Maidan events in Kiev in 2014.

Unknown millions had been donated by the Harbinger Foundation to foreign 'sister' foundations and other organisations with whom close relations were maintained in return for collaboration on humanitarian-interventionist adventures.

Around 5 million dollars had found its way into Loretta Farelli's relaunch of *The Chronicle* newspaper; this figure later expanded to over 10 million dollars to cover the exorbitant rent for the London office, 'miscellaneous expenses', Edward Ollerson's £250,000 per year job and the costs of reinvigorating *The Chronicle* under Taylor Snow's leadership.

To wit, *The Chronicle* was to be commandeered – as an ad hoc UK-based 'baby sister' for the Harbinger Foundation; it became a proxy where the blurring of boundaries between bona fide business and charitable status provided fertile ground for 'creative' accounting, as well as 'creative' reporting.

However, the funds never seemed to be enough, and, when Taylor Snow saw the opportunity to rearrange the finances by reducing the salary of Edward Ollerson from £250,000 to £40,000 per annum, she grabbed the bull by the horns and thereby alerted Loretta Farelli, who was responsible for overseeing those activities of the Harbinger Foundation that were related to *The Chronicle*.

This, in part, explained Loretta's frantic to-ing and fro-ing between London and Washington DC in a vain attempt to make the money work in the way she wanted it to. It also explained, in part, the zeal and the ruthlessness with which Loretta was obliged to act: overtly with regard to the formidable Taylor Snow; and covertly in the case of the gullible Edward Ollerson.

The Republican candidate in the US presidential election claimed to know all about "this swishing around of money like confetti," as he labelled it, within the Harbinger Foundation.

And where it had come from.

And what it was used for.

But how was he to turn this intelligence to his advantage?

The Republican candidate looked for a weak link – and fastened quickly onto the disastrous outcomes from every single one of the allegedly 'humanitarian' overseas projects that had been funded by NGOs such as the Harbinger Foundation. By following the money, the Republican candidate was determined to expose and to frame this whole aspect of Harpy's little world as a succession of hitherto unpeeled layers of (alleged) corruption.

In addition, he claimed another key bit of dirt on Harpy Harbinger...

Information had found its way from sensitive government institutions into the public domain. According to Harpy Harbinger, this could *only* have been achieved by computer hackers and – in line with the dominant narrative that was designed to propel her into the White House – these hackers absolutely *must* be Russian hackers and absolutely *must* be in the direct service of the Russian president himself.

No solid, testable evidence to support the claim of alleged 'Russian hacking' was put forward, but the corporate media picked up the meme about alleged 'Russian hacking' and willingly ran with it – before, during and long after the US presidential election campaign.

Harpy's Republican rival for the hot seat did his homework very well. He rose early every day to scrutinise every word that had been uttered by 'Team Harpy'. With a background in business (and a charitable foundation of his own), he found it easy to follow the money and to work out what he thought was going on inside the Harbinger Foundation and its myriad offspring.

However, computers were a different beast, of which – aside from his social media accounts – he understood very little. He consulted specialists in the subjects of computer networks and communications security. With their assistance, he worked out the truth or, more accurately, some possible truths to explain what might have happened.

Either the leaks had been deliberate and part of a concealed plan – in which case, there had been no hacking at all and it had been an inside job all along, almost certainly by a disgruntled whistle-blower within the Democratic Party machine – or key government ministries had been hacked into, which would imply that the network and communications security of the US was in an appalling state and would not do justice to what the Republican candidate referred to as a banana republic.

When, during one of the televised debates, he challenged Harpy Harbinger with this precise analysis and terminology, he was immediately slapped down by Harpy's allies in the corporate media for using the phrase 'banana republic' – which they characterised as "racist language from the gutter that did not sit well coming from the mouth of a presidential candidate".

Harpy Harbinger sought to capitalise on this gaffe by attempting to link the alleged Russian hackers to her rival for POTUS, together with a host of allegations of malpractice and corruption that, Harpy believed, must have come from the fertile imagination of the Russian intelligence services.

"Why," the corporate media gleefully chirped, "the surname of Harpy's presidential rival – Dirk Volzanger – is almost an anagram of that of Russia's President Glazenov."

※

Harpy Harbinger seemed to be on to a winner.

Dirk Volzanger habitually seemed to put his foot in his mouth at every opportunity.

He complained about mass immigration – which, according to him, had "taken away American jobs" – and he was slapped down as a racist.

He highlighted the offshoring of American jobs and threatened to cancel the contracts and "bring the jobs home" – remarks for which he was disparaged as one who had "lost touch with the globalised reality of the modern world".

He stressed the US's lack of sovereignty and the way other countries played 'wag the tail of the dog' at the US's expense, reducing the US's perceived status and expecting the US to pay for the defence of the Western world, with the US supplying nearly all the military hardware and military personnel required by NATO.

In response, the corporate media accused him of wanting to weaken NATO in the face of alleged 'Russian aggression'; he was rewarded by being chastised in a cartoon while wearing a dunce's cap and facing the corner of the classroom with a notice pinned to the back of his shirt reading: "GLAZENOV'S USEFUL IDIOT".

With one eye to the religious groups who formed a core part of the Republican voting public, he outlined his views on birth control and abortion – and received almost universal condemnation in the corporate media for trying to turn back the clock on women's rights.

In short, in the eyes of much of the corporate media, Dirk Volzanger could do nothing right.

Afraid of challenging the dominant narrative peddled by the corporate media, many Republican senators drifted away from Dirk Volzanger and, in an unprecedented move, pledged their allegiance to Harpy Harbinger.

But Dirk Volzanger had been nominated by the overwhelming majority of members of the Republican Party. They did not take kindly to what they saw as an act of treachery that was being perpetrated from within against their beloved Grand Old Party. There was dangerous talk of not accepting the result of the US presidential election, and forms of protest and armed insurrection were even mooted throughout all media – both corporate and alternative.

At a time when both candidates were addressing the threats and risks of a world filled with tension, the US – the self-appointed 'Exceptionalist' leader of the Western world with its role of self-appointed 'global policeman' – seemed to outsiders to be rent internally with divisions and hell-bent on fratricide.

Something had to give.

There was one notable fly in the ointment. A fly that Team Harpy erroneously thought it had swatted: a series of FBI investigations into the Harbinger Foundation, and the leaks and alleged hacking into computers that contained information that was sensitive to the national security of the US.

Moreover, not all the leaked information was *necessarily* stored on secure systems configured to the exacting standards of the US Department of Defense. Much of it had been stored, allegedly, according to the critics of Team Harpy, "on the poorly secured laptops and other electronic devices that were the personal property of members of Team Harpy itself".

26

TOO MUCH INFORMATION

Monday, 7 November 2016.
Morton set aside a whole day for his trip from London to Cheltenham, to the retirement bungalow of Sir Tom Hamble, in order to help Hamble to prepare his speech for *The New Times* Christmas party.

Aware of his host's propensity for an overly large snifter – the 'liquid largesse' commonly bestowed by Hamble upon host and guests alike – John Morton decided not to drive the family car but instead opted for train and taxi.

On his arrival, he was ushered into the house and taken to Sir Tom Hamble's conservatory. The view from the conservatory was breathtaking.

"He will have his gardens," said Hamble's wife, Lady Joy, "even though he can't bend down to do any work."

"Oh, I wouldn't say that," Hamble interjected. "I have been known to come down on bended knee to curtail the mournful weeping of the drooping flower heads more than once this summer."

Morton was pleased that Hamble had found the time once more to indulge in his library of unread novels and the writing of poetry – even if many of his ramblings were distinctly cheesy when compared to the dazzling compositions of professional rhymesters.

Dinner comprised home-made pâté, which was strong and gamey, with salad and wholegrain toast for the starter; followed by a main course of steamed fish and scallops pan-fried in butter, served with plenty of greens and a little garlic mash; and there was home-made banana-flavoured ice cream for dessert, served with a hot slice of rich fruit cake flambéed in brandy – Joy Hamble was a master chef whose culinary delights Morton had experienced on precious few occasions.

Then came the aforementioned snifters – brandies, which were rather generous in their proportions, and it was only three in the afternoon.

When the over-imbibed Hamble's guard was dropped, the conversation drifted toward current affairs and the uncertain state of the world. In his retirement, Hamble was a world away from *that*. The company of his wife, children and grandchildren; good food and drink; his garden; his books; and his poetry – these were all he needed, and these were all he knew these days.

During a moment of reminiscence, Hamble led Morton to his library, in which a table was covered with a cloth that reached to the floor.

For months on end, Joy Hamble had kept on at her husband to do something with the books which were boxed away under the table – she demanded, "Either find a place to store them or give them to a charity shop."

Among the boxes was a large plastic bag from one of the big department stores that Tom and Joy Hamble frequented on their shopping trips to London, or – more frequently these days – to Cheltenham, Gloucester and Bristol.

The bag seemed light as Hamble lifted it effortlessly onto the table with one hand. Using a small pair of scissors, he clipped the twine that held the two handles of the bag together. Inside the bag was a box. In a past life, it had contained five reams of A4 paper. On top of the box, beneath a layer of encrusted grime disturbed by finger marks imprinted during the house move earlier in the year, was inscribed "To the editor-in-chief, *The Chronicle* newspaper".

It was Carl Waggoner's missing twenty-fifth box.

The box had never been opened. Masking tape stretched over and round it.

"You might as well have this, John," suggested Hamble. "It was Carl's, originally. It landed on my desk sometime after his funeral. I brought it home one evening, but I must have mislaid it and never got around to opening it.

"Carl had so many crazy ideas at the time. I loved the boy like a son and I will always think of him as one of my own, but there was a limit to what I could accept, particularly if I was in the hot seat responsible for running a newspaper and its office."

Morton snipped the masking tape and opened the box. It contained junk covered with inordinate quantities of tissue paper: small plaster busts and statues, which were chipped and broken; mould-covered portraits of the great and the good from World War II – Hamble's favourite historical period.

"There's a framed picture of Churchill, Roosevelt and Stalin at Yalta in here," Morton enthused, "in good condition."

Hamble looked at the photograph and smiled airily. "I've got one. Somewhere."

"I suppose these can go to a charity shop if you don't want them," Morton suggested.

Hamble nodded. *One more little job out of the way, to keep the missus happy*, he thought, as he left the room to retrieve a decanter of brandy from the lounge.

The dust from the box's lid was making a terrible mess of the tablecloth (and the carpet), which was made even worse as Morton removed the junk and piled it onto the table.

At the bottom of the box there was a white plastic bag. Morton opened it to find a second plastic bag inside it. Inside the second bag, Morton found some documents; about forty or fifty pages in all. They were printed in Russian, which Morton could not understand. However, he knew enough of the Cyrillic alphabet to be able to decipher some of the names at the bottom of one of the documents.

The list of authors included Andrey Vladimirovych Talpin, the former advisor to the Kremlin who had prompted Morton to release declassified Russian battle plans twelve months earlier.

✳

Early the following day, Morton paid an unannounced visit to Dmitry Krejevsky at his home in Harrow-on-the-Hill.

Although Morton was officially the Middle East correspondent for *The New Times*, coverage of the Syria crisis had been taken over by Dmitry Krejevsky to enable Morton to dig up as much information as possible about Carl Waggoner's twenty-fourth box of documents and to help Sir Tom Hamble to compose his speech for the Christmas party.

Since Russia's involvement in Syria, the perspective and the narrative had shifted away from the local and the regional to include the geopolitical. To keep track, Dmitry Krejevsky found himself having to consult dozens of political analysts and military experts, particularly those with an understanding of Russian national security and defence strategies. He had become snowed under with work.

Morton handed over a plastic bag that contained a USB flash drive and paper copies of the documents he had found in Carl Waggoner's twenty-fifth box; a box that had remained, disregarded, in the custody of Sir Tom Hamble for two and a half years.

"Just put them on that chair will you please, John," Krejevsky directed, and he asked Morton to set aside empty mugs in readiness for a freshly prepared cafetière.

Morton obeyed, but, seeing that his friend was engrossed in a ton of work, he asked, "You are going to have time to look at this, aren't you?"

"Yes, of course."

Morton was not convinced. He knew that both he and Krejevsky were likely to get up early in less than twenty-four hours to watch the coverage of the US presidential election. Krejevsky would probably not have time to look at the documents until the weekend. Nevertheless, Morton decided to leave the documents on Krejevsky's chair, but the worry nagged away at him all the way home on the tube to Southgate, throughout the afternoon and late into the evening.

✻

Wednesday, 9 November 2016.

Morton rose at four o'clock in the morning and pressed the power button on the TV remote control, fully expecting Harpy Harbinger to have the US presidential election virtually sewn up.

Instead, the tally of early votes revealed a close call. Even more surprisingly, projections for various key states looked like swinging away from the Democrats. A huge vote for the Democrats in California narrowed the gap somewhat, but the sombre mood in the TV newsroom told a story all of its own.

Harpy Harbinger, with her masterful public-relations strategy, with her huge influence in the media, and with her hundreds of millions invested in her campaign and in the campaigns of her political allies in the Senate and the House of Representatives, had failed to convince enough voters to plump for her – even in what used to be the industrial heartland of the US, which was her home turf.

Even the promotion of Harpy's future role as the first *female* POTUS had failed to persuade enough women to get her into the White House, because – as Taylor Snow had predicted during a soirée with Brigita Wolznaski two months earlier – many women decided to abstain, or to vote for the Republicans and against Harpy Harbinger simply because they did not like *her*. Nor did they trust *her*.

A sense of being taken for granted, reminiscent of the Brexit referendum in the UK a few months earlier, had taken hold of large swathes of the US electorate. Not only were they disillusioned with Harpy Harbinger's focus on *her* version of identity politics, which failed to resonate with an electorate that wanted, above all, job security and a living wage – they also felt ignored. These were neglected people reduced to making ends meet in the forgotten, dilapidated ruins of the US's industrial golden age; in the wealthiest country in the world; and in the birthplace of the now-shattered 'American Dream'.

The unusually large turnout reflected the determination of large numbers of disillusioned voters to make the point that they were distinctly unhappy with the direction in which the US had been travelling, and many of those disillusioned voters had chosen this precise time to put their foot down *en masse*. There would be no talk of continuity, and no talk of the 'same old, same old'. There would be no Harbinger family 'Democrat dynasty'.

Instead, the incoming POTUS, the maverick Republican 'populist' Dirk Volzanger, was given a mandate for change.

※

At nine o'clock in the morning, Morton received a phone call from Dmitry Krejevsky to ask if he would like some breakfast.

"The weather is fine, John, so let's say eleven o'clock at the café near the Serpentine in Hyde Park. The café near the lido," confirmed Krejevsky.

※

Morton turned up unshaven and practically in mufti, to be met by Dmitry Krejevsky, who was coming down the path from the opposite direction, as smartly groomed as ever.

Morton half expected his friend to crack open the champagne in celebration, not so much for Dirk Volzanger's victory but for Harpy Harbinger's destruction – and with it the crushing blow that had been dealt to the neoconservatives within the US Establishment.

"Well then, *young Johnny*. *That* was not supposed to happen!" exclaimed Krejevsky.

"It certainly was not, Dmitry, *old boy*," Morton said with a grin, "but the neoconservatives don't usually take things lying down. They tend to refuse to accept defeat and to double down. So, I don't think we have seen the end of this affair; not by a long shot."

"True," Krejevsky concurred with Morton's sober assessment. "Very true."

Krejevsky ordered two breakfasts with a large cafetière of filter coffee. "I've already written my first thoughts on the election and emailed them to the office. It will be interesting to hear any feedback from *The Chronicle*. Is Shirley due to pay them a visit today?"

"Probably. I'll ring up Taylor tomorrow, to gauge her reaction," said Morton.

Two cooked breakfasts arrived.

"Snorkers! Good oh!" Morton enthused, mimicking the first mate in one of his favourite black-and-white war films, *The Cruel Sea*.

The hungry pair tucked in, and ordered coffee refills with extra portions of toast and marmalade.

"By the way," said Dmitry Krejevsky, "I have arranged for those documents to be properly translated; carefully and discreetly, and by a reliable source, of course."

"Of course," agreed Morton.

The most pregnant of pauses followed.

Morton leaned forward and whispered, "Did you get a chance to read them?"

Krejevsky nodded.

"Anything interesting?" queried Morton.

Krejevsky remained coolly motionless, yet an impish glimmer peeked out from his deep-set, brown eyes beneath his heavy eyebrows.

It would need a walk around the park to reveal the secret.

✳

"Let's go back fourteen months, John, to when Russia got involved militarily in Syria," began Krejevsky.

"Addressing the US government in absentia, President Glazenov asked in one of his speeches – I think it was at Valdai, and one of those speeches that are never shown by CNN or the BBC to Western audiences – 'Do you realise what you have done?' Do you remember that, John?

"He was referring to the blowback that had materialised due to the NATO interventions in the Middle East, where NATO destroyed secular Arab republics. This caused the rise of jihadist factions and so-called 'Islamic states' that tried to replace those same secular Arab republics.

"Whether by accident or design, an attempted replay of US policy toward the Mujahideen in Afghanistan during the Cold War against the USSR – when the US supported the Mujahideen, including Osama bin Laden, against the Soviet-backed government of Afghanistan.

"The neoconservatives in the White House – within the Republican Party in 2003 and within the Democratic Party in 2011 – thought that they would arrange a repeat performance; this time, quickly instead of gradually. So, they overthrew Saddam Hussein and Muammar Gaddafi as though they were organising a couple of flash mob events.

"Then, hot on the heels of the Western intervention in Libya, it was Syria's turn. The call went out: 'The president of Syria must go!' But the president of Syria did not go; he hung on in there, and the war in Syria carried on... until the president of Syria asked the Russians for help, and the Russians responded positively to his request, which makes it impossible for the neoconservatives in the White House to remove the president of Syria without the risk of a direct confrontation in Syria between NATO and Russia.

"Now, John, ask yourself this question: would the Russians have become involved in Syria if they thought that there was a risk, a high risk even, that it could lead to a war between NATO and Russia?

"In my view, John, the Russians must have factored in this risk, discussed it at length among themselves, and come to the conclusion that it was either a lower risk than might be expected or that the risk (even a moderate-to-high risk) could be... in some way... 'managed'...

"And I began to turn this thought over and over in my mind; to observe the behaviour of NATO and the behaviour of the Russian government; and to determine how these different behaviours might inform my research, and might either tally with or contradict my expectations..."

Dmitry Krejevsky paused, raised an eyebrow to invite a contribution from John Morton and, after Morton did not respond, resumed his line of enquiry, albeit from a fresh angle. "Have you noticed that Russia's President Glazenov always gives NATO leaders a chance to do something positive, often after the two opposing sides have met and thrashed out an agreement?

"President Glazenov waits to see what NATO's leaders will do, in the near certainty that they will do what he expects them to do – to break the agreement – which they invariably do.

"That is the precise moment he chooses to pounce, and when he pounces, he introduces something new to the ball game: a surprise factor and a *game changer*.

"The element of surprise is maintained, right up to the announcement of the game changer. And President Glazenov does not do anything by half measures.

"In September 2015, the Russian government quickly deployed anti-aircraft defences in Syria and announced a range of security measures that were designed to prevent NATO from implementing a no-fly zone. With joint Syrian–Russian control of the skies over much of Syria, the Syrian government is better equipped to defend itself.

"Now, let's examine how Syria figures in the US presidential election.

"The Republican candidate, Dirk Volzanger, is in favour of US withdrawal from Syria.

"On the other hand, the Democrat candidate, Harpy Harbinger, wants NATO to impose no-fly zones over Syria. However, Harpy Harbinger was warned by some of the top brass at the Pentagon not to even talk about NATO no-fly zones unless she was truly serious about the proposal, that it was not simply a gesture or just talk, and that she was prepared to go ahead and put no-fly zones in place.

"Also, the Pentagon told her that, even if she wanted to set up no-fly zones, it was not prepared to help her, because the Pentagon baulked at taking any action that might lead to a direct confrontation in Syria between NATO and Russian military forces.

The top brass at the Pentagon apprised Harpy Harbinger of their conclusions and advised her to work out an alternative plan.

"So, what did Harpy Harbinger do during the televised debates, toe-to-toe with Dirk Volzanger? She advocated a US no-fly zone over the whole of Syria, live on American TV and in defiance of the Pentagon top brass.

"Now, John, how do you think Harpy Harbinger's antics would have been received by the top brass at the Pentagon?"

"Obviously, that would have not gone down too well," Morton replied.

"That's right, John," concurred Krejevsky. "In fact, the Pentagon made no official comment about Harpy Harbinger's desire to impose a NATO military solution on the Syria crisis. The Pentagon just ignored her!

"And, as part of the turning over of thoughts in my mind, I wondered why the Pentagon made no comment, and just ignored her—"

Morton cut in, unwittingly interrupting Krejevsky's train of thought, and said, "In the absence of support from the Pentagon, how did Harpy Harbinger intend to go ahead with a no-fly zone over Syria?"

Krejevsky shrugged. "I have no idea. Maybe she thought she might buy some drones at the airport duty-free shop – they are only $1,000 apiece, which is a pittance that would scarcely look out of place in the accounts of the Harbinger Foundation, perhaps under Christmas presents for deprived children."

Morton chuckled. "She could have attached a .44 magnum revolver to each of the drones – Dirty Harpy!"

Krejevsky threw back his head and laughed silently in response to Morton's witticism.

Dmitry Krejevsky smiled as he scanned the lake, the eddies and ripples illuminated by the bright autumnal sunshine. Then he took a swig out of a bottle of water, and threw the last bits of his uneaten toast to the hopeful ducks and geese bobbing around among the carpet of entangled twigs and fallen leaves swirling about in the windswept waters of the Serpentine.

He continued, "But, seriously, John, I'm still left wondering; not so much about how Harpy Harbinger might implement her pet theories but more so about the behaviour of the Pentagon. And we are talking about the top brass here, not just a spokesperson who is wheeled out in front of the cameras to say something for public consumption… to say something that would reinforce a dominant narrative… but nothing more than that.

"The top brass at the Pentagon kept mum, as though something made them stop and think, and I am left wondering what that 'something' might be…

"As you can probably deduce from my ramblings, John, I have been trying to piece together an alternative narrative for several months, but there was something missing…

"But, now, some good news! The documents that you have obtained from the two boxes owned by the former editors-in-chief of *The Chronicle* – that is, from Edward Ollerson and Sir Tom Hamble – have shed some light on what is going on behind the scenes.

"*Fact*: NATO preferred an arms race with Russia, similar to the arms race that undermined the Soviet economy in the 1980s, based upon the assumption that Russia would have to keep up with the Joneses and match NATO bullet for bullet, and warhead for warhead.

"*Fact*: the Russian government knew that it could not afford to respond in kind, diverting much-needed resources from the civilian sphere to the military sphere, thereby undermining the Russian economy.

"So, from the Russian perspective, an elegant solution was called for… and, from the Russian perspective, an elegant solution has been found.

"The Russian government has, in fact, managed to upgrade its armed forces and equipment to a sufficient level to deter NATO from encroaching closer to the Russian border. Plus, Russia has much to spare, with its modern aircraft and mobile missile defence systems, many of which are on display in Syria.

"Mobility and flexibility are the watchwords, and they comprise the core of the Russian government's elegant solution.

"This, alone, is big news. The top brass at the Pentagon know it, but the neoconservatives and their friends in the corporate media are in denial about it.

"The neoconservatives in the White House cannot believe that Russia has devised an elegant and cost-effective solution to its defence, without having to engage in an expensive arms race; the neoconservatives in the White House refuse to believe it, so guess what?"

Morton had his answer ready. "They fall back to their default position – they go into denial and they double down, as though nothing is wrong."

"They fall back to their default position," Dmitry Krejevsky repeated Morton's statement, word for word, "they go into denial and they double down, as though nothing is wrong."

"Precisely, John. That was the response I expected from the neoconservatives, and that is precisely what they did. "But – for me, John – the response of the neoconservatives is not big news. It is merely what is to be expected.

"This means that, okay, we need to note it down, file it away and archive it for future reference.

"But, meanwhile, we look for the *big* news. Ask what the *big* news is – the *really big* news – and work out the *really big* question that we need to ask...

"And the *really big* question is this: *how?*

"*How* did the Russian government manage to bring its armed forces and equipment up to date; plan and execute all of this without the Pentagon getting wind of it; and keep it secret until the last minute, until it was the *right time* to reveal it to the Pentagon and maximise the impact of the revelation? How did they time it right, so that the announcement became a *game changer*?

"Now that we have those documents that you received from Sir Tom Hamble, we are closer to the answer. And here is the answer, as near as I can work out, making use of the available evidence...

"At the end of every year, the Russian Ministry of Finance publishes audited accounts, just like any other organisation. Those reports are accurate and above board. They include summaries of the income and expenditure of the other ministries – the Ministry of Defence, the Ministry of the Interior, and so on.

"We know that, for many years, there have been many officials with pro-Western sympathies in the Russian Ministry of Finance, so it should come as no surprise that the Americans find out about Russian budgetary comings and goings before the Russian president himself has had a chance to review the final report.

"One item that the Americans picked up on was the amount of trade that is being done now and is planned for the future between Russia and China, between Russia and European countries, and between Russia and other countries.

"Another item concerned the amount of gold that was being bought and stockpiled by the Russian government, as a simple expedient to counteract sanctions and other forms of economic warfare.

"Apparently, the US government became consumed with interest in these two pieces of information about international trade and gold reserves. For the Americans, these pieces of information were inextricably linked, and they became a dual obsession, merging into one single *idée fixe*.

"The Americans checked how much of the total Russian budget had been allocated to the Ministry of Defence. They discovered that it was not, in their opinion, excessive; it was not enough to constitute a threat to the US or its global dominance.

"Furthermore, since the Russian military budget seemed to be relatively low, the Americans assumed that the Russian military was operating more or less on a shoestring budget, as a hand-to-mouth existence, and posed no serious threat to NATO.

"Consequently, the Americans felt self-assured, but this self-assurance turned out to be merely a face-saving exercise, hiding the Americans' complacency from view.

"But, once again, I come back to this question: *how*?

"Nobody on the American side seemed to have factored in *how* the Russian Ministry of Defence had produced sophisticated weaponry on a sufficiently large scale and with such a small budget. And, crucially, how this remained *undetected* by the US government and NATO.

"And now I know the answer to the question of *how* this was done.

"Consider the American neoconservatives, who ride high in positions of influence throughout the key institutions in the US.

"Consider these same neoconservatives, who love to play identity politics; for whom any insult against a particular social group is regarded as sexist, racist, misogynist, homophobic and so on; and who produce huge demonstrations on the streets of Western capital cities to campaign on behalf of those social groups.

"Consider these same neoconservatives, as they look down upon the Russian people, and see them as no better than stupid, backward and ignorant people who are not supposed to be able to produce anything with a high degree of sophistication.

"Consider these same neoconservatives, with their attendant Russophobia – which is a form of racism; however, these same neoconservatives are oblivious to that discomforting fact, and they have blocked that discomforting fact out of their minds and replaced it with their own home-baked... for want of a better word... *mythology*.

"In their history classes, for example, the war against Nazi Germany was won by the Brits and the Americans, on the Western front, with the Eastern front imagined as merely a sideshow. Period. *Mythology*.

"According to this narrative, the Russians won *their* bit of the war with Germany *primarily* or even *solely* because of the lease-lend arrangements, and the convoys of ships that transferred the stuff across the dangerous Atlantic and the perilous Murmansk run. *Mythology*.

"This line of reasoning *implies* that all of the T34 tanks that won the Battle of Kursk in 1943 and destroyed Germany's Army Group Centre during Operation Bagration in 1944 were made in Pennsylvania, Michigan and so on, in American factories. It does away, too, with any idea that the Sturmovik and Yak aircraft, or the Katyushka rocket systems – even the AK 47 Kalashnikov – could have possibly been conceived, designed and mass-produced by the incompetent, 'stupid Russian' *untermenschen*. *Mythology*.

"*Mythology* that is not always clearly stated, but is implied. Note that, John. Not stated, but *implied*. Subtle and cleverly done, but, nonetheless, *mythology*.

"Of course, it is absolutely out of the question that the 'stupid Russian' *untermenschen* could indulge in the merest smidgen of creative accounting without it being found out. Yet that is what happened.

"However, the ingenuity displayed by the 'stupid Russian' *untermenschen*, in terms of creative accounting, is not *mythology*... it provides us with the answer to the question of *how*.

"The Russian government – with its well-educated *nomenklatura*, and its carefully honed good manners and politeness – smiled and put up with the arrogance and the insults from the West while secretly putting in place a comprehensive system of defence right under the noses of the NSA, the CIA, the Pentagon, and all the rest among the sixteen or seventeen US intelligence agencies that have a responsibility for the national security of the US.

"And what a thing it is that the Russian military has put in place. NATO has only managed to roll out the first phase of its missile defence shield and – even when it is fully rolled out – it will be useless, because Russia has fully rolled out its own missile defence shield based upon tried-and-trusted systems, such as its Pantsir series, and its S-200, S-300 and S-400, which are topped up with the next generation S-500 systems and already backed up with a full range of electronic warfare capability.

"This is on top of the fact, which we discovered almost one year ago, that it would be possible to overwhelm any missile defence system by flooding it with 10% real tactical nuclear weapons and 90% dummies.

"And all of this has been fully financed – but with the true finances hidden carefully from prying eyes, courtesy of creative accounting; meanwhile, the main reports from the Russian Ministry of Finance provide an attention-grabbing diversion.

"The documents you received from Sir Tom Hamble also refer to some highly sensitive reports from the Pentagon; reports to which we do not have access. Apparently, the top brass at the Pentagon is reluctant to go to war with Russia, using guns and bombs, because the top brass does not believe that the American military will prevail in such a war.

"Moreover, the Pentagon is – to quote from a document I managed to obtain from a very sensitive source – 'really pissed' that the numerous US intelligence agencies failed to detect the true scale of the advances in Russian military technology. The Pentagon top brass think that the politicians (the neoconservatives in particular) have not been doing their jobs properly.

"It's checkmate or, rather, only stalemate – which is a win for Russia. And, because Russia merely wants to quieten everything down so that Russia can focus on its economy and the long-term project of Eurasian Integration, *stalemate means game over.*"

※

The documents from Carl Waggoner's box number twenty-five were translated in full. It became immediately obvious to Dmitry Krejevsky that it would *not* be possible to publish them in *The New Times*, nor to leak them in any way.

They were simply too sensitive. They would give an impression that Russia was a match (and perhaps even more than a match) for the US. Dmitry Krejevsky – a man with a foot in both camps, the West and the East – would be quite happy for the global public to realise that this was the case, for a sense of realism to set in, and for a pathway to open up leading toward a détente between the East and the West.

However, on reflection and after discussions with John Morton, he felt that this process of realisation should be allowed take its own course and to reach maturity under its own steam without any prompting from a third party.

Another reason for withholding the documents was their sensitive nature. Not only because they were the property of the Russian government (and, in some cases, also the property of the US government) but, critically, because – in combination with what he had heard from his expert advisors, as well as what he had gleaned from the documents in Carl Waggoner's twenty-fourth box – they might cause embarrassment to senior officials in the US government in front of the entire world's population.

Should the Americans, in 2017, seek a rapprochement with Russia, neither the US government nor the Russian government would thank *The New Times* for revealing a set of documents that would make their job more difficult.

Eighteen months earlier, Dmitry Krejevsky and John Morton had met with the Russian president and his foreign minister. President Glazenov had told them that Russia was going to drive forward the inauguration of a new world order – a multipolar world order.

The Russians were encountering great resistance from the American neoconservatives. If the obsessively Russophobic Harpy Harbinger had won the US presidential election, that task would indeed be an arduous one; however, with Dirk Volzanger in the White House, the game *might* be a little easier. It just *might*.

The 'deep state' within the US elite might have realised that the original game was up. Sure, NATO has more of anything that the Russians have in terms of military might, but it is dispersed throughout the world to 'protect American interests' worldwide. The imposition of US or NATO no-fly zones over Syria could lead to war with Russia, and key figures in the Pentagon had pointed out this assessment to many a deaf ear in the US State Department.

Harpy Harbinger had campaigned vigorously for NATO-imposed no-fly zones over the whole of Syria. Her Republican rival, Dirk Volzanger, expressed a lack of confidence in the so-called 'moderate opposition' in Syria, and preferred (in flagrant opposition to the CIA and the hawks in the US State Department) to ignore the moderate opposition and instead opt for a common approach between the Americans and the Russians.

Dirk Volzanger could see for himself that the CIA backed the Islamist moderate opposition, while the Pentagon preferred to back the Syrian Kurds. Since these two separate and unconnected groups often ended up fighting each other, the CIA and the

Pentagon were effectively waging a proxy war against each other. The more cynical analysts in the corporate and alternative media thought that keeping the war alive might have been the plan all along, with huge profits coming the way of the Western armaments industries.

Furthermore, there were other factors to bear in mind, about which Dirk Volzanger expressed his disquiet.

Suppose that, further on down the line, the Syrian Kurds felt strong enough to champion the idea of a separate, independent Kurdistan? Put yourself in the shoes of a senior NATO negotiator. You could decide to back this project and promote the cause of an independent Kurdistan actively, but then you would have all of the countries with a Kurdish minority against you: Iran, Iraq, Syria and... Turkey – a key NATO member and ally.

Sooner or later, all spruced up like James Bond in your tuxedo and bow tie at the casino table of geopolitical risk-taking and brinkmanship, you would have to call 'banco' and find out if you had won your bet. If you lost, you might decide to call *'suivi'*, to exercise your right to win back your losses without delay. But how many *suivi* calls would you need to make before you realised the game was blown?

The Pentagon had advised the White House that it would cost at least 1 trillion dollars over a ten-year period to achieve a decisive military superiority over Russia – assuming the Russian Ministry of Defence induced itself into a comatose state during the period of reconstruction and left its armed forces without a future upgrade (which was an unlikely scenario).

One of the documents from the box that Morton had obtained from Sir Tom Hamble was of pointed significance. It showed that, by focusing on what it *needed* rather than trying to match NATO bullet for bullet, Russia was able to develop new weapons within a relatively short time frame, between five and ten years, in line with Russia's *limited* military requirements.

NATO, in contrast, took between twenty and thirty years to fully re-arm across the board, in terms of expensive weaponry, in line with its globalist and full-spectrum-dominance requirements

– by which time the new planes, tanks, aircraft carriers, strategy and tactics of NATO would be obsolete.

Given that Russia had already put in place all that it needed, after it had called banco over the Syrian crisis to find out if their gamble had paid off, there was no need for the Russians to follow up with a *suivi*, to exercise their right to win back their losses without delay. If the top brass at the Pentagon did not know this when they were preparing to up the stakes in Syria between 2013 and 2015, they were surely having second thoughts now, in November 2016.

※

The only people who knew that Carl Waggoner's *twenty-fifth* box was in the hands of *The New Times* were Dmitry Krejevsky and John Morton – plus Krejevsky's translator, who remained anonymous and sworn to secrecy.

Sir Tom Hamble had never inspected the contents of the box; for Hamble, immersed in his new life as a hobby-driven senior citizen, the unwanted box had already faded from memory, never to return.

Morton and Krejevsky, in addition to Vivienne Eissinger and Hugh Lombard, were also aware of the contents of the *twenty-fourth* box, which had been discovered in a wardrobe on the Ollerson family's canal barge.

According to Shirley Bould, a box that fitted this description found its way into the offices of *The Chronicle* and was delivered subsequently to Loretta Farelli, in Washington DC, via Katy Drake.

"I would bet my house that Taylor Snow opened that box and made copies of all the documents inside it before allowing it to be sent on to Loretta," John Morton declared.

Dmitry Krejevsky agreed. "But none of them know that *we* know about the contents of the twenty-fourth box, and none of them are remotely aware of the existence of the twenty-fifth box."

Krejevsky splayed the fingers and thumbs of both hands together, and gripped and released his lower lip several times in contemplation. He thought, *It's too much information. To publish would be counterproductive... so it's time to behave responsibly, to indulge in an act of self-censorship and to fight the information war, not only by thinking hard but by thinking* smart... *Truly, in the spirit of* a phoney war.

"Let's keep it that way, John, shall we?" he suggested.

27

QUEEN BITCH

The year 2016 was coming to its end.

The year of *a phoney war*.

A year during which the outbreak of global hostilities had been risked by certain hawks in the US governing circles, only to dissolve in total disarray before it had "gotten off of the ground," as President-elect Dirk Volzanger was reported to have said in a conflab with his tiny group of allies within the political Establishment and the Pentagon – truly a *minority* faction, if ever there was one.

Consequently, instead of a hot war, we were treated to *a phoney war*; a war fought predominantly with non-lethal weapons, including jaw-jaw and 'soft power'.

The year 2016 began to wind down.

The Americans would have Thanksgiving to draw their polarised nation together – as far as that was possible.

Christmas was coming, the geese were getting fat – hopefully, to the benefit of many an old man's hat. Seasonal displays that had long been in preparation behind many a temporary hoarding in shopping malls all over the world were now open for public viewing. 'Santa' was being visited by long queues of children, for them to let him know what he should deliver during his twenty-four-hour sleigh-ride across the globe.

It was a time to get ready the port, the crackers and the stilton.

Except that, for *The New Times*, a surprising and quite bizarre challenge was in the offing.

Perhaps unsurprisingly, this challenge was the product of a tantrum.

Unable to take the electoral defeat of Harpy Harbinger a moment longer, vociferous in her denunciation of the incoming President Dirk Volzanger and seething with rage at being denied the prospect of a key position within the Harbinger clique in the White House, Loretta Farelli decided to make someone pay for her discomfort.

Loretta had fought and won a similar battle once before. Her opponent was easy meat at the time. He would be unable to refuse the chance to get even, if she threw down the gauntlet.

She would ambush him again. Last time, he was struggling to come to terms with the early stages of the Ukraine crisis. The Ukraine crisis had not panned out the way Loretta had hoped. So, this time, Loretta decided to steer the narrative away from geopolitics and toward ground on which she felt comfortably at home: identity politics.

Prior to launching her latest dubious initiative, Loretta did some homework. She researched the strengths and weaknesses of her target at *The New Times*. She also scrutinised the performances of Harriet 'Harpy' Harbinger at the Democratic National Convention and face-to-face in the televised debates with her rival in the presidential race, Dirk Volzanger.

Painfully but earnestly, Loretta noted some of the shortcomings in Harpy Harbinger's *style* and determined to eliminate them from her own presentation. The *content* of Loretta's presentation, however, would remain identical to that of Harpy Harbinger – as strange as that may seem to the attentive observer.

When Loretta was ready, she assembled a bunch of soundbites on sheets of paper and rehearsed in front of a mirror – a talking head in a verbal duel to the death with its reflection. Loretta ran an idea past Katy Drake, without letting her know entirely what she had in mind, and asked Katy to book a venue in London in the name of *The Chronicle* newspaper for a full-blooded verbal confrontation with the top boy from *The New Times*. This was almost certain to be John Morton, but if they put forward Dmitry Krejevsky, so much the better. Loretta was ready for them.

She even took account of the possibility that *The New Times* supporters in the audience might be a bit on the flat side and unresponsive. They, particularly the men, would need to be provoked into a reaction that would be abhorred by the women among the onlookers.

Loretta could turn that to her advantage.

At the end of the day, after Loretta's provocative game plan would have played out to its logical conclusion, John Morton would be tarred and feathered, and held up to public ridicule, not only as a collaborator with the enemy but also – of equal and perhaps greater importance to Loretta's caprice – castigated as a sexist, racist, misogynist, homophobic relic who should be put out to grass.

The only problem for Loretta was that the staff at *The New Times*, during a lengthy team talk about the proposed event, smelled a rat. They knew they could not back down, but why should they? They were hardly overpopulated with shrinking violets. Some lateral thinking was called for – which is quite a challenge when you have no idea exactly what to expect.

Not for the first time, the day was saved by a volunteer. This was someone with a thorough grasp of his field of expertise and who could hold his own in a debate; a man who could think on his feet; and a man who, despite appearances to the contrary, remained – in a manner of speaking – male.

※

Wednesday, 14 December 2016. London.
Loretta Farelli thought long and hard about what to wear for her big occasion. Courtesy of the generous philanthropy of the Harbinger Foundation, and accompanied by Katy Drake, Loretta flew to New York, Milan, Paris and London to make sure that her look was right.

After the failure of the brand 'Harpy Harbinger', white was out, but what, Loretta wracked her brains, was in?

A little black dress – what else?

Being hip and 'killer' apparel – simple and subtle – it had never failed her in the past, so – for Loretta – a little black dress was the obvious choice for her big night.

She tried on several of her little black dresses, which had been accumulated over the years and retained by Loretta as trophies to remind her of the 'down and dirty' male conquests she had made over the years.

Katy Drake was dragooned into Loretta's apartment. The pair spent over three hours with Loretta trying on one dress after another, before Loretta decided eventually that none of them were fit for purpose.

Loretta conceded an unpalatable observation, grudgingly, which was clearly visible to Katy; namely, that, in addition to the little black dress, black leggings should be worn to, as Katy put it, "emphasise the finer points while hiding one or two disagreeable features".

Okay, Katy. Anything you say, thought Loretta, eagerly. *We're almost good to go.*

Now, there was one last thing: should her hair be put up or hanging loose? Or what about that black Spanish-style cowboy hat, which was an impulse buy acquired during a recent shopping trip? This was a Spanish Stetson that Loretta and Katy had at first dismissed contemptuously because it created an image reminiscent of an on-screen upmarket female companion of a bad boy gunslinger in the mould of Lee Van Cleef, but it was a hat that the compulsive Loretta simply could not stop trying on.

On her big night, Loretta positioned herself on a tall stool to the right of the stage, from the audience's viewpoint. "Right is might, and might is right," was the message she wanted to send out.

The representative of *The New Times* – billed simply as 'Roland' – approached the tall stool to the left of the stage.

Roland had been shopping with Shirley Bould again; this time with the full permission and connivance of Dmitry Krejevsky, who

– together with his wife Catherine – had situated himself at the rear of the auditorium next to Sir Harold Nevin and his wife, Lady Miranda.

Miranda shed a tear to see one of the grandchildren of her dearest of dear friends at last taking his rightful place in the world. Miranda fretted a little as the time passed inconceivably slowly, her hands interlocked tightly with a handkerchief clasped in her frail fist. She asked her husband nervously if he had submitted the drinks order for the interval – only to be courteously informed by him that, "This is not that kind of event, my dear."

Dmitry Krejevsky noticed this bout of anxiety and was about to offer Miranda some reassurance, when extraordinarily loud music started up without warning, seeming to summon the gladiatorial contest into being from a netherworld of imaginary demons. Dmitry Krejevsky settled back in his seat. Yes, he was expecting a white-knuckle ride, but this was no time for the stressful gripping of armrests.

This was a time to get out the popcorn.

※

Having temporarily offloaded the guise of his alter ego, Vivienne Eissinger, Count Roland von Eissinger the Third bent low to shake the hand of Loretta Farelli – who proffered it in readiness for a sweet kiss. The count thought that a handshake would suffice; released his placid, cold-fish grasp; and twirled round to position himself on his high seat to the left of the stage.

He and Shirley had done each other proud. The suit was purple velveteen, the shirt a darkish shade of mauve, and the scarlet-and-blue old school tie with the black-and-gold crest set the whole thing off to a T. Black socks and black shoes with a Cuban heel completed the outfit.

His hair raised and secured in place with one of his favourite Japanese hair clips, a minimum of make-up in place, and Roland was ready to roll.

※

Sir Tom Hamble relished the prospect of compering the lavish occasion, yet he did not overstay his welcome. The citizens had become restless and impatient for the games to start – and they were eager to see which of the combatants was ordained to be the lion and which was condemned to be the Christian.

Loretta Farelli stuck to her script. She trotted out, virtually word for word, the political line with which Harpy Harbinger had plunged headlong into the fateful abyss during the US presidential election campaign.

Seated next to her on the stage, the count adopted an indulgent pose, nodding and smiling in the direction of his challenger. A few minutes into her talk, the count noticed that something was not quite right with Loretta's Spanish Stetson. Something white was sticking out at the junction where the hair met the right side of the brim. He tried to ignore it, but he found it difficult to avert his eyes. He simply had to get a better look.

Now, he pondered, *can I get her to shift her position? Is it possible for a gay man to play it 'straight'? And to improvise (for the benefit of an alluring, if older, señora) the 'bar-stool tease' routine, which served me well in my younger days?* This involved a little flirting, adjusting his position on his tall stool, rubbing his legs together, and a little cajoling with his eyes and his lips, with a coquettish tongue-in-cheek raised to one side.

Near the rear of the auditorium, Dimitry Krejevsky was horrified.

"What the bloody hell is Vivienne playing at?" he murmured, before recoiling in embarrassment upon hearing a phrase that he seldom used – and worse still in the company of dear friends – and their wives!

Sir Harold Nevin turned to catch Dmitry Krejevsky's sheepish eye and returned the lingering hangdog expression with a twinkle in his left eye.

"As Roland would say, Dmitry, *alles in ordnung,*" Nevin said softly. "*Alles in ordnung.*"

On the stage, Loretta continued her monologue. As the segment of her speech concerning LGBT rights reached its climax, some in the audience began to clap – and, in growing numbers, they initiated a partial standing ovation.

Loretta was forced to pause while the cheering died down. Sir Tom Hamble approached the stage with a hand-held microphone, before deciding that an intervention was not, after all, necessary or appropriate.

On stage, the count patted the palm of his left hand with the fingers of his right hand and expressed glowing admiration for Loretta.

Nothing could have been more discomforting to Loretta. This was supposed to be an event to showcase the trouncing of the alternative media by the corporate media in retaliation for the humbling of Harpy Harbinger, and as revenge for the annihilation of 'Team Harpy' and its illustrious brand.

The count's antics prolonged Loretta's sense of discomfort – notably, his absurdly over the top 'bar-stool tease' routine – and provoked Loretta into an overreaction, which was precisely the short-term objective the count had set himself.

His nodding, flirting, and the movement of his lips and of his tongue over his teeth proved to be most unsettling. He seemed to be making eye contact with some of the rainbow-bedecked cohort within Loretta's entourage among the spectators, causing much simpering and swooning at the prospect that their candidate might have defeated her opponent by winning him over – which, of course, was *not* Loretta's aim, nor was it what the count had in mind.

During her summing up, Loretta lost her composure briefly before regaining it – but not before the right side of her hat separated itself momentarily from her hair, thereby revealing the anomalous object.

Oh, my Lord, thought the count. *You can see a bit of the price tag.*

The count continued to manoeuvre himself on the high stool. At a critical point, a certain jerkiness of his right leg accompanied by a little tittering from the audience distracted Loretta sufficiently for the count to achieve his second objective. Loretta's Spanish

Stetson dislodged itself and fell onto the stage floor, whereupon the count was on it in a flash, retrieving it and examining it in detail.

It looks rather cheap, compared to the rest of Loretta's outfit, he thought. *Maybe their budget did not stretch any further. It was not bought in Paris or Milan, that's for sure. It is probably from London – perhaps an unwanted present, dumped by its indifferent former owner for sale... at a knock-down price... in a flea market.*

The count stood perfectly upright and set about putting Loretta at her ease. He placed her Stetson on his high stool, reached around to the back of his head, and removed the Japanese hair clip, thereby allowing his hair to cascade over his shoulders and more than halfway down his spine.

"Oohs" and "aahs" were emitted by the audience, mingled with wolf-whistles, which the count took in good faith while reprimanding the naughty boys and girls with one of his gorgeous sideways glances and raised eyebrows.

After fixing his opulent, flowing, jet-black locks into a ponytail, he set about replacing Loretta's hat, holding the Japanese hair clip between his teeth while making some slight alterations to Loretta's hair (with her permission, of course – how could she refuse the count's obliging persistence?) and used the hair clip to secure the Spanish Stetson in place.

However, this was with two major changes. First, the hat was positioned with the price tag facing *toward* the audience, teasingly not quite in full view but annoyingly noticeable. Second, although the hat was placed ever so slightly at a jaunty angle to one side – which was how Loretta wanted it – it was also positioned to the rear of her head with the front of the brim slanting upward.

Loretta Farelli – a top neoconservative and neoliberal icon within the Beltway – was attired in a way that would not look out of place on an *ole gran-pappy* from an old-style western or the free-spirited lead in a remake of *Calamity Jane*.

Loretta wound up her talk and was rewarded with a second partial standing ovation.

At the rear of the theatre, Dmitry Krejevsky watched the show nervously with his hands joined as if in prayer, and covering his mouth and nose.

Count Roland von Eissinger the Third then proceeded to do something extraordinary. He had his prey where he wanted her to be. He knew the exact sequence of steps that he intended to carry through.

Step one was easy. He had already ripped up Loretta's unwritten rule book and, unconstrained by its tacit directives, he threw out of the window the prearranged format of one speech each, followed by questions from the audience, then a debate.

In place of the designated format, he started a Q&A session with his opponent. Fifteen minutes in, the debate had been transformed into something quite unique – an ad hoc chat show with the count as the host, live in a theatre in front of an audience, and with the whole event being broadcast worldwide courtesy of the advanced technology of *The New Times* website and (by agreement) the website of *The Chronicle*.

"Do you play polo, by any chance?" the count asked, a few minutes into his 'chat show'.

"No," responded Loretta.

"Well, do you ride?" he asked, to a chorus of titters then giggles from the audience, as he reproached the unruly minority amid the audience again with his disapproving sideways glance and raised brow.

"I mean – do you ride horses?" he clarified.

"Sometimes," Loretta declared.

"In that case, you really must come down to one of our estates."

"*One* of your estates?"

"Oh yes. We have several scattered about the country. We also own land and property in Germany – 'the old country' as my dear grandmamma refers to it. She is an extraordinary woman. She is in her nineties, you know. You would love her, and she would love you to bits, bless her. Then there is Mamma. Mamma is in her seventies. Mamma married late in life and I am the youngest of her children. You really must come down to meet them."

Loretta nodded, obliged to go with the flow.

"Now you really must, you know. There's no backing out. Promise?"

"Promise."

"*Pinky swear?*"

"Yes. *Pinky swear.*"

They both raised the little fingers of their right hands.

"Now both together, Loretta," he demanded.

Both together, they shouted, "*Pinky swear!*"

The audience erupted into hoots and whistles.

Roland continued, "Thank you, Loretta. I can give you a tour of the estate; and my private quarters therein. Do you like art?"

"Well… yes," she replied.

"I do apologise. What I mean is, do you *own* any art?"

"Nothing special. Nothing like a genuine Tracy Emin or a Damian Hirst, for example." Although, I do own some prints – copies – of some of Tracy's work."

"Oh," said the count, a mite crestfallen. "No *fine art*? No portraits by Rembrandt? Nothing by Velasquez? No landscapes by Constable; nothing by Turner?"

"No," replied Loretta, completely off-guard.

"Oh," the dismayed count exclaimed. "Oh dear. Oh dear me."

The count resumed. "The Eissinger estate is littered with fine art. I myself own several pieces, including a Titian. Just the one. It is my pride and joy. It was bequeathed to me by my dear grandmamma upon my graduation."

"Really. It must be worth a lot of money."

"It is priceless."

"Priceless? Really? Are you going to sell it?"

"Oh no. I would never sell. It is so dear to my heart."

"But you could make a fortune. As an investment, it must have… it would fetch an enormous price back in the US. You would be able to buy something nice for your… your dear grandmamma to keep her company in her old age."

"A fortune! Oh Lord, no. I couldn't sell it. I simply couldn't. It is a lovely piece. I really should add to it. Some new items are coming onto the market soon. I tell you what, Loretta, why don't you accompany me to *Sotheby's* in London, so we can see what is available. I would love you to help me to select the worthiest item."

"It would be very expensive. You would have to spend thousands to get something worthwhile."

"Not thousands. Millions," the count stated clearly, to gasps offstage as well as on.

"But where on earth would you find that sort of money?"

"I might have to sell one or two thoroughbred horses to cousins to raise a deposit, or I might have to sell some artefacts or some land. It is doable, though."

Loretta Farelli suddenly woke up to the fact that the debate had veered far from her pre-planned agenda. For what it was worth, she steered the debate back to identity politics, during which it became apparent that the count had never attended a gay pride event.

"But how can you win your rights if you don't go to Gay Pride?" Loretta asked. "How can you prevent the world from slipping into the dark ages following the Brexit vote, Russia's Glazenov running wild and the coming to power of a fascist in the White House?"

The count continued to size up his prey, play up to Loretta's massive ego, flatter her and engage her with his finely tuned techniques of seduction.

He was an erudite and learned aristocrat, bold and assertive, glistening with real charm, with no sexual motive vis-à-vis Loretta and, therefore, unthreatening – even when he moved his high stool closer to hers and he took the liberty, from time to time (with a deceptively kittenish chuckle), to touch Loretta lightly with his forefinger on her cross-legged knee.

"Oh, don't flirt, dear," forefinger to the cross-legged knee. "*You're* inviting *me* to attend *Gay* Pride?"

Giggles burst forth from the crowd.

"You do have a smidgen of sassiness about you, don't you, dear? Naughty Loretta," chided Roland.

An admonished Loretta felt obliged to laugh nervously out loud, which the count mimicked in his unthreatening and charming way, by throwing back his head and opening his mouth very wide with his full blood-red lips withdrawn, revealing prominent vampire-like canine fangs, which looked ready to sink in, at a moment's notice.

A short period of silence ensued.

"I tell you what I'll do. My little Hughie attends the Gay Pride event. Sometimes more than one event. It is quite a party, I hear. You are right. I am guilty of a certain dereliction of duty. I will make a point of attending Gay Pride with my little Hughie at the first opportunity," he acquiesced.

"Mmm," Loretta agreed, at the same time seeming to admonish her opponent, while yelps and squeals of delight erupted from the LGBT cohort within Loretta's fan club.

"But you are mistaken if you think I have to attend such events to win or to retain my rights," the count reminded Loretta. "We Eissingers go back a long way. Many centuries, in fact. At our main home in the Cotswolds, on the wall above the fireplace in our ballroom, we have a very large tapestry of one of my great-great-great 'somebody-or-others' in full armour on horseback looking every bit the bloodthirsty Teutonic knight of old."

"But that is far from the truth. Teutonic warrior knight, indeed. That's balls. Queer as a coot, he was.

"In Germany in 1937, the Nazis wanted to put the Teutonic tapestry on public display to promote their cause and to persuade our family to fall in line with them, but my great-grandfather would have none of it. The tapestry was shipped out to one of our English estates and the Nazis had a fearful row with my great-grandfather.

"Great-grandfather pretended to indulge the Nazis, to calm them down and to persuade them to go away – which they eventually did, in return for some bottles of supposedly vintage wine and supposedly rare Napoleon brandy from the cellar, and with worthless daubs masquerading as 'modernist' and 'decadent art', created by an amateur (an 'arty' great-uncle of mine), which the Nazis fancied had been painted by one of the great modernist masters and should therefore fetch a handsome price in the shadow economy of the times.

"Those Nazis had no idea what they were talking about, and that they were being bought off with paltry trinkets – like natives being bought off by early colonisers dishing out coloured beads in exchange for valuable pieces of land. Those Nazis were so easy to bribe.

"And… the Nazis had no *style* and a total absence of *panache*; *that*, for me, was the truly *ignoble* sin."

The count swivelled on his high stool before continuing. "You see, Loretta dear, there has *always* been a 'stately homo' in my family, and nobody has ever so much as lifted a finger to stop it – not even the Nazis. They had other things on their minds – the elimination of Bolshevism and Jewish influence, in particular, and the conquest of *lebensraum* in the East.

"The Nazis left the old aristocrats alone, even when some of my family seemed to be implicated in the plot by the Secret Germany group to kill Hitler, due to some connections with the Stauffenbergs and other followers of the late Stefan George.

"You know of Stefan George, Loretta? No? Oh, you really must familiarise yourself with Stefan George – verily a scholar; a savant. He was such a wonderful aesthete; a poet and a visionary; and a homosexual who advocated and practised celibacy.

"His ideal form of government was some sort of benign aristocracy. I don't suppose there is much call for that sort of thing these days… there's not much call for benign aristocracy or indeed, perish the thought…" to loud and irreverent laughter throughout the auditorium, "… *celibacy!*"

The count homed in for the subtlest of kills.

"The tiny minds of the blond-haired supermen never could clearly distinguish between real and imagined threats. They were compromised, too, because – as they wheedled their way into German high society – they were able to avail themselves of one fresh prospect of corruption after another, leaving themselves open to blackmail and other disagreeable undertakings.

"I, too, became an adherent of Stefan George during my university years, many decades after the savant's demise. I wanted to put behind me the era of my wild youth, and I needed a suitable role model. Stefan George fitted the bill perfectly. I admired his discretion, his ability to keep his true feelings under control and the way he concealed his private life.

"One must maintain a sense of decorum, Loretta, dear. One simply must. All this shouting and parading around and grandstanding and virtue-signalling... it is cheap and uncivilised. Moreover, it doesn't work and it doesn't address the real issues.

"Look at Dirk Volzanger, the newly elected POTUS. He is *not* a gentleman – absolutely, *not* a gentleman. Wealthy and well-connected, yes; but, there again, so was his rival, Harpy Harbinger. In different ways, both have been using identity politics, displaying their bravado in the most uncouth manner. Both *he* and *she* have done this."

Roland touched a finger to the cross-legged knee of Loretta.

He then went on, "Now you tell me, Loretta dear, exactly how Dirk Volzanger intends to implement his 'America First' policy. Another four years of a Democrat-controlled White House would only have produced more of the same, and there would be nothing to show after four years. They'd be standing still. But, for President Volzanger, the future is about anything but standing still. It is all about change, and not necessarily change for the better.

"His easiest targets will be outsiders, foreigners, 'the others' – Mexicans, Latinos and immigrants – and those countries with which the US has certain close relationships. That means pulling out of NAFTA [the North American Free Trade Agreement] or renegotiating a deal that is more favourable to the US at the expense of Mexico and Canada.

"It also means doing something about China and other countries that have benefitted from the 'offshore outsourcing' policies of the outgoing US administration.

"Now this means going beyond identity politics, which, in turn, means formulating policies (and, in fact, a whole approach) that solve the perceived problem.

"But, more of the same will not do; it simply will not. Change is in the air and change is what history demands. Anyone who does not recognise that obvious fact, and who is unwilling to use imagination to create a new vision, will find the world of the future… tough going, indeed."

The event continued in this vein for another forty minutes, with Loretta Farelli struggling and failing to reassert control over events, and producing a sense of *sitzkrieg*.

※

Elsewhere, in the offices of *The Chronicle*, the dependable Erik kept the website up and running at the behest of Taylor Snow, who sat alongside Katy Drake and Brigita Wolznaski in the auditorium. As Loretta's plan began to fall apart, Katy Drake excused herself, allegedly for a 'comfort break'.

Smiling sweetly in the knowledge that Katy was probably up to something, Taylor Snow also left the auditorium temporarily, to make a phone call to Erik.

"Whatever happens, whoever tells you to take a certain action, make sure our website stays up. And, during the rest of the broadcast, disable all user login accounts temporarily except yours and mine. By way of explanation to anyone who attempts to log in, put out a screen message saying that maintenance is taking place," stated Taylor.

Taylor muttered to herself, "I am not going to allow this fucking bitch to get off of the hook."

IN LIEU OF AN EPILOGUE

"I don't have all the answers; nobody does," trilled a downcast female voice.

"I am not saying that you don't have all the answers," came the snooty, highbrow reply. "I am saying that you don't have *any* of the answers. New ideas are needed and, since you seem incapable of coming up with those new ideas, we can expect only one outcome – that *other* people will come along to generate them. You cannot cope with new ideas and differences of opinion. *Ergo*, you are standing in the way of progress."

This snippet was overheard by Taylor Snow as, with three drinks clutched in her hands, she sidled past the erudite Count Roland von Eissinger the Third as he conversed with one of Loretta Farelli's allies during the 'post-event' event in a chic wine bar within walking distance of the theatre. This was a 'post-event' event that Loretta had erroneously intended to be a victory parade.

Among the count's immediate *fan club nouveau* was Brigita Wolznaski, who had almost fallen off her chair with surprise the previous day when Taylor Snow assigned to her the main review of the Loretta-versus-Roland event for publication in *The Chronicle* the following day.

During the performance, Brigita had entered the words of wisdom frantically into her electronic tablet and, when she arrived home, she backed up the data to her private workspace within *The Chronicle*'s website before retiring to bed.

Brigita's first-ever article was reviewed by Taylor Snow, amended and polished by Brigita, and, finally, proudly forwarded to Erik, who uploaded it to *The Chronicle*'s website late in the afternoon.

Loretta had already waded in and insisted that *her* review be posted first – to which Taylor Snow acquiesced, safe in the knowledge that, whatever Loretta came up with, the damage to her credibility had already been done.

The upshot saw Loretta and three of her co-thinkers taking up an excessively large amount of space with interminable waffle under headlines such as 'Is identity politics really dead?' and 'Whither the postmodern era?'

This made use of a simple defence mechanism: don't address an awkward issue – sidestep it.

The next day, during a team meeting attended by Loretta and Katy prior to their flight back to Washington DC, Brigita was taken to task by Loretta for spelling out in her article the significance of the exchange between Loretta and the count. Taylor immediately jumped to Brigita's defence.

Falling back on her university notebooks on identity politics and her copious library of feminist literature, Brigita used her article to highlight the way in which social differences such as race, gender and sexuality often overlapped – sometimes in a collision with each other. Roland was a perfect example of how identities such as sexuality and gender interacted within the same body (and the same mind).

The event introduced the forgotten identity of 'class inequality' into the debate – uninvited by Loretta, Katy and the other event organisers. Moreover, the wealthy, aristocratic count seemed perfectly at home with himself, crystallising in human form what Brigita stated was "asserting the primacy of class" when it overlapped with other social differences.

It was this leaning away from a *particular interpretation* of identity politics that grated on Loretta's sensitive antennae. Class was not supposed to be talked about anymore. The battle of ideas over class supposedly had been won long ago. Why resurrect it now and using the terminology of thirty years ago?

"Asserting the primacy of class", indeed. This was wrong; completely wrong. Except that what Loretta took for right or wrong was based on whether a word or phrase fitted her preferred narrative of the day.

Bringing up class inequality from the dark ages did not fit the dominant narrative; therefore, it was irrelevant. Anyone who raised this issue was in danger of falling into the category of sexist, racist and misogynist; and summoning up dangerous demons that would upset the status quo. The status quo being a Fukuyama-inspired, 'end of history' ideal world of universal liberal values, which was based on the unequal political and economic system of capitalism but, nevertheless, a reflection of the fair-minded way that this unequal world was expected to work (despite the supremacy of an unequal political and economic system) and the way the world should be ordered, at least in the minds of Loretta and her allies.

As for Count Roland von Eissinger the Third, although he had raised the issue of class – perhaps inadvertently, but perhaps deliberately as a reminder to the lower orders of who was boss and what the lower orders would have to do to correct the imbalance – he or she could easily be explained away by Loretta.

Although she would never dream of broadcasting this viewpoint overtly in public, certainly not face-to-face with the self-confessed 'stately homo' Count Roland von Eissinger the Third, who would have relished the prospect of rectifying Loretta's error in an imperious and intentionally discomfiting way.

All the same, Loretta had a simple *exegesis* ready to hand: he, or she, was quite simply the *wrong type* of LGBT – an anachronism who had little relevance to a dominant narrative that supposedly defined and explained all that was going on in the real world.

One morning between Christmas and New Year, John Morton flopped down in his favourite armchair in front of the TV set, alone and with the intention of catching up on some films and TV shows he had missed during the busy year. Alison Morton had decided to spend some extra time with her parents, neither of whom were in the best of health, although they seemed determined to doggedly stick it out – which they had done for many years past and would probably do so for years to come.

Day one of Morton's marathon solo effort in front of the TV began with a travelogue from the 1990s entitled *From the Arctic to the Equator*, which the producer followed up with a second series covering *From the Equator to the Antarctic*. Morton planned to watch the two TV series back-to-back, over a day or two.

The first travelogue brought back a stockpile of vivid memories. The presenter took a train from the Far East through Siberia to Moscow, stayed in a hotel for a couple of nights, then boarded a train that took him to the Black Sea via the Rostov region in southwest Russia and the Donbass in eastern Ukraine.

Thence it went on to Morton's old stomping ground – the Middle East. The train stopped at ancient sites in Turkey, Syria and Iraq; underwent a trip to Persepolis in Iran; then moved on to the Holy Land, to be treated to teas and dinners by local Arab villagers and Jewish Kibbutz settlers. Egypt was entered briefly, but, following a near-fatal altercation with armed jihadists near a desert oasis, the TV crew was evacuated to a place of safety – which was, of all places, the calm and well-ordered state of Libya circa 1990 – in order to continue their journey south.

As a young reporter starting out on his first overseas assignment in the 1990s, Morton had been optimistically preoccupied with the Israel/Palestine peace process. His local acquaintances in the Middle East were talking up the prospect of a thriving tourist industry in the region. A rosy future beckoned.

Now it all seems a world away, thought Morton, *Look at it. It's all changed, and not for the better.*

Morton reflected sadly on the broken dreams, where few Westerners would even look at the region as a prospective tourist destination unless they could be persuaded that it was safe to do so. That would be quite a challenge! Maybe it was just put on hold. All the same, it seemed a forlorn and faraway dream.

✵

Toward the end of 2016, a few matters of concern raised their heads.

The most important was the immediate future of the US presidency.

Leading Democrats – as well as some leading Republicans – were engaged in a conspiracy to prevent Dirk Volzanger from being sworn in as the new POTUS. Meanwhile, President-elect Volzanger was busy filling up his cabinet posts with strong men – no women, as yet, but surely that would change. Surely?

To prepare the groundwork for their proposed 'soft coup', the conspirators needed to create a moral panic throughout American (and world) public opinion. Their main weapon of choice? Good old-fashioned, tried-and-trusted Russophobia.

Public opinion was led to believe that the CIA and more than a dozen other intelligence agencies had incontrovertible proof that the Russian government – nay, the Russian president in person no less – had manipulated the US presidential election to get his man into the White House.

How was this achieved? Simply, by computer hacking and propaganda.

What evidence was there of hacking? A huge amount, we were told.

Were we going to be allowed to see this evidence? No. The evidence was classified.

Could it be declassified, some wondered? Not without putting at risk the lives of certain individuals who had investigated the hacking and not without jeopardising the national security of the US.

So, according to the corporate media, leading lawmakers in the US were expected to take mere unsubstantiated accusations as gospel truth, set themselves up as judge and jury, find the miscreant guilty, and – what next? An international criminal court for Russia's President Glazenov? Or, perhaps, his extradition to face trial inside the US?

These were serious charges. As one senior US senator put it, it amounted to an act of war against the US. There was only one right and proper response to an act of war: to declare war on the adversary.

John Morton suspected that Taylor Snow might have inside knowledge of what was going on behind the scenes, so he invited her out for lunch to quiz her.

"Surely," Morton asked, "the neoconservatives are merely engaged in shadow boxing? The American neoconservatives can't seriously be talking about going to war with Russia? Or can they? Are they really that crazy?"

"It's a hissy fit," Taylor Snow remarked, not entirely convincingly. "Just a hissy fit to let off steam, but I don't know how long they will stretch it out. These neoconservatives or liberal internationalists or whatever you call them… they tried to prevent Dirk Volzanger from being elected president, and they failed.

"But they cannot accept this failure, which was all of their own doing, so they will double down and try to remove Dirk Volzanger from the presidency, starting with a smear campaign based on unproven so-called 'evidence' of collusion between Dirk Volzanger and Russia."

Morton asked, "How come all this alleged hacking took place on the retiring president's watch? Surely it should reflect badly upon him and his fellow Democrats? In contrast, Dirk Volzanger was just another participant in the contest at the end of the day – and, unless collusion can be proved, his hands look clean."

Taylor Snow allowed herself a little chuckle. "I think, John Morton, that you know the answers to those questions. As do I."

※

However, the smear campaign was not confined to Dirk Volzanger.

As renewed accusations of hacking surged then subsided then surged again, like a series of oceanic swells generated by distant weather systems, a website appeared from nowhere peddling another of the memes that had been propagated by the losers in the election: the characterisation of viewpoints that did not fit the dominant narrative, deemed by the corporate media as 'rogue' or 'renegade' viewpoints which were to be regarded henceforth as 'fake news'.

This new website listed its top 100 websites that it described as 'pro-Russian' propaganda sites. Among the top 100 was *The New Times*.

Here we go again, thought John Morton. *It looks like 2017 is already shaping up to be a busy year, even before it has begun.*

✳

As New Year's Eve approached, there was just time for one more notable titbit of scandal.

Perhaps in response to the accusations of negative criticism, the scaremongers who had drawn up the top 100 list of 'renegade' websites followed up with a list of 'recommended' websites – including *The Chronicle*, which was characterised as a 'friend' in the fight against Russian propaganda.

Taylor Snow immediately took umbrage at this unsolicited liberty. She had not given permission for *The Chronicle* to be labelled as a 'friend' for any purpose whatsoever.

She refused to be enlisted as part of a so-called intelligence-led campaign to dethrone the American president-elect before he had taken up his new role.

She declined to join in the smear campaign against the so-called 'renegade' websites, and expressed concern over demands to increase the state surveillance and censorship of such websites.

For, although Taylor Snow had grown up under the umbrella of the dominant neoliberal and neoconservative narrative, she was herself something of an outsider. Potentially, someone to be placed under surveillance.

She regarded herself as a democrat who believed in the rule of law and the US Constitution. She believed in free speech *per se*, and not merely as something to which lip-service was given and that might be restricted if it contradicted the received wisdom enshrined in a dominant narrative.

She also saw herself as a patriot. Not only had she volunteered for a self-imposed national service as a cadet during her teens, upon her university graduation and in the wake of 9/11 she had enrolled in the US Army.

She saw action. She was wounded in action: physically, psychologically and emotionally. She had seen, at close quarters, what humanitarian intervention was really all about.

Perhaps it was these factors that enabled her to connect with John Morton, a civilian who had also encountered the horrors of battlefield conditions in Iraq and in Ukraine. Both she and he knew all about the infamous Operation Total Pacification – a US war crime against the Iraqi people, which had been deliberately exorcised from public view, with the willing connivance of the corporate media.

Taylor Snow was a veteran; an Iraq War veteran. She celebrated her thirty-sixth birthday alone in her apartment on New Year's Eve. But, high up with a glass of Hennessy XO in one hand and with a magnificent view looking east over London and beyond, her solitary existence allowed her time to reflect and to plan ahead.

She determined that her immediate future would be tied up with that of *The Chronicle*, albeit a revised version of *The Chronicle* in transition from the failed liberal internationalism of the past toward her self-styled 'realist internationalism' of the future. She had not yet articulated too many of the basic tenets of her new mindset, but it would come.

Patience, she told herself. *Patience.*

Yes, Taylor Snow knew that it would come together over time.

Unlike her contemporaries with whom she was currently engaged in a battle of ideas to the death, Taylor Snow might live in a residential tower block, but – being a realist and a pragmatist – perish the thought that the tower be made of ivory.

ACKNOWLEDGEMENTS

Samson's Syndrome (2017) was a contemporary political thriller, set predominantly in London in the period from April 2014 to January 2016.

A Phoney War is the sequel to *Samson's Syndrome*, and covers the year 2016 – the year of the referendum concerning the UK's membership of the European Union and the 2016 US Presidential Election.

The uncertainty and surprises which are the hallmark of contemporary politics have already begun to spawn a new generation of 'cold war' style books, movies and TV series.

Samson's Syndrome and *A Phoney War* tap into this uncertainty, introducing fresh perspectives which are rooted in events which have already happened, but whose consequences continue to unfold in surprising ways.

A third novel in the series is in preparation, taking its lead from the posturing around real/fake news and identity politics but also moving on into the years 2017, 2018 and 2019, when ever more dangerous trends can be discerned, leading to the rise of right-wing populism, fascism, and various forms of 'hybrid warfare' as the Western powers struggle to come to terms with the challenges posed by the emergence of a multipolar world order led by Russia and China.

With a whimsical, jocular style of delivery, these novels should appeal to readers who want something other than yet another 'cold war' narrative and the ensuing deluge of pulp fiction.

My thanks to several friends and former colleagues who read the drafts and offer support and suggestions, particularly Caitlin, Faye, Christine, David, Joseph, Sol, Diane, Hannah and Loretta.

The author is indebted to numerous media outlets including the

BBC, ITN, Channel 4 News, The Guardian/Observer, the Sunday/Daily Telegraph, the Independent, the Times, the Daily Express, the Mail on Sunday, MorningstarOnline, CNN, the New York Times, the Washington Post, Der Spiegel, RT (particularly the 'Crosstalk' show), Sputnik, Counterpunch, Asia Times, Consortium News, the Unz Review, thesaker.is, moonofalabama.org, fortruss.com, theduran.com, craigmurray.org.uk, nakedcapitalism.com, and the many individuals who work hard to make it happen behind the scenes.

BY THE SAME AUTHOR
SAMSON'S SYNDROME

A crisis in the Ukraine potentially ushers in World War Three ...

Britain's flagship liberal newspaper, *The Chronicle*, is undergoing an identity crisis, leaving it vulnerable to takeover. The Eurosceptic, aristocratic Sir Harold Nevin has realised that a botched attempt to draw Ukraine into the EU is a heaven-sent opportunity to bolster the campaign for British withdrawal from the EU. Using his 'old school tie' links with the Editor-in-Chief, Tom Hamble, Nevin attempts to gain a foothold in *The Chronicle*. John Morton, a 'nonconformist' investigative reporter, is cast as Nevin's instrument of change.

During a trip to Russia, Morton is introduced to a new concept: the transition from 'unipolar' to 'multipolar' world order. At the same time, he faces the risk that the difficult transition period might lead to 'Samson's Syndrome', a metaphor for Mutually Assured Destruction and global Armageddon, based on the Bible story of Samson pushing aside the walls of the Temple and himself being killed in the process.

The story builds to a climax when John Morton agrees to leak a declassified Russian battle plan to warn the people of Europe of the dangers of depending on the failed neo-liberal policies of Western governments. This is spun into a tale of impending Russian invasion, and the plans are leaked. People throughout Europe take to the streets in terror.

Samson's Syndrome is available on the Matador-Troubador website and Amazon websites.